"Tibetan sand painting, lichen-dappl[ed] and a Mauritian scholar in Stockhol[m] [are some] of the [hundreds of] images contained within *Patterns*. A potpourri of poetry, art, and essays served up. Within the diversity of images and ideas a thematic pattern always emerges. Swedenborg held that we are more than merely human. His spirit of inquiry continues in the patterns of meaning discerned and exposed in this Chrysalis."

—*Jeff Rasley, author, Himalayan trek organizer,*
and president of Basa Village Foundation USA

"The engaging pieces in this anthology tumble through the mind like the varicolored bits of glass in a kaleidoscope. Individually beautiful, they combine to create patterns of endless fascination."

—*Lisa Hyatt Cooper, translator of* Secrets of Heaven
(15 volumes), Swedenborg Foundation, New Century
Edition of the Works of Emanuel Swedenborg

"*Patterns* does what it promises to do in Robert Lawson's editor's note: it enables us to see beyond our prescribed boundaries, to confront our own borders, and to begin the process of seeing opposites as one. The authors reveal the meaning and beauty in crossing boundaries from human thinking to spiritual identity."

—*Sarah A. Odishoo, associate professor of English,*
Columbia College Chicago

"This ultimate Chrysalis bodies forth a world of truth and wonder built of words and drawings, elegantly simple in their architecture and beautiful in their meanings. Six dozen newspaper men and women, financial analysts, psychologists, physicists, professors, ministers, and a pugilist—poets and prose writers all, contributors to America's most vivid little magazines—are here brought together in imaginative reaffirmation of the spiritual-material interconnectedness of all life, a philosophy according to which nothing is lost, everything changes."

—*F. D. Reeve, poet and novelist, Academy of Arts*
& Letters award winner, Golden Rose honoree,
author of the novella Nathaniel Purple,
and poems-with-jazz The Blue Cat Occupies the Moon

Patterns

MAKE 'EM AND BREAK 'EM

Chrysalis Reader

ORIGINAL ESSAYS, POETRY, AND SHORT STORIES
ILLUMINATING THE SPIRITUAL PROCESS

VOLUME 19 (2013)

JOANNA V. HILL
SWEDENBORG FOUNDATION
EXECUTIVE EDITOR

ROBERT F. LAWSON & CAROL S. LAWSON
SERIES EDITORS

SHELIA GEOFFRION
ART EDITOR

SUSANNA V.R. BUSCHMANN
MANAGING EDITOR / DESIGNER

ROBERT TUCKER & JOHN WELLIVER
FICTION EDITORS

ROBERT F. LAWSON
POETRY EDITOR

CONSTANCE J. ELDRIDGE
ASSOCIATE EDITOR

MORGAN BEARD
ASSISTANT EDITOR

PERRY MARTIN & DIRK SPRUYT
CONTRIBUTING EDITORS

KAREN CONNOR
COVER DESIGN

CAROL URBANC
MARKETING

COVER
KAWASE HASUI

Winners of the 2013
Swedenborg Foundation
Bailey Prize for literature:

Katherine Noble, Poetry,
University of Texas, Austin,
"Orpheus After" (p. 96)

Kristin Troyer, Fiction,
Cedarville University, Ohio,
"I Am Elizabeth Proctor" (p. 97)

≈

Chrysalis has been published
annually. Current and back issues,
as well as the entire series
are available for purchase.
To place orders, contact:
Swedenborg Foundation
320 North Church Street
West Chester, Pennsylvania 19380
www.swedenborg.com/chrysalis.

Detail of Snow at Hie Shrine (Shato no yuki [Hie jinja]), New Year's Day *with full image shown on back cover. This artwork is a 1931 Japanese color woodblock print on paper (14-3/16 by 9-3/8 inches) by Kawase Hasui. Virginia Museum of Fine Arts, Richmond, René and Carolyn Balcer Collection. Photograph by Travis Fullerton, ©Virginia Museum of Fine Arts.*

FRONT & BACK COVERS AND PART PAGES
KATE CHAPPELL

The migration of birds marks the seasons on Monhegan Island, off the coast of Maine. Like the birds, Kate Chappell returns every spring to touch down for nourishment, rest, and re-creation. Her multilayered collagraphs are made using a collage method, building up layers of rag paper on board with gesso, incising, and embedding into the plate. Two plates work in tandem: the sea surrounding the island mass, and the bird itself, a two-sided plate that can be positioned freely and printed on both sides.

INSIDE COVERS
LISE AUBRY

Covered in Ice. *Acrylic on paper, 2011.*

Publisher's Statement

The Chrysalis Reader is a journal of spiritual discovery published in honor of Emanuel Swedenborg, eighteenth-century scientist, civil engineer, and mystic, who used his scientific orientation to explore the world of spirit. Respectful of all lives lived according to faith in the Divine, Swedenborg described the ever-present reality of the spiritual world. Individuals who have responded to Swedenborg's ideas with great energy can be found in the arts, especially in literature and painting, as well as in philosophy and the social sciences. The Swedenborg Foundation Press has celebrated and furthered the Swedenborgian connection with the arts by publishing the Chrysalis Reader and by giving the annual Bailey Prize for literature. The Chrysalis Reader is partially funded by a bequest from Esther Blackwood Freeman (Mrs. Forster Freeman Jr.) to honor two past presidents of the Swedenborg Foundation: Forster Freeman Sr. and Forster Freeman.

Patterns

MAKE 'EM AND BREAK 'EM

Edited by Robert F. Lawson & Carol S. Lawson

CHRYSALIS READER / *Swedenborg Foundation Press*

THE CHRYSALIS READER is a book series that examines themes related to the universal quest for wisdom. Inspired by the concepts of Emanuel Swedenborg, each volume presents art with original short stories, essays, and poetry that explore the spiritual dimensions of a chosen theme. Works are selected by the series editors. For information, contact Editor Carol S. Lawson, 1745 Gravel Hill Road, Dillwyn, Virginia 23936.

LIBRARY OF CONGRESS CATALOGING-IN-PUBLICATION DATA
Patterns: make 'em and break 'em / edited by Robert F. Lawson & Carol S. Lawson.
p. cm.—(Chrysalis reader; v. 19)
ISBN 978-0-87785-244-5 (alk. paper)
1. Spiritual life—Christianity—Literary collections. 2. Self-realization—
Literary collections. I. Lawson, Robert F., 1948– II. Lawson, Carol S.
PS509.S62P38 2013
810.8′0382—dc23
2012036993

CHRYSALIS READER
Swedenborg Foundation Press
320 North Church Street
West Chester, Pennsylvania 19380

Contents

Lise Aubry.
Covered in Ice (detail).
Acrylic on paper,
2011.

EDITOR'S NOTE: ROBERT F. LAWSON

The Golden Fish in the Well

Patterns within Patterns

RECENTLY, I HAD THE GOOD FORTUNE to spend my honeymoon on a remote peninsula in the west of Ireland. Behind our cottage, on the slope of Mt. Eagle, is a green patchwork of pastures stitched together by ancient stone walls. The lichen-dappled stones are covered by plant life. In spring, bright yellow blossoms of thorny gorse announce their tenacious hold, and in summer, orange-trumpet montbretia mixed with red-bell fuchsia add a festive air. The colors and shapes of vegetation change each season, but the pattern of durable stone walls remains unchanged.

Before the Republic of Ireland was established in the 1920s, this peninsula's windswept land was one of the last refuges for the Irish language. Now the tables are turned, or should I say, the pattern is reversed. Road signs are in Irish, and all school children are required to take a semester of Irish. Many come to this peninsula's Gaeltacht schools to study it.

Most people living in the nearest hamlet are bilingual, but there are some who speak only "the Irish." If you want to hear English, you must drive to the next town. Patterns are all around us. They provide consistency; but just as Irish is spoken in the hamlet and English in Dingle, patterns can also provide variety.

In a landscape inhabited by people for thousands of years, you witness a rich texture of new patterns overlaid on older patterns. Walking on the back roads, I pass stone beehive huts used by early Christians for shelter when making their pilgrimage to Mount

Brandon. Today, the huts are used by farmers for storage. Pre-Christian wedge tombs and remains of promontory forts are now part of the active farmland. In a culture where nothing is wasted, some stone has been repurposed for newer structures.

Outside our front door, sheep graze on a headland punctuated by an Iron Age fortification with souterrains—underground passages by which defenders could slip away from their attackers. Foot traffic has created a darkened path up to the summit where a large ogham stone, taller than a man, leans into the wind. The stone has a pattern of incised markings, an inscription dedicated to the ancestral goddess Dovinia, protector of the peninsula's ancient people.

These ancient Irish pagans had special sites—burial grounds, solstice or circular stones, and wells—which the Christians sagely co-opted for the promotion of their religion. In early Christian church-

Stone marker in Minard, West Kerry, Ireland, at St. John the Baptist Holy Well. Translation from Irish: John's Well. Pattern of Minard, the 29th of August [a pagan, now Christian, Holy Day]. Photograph by Robert Lawson, 2012.

yards, you can find pagan sundials and ogham stones mixed with crude stone crosses. A short drive from our cottage is the holy well of St. John the Baptist, a well believed to cure aches and said to be the home of a golden fish. If you catch sight of it, you will have good luck and your aches cured. This story probably takes advantage of an early Irish myth—the salmon of knowledge, which the hero Finn eats and gains eternal wisdom—and is an example of incorporating one pattern of thought into another.

Annual devotions at this and other sacred wells are called patterns or patrons *(patrúns)*. Visitors circle the wells while decades of the rosary (ten Hail Marys and one Lord's Prayer) are said. Often pebbles are thrown in—one for each time 'round the well. Until recent times, devotions included not just the saying of prayers but also entertainment with music and dancing. The latter activity, evidence of the wells' pagan origins, was frowned on by the clergy.

High above a remote valley is an 1840s famine graveyard. During the height of the Potato Famine, stillborn and unbaptized children were buried here. At the time it was the belief of Catholics that if a child died before he or she was baptized, the soul went to limbo. The graveyard is overgrown and neglected, but knowledge of these places of little lost souls is well known in these communities.

Emanuel Swedenborg believed that the Catholic Church of his day was out of touch with the realities he was discovering in his spiritual explorations. He reports that the practice of selling indulgences was man-made and wrong. "They [the Catholics] cherish the thought that heaven and hell are in their power and that they can forgive sins at will." (*Heaven and Hell*, paragraph 508 [3]) And innocent children? Swedenborg said they are born with a clean slate. "Every child who dies, no matter where he or she was born, within the church or outside it, of devout or irreverent parents, is accepted by the Lord after death, brought up in heaven, taught according to the divine design, and filled with affections for what is good" (*Heaven and Hell*, paragraph 329).

As for the Protestants, Swedenborg believed Calvin's preoccupation with the concept of predestination (that only a select few are saved) was terribly misguided. On one memorable occasion, Swedenborg encountered Calvin in the world of spirits and held a long discussion with him on this subject. It was clear to Swedenborg that Calvin was not one of the "elect," except in Calvin's mind (*True Christianity*, paragraph 798).

Talk about breaking patterns! Swedenborg's discoveries confronted destructive Christian patterns, both Catholic and Protestant. His conclusions must have been startling and revolutionary to his contemporaries. Rather than a shadowy place of lost souls, the Irish famine graveyard would have been in Swedenborg's view a veritable launch pad straight to heaven. He describes spirits who have a special affinity for the care and upbringing of children, guiding and instructing these heaven-bound offspring. For more on this subject, see the insightful treatment *Children in Heaven* by Ernest Martin.

WE LIVE IN A WORLD LAYERED WITH PATTERNS. Equipped as we are with earthbound sensibilities, some designs are indiscernible until they manifest themselves in the most unexpected ways. *Patterns: Make 'em and Break 'em* has grouped pattern experiences into five categories. For example, in part 1 ("Breaking Patterns") we have a story about a woman who comes from a family of holistic healers who suddenly is unable to use her special gift. In part 2 ("Perpetuating a Pattern"), there is an account reflecting the reverence and esteem Parisians maintained for Charles de Gaulle even after his retirement. A story in part 3 ("Stuck in a Pattern") describes a heroine who moves between descriptions of being an actress in *The Crucible* and life as a university student dealing with her father's illness. (This author is one of our Bailey Prize winners.) A narrative in part 4 ("Patterns in Process"), deals with a soldier's return from Baghdad and his integrating back into civilian American society. In part 5 ("Making New Patterns"), an historian and scholar describes how Swedenborg's first readers in England split in two directions. There were the separatists, who started a new Christian denomination, and the non-separatists, who felt that Swedenborg's concepts could contribute to all forms of worship.

As poetry editor, I am delighted that seven poems are formal verse, ranging from a ghazal to a sestina. Will Wells, author of "Keeping Accounts, Akron," notes a personal pattern—his growing attraction to the sonnet form. "I have sought to link our common patterns of behavior and our dispositions to renew what's broken through an old form, the sonnet, which I hope my content somehow manages to 'make new.'"

From 1985 to the present, many, many accounts of spiritual experience (in both prose and poetry) have been offered by Chrysalis as a service of the Swedenborg Foundation. With the completion of this final edition of Chrysalis, I would like to leave us with the idea that some patterns in our lives can lead to the unexpected. The Chrysalis editorial team has created a legacy of imaginative work, and now it is time for us to launch out into yet-undiscovered patterns of creativity. In the meantime, dear reader, we hope that you will catch sight of your golden fish of surpassing beauty swimming in this well of stories and poems. May it bring you good fortune and great joy.

LINDA PASTAN

Patterns

The way the gulls' tracks in sand—
pattern of bisected triangles—are erased
by the breaking waves;

my mother pinning
the Vogue pattern onto the silky
blue fabric;

the long marching band of numbers: 4
is the square of 2, 16 the square
of 4, and so on;

sex and Samoa—
our adolescent take
on Patterns of Culture;

how history repeats itself:
war, and famine, and quiet
spells of peace;

our fragile days together: toast
and the morning paper, work,
and a glass of pinot gris at 5.

What mortal pattern waits
in these aromatic tea leaves,
in the unyielding lines of my palm?

LINDA PASTAN has written thirteen volumes of poetry, most recently
Traveling Light (W. W. Norton & Company, 2011). Two of her books were fi-
nalists for the National Book Award. In 2003 she won the Ruth Lilly Prize
for lifetime achievement. Pastan served as Poet Laureate of Maryland for
four years and taught at the Bread Loaf Writer's Conference for twenty years.

LAURENCE HOLDEN

Thistle and Seed

In the ruined garden
of late September
one thistle rises.

Above all the rest
from its white crown
seeds take flight, loft

into the emptied sky
like birds
going home.

LAURENCE HOLDEN's paintings and poems are drawn from his connection to
the land—a secluded cove in the Georgia mountains. He believes that paint
and word are two natural dialects for the same thing—bearing witness to the
Creation. His poems have appeared in *Appalachian Heritage, The Reach of
Song: The Poetry Anthology of the Georgia Poetry Society* (2010 and 2011). His
work received an award of excellence from the Georgia Poetry Society (2010)
and an honorable mention from the Byron Herbert Reece Society (2011). His
paintings have appeared in over twenty solo exhibits and are in more than
two hundred public, private, and corporate art collections.

Hello

THE ROAD STRETCHED AND TURNED BEFORE US like a tangled brick-red ribbon. Even the ruts were worn smooth, so unlike the potholed roads in my native New England that threaten to break an axle every spring.

The light, which had been midday bright just an hour ago, was waning. As Kate and I emerged from the village market with brightly colored paintings and carved wooden animals in our reusable canvas sacks, we realized for the first time how far we had to walk to our cabins.

Bright patches of azalea and crown-of-thorn, which had seemed cheery earlier in the day, now cast eerie shadows across our path. The air was no longer heavy with the fragrance of beautiful flowers. Instead, it smelled of ancient dirt and decay. Suddenly, the trees were silent with no monkey or bird calls. All was still and quiet, quite a shock after the constant chatter of our group and the people in the market.

Michael Dietrich.
Curious Children in the Small African Village Tanji, Gambia, Africa (detail).
Photograph.
ALIMIDI.NET.

The women selling necklaces and earrings strung with local seeds and shells had packed up their worn blankets and left. The rest of our own group had gone back earlier with the van. Only Kate and I had lagged behind, talking with the artists, in variations of English, about their works. The market door was locked behind us.

As we left the center of Mua Mission, with its elaborate outdoor cathedral and photos of sad-eyed priests, three goats skittered off the road and into the bush at our approach. We both jumped, startled at the sound of their clacking hooves.

We held our purses and our purchases a little closer as we continued up the empty road. Kate, dressed in a red T-shirt and shorts, was carrying a handmade drum she had bought from a local craftsman. I was wearing my by now very familiar tan capris and a turquoise camp shirt and carrying my camera.

A silent wind picked up. We walked a little closer together and spoke a little more quietly. In a hushed voice, Kate was explaining how she planned to carry her new drum on the flight home in a couple of weeks. Since she had received only one of her lost suitcases from the airline, she was traveling light so far. Adding a large goatskin drum to her carry-on bag didn't yet seem like a big deal.

All at once, we became aware of footsteps behind us. Footsteps quickly became a pitter-patter of many feet, and we both spun around to look. Where they all came from, we didn't know. Somehow, a crowd of about twenty children had fallen in step about twenty feet behind us.

"He-llo," some of them said in sing-songy voices and smiled shyly.

"He-llo," we called and smiled back.

The children ranged in age from about six to twelve. Some smiled as if they were playing a favorite game, while others appeared terrified if our gazes lingered on them. Yet, they all followed us, and the crowd grew as more and more children joined in.

It would have looked to an outsider like some weird version of Pied Piper. Still, we continued turning around and smiling and waving to their "he-llos" as we slowly made our way back toward our cabins, our friends, and dinner.

It became a game, and Kate and I gladly gave up efforts to converse in order to maintain our role in the pattern of call and response. She swung her drum by its flimsy strap, and I was waving for the hundredth time to the kids who squealed with glee every time we turned around. I was wondering if our entourage would follow us the entire mile back to the tall steel gates that separated visitors from villagers when three bigger boys jumped out of the bush to our right.

They each carried a stick; long pointy branches wrenched off scraggly trees. One of the boys, a tall, lanky teenager dressed in dingy jeans and a Chicago Bulls jersey, pointed his stick at us. All of us stopped in our tracks when the big boys appeared. I stole a glance at our entourage, whose voices had become silent and whose faces reflected uncertainty, and maybe fear.

"Give me money," the tall teen demanded, pointing his stick in the direction of Kate and me. The other two boys followed his lead, pointing their sticks and saying, "Give me money," in somewhat faltering English. By now some of the younger kids behind us thought they'd try this new game. Soon the air was filled with voices demanding money. Amid the aggressive shouts, some of the youngest children started to cry.

There had been nothing in my Bradt Malawi guidebook to steer us through this situation. I was at a loss for what to do. My gut said to ignore them, but the teenagers were blocking our path. I wanted to give them money, wanted to give money to everyone who needed it, but I knew to do so would cause a mob scene, and there would never be enough money to go around.

It was Kate who, the first time we talked on Skype, explained she had a tough edge and a mouth like a trucker because she'd grown up in a rough part of St. Louis. Now, she looked the tall teen in the eye and said, "No."

There was a long pause. I stared at the sharp end of his stick.

"Give me money?" he said again, this time with a question in his tone and a wavering smile.

"No," Kate replied again. She shifted the drum-strap on her shoulder, then took my hand in hers and steered us around the teens. We kept walking.

Confused, the teenagers and the little kids began to follow us. There were still some requests for money, but we ignored them.

After a few minutes, we heard a tentative, "He-llo" spoken by one of the youngest voices. Kate began to beat a rhythm onto her new drum, and we resumed our game of singing "He-llo." The kids, visibly relaxed at the familiar drum sound and a familiar game, responded back in unison.

We continued our call and response until we'd wound around a big bend. I turned back and glanced at the crowd. The big boys were still with us, but now they were smiling and participating in the game. They had dropped their sticks. We slowed near the edges of an ancient baobab, and Kate began a new beat. "He-llo, we're walking down the street," she sang.

Behind us, many variations on Kate's song erupted, along with a lot of giggles. On and on, we walked and sang as the sun began to sink behind a pointy purple mountain. Kate and I walked backwards much of the way, giggling along with our new friends, all thoughts of anything serious long forgotten.

When, at last, we arrived at the steel gates, our entourage stopped about ten feet from the barrier. Probably they knew they couldn't come any farther. Probably, if we spoke Chichewa, we would have told them how much we wished they could all be our guests at dinner. Probably that would not have been proper.

In the end, the children were the ones who saved us all from embarrassment. With smiles on every face, they each waved and yelled "He-llo" to bid us farewell as they disappeared back down the lane and into the village.

KARI KYNARD-RIDGE is a journalist, editor, photographer, and fiction writer. Her work has been published in literary journals, metropolitan newspapers, national magazines, and on websites. She leads Amherst Writers and Artists-based writing workshops in Massachusetts. This story is from a chapter in her book about Malawi experiences in Africa, volunteering with the nonprofit VoiceFlame, a program to help women create writing workshops in their villages and towns.

PART I
Breaking Patterns

Remission

In sun-bleached fields, the fragrance of late honeysuckle
floats like a prayer snatched from a mother's lips,
lost in time's loose breezes.

Who can explain the patient who rises well one morning,
clean cells singing in her skin, or how a soul
sheds sadness that has buried its spores and spread
To all the chambers of memory and pleasure?

A bluebird singing in a sapling
parts depression's curtain to reveal the true sky,
and I slip through, like a salmon through Kodiak claws.

As I walk mown trails to my childhood home,
locusts leap from underfoot to blowsy weeds.
Blond plumes of long grass stroke the belly of September.

Queen Anne's Lace shines like a carnival of brides;
yellow cabbage moths pleasure the blue chickory.
The sky repeats its reckless promise
to hold this earth through another season.

I grasp these unsought grains of joy in my palm,
the way my mother held the seeds of my self
in her womb's tight fist.

At my cradle, she spoke the wayward prayer
that greets me here, warm, still moist from her young breath,
and sweet with all her hope for my life.

AMANDA LEIGH ROGERS teaches theater and writing at Bryn Athyn College. She loves poetry as an art form that marries the sensual and the cerebral, and as a spiritual practice that invites writer and reader to move between states of quiet presence and energetic expression. Her work has most recently appeared in *Tipton Poetry Journal, The Mindful Word, Ruminate Magazine,* and *Sojourners.* She is a recipient of the Hopwood Award for major poetry.

DAVID S. RUBENSTEIN

Time Gate

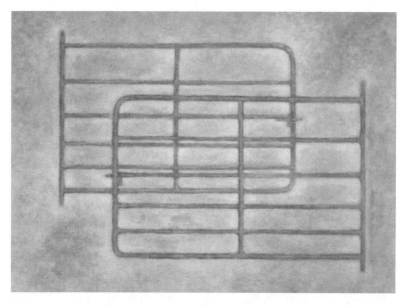

AS HE PLACED HIS SUITCASE IN THE TRUNK of his twenty-year-old
Trabant, he found himself wondering idly if his wife could hide in
there with it. He quickly rejected the idea: the exhaust fumes from the
rusty old car would undoubtedly get to her long before the Grepos
found her.

Pat Owen.
Farm Gates.
Oil on linen, 2010.

He glanced around nervously, half expecting the Stasi to leap
from the shadows and arrest him for even thinking about escape. In
the gray street of gray buildings under ominous gray skies, the eyes
were everywhere, burning into the back of his neck and rendering his
face the same ashen color as his world.

When he and Anna wanted to talk about escape, they left their
apartment, which was undoubtedly bugged, and went to a nearby
park. There they strolled to an open area where they spoke in hushed
tones of the lives they craved in the West, of the freedom, and of the
color. So drab was their world that they themselves felt sodden and
faded.

But talk as they would, they were still there. He was allowed to
leave but only by himself. The authorities knew full well that he
would always come back. Back to his Anna. Back to Anna. How could
they ever get out together—to start the new life they yearned for in
the West? They'd had endless discussions and proposals and schemes

3

over the years. Each one they contemplated for weeks, unspoken in the days of their lives but hinted at with a raised eyebrow, a nod, each knowing what the other was thinking. But every idea was in turn dashed when some more desperate East Berliner would actually try it and either be dragged away in chains or left to lie bleeding in the no-man's-land gravel as an object lesson. Somehow he would get her out. It was his solemn promise to her. To himself. He would get her out.

So he placed his sample case into the trunk next to the suitcase and closed the lid. Anna would not be coming. Not this time.

Darkness had fallen unnoticed in the perpetual gloom, and behind the curtained windows of the soot-blackened buildings, some still showing the scars of Soviet bullets from three decades past, few lights winked on, as though the inhabitants had long ago given in to the perpetual twilight of their existence. In The People's Paradise.

He checked his watch. He needed to be at the Brandenburg checkpoint by 8 PM for his exit visa to be valid. It was only 5:30 PM. He would wait until Anna returned from work, say goodbye, and go. Back again in a week. Back again to his Anna, hostage. Back again.

He trudged into the tenement building and up five flights of stairs to their two-room flat. He was so tired. From the dim hallway he opened the door into the empty apartment. Of course no children, he thought again to himself. He and Anna wanted a family desperately, to replace all those they had lost. Both of them had come through the war without a single living family member. But who in their right mind would bring a child into this, this . . . Purgatory? No, they had to get out. This time, they had agreed, he would contact someone in the West who might be able to help. This time they would take the risk. This time. Doing nothing was tantamount to accepting. And they would not accept. Never accept.

He set a kettle of water on the stove, lit the burner, and took down two teacups. She was due any minute, and they had time for a cup before he left. When the kettle began to whistle and she hadn't arrived yet, faint pricks of unease furrowed his brow. The five-thirty train stop was always on time. Always within a minute of the posted schedule. And she was always on it. Every day, like clockwork. There was some small comfort in the absolute, tedious regularity. But the rigid pattern of each day caused alarm in its smallest deviation. He turned down the gas, and the whistle trailed off into the silent room.

He could see her, sitting on the train, crammed in with some malodorous oaf next to her. The train obviously delayed. All the gray people sitting silently, compliantly, as the delay went on. What were they late for? Another gray night in their gray apartments? Knees together, purse on her lap, she would be thinking of him. Knowing that he had to leave. Knowing that he would be on the green side of the Wall that very night, while she stayed behind, the long chain that kept him from freedom. Knowing that, as they had agreed, he would take the chance. She would wait while he was gone, wait for the boots on the stairs, the pounding on the door if he failed. Or the wordless look of hope in his eyes if he succeeded.

By six-fifteen he began to pace. He went to the front window to watch for her in the street, but the only working street lamp was half a block away, so he could see little. Moving traffic swept the sidewalks with light, and he could make out figures. None looked like Anna. None moved like Anna. At six-thirty, he realized that he would have to leave without saying goodbye. A note, on the table. But what had happened to her? With a pencil above the paper, he noticed that his hand was shaking. Had she ever been late? There was that one time; but actually, she had told him that she would be late, and he had forgotten. He stood and walked to the window again. Peered into the darkness.

The jangling of the telephone startled him. He looked at it from across the room in confusion, then rushed to pick it up.

"Anna?"

"No, it's Kirt."

He stared, not comprehending. "Oh, Kirt. Sorry, I was expecting Anna."

"I know. That's why I'm calling." Pause.

"Kirt . . . ?"

"There's been an accident. A train wreck."

"Oh my God . . ."

"I'm afraid it's Anna. I'm so sorry."

The room rushed inward, time stopped.

"Hans?"

"Hans?"

"Uh, yes. Dead?"

"Yes."

Static on the line. Popping. Other conversations fading in and out like voices from across the universe.

"Are you sure?"

"I'm a doctor, Hans. I was there. Three cars back. I went up to help."

"Did she . . ."

"I'm quite sure it was instantaneous."

"And it was Anna? For certain?"

"Yes. No doubt. It was she."

He sank to his knees, the phone pressed to his ear.

"Hans?"

"Yes."

"Hans, they're taking her to the People's Police Hospital. She'll be in the morgue." He paused. "If you wish to identify her."

He was in the Trabant. At a dark intersection, traffic from the right not stopping, honking as he drove through, tires skidding. He drove on, oblivious. Where was he going?

Morgue. He was going to the morgue. To the hospital.

At the next intersection, he saw flashing lights off to the left. He gazed there, until an impatient horn behind startled him into action. He turned left and drove toward the lights. A block on, he could see the wreck. Jumbled train cars, accordioned. On their sides. Steel wheels gleaming in the harsh emergency lights. He stopped and stared.

A woman walked past him on the sidewalk, pushing a pram and holding the hand of a small child, hurrying against the darkness. Anna was in the morgue; life went on.

Some time later he turned the car around and drove on to the hospital.

In the basement. In the chill of the morgue. A white-coated attendant had led him through the room, a room full of steel tables upon which rested sheet-covered forms, blood showing through in drying red testament. Knots of somber people in quiet discussions or muted anguish. The attendant consulted a clipboard again, then checked a toe tag. Moved on to the next table, another tag. Squeezing past a group of red-eyed people to the next. The right tag. The man pulled the sheet down unceremoniously, and there lay Anna.

He gasped at her paleness. And her beauty. Her face uninjured. His eyes trailed down the length of the sheet to her blood-soaked torso, and he felt dizzy. He leaned heavily on the table, which rolled on its wheels. The attendant grasped him under an arm, and he steadied.

"I'll give you a moment," the man said, suddenly sympathetic. He moved off toward a group of people who had just appeared in the doorway.

He gazed upon her pallid face and suddenly saw her twenty years earlier, her smooth, line-less face blushing at something he had said in the hallway leading to the high school auditorium. He saw her in the sunshine as they walked between buildings at University, laughing at his seriousness. He saw the decades as they descended upon her like a darkening haze, sapping the color from her cheeks and the delight from her smile. He thought about their plots to escape, becoming more urgent as time went by, and finally their decision just last week to risk making contact in the West. Finally, to break free or die trying. Then the phone call. And then she was gone.

"So, Herr Wagner. Is this your wife?" The attendant was back, clipboard in hand, form filled out and ready for his signature.

What had he said?

"I said, is this your wife?"

What had Kirt said? Something odd. If you wish to identify her. Yes. That was odd. What did he mean by that?

If you wish to identify her.

"What time is it?" he asked suddenly, looking at his watch. Seven thirty-two.

He looked around, panicked. He started for the door.

"Is this your wife?" the attendant called after him, confused. All around, people looked up from their grief.

"No," he yelled back over his shoulder. "There must be some mistake."

He sprinted up the stairs, out into the night and to his car. He cranked the engine. It did not start. He forced himself to calm, then held down the accelerator and tried again. The engine bucked and coughed, but then smoothed. He shoved it into gear and sped out into traffic.

He looked again at his watch but couldn't read it in the darkness and dared not struggle with it, as every iota of his attention was needed to keep the car on the road as he swerved around corners, ran traffic lights, and violated every speed limit. The gate was closing. If he did not get out tonight, they would never let him leave again.

Even if he made it by eight, before his visa expired, how long before the Stasi, the dreaded Staatssicherheitsdienst, would sense the tear in the fabric of his pattern and put together the death of his anchor with his exit visa?

But he had said it wasn't Anna. Maybe that would buy him time. If they hadn't already assumed it was she and started the process an hour ago.

But how could he leave her there, on the cold steel table? He should be there, see to a decent cremation. What of all their things? He had nothing but the clothes in his suitcase. One picture of her in his wallet. Everything else would be lost. A lifetime of memories. He slowed. This was not right.

But to stay was to be condemned to life alone, in this place. Alone. The thought was unbearable.

What would Anna want? All that was left of Anna was in his head. Back there on the steel table, that was a husk. Anna would say "Go! I'm with you." In his head, "Go!"

He floored the gas pedal again, skidding on the cobblestones as he entered Potsdamer Platz and saw the lights of Checkpoint Charlie ahead.

They'll never find her. He pulled into the line, checking his watch. Seven fifty-five. In front of him, two Grepos were stepping back from a car as a third raised the gate and motioned it through. It moved off into the bright roadway toward the blue sign reading "You are entering the American Sector."

They'll never find her, he thought again as he pulled his car forward.

"Papers!" Papers! He panicked. He'd left them at home in his fog-shrouded journey to the hospital. He patted his pockets in horror, a caricature of the absent-minded. But then, there they were, in the breast pocket of his coat. Sweating, he handed them to the guard, who looked at him more suspiciously than usual.

"Step out of the vehicle."

He stepped out. _They'll never find her._

A Grepo rolled a mirror under the car, looking for stowaways. Front, sides, back.

The Grepo with his papers patted him down, finding nothing. _They'll never find her._

Finally the man handed him back his papers. He got back into the car. The mirror man was searching the trunk, while a third had lifted the back seat, looking under it at nothing but rust, and dropped it back without pressing it into place. The searcher had then backed out of the car and nodded to the first Grepo, who nodded in turn to the man at the gate.

The gate rose slowly, and he started the car through it. As he did, a telephone in the guard booth rang with a loud jangle, and the guard went inside. Picked it up, listened for a moment, then yelled at the gatekeeper. As the gate reversed its upward movement and began to descend, the old Trabant belched smoke and lurched forward, the black-and-white barrier scraping across the roof.

He drove, pedal to the floor, knowing he would not hear the shot that pierced his brain. Through the haze of his exhaust he could barely make out the Grepos as they unshouldered their Kalashnikovs and aimed in his direction. _Anna. Anna, we're almost there!_ If he did not make it, she was gone forever.

Then ahead he saw two American soldiers watching the scene unfold rush forward, their M-14s raised and pointed back toward the Grepos. The harsh light made the road between the two sectors like moonscape, all shadows washed out, all detail in blinding clarity. He drove on, white hands clutching the wheel, the ancient Trabant as if plowing through mud, he and Anna, on across the moat to the bright colors of freedom.

DAVID S. RUBENSTEIN is an American writer and painter.

CAROL KANTER

two birds

in counterpoint, they spiral couplets upward,
too high, too swift to name; they tryst unknown,
every body contour, marking blurred
into a loopy, undistinguished brown

neck rings, beak hooks, leg bands, darker spots
elide in flaps of perfect synchrony
braiding the maypole air with lovers' knots;
chirps grace note a romantic symphony

for muted winds; while far off in the sky
a shrinking wedge of cousins, sibs, grown chicks
hardly seem to miss this pair; those fly
with vee filled in, snub these eccentrics

who tour jêté adieux to journeys gone,
a-dance with all they've been and seen and done.

CAROL KANTER's work has appeared in numerous literary journals and anthologies. *Atlanta Review* gave her three International Merit Awards before
publishing two of her poems. Her two chapbooks were published
by FinishingLine Press, *Out of Southern Africa* (2005) and *Chronicle of Dog*
(2006). *No Secret Where Elephants Walk* (DualArts Press, 2010) presents
Kanter's poetry with her husband's photography from Africa. She is a
psychotherapist. Kanter says, "I used a sonnet format for 'two birds' to in-
voke the larger formation in which birds navigate and from which the cou-
ple(t) has chosen to break off in the end.

C'est l'Heure

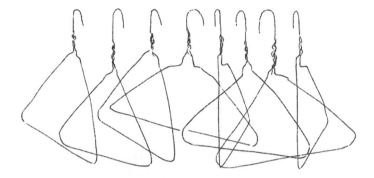

SURELY SHE CAN HEAR MY HEART POUNDING against the wood floor.

What will I say when she looks under the bed?

"Well, Madame," I could say, "I left something—*quelque chose*—under this bed."

But Madame is no idiot. "*Vous* are the only *quelque chose* under that bed," she would reply. This bed has been stripped, cleaned, sanitized, and is ready for another student. A student who is not me.

Madame's brown oxfords cross the room. Heavy stockings wrap her legs, even in May. She never wears pants. Pants do not suit the headmistress of an expensive international girls' boarding school.

My high school junior year abroad is over.

Terminée.

I am being sent home.

This is not the only time Madame has come looking for me.

THE FIRST TIME IT WAS EARLY OCTOBER. Still giddy from my new-found freedom, I tiptoed across the room to awaken Elisa. A room-mate was more fun than a sister, better than a friend. A roommate was a school-year of sleepovers. My sister, Helen, would have her overseas adventure in a few years. That had been the plan.

Elisa and I stacked pillows and blankets on our window seat to take in the midnight view. Through the gaping windows, down the old stone wall of the château-turned-dormitory, beyond the mani-cured school grounds, over the gentle slope of a hill cluttered with shingled roofs, pointed church steeples and evergreens, lay Lake

Geneva. Its crinkled waters reflected the snowcapped French Alps
and the harvest moon. We feasted on treats lifted from the dining hall:
French bread and unsalted butter, plump grapes, *jus de raisin*, pas-
tries with chocolate, almonds, apricot jam . . . a late night *fête*.

Our mistake? Turning up the volume of Eddie Money on my
boombox. "Baby hold onto me," we howled at the moon.

The door swung open and there Madame stood, her worsted
wool slippers just visible under her gray bathrobe.

"Children!" she said. "It is midnight! *C'est l'heure de dormir!*"
Time to sleep. She pointed to our beds. *"Au lit!"*

What will I say when she looks under the bed?

Madame walks to the closet, the one with the door that sticks. My
closet. My ex-closet. Two tugs and it gives. Nothing left in there but
hangers, that chipped mirror, and my initials engraved with the Swiss
Army pocketknife Helen had given me. A going-away gift.

Next to my initials, I had scrawled: *J'étais ici.*

I was here.

"Madame," I could say. "This room was mine for eight months. I
was just bidding *adieu* to every last corner."

But Madame isn't sentimental. She doesn't care about small
things like corners and big things like goodbyes. She is as tight as the
laces on those oxfords. Does she even remember high school?

I should be downstairs, ready to leave.

The taxi is coming.

THE SECOND TIME Madame came looking for me, Elisa and I had
skipped French class. Some days we really weren't in a subjunctive
mood. Did we think anyone would notice? No. We were free agents.
She was fun, adventuresome, my partner in crime. Like sisters, only
without the bickering. Instead of doing *dictée*, we tried on her skinny jeans and satin tops. I grabbed my Polaroid camera, Elisa grabbed
her hairdryer, and we took turns blowing our hair back and posing
for the fashion shoot. That is, until Madame flung open the door,
those oxfords flat on the floor but somehow staring us down.

"Girls! You should be in class! *Toute de suite!* Next time, I will call
home! *Allez!*"

What will I say when she looks under the bed?

Goodbyes are important. Elisa and I already had ours. We hugged
each other until they peeled her away to send her back to class. I was
supposed to wait for my taxi. Instead, I bolted up here. This bedroom
knows me. It has seen me laughing and crying.

When Madame called me, I dove under this bed because I didn't want the lecture. Not in French. Not a French hardened by her thick German accent.

Not on my last day.

"Madame," I could say, "some of the coils under this bed have not, *je répète*, have not been dusted . . ."

If my heart pounds any harder, I will knock a hole through this floor and land on top of my bulging suitcase in the front entrance.

Those oxfords click over to the other closet. Elisa's closet.

THIRD TIME. I knew it wasn't okay to smoke. But our own little store around the corner—*le P'tit Mag*—sold cigarettes to anyone. To fifteen-year-olds. To us. Elisa and I opened the window in spite of the snow that drifted in from the February sky. I lit a match, anticipated the moment, took a puff, and coughed it out at the world. We took one hacking puff after the other. (Helen would never have dared. She was a rule-follower, the good child.) How did we know that the smoke would ricochet back into the room, under the doorway, into the hallway, and down the stairs, seeking out Madame in her office below?

When our door flew open, I fixed my gaze on the pointed toes of those oxfords. How many pairs must she have? One? Fifteen?

"Young ladies!" she said, her voice raised. "*C'est strictement interdit!* Forbidden for girls to smoke! Your parents will be notified and the next time . . . suspension!"

She clamped her hand over the pack and crumpled it.

What will I say when she looks under the bed?

She opens the closet.

Not in there, Madame. Why would I hide in Elisa's closet? It is still full of Elisa's clothes and shoes, which, by the way, do not include brown oxfords like your own. Elisa is the lucky one—no one is plucking her from here, no one is curtailing her stay. She will leave at the right time, in June, at the end of the school year, before summer break. And when she goes home? She will be with her family and everything will be normal.

"Madame," I could say, "don't make me go home yet. I'm not ready—*je ne suis pas prête.* Just give me . . ."

Give me what?

A moment?

A break?

A different ending?

FOURTH TIME. Late afternoon, Elisa was playing cards downstairs. Alone, I preferred inspecting myself in the mirror. Should I grow out my bangs? How would eyeliner look? Lip gloss? Blush? . . .

A knock. I opened the door and came face to face with Madame.

Saturdays were sanctioned free time. What rule had I broken? Didn't eat the anchovy paste on toast at lunch? Took too many stairs at once? Spoke too much English?

She motioned for me to sit on the bed. Pulled up a chair. Her hand reached out, hovered, then rested on top of mine. Above, her fingers were wrinkled. Underneath, smooth. Her oxfords were tucked under her skirt.

"*Mademoiselle*," she said, her look serious. Her voice was quiet, not angry.

"*Votre sœur* . . . your sister . . . Helen . . ."

Helen's image popped up. Saturday morning in Virginia. She must be eating breakfast. No, it's later than breakfast. Maybe she's at a soccer match?

"*Oui?*" I asked.

"Your parents called. I have some . . . *mauvaises nouvelles* . . . some bad news."

I was confused. Not a scolding?

"Your sister was in an accident this morning . . . a very bad car accident." Madame's hand clenched mine. "*Elle est décédée.*"

"*Je ne* . . . I don't understand," I said.

"*Elle est morte.* She died. It was a very bad accident. I'm so sorry."

Her mouth continued to move. English? French? No language made sense anymore.

What will I say when she looks under the bed?
I hold my breath.
She pauses.
Sighs.
And then . . . leaves.
My cheek rests against the floor. Gazing across the room, I see my own naked footsteps over these past months, so light, now heavy. *Let me stay under here forever, Madame. I don't want to go home.*
J'ai peur.
I'm scared.
Her oxfords clack, clack, clack down the stairs to the first floor where I am supposed to be so I can go home to a home without a sister. I gasp and hot tears pour across my nose and cheek onto the floor. My younger sister, my only sister . . . how can it be? Just a few months ago, at the end of Christmas break, she was jumping and waving see-you-soon. Just last week, she called and told me she had a crush. Just

yesterday, I got her letter filled with smiley-faced confetti. At the end of school, she was supposed to come with Mom and Dad so we could see Europe, but . . . my curly haired sister who raced tricycles with me down our long driveway, who poured dry cat food in the doll carriage to play baby with our cat, who hated bananas and loved mustard on her fries, who quarreled with me over things big and small, the chipped barrette, the stained T-shirt, the putt-putt golf game that I won, the borrowed money, her talent with the viola, the infuriating manner in which she always got her way with Mom and Dad. . . .

This year was my break. It was only supposed to be a break though.

Not an end.

I would scream if I could. I want to empty out my fear and sadness.

My taxi honks. Madame calls for me, insistent. This tiny bed frame cannot hide me here forever. Reluctantly, I slide out from under the bed. I breathe. I can still breathe. "Goodbye, room," I whisper, trying to inhale its protection one last time. I open the door, slip through, and shut it as quietly as I can.

Madame watches as I descend the steps. Her lips are pursed. She doesn't ask me where I have been. She places firm hands on my shoulders.

"*Êtes-vous prête, Mademoiselle?*" she asks.

Am I ready? What do I say? I can't look at her face, so I look down. Her oxfords are pressed together, the polished leather tidy in front of the scuffed rubber of my sneakers.

My stomach muscles tighten.

I want to shout that I'm not ready.

Instead, I say, "*Oui, Madame. Cest l'heure.*"

It is time.

And that is what I repeat silently to the stone threshold . . . to the gravel on the driveway . . . to the back of the taxi driver's seat . . . to myself.

It is time.

Time to leave.

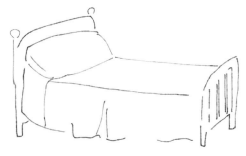

Vincent Desjardins.
Digital pen and ink,
using Corel Painter,
2012.

ABIGAIL CALKINS AGUIRRE holds a master of fine arts in writing from Vermont College of Fine Arts, as well as a master of public administration from Columbia University. Her story, "Development Is Down This Road," won the 1992 Peace Corps Experience Award from *RPCV Writers and Readers* magazine and was published in three Peace Corps anthologies as well as by two magazines. She has studied and worked in numerous countries, including Cameroon, France, Haiti, Mexico, and Switzerland.

RICHARD SCHIFFMAN

The Transmigration of Tools

He directed his next of kin to give away the tools—
the sanders and mallets and scrapers, bit braces,
chisels and fluters assembled lovingly over decades,
many impossible to come by, nowadays,
or custom-made by himself for tasks endemic
to his work as a shaper of primordial elements—
wood and stone and metal and bone.

So they threw a party when he died—
"the great tool divide"—for that tight co-fraternity
who spend their days—as he had—gouging and forging,
stripping and finishing. His assistant brought
a flatbed truck to haul away the welding station,
others crammed burlap sacks and shopping carts
with planes and brackets, spools of heavy twine,
drills and drill bits, blocks of poplar, pots of glue.
In no time, the plywood boards stood bare.
Only the outlines remained of handsaws and pliers,
and reamers, penciled ghosts of a life given
to excavating the stubborn densities of matter.

His place of assemblage now swept and silent.
His works scattered—though some few remain
in cyberspace and yellowing catalogues.
The universe he made increasingly
unmade. Yet it doubtless eased his dying mind
to know the tools were one of a kind,
and would survive in other hands.

Author of two spiritual biographies, RICHARD SCHIFFMAN is an environmental journalist and a poet whose work has been published in a wide variety of print and internet journals. Like the protagonist in this poem, he believes that we are here on earth to pass on our tools, to enrich the world with
our own unique gifts and ways of being.

Delaware and the Rip-off King

THE TELEVISION WAS HOT—no doubt about it. A plasma in this neighborhood? Not likely. Not this time of year. No way.

"Where'd you get that from?" I ask.

"Delaware."

I start laughing; I can't help it. "Delaware!?"

"That's right, man. Delaware." He's serious.

"All right," I say, gathering my breath. I put on my wheeling and dealing poker face and tell him I'll give him three hundred for it.

"Three hundred?! You high man? You on drugs? It's worth ten times that."

"It ain't worth squat when the cops come take it."

"I'm telling you, I got it from Delaware. It's cool."

"Sure it is," I say. "Two-fifty."

"Man." He looks around; his eyes focus on the alto sax hanging on the far wall, then on the video camera in the case beside him. "Three hundred?"

The Monopoly® Man is the logo used on the game and created by the Parker Brothers.

17

I write out the ticket quick, like I usually do. I open the till and slowly hand over the bills. I think there's no way he's gonna remember this afternoon as it is, but five minutes off the junk is five minutes clean, ain't it?

The phone rings as he leaves my shop. I hear him mutter and call me a "rip-off king" as he shoves the bills into his back pocket. I don't say nothing.

Later, I'm ready to shut off the lights and climb up to my empty apartment. As I'm walking to the door to pull over the metal bars to lock up, the bell jingles. In walks this guy, suit, tie, loafers for crying out loud, and he says, "I believe you have something of mine."

Danged dog if he doesn't hand over the ticket for the plasma TV and three hundred bucks.

"Certainly," I say—nobody can say the "Rip-off King" don't have good manners. I bring the television out; it hadn't moved very far away from my counter that afternoon.

"You need help with that?" I ask. The guy is older than me, but I don't guess by how much.

"Yes. Thank you." We carry it out of the store. His dark Lincoln Town Car is parked right close. He opens the back passenger side door, and we slide it gently into the back.

"Thank you," he says again. He even shakes my hand before he drives away.

About a month goes by, and I don't think anything more about it. Suddenly, I'm looking at a Bose stereo sitting on my counter, and the guy that brought me the plasma is standing behind it. His brown eyes are bloodshot like you wouldn't believe.

"Where'd this come from?" I ask, "Rhode-freaking-Island?"

I know this particular system sets a body back at least nine hundred bucks. "Seventy," I say. I'm not in a generous mood, though I am dying to see where this goes.

"Man," he mutters. "Two-fifty. I'm good for it."

"Seventy-five."

"Screw you."

"Screw me! Screw me? That'd cost more than this piece of junk will *ever* be worth."

"Whatever, man."

After a while, we settle at one and a quarter. He takes the money and leaves.

That night, the same thing happens. Just before I'm going to close up, the older guy walks in holding the ticket and the cash. I help him out. I carry the stereo and put it in the trunk. This time I ask, "What's the deal? How you know that horse humper?"

The guy's eyes get all distant looking, and he clears his throat. "He's my son."

"No way."

He smiles at me, "I was young once. I made some questionable choices. Now I'm living with the aftermath."

"You want for me to not take the stuff?"

"Oh, no. Please, take what he brings you. As long as you do, I'll be able to retrieve it. Otherwise, I'd never see these things again."

"They're just things," I say. I feel all philosophical at the moment.

"It's just chemicals," he counters.

We stand there on the sidewalk for a minute, looking at our shoes.

"I've tried to get him into programs. Perhaps, in time, he will change."

I don't say nothing.

So, this keeps going on. Once or twice a month, tie tacks, TVs, anything that can't be bolted down floats into my shop. He asks for too much; I give him some cash. He cusses me as he walks out of the store and a few hours later, right around closing time, his father shows up with the money and the ticket. I start feeling sort of bad about the whole situation, then boom! They both stop coming. Just disappear. I don't see or hear from them for months. I think maybe it's on account of the weather. I don't want to think about the other possibility.

Spring comes along and guess who walks in? Both of them, but this time they're together. The horse humper looks good. His skin has cleared up and his shirt is clean. He begins apologizing before he's anywhere near my counter.

"Mister, I am so sorry for swearing at you and calling you names. It wasn't me. It was the drugs talking."

I raise my eyebrows.

"You were very helpful," The older guy tells me. "With your help I was able to have the time I needed to build up his trust in me. The detox wasn't pretty, and the counseling has been rough at times, but he's been clean for three months now." He looks over at his son and smiles wide. I really want to believe it with him; that his kid will stay clean.

"I'd like to reward you for your indulgence." He pulls out a check and hands it to me. Five hundred bucks. Drawn from the account of "William J. Delaware."

Go figure.

T. I. SHERWOOD lives beside a creek in western New York and enjoys gardening, reading, and working with glass. Her writing has appeared in many venues and she has won several prizes.

DUANE TUCKER

The Blade
of Solitude
for Sue

One day after so many days
Of scraping and planing, the blade of solitude
Scoured me clear the way fasting does
And in the emptiness I noticed a buoyancy

Here and there were no longer
Tugging at me
This and that had let me be →
I felt the fingers of light that were spinning the shivering birds

Out over the valley, spinning me →
Out of my loneliness. Even though the air was frigid,
Even though, surely, they were near starving
They curved and spired in perfect prayer

And I with them.

Later a drift of moonlight parted
And beyond, in the cobalt dark, stood my father
Still wearing his *de riguer*
Brooks Brothers suit, still carrying his leather briefcase →

He smiled that quivering, Depression-scarred smile
So rare it used to make me soar
And I knew
At last, he understood

DUANE TUCKER is a screenwriter, playwright, critic, essayist, and poet. He has reviewed theatre for the *Hamilton Spectator* and written art criticism for *Canadian Art* and *Border Crossings*. In a previous incarnation, he played far too many cops and crooks, appearing in over forty films and television shows. His poetry and prose have been widely published. *Passager* journal (University of Baltimore) voted him poet of the year (2002).

Workin' on Woodstock

Setting the Stage

THIS MEMOIR IS ABOUT WHAT HAPPENED BEHIND THE SCENES—*leading up to and during the 1969 Woodstock Festival in upstate New York. I was artistic coordinator of the field crews who built the environmental setting for the festival.*

Unexpectedly, in its spectacle and drama, the Woodstock Festival was an immense, sprawling opera, with a cast of thousands. The performers sang and played their hearts out, their multicolor costumes on stage flying and flashing, the music booming and rolling over the hills. The audience—in fringe, paint, filmy dresses, beads—was singing and dancing: they were performers too.

Woods and fields surrounded the stage. This country setting hosted an unparalleled three-day extravaganza, spun out in the open, with sun, rain, heat, cold, and the smell of the crowd. All of this was made more dramatic by low-hanging veils of smoke from campfires scattered about, creating the atmosphere of a Civil War battlefield.

Sustaining the energy and needs of these 500,000 performers was like attending an opera. There were breaks for food, visits to outhouses, and time to mingle and make new acquaintances. Woodstock was performance art in the finest sense of the term. It was alive.

Max's farm is just what you would want a farm to be: quiet, no sound of cars or trucks. Airliners would have to shut down their engines and glide through the air space. We felt a soft breeze as it gently moved the tall grass, like the sound of corduroy pants brushing against your legs while walking.

Bill Ward

People everywhere . . . everywhere. From where I stood outside the operations trailer on the top of the hill, I could see people from horizon to horizon. Bodies were spread out across the landscape like a brightly painted Chinese fan. Hundreds of thousands of faces were surrounded on all sides by trees, and above the dark line of trees, the darkening afternoon sky made a dramatic frame.

I was standing at the top looking down at the stage below me. It was hard to take it all in. Inside the operations trailer, my wife Jean, Mel, Penny, and the others were all waiting, disconnected. They had to just wait. It was all up to the staff on stage.

When it was time to start the show, none of the performers were ready. After some discussion and shuffling of acts, it was decided John

The first arrivals staked out their territory like early settlers. Small groups congregated on blankets with a few meager belongings.

Sebastian would be first. But when they found him, he was in no shape to go on.

Richie Havens must have drawn the short straw because he came on stage first. He sat down and, as he said later, he had no idea there would be that many people. He was really surprised to see that crowd. When he started to play, everyone on the staff let go of the breath they had been holding since mid-summer.

The enormous sound system speakers on the towers spread music across the landscape. Richie Havens looked so small on that stage—but his music came out big.

Wearing my blue staff jacket with its white dove and guitar logo on the back, I made my way down to the stage. Because of that jacket, I was able to get close. By that time, Havens had gotten over his jitters and was finding his groove and feeling more at ease.

The strumming of his guitar boomed out over the speakers, and the lyrics of *Motherless Child* rolled over the audience like waves breaking on the beach. His music produced a feeling of joy that spread over the crowd and reached deep down into the soul of everyone.

In the words of those times, "good vibes" spread through the crowd. It was contagious. You could see it in the faces, hear it in the voices, and see it in the body language. There were smiles, relaxed laughter, dancing. People reached out to each other and swayed in place to the rhythm. All of the music that came after that moment, no matter how great it was, could not match Richie Havens playing and singing on that stage.

When Havens finished his set, he kept trying to leave but was begged for encores as the next band was not ready. As the festival's first performer, he held the crowd for nearly three hours. Having run out of tunes, he improvised a song based on his opening spiritual that became *Freedom*.

That first evening of the festival was tremendous. There would be "three days of peace and music" on Max Yasgur's farm. Live music, made intimate by the singers and musicians I had been hearing about all summer, had arrived. Here it all was, in person and all around us.

Changing Times, Time to Change

In June 1969, Jean and I had arrived at the planned festival site in upstate New York. With me was Ron Liis, a colleague from the University of Miami art department, and his wife, Phyllis. I was leader of the art crew, one of the advance parties preparing for the mid-August festival. Up to that time, except for the people who lived there, nobody had ever heard of Woodstock. Nothing would hint that the very name would soon be synonymous with a new radical political stance.

Who would have thought that answers to all important questions a generation might ask would come from television, the movies, and a rock fest? This generation's heroes were pop musicians. Anti-establishment, anti-war, free love, and anti-adult was its creed. How is it they came up with so many influential answers? In their idealism they stopped a war, reforged a nation's concepts of law, and raised our social consciousness.

Off to History, Country Roads

Ron and I wandered around Mills Farm, the original site before moving on to Max Yasgur's farm. We were trying to decide where things were to go. The stage position was already set, and plans for other things, such as places for service roads and parking, were fairly obvious. Our decisions, as expected, were mostly aesthetic. While we walked, crushing wild strawberries under our feet and feeling so great to be out of the city, we knew that the giant steel and wood sculptures we had built for the Miami Pop Festival were not right for this peaceful countryside.

We set up a teepee, which was a symbol of simpler times and our connection with the American Indian culture.

Driving the back roads, we saw beautiful old stone barns and farmhouses, worn stone fences, lush orchards, and rusty farm machinery overgrown with weeds. It became clear that we should celebrate the land and develop the festival site by putting in all of the things we liked from the countryside. We thought if we could bring the feeling of a rural setting—something peaceful—into the site, the festival-goers, especially those from cities, could have the best of the country all in one place.

At this time in the art world—for galleries, artist studios, and museums—conceptual art, happenings, disposable art, and junk sculpture were the focus. It all made sense to us.

Mel Lawrence, our contact with the festival front office, said, "Go for it!" Woodstock Ventures billed the concert as a "weekend in the country." Ads ran in newspapers, both establishment and underground, and on radio stations in Los Angeles, San Francisco, New York, Boston, Houston, and Washington, D.C. A concert ticket also bought a campsite. Tickets for the three-day event cost $18 in advance and $24 at the gate.

The crew started hauling in old John Deer plows, cultivators, and farm machinery to become part of the site.

Carol the Cook

Lots of new people were arriving daily, and getting to know everybody was tough. About that time, we needed more living space, so we moved to the Red Top Motel. We'd have our own dining room and kitchen there. Carol Green would take on the task of feeding the multitude.

Carol had some help from a commune that had not made it on its own. The group almost starved and froze during their first winter together in Canada. I heard stories about their problems, which were mostly a result of different ideas about how things were to be done. Now the remnant of the group—about seven or eight people—had hooked up with us to earn (and learn) something.

Imagine a small wooden building the size of a toolshed with everyone hungry, tired, the sound at Hendrix levels, the smell of food, and the weirdest people on the planet. Every now and then, I would hear Carol losing it in the kitchen and coming out and shaking a big wooden spoon at no one in particular. Then she would turn and run screaming back into the kitchen.

Outrageous Costumes

As work progressed on the festival site, more people were showing up daily. One evening, the crowd arriving at dinner was the hippest hippies in all the land, each one stranger than the next. Tall ones. Short ones. Colorful and artfully raggedy ones. Each seemed to be vying for first prize for outrageous costume.

The talk at dinner was about the arrival of the legendary Hog Farm. Most of the kids thought the flamboyant folks on site were real cool until the Hog Farm arrived. The Hog Farm was a group of about eighty-five members who had started a communal pig farm in California. They had managed to survive while other experimental communes did not. They were creative and led by several strong personalities. Their spokesperson was a skinny, toothless hippie, Hugh Romney, who used the name Wavy Gravy.

Earlier that day I had sent one of the girls to Kennedy Airport with a bus to pick up the Hog Farm group. She called, frantic on the phone. "They are wandering all over the airport, and I can't get them on the bus!" As soon as some of them got on the bus, and she left to get the rest, the others would get off. What a zoo! At the same time their looks were scaring other travelers. "What do I do?" she pleaded. I told her to get some help from airport security. By the time she got back, they were all on the bus. Timing is everything.

Despite their unruliness, the Hog Farmers had been hired to assist with the medical tents, security, food services, stage activities, and information booths. They built their own shelters and drove around in a raggedy school bus painted in psychedelic colors.

They knew more about the drug culture than almost anyone. They knew how to use it and how to make it. During the festival, they were more help with bad drug trips than the doctors we had on site. They put up a free vegetarian kitchen and fed thousands.

Alarmed by possibilities of food shortages, one of the Hog Farm women decided to make an emergency run to New York City to buy basic food and supplies. She approached one of the organizers, wanting $3,000 to go into town to buy food. She got the money, commandeered a truck, and bought thousands of pounds of bulgur wheat, rolled oats, currants, wheat germ, as well as 160,000 paper plates and a Jade Buddha to bless their kitchen.

The official food concessions ran out of food on the first day of the festival. The Hog Farm kitchen crew hand-mixed muesli (now called granola) in new plastic trash cans and doled it out to half a million hungry kids. Granola thereafter became a popular new American food.

At this point, Mel was out of town, and I was in charge. The day ended with me on the phone, listening to an angry motel owner yelling, "You better get these people (the Hog Farm) out of my motel! They've only been here twenty minutes, and all the toilets are stopped up!"

On cue, Carol Green popped out of the kitchen again, waving her big wooden spoon and shouting. I couldn't understand what she was saying, but she felt it was important.

Jean and I looked at each other and laughed. It was surreal. Jean reminded me, "Mel is out of town, and you are in charge of all this," and continued to laugh.

"In charge of what?" I said, "No one can be in charge here."

Members of the Hog Farm commune arrived from California to assist in the management of the event. Experienced in the drug culture and communal living, they handled food crises, bad drug trips, and security. One of the commune's leaders, Hugh Romney, nicknamed "Wavy Gravy," would get on stage at times to calm people down. It was, indeed, a giant experiment in controlling 500,000 young Americans.

Security: The Please Force

Wes Pomeroy was head of security at the festival. A former Marine, Wes was a dignified man in his fifties, trim, and taller than average.

He was given the enormous task of keeping thousands of people from doing their worst. He must have known when he signed on that this was virtually an impossible job.

Surely luck and divine intervention would be needed to deal with hippies, police, local politicians, people with power, your everyday mob, and fans excited by superb music. Add to the mix the usual jerks and conartists who are attracted to high-profile events as Woodstock turned out to be.

Wes treated everyone the same. He listened to everyone with respect and seemed to answer their questions to their satisfaction. I never saw him show any prejudice toward anyone.

The security force he built consisted of off-duty police, who carried no guns and were not dressed in cop gear. All of the staff and other workers had the Woodstock jackets with different colors: blue for staff, green for security, and so on. Our "police force" milling about in the crowd didn't attract too much attention except that they were older than the average festival-goer. After a few days in mud, however, everyone pretty much looked alike. Wes's job was to keep the peace without appearing to do so.

This new method was an experience that the personnel who worked for him took back to their different departments. Most were off-duty NYPD. Woodstock was, among other things, a giant experiment in crowd control. The premise was *be patient and count on the hope that most of the people will do the right thing. Don't let a few crazies and mob rule get started.*

Some of the bad possibilities were derailed ahead of time. Aside from the large number of nonuniformed police, the Hog Farm commune was part of the security plan. These individuals quelled disturbances by throwing pie in the face and spraying seltzer water. Hog Farm leader Wavy Grav, went on stage during difficult times to calm things down and to point out that everyone needed to be cool. Wavy Gravy called this method the "Please Force."

A deal was made with political activist Abbie Hoffman, who believed everything should be free. He and his radical group threatened to tear down fences and break things up. Money and a copy machine to print their flyers bought off their threat of disruption.

Other than Janis Joplin trying to stir up some trouble late at night when everyone was too tired to riot, things went well. In the end, 500,000 young Americans met the challenge of three days of peace and music.

Free Festival

July turned to August, and before we knew it, it was show time. Jean and I left the motel for the first day of music. Jean knew a back way into the site that would miss most of the traffic. We parked the car and walked to the operations trailer.

The citizens of Woodstock Nation had started to arrive. The grounds were filling up with people. We had worried about the farms nearby. In the middle of all the campers and people sitting around waiting for things to start was a little farmhouse with two elderly people sitting on the porch with their untouched garden of greens in front of the house, surrounded on all sides by kids from outer space.

As we walked down West Shore Road, we could see the stage still had people working on it, but it seemed to be ready enough. We turned up Hurd Road and made our way to the operations trailer. As we got close, we could see people streaming in through the gates. It was a tsunami of humanity, a tide of people pressing through the downed fences. We had on our blue windbreaker staff jackets. Seeing our official jackets, the boy working the gate hollered out, "What are we gonna do?" The answer seemed obvious. I yelled back, "Get out of the way and let them in."

Free Kitchen, Well Organized

Later that day, I drifted over to the Hog Farm food area to get something to eat. They had plenty of food, all veggies and always lots of rice. They fed the multitudes free. Well organized, their Free Kitchen fed five thousand at a time with fifteen cauldrons of rice-raisin combo. Granola was made and passed out when other foods ran out.

Finding food vendors had been problematic. Two weeks before the opening, the festival principals hired three guys with scant experience in the food business who optimistically called their enterprise "Food for Love."

The first day of the festival, Food for Love was running out of burgers, so it raised prices from 25 cents to $1. Free-thinking festivalites saw this as capitalist exploitation and against the spirit of the festival. Two of Food for Love's stands were burnt down. Prices stabilized.

In the End, Music

Beautifully engineered, the sound system contributed to the top-quality music. At the amplifier's lowest setting, the Woodstock speakers would cause pain for anyone standing within 10 feet. It kept the massive crowd at peace.

The field we had selected was a natural amphitheater. Because most of the audience would be high on the hill facing the stage, the sound-system designers built two speaker towers, each with two levels of speaker clusters, one high (about seventy feet, to reach the middle and top of the hill), and one much lower for the near audience. This genius geometry sent the music directly to everyone's ears, without causing any echo. Grass, earth, and the bodies of half a million fans absorbed the sound.

Jimi Hendrix was the most talked-about performer before and after the concert. The staff had discussed how loud his music was and how radical he was as a musician. Today he is called the greatest instrumentalist in the history of rock music.

Hendrix's set was slated for the festival finale and was supposed to start at 3 AM. Due to bad weather, a poor "pick-up" band, among other things, Hendrix didn't get rolling until 8 AM on Monday, August 18. Some crews were actually beginning to clean up on the edges of the crowd.

Hendrix closed the festival with an iconic performance of our national anthem. His mesmerizing take on the classic was among the most controversial renditions of the anthem ever and is now considered one of the most memorable rock-and-roll performances of all time. In fact, Hendrix's version of "The Star-Spangled Banner" has become a symbol of the 1960s era.

Epilogue

Many of the people who worked at Woodstock went on to be in show business. Jean and I were not tempted, but for the rest of our lives, Woodstock would be there. It didn't define our lives as it did for some of our friends, but it would never go away. The Woodstock crew came together for that one brief summer. Most didn't know each other before the event and never saw each other again. Yet the earth and sky, the fire and water of those intense, game-changing, tumultuous days remain with us like faithful dogs, resting beside us, ready to give chase at the slightest stir of memory.

A citizen of Woodstock Nation stood in the doorway of the barn in long tangled hair, bare feet, and blue jeans. He had traveled a long distance to see if there were others like him. He found about 500,000.

Sculptor and artist BILL WARD served for thirty-two years on the faculty of the University of Miami, where he headed the undergraduate and graduate programs in sculpture. During part of his tenure, he was chair of the University's art department and director of the Lowe Art Museum. "Workin' on Woodstock" is excerpted from his full-length manuscript describing his summer 1969 experiences as field art director of the Woodstock Music Festival. He provided the pen-and-ink illustrations for these excerpts.

TIM MAYO

Time, Bomb

For Whitney

That summer I live in the cabin nearest the latrine,
where they are planning to blow up the boulder
we have to skirt each time we have a need.

It stands about even to my nine-year-old hip.
Partly covered by greenish lichen, it has that uneven
mottled gray patina so common to granite,
and for as long as anyone can remember,
it has just been there: an inert presence
we've always tolerated.

For weeks before the big event, we watch them
slowly chip a hole deeper and deeper into the rock,
letting the salt air into the whitish wound of its center,
and all over the camp you can hear the slow, arrhythmic
clunking chime of the sledge against the top end
of a steel rod they are using to tease open this hole.

With each strike and ring of the sledge, the rod's
thicker point gouges a little deeper into the rock.
The hole they pound into this stone has to go
down at least a foot before they can put a stick
deep enough into its heart to blow it so far apart
only the eye-stinging dust of its memory will remain.

And so this goes on: each day the camp air
fills with a constant, out of step, ding and
stutter of something like a town clock gone
awry, its clumping sounds echoing back
and forth, no longer able to keep time
in a place where time has lost its standards.

Here, we rise to "Reveille" and sleep at "Taps,"
the bugle blows out the only hours we need to know,
and twice a day a little toy cannon, so real our hearts stop,
puffs and booms a bright flag up and down a pole
so nobly we all snap stiffly to attention—we all salute.

Finally the time comes at the quiet hour, just after lunch,
when, usually, we nap in our cabins, but, today,
we are *admonished* to stay inside and to especially
keep away from the windows.

                                      They have no glass,
these windows. They are just squares of air:

each with its own wooden flap that hinges down
only at summer's end to close the cabin for winter,
to keep out all the unwanted critters,
but no one thinks to close them now.

So, if a piece of stone flew through
all the filtering limbs of the forest,
to strike its rough and heavy fisted hand
like an annunciating angel against a child's forehead,
gesturing in that mute crushing language of rock,
so that the idiocy, once and for all,
would be teased out of his head,

then the child it touched would just keel off his cot,
roll off like a pebble falling from the sill
of this one square frame of reference
which had become his last knowledge
of how everything with a heart of stone
moves through the world
at an absolutely inhuman speed.

TIM MAYO'S poems and reviews have appeared in *Atlanta Review, 5 AM,
Poetry International, Poet Lore, River Styx, Web Del Sol Review, Verse Daily,
Verse Wisconsin,* and *The Writer's Almanac.* His first full-length collection
The Kingdom of Possibilities was published by Mayapple Press (2009). He has
been twice nominated for the Best of the Net Anthology, three times for a
Pushcart Prize, and was chosen as a top finalist for the Paumanok Award.

Curve
of the Earth

"THIS IS IT," the real estate agent said. Tim swung his big station wagon off the country road into a narrow gravel and dirt lane. Dry grasses as tall as the car's hood pressed in on both sides.

"This is a driveway?" my wife, Carol, exclaimed.

Tim nodded as the car crawled up the slope. Pebbles kicked the floor, and the leaning grasses swished against the doors. Tim maneuvered to avoid foot-deep ruts. We passed a derelict, tan mobile home set crookedly on blocks, its windows broken. Beside it sagged an ancient Volkswagen Beetle with four flat tires and no windshield. "The farmer who owns the field plans to move this stuff," the agent said without conviction.

We crept another half mile, still no house in sight. I envisioned pushing through here against blizzards and spring mud. "Who plows this driveway?" I asked.

"You. It's not town property." The idea was ludicrous. Me keep open this narrow lifeline to the outside? The station wagon climbed a small hill, putted a hundred level yards, then labored up a steeper hill. The wheels spun momentarily, and a rock clunked in the wheel well.

Scrub willows and vines as thick as my arms now formed an impenetrable wall to our right—a tangle like the one over Sleeping Beauty's castle. But to the left, long-abandoned fields sloped away, revealing a wide view of the valley and hills beyond. A breeze rippled the wispy meadow grass, which was dotted with islands of sumac and honeysuckle. The undulating roll of the land gave it the feel of sea dunes. The space and distance was breathable, touchable.

Earlier we had viewed two houses with Tim. The last was a log cabin on a quiet, paved road, a cozy private ten acres with a pond. No neighbors behind. "Good value!" Tim whispered. "They're motivated to sell!" We went far enough to discuss mortgages, contingencies, escrow, appliances—the usual tangle. If you were to ask why the place finally left me cold, I couldn't have told you. I felt unreasonable not wanting it.

Now came this crazy place hanging in the air. To the left the field opened wider, offering a panoramic view of maybe two hundred square miles spread below—dark green forest, pale hay fields, rusty wheat fields. Houses were mere white dots. Then I saw it—the curve of the earth's horizon. The blue hills arced from west to east. Seeing the curve of the earth through an airplane window is like watching an image on television. But this was palpable. I felt for the first time that I was actually riding the planet, rolling through space.

"Can you imagine this driveway with a foot of snow?" Carol said.

Tim replied, "You'll want a four-wheel-drive vehicle."

I laughed.

"What's so funny?" Carol said.

"The whole thing." We were flying through empty space on a spinning sphere and worried about navigating snow. We ought to be clutching the earth to hold on.

Nearly a mile up the lane, the scrub trees on the right ended at a fenced field. A ghostly white horse stood atop a pond embankment and watched the station wagon. Behind the horse, set into thick woods, a chalet roof was visible.

"The neighbor," Tim told us.

Carol and I waited, and when he said nothing else, we exchanged a look. Tim crunched another quarter mile as the lane curved left into trees, crossed a culvert, and ended. Tim parked the car, which was now powdered with clay dust.

As we got out and stretched, I glanced at the house—a dark brown chalet with white trim like the neighbor's. It was a house, that's all. Nothing built of sticks and shingles would have impressed me then. I turned to that magnificent space between the house and the distant hills. I was riding on a planet rotating through the sky, not just penned between my neighbor's fences. It's no wonder the ancients thought something—a gigantic turtle or a Titan—held it up. Something more tangible than gravity ought to support a planet. It was so quiet I could hear the meadow grass sifting in the field. The stillness was immense. It was not just the absence of human noise, but the presence of something ancient—both soothing and threatening.

To live here would require stripping away the noise that disguises our true condition. Men have banded together a long time against

Kevin Russell.
Coumeenole, Ireland.
Photograph, 2011.

the beasts, the darkness, and each other. To choose a home here would mean choosing a different relationship with the world. I had visited wilder, more dangerous, and exotic locations; but to live here would mean changing our inner address as well as our street number.

We toured the premises. Its three bathrooms would be wonderful with our four children after sharing one tiny bathroom. The ten-year-old house was sound, but when Tim told us it had already had three owners, Carol and I exchanged glances again. This place had been too far away for the owners. Seven sliding glass doors pulled the vista inside. Did the builder think it was only a nice view? Didn't he see what he was letting in?

One thing that puzzled us was that the closet doors had locks on the inside—heavy-duty latches or dead bolts. I checked—all the closets had inside locks. What kind of person would lock him or herself inside a closet? Was it a refuge from some imagined attack, or an isolation chamber from family? Did they retreat to these womb-like holes when the borderless space outside became too much? Tim shrugged his shoulders, but I saw darker puzzlement touch him too.

Although the aura of the house unsettled me, when we walked the land, I fell in love; seventy-five acres with a one-acre pond. Hemlock, beech, hickory, oak, and dogwood dominated the woods. The half that was field bloomed with midsummer trefoil, daisies, jewelweed, devil's paintbrush, and chicory. Aster, Queen Anne's lace and yarrow were coming on. Withering trillium, jack-in-the-pulpit, May apple and Indian pipe in the woods told us spring would be glorious here. A trail through the woods ended at a bench overlooking a sheer ravine perhaps a hundred feet deep. At the bottom shone a wide, flat creek and a thirty-foot waterfall. I leaned out over the drop to follow the gurgling creek, but couldn't see far.

"It's got a name," Tim said. "Wildcat Gully and Wildcat Creek. The owner says bobcat still have dens here. It's your eastern border."

Mine? Does he know what he's saying? A deed doesn't mean anyone owns this. Living here should convince a person that we are all
mere tenants, squirrels holed in trees for a few seasons.

"Who would live in a place like this?" Carol asked.

"Not us," I said.

Carol grew up in the country, so the site was not totally alien to
her; but I was raised in the center of the crumbling industrial city of
Paterson, New Jersey. It was a dangerous place with crime and vio-
lence all around us. Our city house was armored by fences, chain link
on one side, wooden along the rear, concrete to the other side, and a
huge, prickly hedge along the sidewalk. Our narrow driveway sym-
bolized my family's approach to life. There was only one way in or
out, and you put fences around things you owned so you and other
people knew exactly what was yours. We marked our borders well.

My father was born on the kitchen table of that house and lived
there until he was forty. His baptism, wedding, and funeral all took
place in Paterson's Saint Paul's Episcopal Church. You would think
that the smaller and more defined you made your world, the more
secure you would be, but sometimes erecting fences only intensifies
your terrors.

Our walled existence was battered when I was five months old.
My grandfather owned an ice business. One day, in his customary
blue uniform, he hauled ice into a doctor's office. A demented patient
mistook grandfather for a policeman arresting him. The man
snatched an ice pick from my grandfather's belt and stabbed him sav-
agely. Grandfather left the house whistling one morning and never
returned. But in my imagination, he stared from on high like a stern
angel, watching and warning how dangerous life was, and how you
could never be too careful.

Does this explain our purchase offer? A city boy taught to fear
wildness in all its forms needs to explain why he chose to live on a re-

mote hillside. It took me thirty years to knock down the fences my family nailed around me. This was marked by my steady moves from city to suburb to rural town. Now I would find out how many more fences I could live without.

The summer day we moved in I dragged our cardboard boxes to an old burning spot downwind from the house. This beautiful countryside had no cardboard recycling. As I burned, a man in a camouflaged hunting outfit tramped through the trees toward me. Two dogs, a big Doberman, and a small mutt, trotted beside him, and a gray cat trailed behind. The big man, easily three hundred pounds and six-foot-two, introduced himself as our neighbor, Rudy. Balding in front, with Michelin Man neck rolls, his remaining hair was pulled back into a ponytail. The sleeves of his T-shirt strained against bulging arms.

After affirming I was the new neighbor, he said, "The last family only stayed three years."

"Why?" I asked.

He grunted. "It can be rough. Count on getting snowed in. Last year's ice storm trapped me here two weeks. We ain't first on the electric company's list when power goes out. And it goes out a lot. I had to hack ice from the pond to get water to flush the toilets and for my horse. Telephone line went down—1,200 bucks. I hiked out to get a snowmobile to bring in food. Trees went down all across the driveway. You watch this summer. Thunderstorms have rockin' parties up here. Lightning blew my TV three times. Zapped the well pump too." I couldn't tell if he was complaining or bragging.

I led him inside to meet Carol, and he announced it was the first time he'd entered the house. I was shocked. "Really? How long have you lived up here?"

"Six years. The people before you didn't like company, my company especially. The first time I meet the mister, he says, 'I don't want you hunting my land, skiing my land, walking my land. I don't want nobody on my land.' He was a real sweetheart. The wife taught the kids at home so school didn't contaminate them. They'd all parade around the field in dresses and suits. They were something. The eleven-year-old wrote a book on religion."

Perhaps to slow the stream of information, Carol asked, "Is your wife at home?"

Rudy snorted. "She left me last year. Just walked. Left everything behind—jewelry, clothes, cat, even her underwear. Didn't want nothing I had touched. It was a rough year up here all alone, snowed in, iced in, nobody next door even, not that they were company, but it helps to have something that talks nearby. My dogs listen, but they don't talk to me yet."

I was trying to calculate how much of what Rudy said I should believe when he said, "Now, fall's like the OK Corral up here. Hunters blast anything that moves. I chase off a hundred maniacs every year. Mister who lived here, he strapped on a pistol and patrolled his property like a sheriff." He laughed. "You'll see his posted signs all shot to bits. He used to have a fence around the yard for the kids too. They were weird ducks. Made me feel almost normal."

This jogged Carol's memory. She walked away, then returned with a ten-inch hunting knife she held out. "I found this on a ledge over the door of one of the closets."

Rudy whistled in admiration. "That'll do a nice number on a throat." Carol and I glanced at each other with a married couple's oneness of mind. Did he say "throat"?

Outside, the dogs ran happily to Rudy, and the cat emerged from under the steps. "This is Joey," Rudy said, stroking the shaggy, hunch-backed old dog that walked tiptoe. "He's not doing too good, but I give him six pills a day. He's almost blind and has arthritis." Then we were introduced to the sleek, chocolate, brown Doberman. "People think they're vicious, but Sunny's a baby." She nuzzled me politely for a pat, and I hoped the gentle animals revealed more about our neighbor than we might surmise from listening to him.

"And who's this?" Carol asked, stroking the gray cat rubbing against her ankles.

"That's Mom," Rudy said. "I named her 'Mom' 'cause when she had kittens, she took them all off for a walk in the woods one day and came back alone. I never saw the kittens again, and she didn't go looking for them. She didn't want them getting any attention she might get. It reminded me of my mother, so I called her 'Mom.'"

I thought, *now we have it.* This is where square-peg, paranoid, or abandoned people make their last stand. I had hoped living up here wouldn't be just an escape, but a search for new ways of thinking and connecting to larger patterns. What's the point of living on the edge of the earth if you hide in a closet or if the old demons still pound on your house?

"Women don't last long up here," Rudy said. "Too lonely. My wife left me. Lenhard—he lived in your house—his wife left him. The first guy who lived in my house, his wife ran off too."

Carol smiled and said the right thing, as usual. "We'll be here a long time together."

That first night, our goods piled against the walls, our backs aching, Carol peered out a window. "It's so dark out there!"

"Let's see how dark," I said. When I flicked off the lamps, a sea of blackness flowed through the sliding glass doors, a deep, silky darkness. Until you live this far apart, you don't realize how much other people's lights illuminate your existence. We held hands tightly on the couch. As our eyes adjusted, tiny specks appeared on the hills out past the black fields.

Carol curled her feet under her and laid her cheek against my upper arm. Beyond our field, the land dropped two miles to the north to the tiny village of Tuscarora. From here we could not see its houses, and only after the leaves fell might we glimpse the tip of the church steeple. That night the hamlet's dozen homes radiated only a weak glow—like an ancient, feeble campfire.

Beyond that glow, tiny twinkling lights scattered across the hills that receded like waves at sea. Yellow yard lights, farmers' blue mercury lights, the string of lights we later found out was a country airport on the ridge twenty five miles away. Once in a while, car headlights bobbed on the gravel roads. We couldn't see the curve of the earth now—the darkness of the land and the darkness of sky had become one. A bright star might be mistaken for an electric light or a lamp for a star. A small airplane's red light winked below us as it crossed the valley. Somewhere above the human lights, the real stars began and spread across greater, emptier wild areas than I could grasp. All of them were little islands in the night—all unique and all part of a vast, incomprehensible pattern. It almost seemed possible to step out into them. From this time, we would be farther apart from men and closer to everything than I had ever imagined. I sensed now why the closets had inside locks, and I hoped we would never want to use them.

Carol's warmth felt good. She lay her head on my lap, and I combed fingers through her hair, lifting and letting it fall back. I combed slowly enough to drop just a few hairs at a time, continually, like cascading water. For an hour we stayed like that, on the edge of the dark hillside—and on the edge of the earth that rolled through space. People in houses across the valley seemed far away. Maybe they sat in the dark too, staring our way, wondering why the lone light in the dark mountain had suddenly come on again.

M. GARRETT BAUMAN and his wife have now lived on their part of the curve of the earth for twenty years. A retired professor of English, he has recently published the eighth edition of his popular book on writing, *Ideas and Details* (Cengage 2012) and contributes fiction and essays to *The Chronicle of Higher Education, Sierra,* and many books and literary magazines. He writes frequently for Chrysalis because more than any other publication, it makes him look for moments that make us more than what we are in our ordinary hours.

Wrecking Ball

i.

I like to think of things breaking down:

particles of skin that slide off my hand
and cling to doorknobs, books, other hands,
or roll on the ground like little ball-bearings;

the slab of rock that disengages from a cliff
where there are no witnesses;

hairline cracks fanning out
from the basements of public buildings;

the tractor that stops one day
in the middle of the hayfield
where no amount of coaxing will move it.

ii.

Once in Denver I was standing on a railroad bridge.
A woman at the liquor store had just said
Martin Luther King was better off dead,
and I was thinking of him, and of the bridge

he'd built, when, above the junked-out prairie,
there came a sound, a thud, like a fist
aimed too low, and a prolonged fizz.
Twice more the sound, before I saw,

amidst the grey shapes downtown, suspended
from a derrick that outreached everything,

a wrecking ball. Quietly it moved along
the gutted building flank, nuzzling, probing,

a conscious thing. It paused, swung back,
delivered, then disappeared in the spray
of debris. All afternoon I stood there,
while the wind swung around full-face,

the sky thickened, snow—that winter's first—
commenced, the wrecking ball persisted,
and the building was reduced. In my notebook
I wrote, *nothing is broken.*

iii.

Nothing is broken. The cliff is just as much a cliff.
The boulder rooted in the bottom of the gulch
is host to packrats, trellises, geographies of lichen.
The tractor grows more permanent. The bridge
survives its architect. Particles
all filter down, become the ground.

Poet and essayist RICK KEMPA lives in Rock Springs, Wyoming, where he directs the Honors Program at Western Wyoming College. A book of his poems, *Keeping the Quiet* (2008), is available from Bellowing Ark Press, and a second book, *Ten Thousand Voices,* will be released in 2013.

Theopoetics of Healing

WHEN I WAS SEVEN, every night before I prayed, I took my dolls off my pillow and situated them on a chair. Placing a blanket around them, I said goodnight to each in turn, taking special care with one small doll with a missing leg. She was my favorite. How had she lost her leg? Did she come to me in that state? After making sure the dolls were comfortable, I knelt by my bed. Beginning with being thankful for everything, I asked Heavenly Father to bless my grandparents and Greatmama who lived across the world in Wyoming that they would not die. At the end, I asked, "Please give my doll back her leg." After that, I got into bed and soon, as if there was a hidden camera, my parents appeared. They kissed me goodnight and tucked the covers around me. My father had told bedtime stories earlier on the couch with all of us around him. They were only there to say goodnight. "Sleep well, Patty dear," they said, and were gone. The tap of their footsteps receding on the terrazzo floor, I untucked myself, turned on my closet light, and read.

In the morning (I don't know when I found my way back to bed, but I always woke up in it), the first thing I did was check for my doll's leg. During one of the moves of my childhood, my doll was lost.

IN A PHOTOGRAPH, my great-grandmother Patty, Greatmama to us, stands in between my elder brother, Wes, and me. Her red-and-white flowered muumuu is moving in the wind. We are smiling. My brother at thirteen is showing the beginnings of acne. As she smiled, Greatmama was thinking of what to do. She took us on a drive in her old rounded black car, the leather seats retaining the shape of people

41

she had loved and lost. We rolled up the windows to prepare for passing through the fertile land around the sugar beet factory and its pungent, manure-like smell. The furrowed beet fields gave way to corn and buckwheat whose flowers yielded the best honey in the world. The two-lane road dropped off on each side into irrigation ditches, one of the first colonizing efforts of Greatmama and her fellow pioneers. Sixty years before, my grandmother had been held under the water of those ditches by her friends and almost drowned. "We'll cut asparagus on the way back." Greatmama pointed at the feathery bushes floating among the cattails like pale green clouds.

When the sugar beet factory and beets were far enough away, I cranked the window down and breathed in the air that mingled the diminished scent of beets with the sweetness of flowers. This was the smell of the Big Horn Basin, the scent of my mother's childhood and our days with grandparents and Greatmama. A cemetery sat on the edge of the civilized world. As we passed, Greatmama told us, as she did every year, that a plot was waiting for her next to her first husband Wilder's grave. She was eighty-nine.

As if exiting the gate of the garden, the cultivated landscape transformed into the dry Wyoming desert of rock, sage, and antelope. That was where Aunt Loretta taught us how to shoot. Greatmama pulled her big car over and stopped on the roadside. Taking a pocket knife from her purse, she surveyed the clumps of vegetation and choosing the right stalk of sagebrush, cut it down. "It's for your brother's spots," she announced when I helped her open the trunk. The sage scent traveled with us back along the same road, passing from desert into garden. We picked a bag full of asparagus and placed it next to the sage. Back at her bungalow set in a wide lawn that she mowed each Saturday of summer in a muumuu and straw hat, edged with roses and a strawberry patch and rows of corn, Greatmama whistled. In her kitchen, she was happily making Wes a stiff cup of sage tea.

"This will clear up your blemishes by cleaning your blood." She pronounced the words carefully, and, set the mug of dark green liquid in front of Wes, she turned her attention to delicate asparagus spears. Cooking them only for a moment, she arranged them in a small bowl for each of us with a pat of butter and a baptism of cream. Wes obediently drank the liquid, and she gave him a spoonful of buckwheat honey for his efforts. Our suitcases crammed with sage and instructions on how to make the tea, we returned home. To my knowledge, he never drank the tea again.

Greatmama had learned about herbs from *her* grandmother Patty. Sharing a name, they had been friends, and Patty had taught her what she knew. Some say Molly Ockett, an Indian woman, taught

Patty about herbs. Molly also may have been the one who caught Patty in her arms when she pushed out of her mother's womb. But for Patty, herbs were only a small part of what she did. They were some of the craft of healing, but the heart was in God's hands. When God told her to go to someone and heal them, she did not mince words. "Do you want me to make you well, Sister?" she asked. Anointing and laying her hands on friend or stranger, she told them to get up and walk. And they did. God reached out to the sick through her hands.

I TRAVEL TO HEAL. The cracked leather of a taxi seat behind my back, the smell of diesel coming in the window, horns blaring, humanity teeming around me asking me for money, for my attention, I can return to joy. When my heart is broken, my forehead deeply furrowed between my eyes, movement through the incarnation of humanity is salve for my soul. It is the elusive, impossible glue that Humpty Dumpty will never find. Yet in the middle of my own healing, I have failed.

In a castle town on the edge of the Thar desert, the proprietor of the Jaisal Castle Hotel told me I was lucky. I had come to go on a camel safari and there was one place left. With a down payment, he would hold the place. "Thank you, Madame," he said as I handed him the bills and went to my room. The next morning, early, I left the safety of my hotel. Notes that I had written in the dark to myself to prepare for the safari held only scratches. My pen had run out of ink. Into the darkness of the town I walked to fulfill the only part of the list I could remember: I must call home to say that I would be out of communication for four or five days. I would be crossing the desert. "Do not worry," I said over and over, willing my voice to be heard across thou-

sands of miles as I walked the dark streets slowly, unable to see cows or avoid the gutters I had seen the afternoon before, filled with sewage and things I could not name. I walked until I found the telephone shape on a sign and knocked. A woman appeared at a window. Smells of burning ghee and breakfast emerging with her, she kindly opened up her shop one hour early to let me use the phone. Thanks to her, I could say, "Do not worry. I will be safe. Angels have always followed me. I can hear their wings."

An hour later, I was on the back of a camel, going along the cobblestone streets gingerly, my hat shielding me from the rising sun, the guide on a camel ahead of me, another younger man leading mine by a rope. Soon, the other participants on camels would join us. When we reached the edge of the city, our tiny caravan entered the desert. I had heard of expensive tent hotels, managed by fancy European resorts. That was where we would meet the others. The young man who had led my camel hopped on with the guide, and with a crack of his whip, the three of us trotted over the barren ground. My hat flapped behind my head, tethered by the string tied under my chin. Every few minutes the guide looked back at me. I smiled, completely occupied with keeping myself in sync with the camel to avoid the painful rubbing of my legs against the rough blanket and saddle. This was very hard. After a half hour I managed to signal to the guide. He slowed his camel and riding alongside, he said, "Yes, Madame?" "Where are the others?" I asked. "Oh, Madame," he said. "There is no one else. This year, there is the plague. That is keeping everyone away. And," he added, "There is a malaria right now. In three days you are dead."

An hour later, we stopped for tea. The young man cared for the camels, feeding them a little grass while the guide spread a blanket under a lone tree and made a fire to boil water. As soon as the tea was in front of me with a plate of biscuits, two old men in white cotton breeches and loose cotton shirts appeared with a young girl. I did not see them coming until they were close. As I sipped my tea, the old men played, one on a drum and the other on a flute. The young girl, an anklet of bells jingling, danced for me. As a child of three, taps on my cowboy boots and a white cowboy hat, I had danced to *Let a Smile Be Your Umbrella* for a crowd of parents at a hotel on Lake Maracaibo. The costume hangs in a closet of my parents' home with my miniature ballet tutu and shoes. Did this young girl have butterflies before her performance as I had? Did her heart start pounding from twenty feet away? She smiled and twirled and then it was time to pack up our picnic. When I turned to wave, she was gone.

An easy peace settled among the three of us humans and two camels. The guide let me walk sometimes but only if I trotted as fast as the camels lumbered along. When our path took us through villages, people came out of their mud-and-stone houses and asked me questions. The guide translated, "Do you have aspirin? Tylenol? Anything?" "Medicine" had been one of the words scribbled unidentifiably on my note to myself. I had left it all at the hotel. The villagers were looking to me for something to heal. In the evenings, around a campfire, the two men drank tea with me after a delicious dinner of curried eggplant and bread hot off the fire. From my tent, I heard them talking long into the night. I had never seen so many stars.

One afternoon, the young man, his hair standing up from the wind as mine would have if I hadn't braided it close to my head, was limping, his foot obviously in pain. I asked the guide what had happened. The young man walked up to me, his dark eyes looking into mine. He quickly took off his shoe and sock and put his foot almost in my lap. One of his toes appeared infected. What could I do? I looked at it on the edge of my skirt. My hands to my side, wanting to reach out but not able to, I told him through the guide, "I am sorry. There is no water. I do not know what I could do." The young man put on his sock and shoe and walked away.

His foot has appeared to me in dreams. It is the only part of the journey that I cannot fit into the whole. I returned from my own journey healed and in the middle of my own healing, I had not reached out my hands. Why? What had happened between Greatmama and her grandmother and then again with me? The conviction of healing had diluted thinner and thinner through the generations until I, the third Patty, could not even hold out her hands. The young man looking into my eyes saw that the habit of healing was gone.

In my imagination, I take his foot and wash it tenderly with whatever I have: a handkerchief from my purse or a wet towelette (surely I had one someplace). Instead of saying I am sorry, I say, "Wait until we reach the watering hole for the camels, I will tend to it there." I take out packets of soap and wash his foot, drying it with my skirt. I look into his face and do not turn away. As I wash his feet, I bless him with prayers.

When he was in front of me, not in a dream, a barrier separated us, like a stone in my heart. When was the stone placed there? Was it passed down generation to generation in the women of my family like a fancy brooch? Could it be the stone that lightning split away from the tomb? Does the stone keep the miracles inside, the resurrection, the healing, locked from view? What would it take to roll the stone away? If I pushed and pushed, what would I see? Or, instead of pushing, what if I held my hands above it and warmed it until slowly it rocked out of the way?

*Patty Christiena
Willis*

The first morning of the safari, when I lost hope of fellow travelers, the guide stopped our procession and, getting off his camel, he picked up round, iron-like stones from our path. "This is the currency of the desert," he told me. I filled my pockets with them and now find them unexpectedly in a basket of earrings, in my box for paints and with childhood marbles.

Are these the stones I must roll away from my heart? What do the stones hide, encapsulate? Behind them would I find an angel waiting? Would sunbeams crossing the threshold beckon me to dance in their light?

PATTY CHRISTIENA WILLIS' play *Just Between the Three of Us* was hailed as the "great east-west event of the Edinburgh Festival" by the *Sunday Times* (of London). Her book, *The Village Above the Stars,* is recommended reading by the National Japanese Library Association. The *Los Angeles Times* wrote that her work "showed the power of the folk tale to create wonder." Most recently, she wrote a musical theater work *Man from Magdalena* based on a true story that occurred in the borderlands of southern Arizona. As of June 2012, the play has raised over $60,000 for micro-loans in Mexico and Central America. She is now developmental minister of the South Valley Unitarian Universalist Society of Salt Lake City.

DONNA PUCCIANI

Holding Your Leg

The physical therapist wants
all the weight on the bad leg.
You need to regrow the muscle
that disappeared as you limped
for five years bone-on-bone.

I help with the exercises.
You lie flat on your back
with ankle weights strapped on.
I hold the good leg to make sure
it is not doing the work.

I cradle it in my arms
like a newborn, a warm loaf of bread,
a favorite book, a spring bouquet,
folded laundry. It is not
swollen or red as the other,

that wounded animal trying so hard
to lift itself from the bed.
The specter of disintegration haunts us
in old age, with death waiting
just behind the scrim.

But now we perform, you and I,
counting repetitions and sets,
your brow furrowed against pain,
as if all this mattered, spotlit,
in the greater scheme of things.

The sunset appears
in crimson blush, embarrassed
by its own brevity but as proud
of its brilliance as you, lifting
your leg to feel new strength,

welcoming the strange metallic hip.
I hang on to the other, owning
its goodness for a few minutes,
praying for equilibrium
while night obscures tree, flower, sky.

DONNA PUCCIANI's poetry has been published in the U.S., Europe, Australia, and Asia in such diverse journals as *International Poetry Review, The Pedestal, Shi Chao Poetry, Spoon River Poetry, Journal of the American Medical Association,* and *Christianity and Literature.* Her work has been translated into Italian, Chinese, and Japanese. Pucciani's books include *The Other Side of Thunder, Jumping Off the Train* (Windstorm Creative 2007), *Chasing the Saints* (Virtual Artists Collective 2008), and *To Sip Darjeeling at Dawn* (Virtual Artists Collective 2011). A four-time Pushcart nominee, she has won awards from the Illinois Arts Council, The National Federation of State Poetry Societies, and Poetry on the Lake.

PART II

Perpetuating a Pattern

KATE CHAPPELL

IPH

Whenever I get up to bat I always try to get an inside the ballpark homerun (IPH). Triples are good, but I'd rather go for the IPH. I have four of them lifetime, all hit in Fenway Park. I played for the St. Louis Browns when I whacked the first one, hitting the edge of the wall in center field where the bleachers join the left field green monster. It bounced way back onto the field, and I came home standing up.

The next one (I was on the Red Sox then) was a sneaky hit pulled into the left field corner, sticking in the drainpipe there. It was a close call, me having to nose-dive under the catcher.

The third IPH came playing for the Washington Senators. A liner, inches over first base, landed fair, curved foul, caromed off the right field fence, rolled all the way to the bullpen. There was a drizzle; the ball and field were slippery. Even so I still had to slide for it.

The last one was a doozer. I was back with the Browns again. It was an inside the infield homer (IIH). We had a man on second. I hit the first pitch, a low scorcher down the first base line, striking the first baseman on the ankle, bouncing off into the Bosox dugout, indeed rolling all the way down the passageway into the shower room. Of course, the first baseman was writhing on the ground, so the pitcher had to go after it. By the time he found it, the man on second had scored, and I had rounded third headed home. The pitcher tripped on the steps coming out, so the throw was just wide enough to allow me to score.

Like I say, I like triples too. Actually my IPHs are all triples stretched into homers. My triples (758 lifetime) are all stretched doubles. I don't do singles.

DUDLEY LAUFMAN played sandlot ball. He batted righty. Blind in his left eye, he always swung late. A Quaker elder suggested he bat left to see the ball. He did and became known as "Dud the Kid." A National Heritage Fellow, he has translated some of Aloysius Bertrand's *Gaspard de la Nuit* pieces. He and his wife play fiddles for New England barn dances.

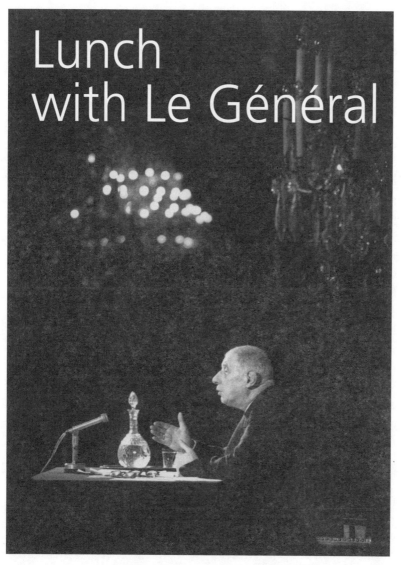

Lunch with Le Général

ONE NIGHT AFTER DINNER, Roland smiled. "Did I ever tell you . . ." He sipped his wine.

Marc Riboud.
Charles de Gaulle.
Photograph, 1959.

"He was very, very tall," said Roland, not a very tall man himself. He raised his hand above his head to a six-and-a-half foot height. *"Grand comme ça! Très imposant."*

Charles de Gaulle came for lunch at 3 rue de la Terrasse in Paris on July 2, 1953.

Although Le Général was no longer involved in politics—his RPF party had been voted out of power—he liked to keep his hand in and visit the capital whenever possible. He was still considered a hero there, still revered, still acknowledged as the personification of his nation.

This was the day that Madeleine, open-mouthed and terrified at the sight of the giant soldier in her mother's dining room, allowed the pasta she was carrying and that was to be the meal to gently slide off its platter onto the rug beneath her feet. She knew who he was, of course. There wasn't a man or woman in France—adult or child— who would not recognize *Le Général.*

The pasta, thin strands gathered about Madeleine's brown and white saddle shoes, steamed on the carpet, the butter and garlic sauce sinking into the weave. Marité was speechless; Roland had turned ashen white. Only de Gaulle had an overt reaction. He shook his head ever so slightly, grimaced a smile at Madeleine and sat down. He was not known for the warmth of his features and the girl, holding the now-empty pasta platter, burst into noisy weeping and ran from the room, pasta clinging to her shoes.

Roland reverted to what he knew. He leaped to his feet and stood ramrod straight and at attention, chin tucked hard into his chest. De Gaulle beckoned him to sit and turned to Marité. "Madame St. Paul. May I call you Marité? Do you have wine? Bread and cheese? Yes? *Magnifique!* We will eat here as Roland and I ate many times in London. Simple fares are the best for old soldiers. And please find your daughter. Tell her I am not an ogre, just a poor retired military man."

So the three, Roland, Marité, and Le Général sat and ate and drank, and if Roland remembered that de Gaulle had never, not once, deigned to eat bread and cheese with his staff while in London during the war, he did not say so. Le Général made it sound as if Roland had won the war by himself and flirted gently with Marité. When he learned that she, too, had been in the Free French, he stood and hugged her, kissed her on both cheeks and told her women like her were the backbone of France. Marité became lightheaded and rushed off to the kitchen for more cheese. When Jeanot wandered into the room, de Gaulle scooped him up like a cat and asked, "And this one? Who is this one?" Roland told him that, yes, that was their son, a good boy. Jeanot squirmed, and when de Gaulle put him down, the boy saluted and ran from the room. It was a nice touch his father liked.

Most of the residents were in the courtyard; they'd heard from the concierge that de Gaulle was visiting the St. Pauls. Clovis Répaud had put on his World War One uniform, although the dress trousers were so tight he'd almost fainted buttoning them up. Louise and Mathilde, the maids from Brittany, were in full regional regalia, black skirts billowing beneath their aprons, starched white *coiffes* hurriedly pinned to their graying hair. Monsieur Boyer, the retired butler who lived in one room on the servants' floor, incapable of deciding between his blue and brown suits, had put on the pants from one and the jacket from the other. Louise was trying to button the man's fly, which was open.

Soon word spread to the street and a crowd of fifty-odd shop-keepers, passersby and residents of adjoining buildings gathered at the entrance of 3 rue de la Terrasse. De Gaulle's black Citroën Traction Avant was surrounded, and the chauffeur, a former lieutenant in the army, tried vainly to shoo the curious away, but the people wouldn't go; they touched the shiny car and left fingerprints on the glossy paint; they pushed each other to get closer to the building entrance. A *clôchard* in the vicinity had an excellent morning, and after begging enough for a bottle of vin *ordinaire,* did not wait around even though he'd been a decorated soldier during the war. In time three policemen on bicycles managed to move the crowd from one side of the street to the other. But still the word spread. *"De Gaulle est là. Il est au 3? Regardez sa voiture! Oui, c'est lui! Aucun doute, c'est bien le Général!"*

The crowd became bigger. A man carrying a large bouquet of roses began selling the flowers individually to gawkers. Le Général was known to favor roses, calling them a symbol of French courage.

When de Gaulle finally walked through the *porte cochère* holding Jeanot's hand and flanked by Roland and Marité, the crowd burst into applause. A few threw roses. Le Général appeared mildly taken aback but wasn't. In public he had two looks: startled that anyone would recognize him (as if uniformed French generals who stood 80 inches tall were commonplace) and offended that anyone might not.

He lifted Jeanot above his head, which could have been fun for the child had the general's grasp not been so talon-like, then handed the boy to Roland. The chauffeur opened the back door of the Traction Avant, and the general folded himself into the car's modified interior. He waved at the crowd, smiled showing gapped teeth, waved a second time, and was off. The crowd watched the car until it turned right onto the Boulevard Malesherbes. In the stairway back to their apartment, Marité burst into tears, hugged Jeanot until it hurt, and then locked herself into her bedroom for the rest of the day. Jeanot and Roland had hot chocolate and some Biscuit Lu. They nibbled the corners off the cookies and agreed that, aside from the pasta incident, it had been a remarkably good visit.

THIERRY SAGNIER was born in Paris and grew up surrounded by an eclectic collection of lead soldiers, cowboys, Indians, and Eskimos, all of whom inhabited the same tabletop. He came to the United States in his early teens. His work has been published in numerous newspapers and magazines both in North America and Europe. He is the author of two books published by Avon and Harper & Row.

FRED YANNANTUONO

The Narragansett

Summer's coming. Springtime spirits swell.
One more year, so much rapid transit.
Presently, the bell begins to knell—
Time to head out to The Narragansett.

Nowhere else, no travel agent's sell,
Lebanon? Beirut? I wouldn't chance it.
Martha's Vineyard. Cancún. Cozumel.
No comparison. The Narragansett.

When in March I thirst for what's afar,
Parched and dry, all at once entranced, it
Calls to mind the fundamental bar—
Plump martinis at The Narragansett.

Let the uninformed go waste their time
Traipsing through The Hague, Oslo, or France. It
Only leaves more ferry room betimes.
Summer's coming to The Narragansett.

FRED YANNANTUONO's work has been published in eighty journals in thirty states. His book of poetry, *A Boilermaker for the Lady* (NYQ Books 2009) has been banned in France, Latvia, and the Orkney Isles. Yannantuono is currently featured in *Light Quarterly*. His book, *To Idi Amin I'm a Idiot— and Other Palindromes* is due out this year.

Manila
The Noble City

———————————————————————————————————————

Even I,
how am I to speak
for them, to open my hands
and say here,
here are lives.

—MARIA LUISA AGUILAR CARIÑO, "TO AMERICAN FRIENDS"

EVERYONE WAS POOR THAT YEAR. Everyone wore shabby, patched-up clothes. Everyone was sad and bitter and had a bad temper.

All the boys that were growing up to manhood that year were thin, pale, and melancholy. They went around with hunched-up shoulders as if a chill wind were forever blowing.

"Why don't you go look for work?" was the eternal refrain that greeted the poor young men. But there was no work; there were no jobs. The young men would gulp down the breakfast coffee and hurry out of the house, followed by the bitter voices of fathers and mothers.

That was the year Ernesto Ortega turned seventeen.

Every morning, when he woke up, he had to make an effort to remember where he was. Every day, on opening his eyes, he would wonder: "Why does the room look so strange?" And then, slowly, he would recognize the discolored ceiling, the ugly walls, and the cockroaches crawling up the walls.

"It's only a dream, a bad dream," he would tell himself, shutting his eyes tight, trying to get back to that older house he occupied every night in his dreams—the lost house of memory, the house where he had been born and had grown up. He would see the old-fashioned garden and his mother in a white dress strolling among the flowers, and he was calling out to his mother in the garden. She peered up from under the parasol and smiled and waved at him. He was a little boy in a sailor's suit. His mother picked a flower and looked up again and showed him the flower. She was as clean and bright and beautiful as the sunny day gleaming in the garden.

Then a big, old-fashioned automobile appeared at the garden gate, and his father stepped out with a cane, wearing a coat buttoned right up to his neck. His mother ran to meet his father. They stood there talking and laughing at the gate. His mother turned around to point to him there at the window, and his father laughed and turned around to look at him, too.

He was a curly-haired little boy at the window of a big, beautiful house that was clean and fragrant. There it was: the house. Even as he looked at it, it dissolved into a discolored ceiling and ugly wall.

Outside, in the foul alley, he could hear the women quarreling and the cats and dogs fighting over garbage. From the public shed, two doors away, came the vile stench of this day, this year, this life.

He rose and went to the window and saw his mother. She stood there in a faded dress bargaining with the old man who bought old bottles. Tears rose to his eyes. She was not young or beautiful anymore. She was thin and haggard and needed money so she could go to the market. His father had died long ago.

He was a sad young man going downstairs to wash his face in a stinking tin sink. As he groped for a towel, his mother came in.

"Ernesto, are you going anywhere today?"

The street corner, rock by the bay, Luneta park.

"No, Mother."

"Ernesto, you're wasting your life. You're young and . . ."

"Please, Mother, must we start so early in the morning?"

"All your other brothers are working."

"I can't do anything."

"I want you to go to your godfather."

"That crazy old man? What could he do for me?"

"Maybe he can help you. You're young. You're wasting your life."

"Please, Mother, if you want me to go to him, all right, I'll go, but let's not quarrel."

Suddenly she began to cry.

"Oh, Ernesto—I'm so worried! How are we going to live? I'm not used to living this way. I shall die! I shall die!"

The wet towel in his hand, Ernesto stood grimly silent by the foul sink, his young face turned away from the anguish of poverty.

DON SALVADOR GARCIA still lived in a big, old-fashioned house on Carriedo. The other big houses on that street had become bazaars or Japanese refreshment stores. But Don Salvador still kept his house and the ancient bookstore on the first floor although no one ever came now to buy anything. All the books were old—Spanish classics or books by the revolutionary patriots or books of devotion. On the walls where cobwebs hung thick were faded paintings of the heroes and the saints. Poverty, too, lay heavy here—but it was not sordid poverty. It was poverty with an air of magnificence to it.

Don Salvador Garcia was Ernesto's godfather.

"Hola, Ernesto," he said wiping the ink off his fingers with a perfumed linen handkerchief. "How is my godson?"

"Okay, Godfather."

"And what can I do for you, young man? Ah, you don't have to tell me, you young rascal! You need a little money for a dance, a girl, eh?"

Ernesto shuddered. Don Salvador was just as poor as everyone now, but he spoke like a millionaire.

"No, Godfather, I don't need anything. I just came to visit you."

"Well, sit down, sit down, son! And how is your mother? How is the widow of my good friend? A beautiful and elegant woman."

Ernesto shuddered again, remembering his mother among the slum women, the old-bottle man, the fighting cats and dogs in the refuse heap, the public shed . . .

"She is fine, Don Salvador—thank you. And how is the history?"

"Oh, I shall finish it soon, soon! It shall make me famous! I am writing the greatest history ever written. Manila shall be known all over the world when my book is finished! Here let me read to you the opening lines . . ."

Ernesto turned his face away. How many times Don Salvador had read him those opening lines! The old man fumbled through his manuscripts, spread one, and began to read:

"As Palmyra to Arabia, as Alexandria to decaying Hellenism, as Rome to the classic world and Carthage to old Africa, as Byzantium to the Eastern Empire, and as Venice to the Europe of the Renaissance, so was this noble and ever-loyal City of Manila to the Orient. . . ."

From somewhere in the house, Ernesto heard a scream. But the old man never gave heed. He continued to read—slowly, sonorously, with emotion and with majesty.

There was a clatter of slippers, and three women appeared. They swept in, full of cold wrath, full of disdain and bitterness. They were the old man's daughters, and they had his beauty and his majesty. But they were growing old. Poverty had marked them. It embittered them.

"But we could be rich!" they said. "People are offering to buy this house, to turn it into a department store. But Papa will not sell! Oh, he is a hard man! And you know his reasons? Because he wants to finish a ridiculous history that no one will ever read, that no one will ever buy, that no one in the world is interested in! And for that he is killing us! Oh, if only we were free! Oh, if only he were dead, dead! We would sell this house at once and go far, far away!"

Now they swept in and stood in a row before the desk. Don Salvador never lifted his head. He went on reading, intoning the majestic Spanish words. They looked at him with cold fury, with bitter disdain. They cast not a glance at Ernesto, who sat rocking in his chair. From outside, in the street, came the sound of a passing streetcar.

The old man paused and looked up.

Suddenly the three daughters screamed in unison.

"Oh, you hard man! You cruel man! You old devil!"

The old man turned his face toward them and smiled.

"Is the *merienda* ready?" asked the old man, smiling majestically.

A LONG, LONG TIME AFTERWARD, Ernesto returned to that house in Carriedo. It was not there anymore. Only the ruins of it were there—a great heap of rubble and twisted steel. It was August 1945, and Ernesto was a grown man now, dressed in olive-drab clothes. The war had just come to an end, and he had just arrived from the provinces to see the city for the first time in a long, long time.

Ernesto walked down the piteous horror that was Carriedo. A street of desolation, a street of death. He stopped before the house that had once been the fine and mighty house of Don Salvador Garcia. It was late afternoon. The rumble of passing army trucks echoed through the streets.

Ernesto stood there looking at the ruined house, and suddenly his heart gave a leap. Lights had sprung up within the ruins. There were people inside.

He had not been to that house since that day long, long ago when he was seventeen. He knew that Don Salvador had long been dead. Of Don Salvador's daughters he had heard nothing. He had left the city when he was seventeen and had not come back till today, to see what war had done to it.

The lights within the ruins grew brighter as evening gathered and Ernesto heard a murmur of voices. His heart beating fast, he walked into the ruined house.

In the very heart of the ruins, a space had been cleared of rubble and a roof of galvanized iron had been set up. Under that barong-barong stood a few old chairs, a table, and some bookcases. At the table the three old women sat—Garcia's daughters.

Ernesto stepped nearer and coughed. The three women looked around, and their faces brightened.

"Why, it's Ernesto!"

Ernesto went forward. They had all risen with glad cries and were dancing around him like young girls.

"Sit down, Ernesto. We were just having *merienda*. Won't you have some chocolate?"

"No, thanks."

Ernesto looked at the table. It was set with three dainty cups.

"You must excuse us, Ernesto, but we're not dressed to receive visitors," said the three women, laughing.

"I didn't know you were still here."

"Oh, but we have always been here. And we will never go away. This is our home. This is our father's house."

"You never sold it?"

They looked at him with shocked faces.

"Why should we sell it?"

"But when your father died, you were free to sell the house."

"Never, never did we ever think of doing so!" they cried together.

"But I thought . . . you had always wanted to sell it. . . ."

"This is our father's house, and we have kept it exactly as it had always been."

"And you have been living here since he died?"

"All the years since he died, here we have been. Oh, there were people who wanted to buy this house, but we would not sell it. Our father was a great man. This is his house, but we would not sell it, and we have kept it as a shrine to his memory. He was a great man."

Ernesto stared in horror at the three women.

"Oh, he was a great man!" they chanted in unison. "And he wrote a great book, a history of Manila. Would you like to see it?"

They ran to one of the bookcases and lugged out a bundle of papers. Ernesto stared at the bundle. The sheets were yellow with age. The fire of war, the tears of the rain had touched that treasured bundle of paper that those three crazy old women had rescued from the wreckage of the house.

Ernesto stared at the yellowed pages of the manuscript. Every single word had been blurred. The ink had washed away. The labors of Don Salvador had been lost, had been in vain. No one would ever read what he had written. Not one word remained legible.

But the three women were hovering over the pages, their eyes full of love. "It is a magnificent history, Ernesto. Would you like us to read you the opening lines?"

Ernesto began to tremble.

"Light another lamp," said the eldest sister.

When she had put on her glasses, she bent over the page where not one word remained, where every single word had been effaced.

Ernesto gazed with growing horror as the old woman began to read, her fingers moving over the yellow page, tracing the words that were not there. Her voice rose clear and sure: "As Palmyra to Arabia, as Alexandria to decaying Hellenism, as Rome to the classic world and Carthage to old Africa, as Byzantium to the Eastern Empire, and as Venice to the Europe of the Renaissance, so was this noble and ever loyal City of Manila to the Orient. . . ."

Outside in the street, a truck rumbled past as the dark devoured the ruins.

ALEXANDER N. TAN JR. received his doctorate in medicine from the University of the City of Manila (Pamantasan ng Lungsod ng Maynila). He also holds a bachelor's degree in physical therapy from Our Lady of Fatima University. He was a fellow at the 36th Dumaguete National Summer Writers' Workshop (1997). His short stories and poems have been published by several literary journals throughout the Philippines and the U.S. A practicing physician and physical therapist, he writes and lives in Mandaluyong City, Philippines.

Keeping Accounts, Akron

His notes were scrawled on the back, the bottom
or margins of some used scrap of paper.
A clean sheet seemed a vanity item,
an indulgence for a record keeper
of greater means. His ragged stacks were tied
with bits of thread and teetered on his desk,
pagodas of ephemera. He took pride
in recalling just where to look when asked

to locate this acquisition, that receipt.
The heraldry of his junk dealer realm,
those crumpled accounts told all he had swapped,
bought, appraised, or sold. I take after him.
I pile up words, scratch through some, and rummage
my pockets for first jottings of this page.

WILL WELLS' volume of poems, *Unsettled Accounts* (Ohio University/ Swallow Press, 2010), won the 2009 Hollis Summers Poetry Prize. He was the 2010 Ohio Poet of the Year (State Library of Ohio) and served as a Walter Dakin Fellow in Poetry at the Sewanee Writers' Conference in 2010. His work has been published in *32 Poems, Tampa Review, Image, Birmingham Poetry Review, River Styx, Soundings Review,* and *Cimmaron Review.* Will Wells writes, "The sonnet's octave/sestet pattern is both compelling and amazingly conducive to innovation. I enjoy raising an issue in the octave and trying to endow the sestet with some element of resolution—a form which mirrors the fundamental human inclination to raise a question and try to answer it. 'Keeping Accounts, Akron' explores human identity and the compulsion to preserve what has been damaged. My junk dealer grandfather is profiled in this poem. And what is a lyric poet but someone who barters scraps and pieces of experience with his audience, much as my grandfather bartered scraps of cloth and metal?"

EMILY KLEMMER

Dad and New York City

WHILE MY BROTHER NORMAN AND I WAITED for my dad to take us to the Leroy Street Pool, a public pool in the West Village, we threw our Spalding up against the front of our building to try to knock the paint chips off the pink facade.

Our dad would come soon. He'd be wearing his square plastic sunglasses crooked on his thin nose. He'd have on his banged-up white boating cap, a grungy T-shirt and bell-bottom jeans. A real hipster. When he'd see us, he'd brush down on his thick mustache with his fingers and grin without showing any of his teeth. He'd say, "Hi Pelican," calling me his pet name because my legs were as thin as a bird's. Then he'd say, "Hi Norman, like that ball, huh?" and we'd grab our towels from the curb and head down Seventh Avenue for the pool.

My father was a creative man. He could paint and draw. He had spent two years in Germany in the army and then finished his college degree in architecture at the University of Michigan. He started his architectural business out of his small, one-bedroom apartment in New York City after he left my mother and moved out of our apartment. He took calls from clients from the phone on the wall in his

62

kitchenette. Eventually, he found an office on 30th Street, where he put in a conference table, three drafting boards, and a wall of filing cabinets. Tall chrome stools sat at each drafting table, T-squares breezed up and down their edges. Eraser dust flew about as my father brushed and blew the bits off the large sheets of paper.

Dad said that walking downtown on a summer morning was a beautiful sight with the restaurant owners unwinding their awnings over tables set up on the sidewalk. It reminded him of Spain when he was there with my mother for their honeymoon. At that time, my father was on a scholarship to work in Madrid for the summer, but first they had traveled to Scotland, Sweden, and Amsterdam. Then they took a train down the Rhine River and went over to Frankfurt. He told us how that town was completely bombed out during World War II.

Then my parents went to Zurich where a friend of Dad's picked them up in his car and right away they got into a car accident. My mother was sitting in the front seat between the driver and Dad when the other car hit. My mother smashed her face into the rearview mirror and whacked her knees up against the dashboard. Blood ran down her face. An ambulance took her to the hospital where she had forty-eight stitches put all around her eyes and eyelids. After she had healed some, my parents continued their journey on a train to Italy and France. They flew to Madrid where my dad started his work drafting for a couple of architects.

My dad told my brother and me a lot about his life. He liked to talk, and Norman liked to ask a lot of questions. Dad didn't mind the scalding waves of heat from the pavement as we walked downtown. He had stories to tell and other things on his mind, but I felt the rubber of my worn-out flip flops softening. The dirty air hurt my lungs most of the time, which caused me to cough, something that I'd been experiencing all that summer of 1968. The sky was black because of all the soot.

What I liked best about living in Greenwich Village was the way the streets zigzagged around each other in triangles that led me back to where I once started if I made all the right turns. I knew where all my friends lived and what kind of apartment buildings they lived in: brownstones, high-rises, tenements, townhouses. Ours was an old, four-story townhouse that was once a single-family house.

There were scrappy "garbage trees" in our yard. My dad called them that because they were like large weeds that grew two stories high. They were smothered in white caterpillar nests where the leaves had been eaten away and dangled long and loose like confetti. When Norman and I would cut through our yard to climb the brick wall to get to the parking lot on the other side, we ran fast to keep the caterpillars from dropping down onto our shoulders.

When we stopped to look at a building while walking downtown, Dad especially liked to arch his head way back to look up at the gargoyles high up under the eaves of an old structure. When I'd squint up with him into the ugly gargoyle faces, laughing monkeys, or devils with turned-down lips, I felt glad they were away from my reach. I didn't have to worry about them swooping down on me the way the dirty pigeons did when they fluttered up into my face from the street.

Dad pointed out something simple for us to look at, a new addition going up, a storefront getting new glass. He would be the first one peering through a hole or crack in the boards that were put up around a construction site. On the mornings he picked us up for school, we'd look at the modern Maritime Union Building, a skip and a hop across the street past St. Vincent's Hospital to P.S. 41, our school—a modern building at the corner of 11th Street.

"Not the best-looking thing," he would say about our school. I didn't mind the way my school looked. It was beautiful to me with its huge cement playground in the back, which held an abundance of space for the girls to chase the boys around and then kiss them on their soft, pink cheeks, something I had the honor of doing to Eric, my first crush, last year in third grade.

On a school morning, when we had time, Dad would swing us by one of his favorite buildings, the Jefferson Market Courthouse, so we could gaze up at its unique architectural details. The women's prison behind it, however, would distract him, and he'd jerk us away, protecting us from the women inside who screamed down to their pimps or prostitute friends on the street. The women behind the meshed windows were shadows, coming and going like ghosts, their faces appearing and then disappearing, their lips moving when they'd lean down to the open windows to yell out. I couldn't help but stare up at them and wonder how long they'd have to be stuck inside that dark place. I wondered if I was like them somehow, an outcast maybe.

"Wearing any suntan lotion?" my dad asked me when we got to the pool house.

"No," I said.

"Didn't your mother put any on you?"

And then the mood changed. Norman stopped tossing the ball up and down. He gave me a sly look from the side of his eyes. I shut up about my mother. I had learned not to say too many things to Dad about her or to say too many things to her about Dad. But when I would forget, I got scared that one of them would start talking about each other behind their backs. I froze up, and even on a summer day I felt cold inside.

It was a relief to get out of the sun and get my locker tag. The girl behind the counter took her time, enjoying her cigarette. I liked the mod paisley scarves she tied around her afro that made it rise up like a balloon on top of her head.

It took a minute for my eyes to adjust to the darkness of the locker room. I hated taking a shower before going into the pool, cold and sharp against my skin. I ran out into the bright outdoor light, squinting against the sunshine.

I searched for Norman and Dad who were already down at the other end of the pool, standing on their towels that they'd smoothed out on the cement deck. My brother and I ran to the pool and slid under the surface of the water. We looked at each other with bulging fish eyes, his blue, mine brown. I saw in his eyes a mirror image, paired together like we were forever linked.

"Where's Dad?" Norman said.

I looked around.

Dad popped up between us and let out a long relaxed breath. All morning we swam in the shallow end as Dad came and went doing his butterfly laps, water spraying from his arms as they stretched across the water.

When we decided to leave, I went into the locker room and said, "Locker!" and then sat on a wooden bench to wait for the attendant to come in with her huge ring of keys. That was the routine, everyone called out "locker" when they were ready to have their locker opened. But she never came. I got up and went out front to the mod girl with the head scarf and told her I needed my locker opened.

"Who wants their locker opened?" A voice from behind me asked.

I turned around and faced the big white dress. Inside it was a large African woman with a much shorter afro than the mod girl's.

"I do," I said.

"Next time, just ask," she said.

I followed her back into the locker room.

"Now listen, honey," she said as I pointed my locker out to her, "all ya'gotta do is say 'locker' real loud, and I'll come."

But I knew I couldn't say "locker" real loud, not as loud as I needed to. It was the worst part of coming to the pool.

I got dressed and rolled my suit up inside my towel. Norman and Dad had their hair parted and combed neatly to the side. They looked cool and refreshed. If my mother were here, maybe she could have helped me comb my hair and put a part in the middle like I usually wore it.

"How was it, Pelican?" he said.

"Okay."

"What took so long?"

The heat outside made me feel sticky all over again. Dad had put on his crooked sunglasses, and we walked up to the pizza parlor on the corner where we usually went after the pool. The smell of pizza sauce made my stomach flip with hunger. We sat at a Formica table, with a fan spinning overhead, and waved the flies away. Being out of the sun and sipping a little can of apple juice, I started to think again about things I didn't know, asking myself questions about why Dad left or if he was ever coming back. I could see us sitting there talking, but it was like I wasn't there at all. I saw my brother talking to my dad but heard no words. I saw pizza, stringy cheese, hands, lips moving.

Dad bought us Italian ices. I ate mine fast, but the lemon juice still dripped down my arm.

At our corner we said goodbye to Dad.

"We'll do this again next weekend," he said.

Promise filled his face behind the facade of glasses, mustache, and boating hat, as he nodded his head. I watched him cross 14th Street until he blended in with all the other people on the street, until the buildings engulfed him and he disappeared into his own life.

This chapter is from EMILY KLEMMER's full-length childhood memoir about growing up in New York City in the sixties. Her father would take her and her brother to the Swedenborgian Church on 35th Street when they were six and seven years old. As children, they especially liked sneaking up the back stairs to explore the balcony with the organ and the rooms above the congregation. It was her father who walked Klemmer down the aisle of the same church twenty-three years later, and it was the same balcony from which the music came and the same rooms above that held her wedding reception. The 2012 pen-and-ink illustrations are by Carolyn Judson.

BETH PAULSON

Inheritance

Mother taught me what her mother had showed her,
to press a double hem to make it neat
before you sew it down in even stitches
that barely show through on the other side.

She taught me how to make hospital corners
with sheets dried on a line that smelled like summer
air in trees or just-mowed grass. I learned
to fold each side into a neat triangle
and tuck it in tightly like nurses did.

I learned what my grandmother once taught her,
to roll out pastry thin, but not too thin,
and cut a Bethlehem star in the top crust
before you lift it over the filled pie
and crimp between two steady forefingers
its trimmed and folded edge circling the pan.

She taught me as her mother once taught her
in country kitchens or when they moved to town
where women wore bought dresses and white gloves
and knew all the people they were related to.

BETH PAULSON'S poems have appeared nationally in magazines and anthologies. She has received three Pushcart Prize nominations. Her collection *Wild Raspberries* was published by Plain View Press in 2009. Beth taught college writing for over twenty years at California State University Los Angeles. She lives on Colorado's Western Slope where she teaches writing and creativity workshops. She recently published a new collection called *Canyon Notes* (Mount Sneffels Press, 2012).

MICHAEL HOPPING

The Triple World

Newgrange (below) was built about 3200 BC, during the Neolithic period in Ireland. It is made of earth and stone layers. Once a year during sunrise at the winter solstice, the sun precisely illuminates the mound's chamber floor, if weather conditions are favorable. The origins of this prehistoric tomb remain a mystery. Photograph, 2006. Creative Commons 2.5 Attribution.

THE VEIL BETWEEN WORLDS is thinner at some places and at certain times, or so believed the ancient Irish Celts. Celestial markers of seasonal change and the rising and setting of the sun were among the times when worlds might intermingle. I can't vouch for much of that from personal experience, but I do know the veil was thin at my house when the alarm clock buzzed at 3:30 AM on December 21st.

The occasion was a live webcast of the winter-solstice dawn at Newgrange, a five-thousand-year-old megalithic passage tomb in County Meath, Ireland. Ages before the Celts held sway, a millennium before the great stone circle at Stonehenge, and five hundred years before Egypt's renowned pyramids, Irishmen hauled hundreds of thousands of tons of rock and soil to create Newgrange and other

monumental cairns on the hills overlooking a bend of the River Boyne.

Today, Newgrange is a graceful grassy mound 260 feet across and 40 feet in height. Around the perimeter, a line of gray kerbstones, each weighing a ton or more, supports the base of a white quartzite retaining wall. A stone door leans beside what appears to be a mine entrance "timbered" by stone pillars and a platter-like lintel. Above the lintel, the wall is set back to frame a rectangular transom or "roof-box" opening. Like the doorway below, it accesses a straight and proudly rectilinear up-sloping passage into the mound's interior. Massive stone walls and ceiling slabs traverse sixty feet to a small dead-end chamber where the ceiling sweeps upwards twenty feet into a conical dome. At floor level are three squarish recesses. In the largest of these, a wide granite basin once held the ashes of the dead and items sent with them to the afterlife.

Many of the large stones inside and out are decorated with incised pictographs, often spirals. Some are doubled, winding inward only to reverse course at the center and wind out again. Newgrange's signature design is a set of three doubled spirals interconnected in a cloverleaf arrangement. Tri-spirals occur on both the entrance kerbstone and a wall of the rearward chamber recess. The triangular pattern echoes the three-recess floor plan. (Scholars describe the passage and chamber layout as cruciform, cross-shaped, a term out of keeping with the site's antiquity.)

The number *three* was evidently important to these Stone Age farmers. They knew the moon was dark for three days each lunar month. Perhaps the tri-spirals depicted a three-day sojourn in the underworld or the related trinity of birth, death, and rebirth, a

The threshold stone at the entrance of Newgrange is about five thousand years old, 10x4 feet, and weighs five tons. Carved on its surface are spirals, concentric circles, and diamond shapes. Three concentric spirals have become associated with the legendary Celtic design. Photograph, 2005. Creative Commons 2.5 Attribution.

concept often central to the beliefs of primitive agricultural communities. For them, the trajectory of existence went round and round. The Celts revered their megalithic tombs as portals to the otherworldly home of the Tuatha Dé Danann, the people under the hill.

The monument builders were almost certainly animists, people who recognized a profusion of spirits in nature: rocks, salmon, and barley, as well as spirits embodied elsewhere. Pre-colonial indigenous cultures have left us examples of rites designed to maintain harmonious relations between spirits and the human community. Proper behavior of the sun, moon, and rain gods depended on people doing their part. Animals and plants offered themselves to mankind's service in return for prescribed demonstrations of appreciation.

The mounds once served another purpose. They were astronomical observatories. From December 19 to 23, when solar fire is weakest in northern latitudes, sunlight streams through the Newgrange roofbox at dawn, briefly lighting the recess at the rear of the chamber. If the door is open, a second golden beam illuminates the passage floor.

Shadows in the Mists of Dawn

WHAT MOTIVATED ANCIENT IRISHMEN to take such pains for a fleeting display spoiled more often than not by cloudy skies? It may have been important to prove that the sun, like the doubled spiral, reversed its dwindling autumnal course and wasn't abandoning the world to privation in an endless frigid night. And, as it happens, salmon run on the Boyne at midwinter. Despite the damp Irish cold, winter solstice may have heralded a time of plenty.

The sun's penetration of the earthen mound might have been an act of fertilization. Such notions are common in stories explaining how a spirit world can affect life on Earth. The Babylonians said a ray of light impregnated the mother of Tammuz, an agricultural deity who cycled annually between birth and death. Mitra, an antique sun god of Indo-Iranian origin, was born in a cave at winter solstice. In Greece, the virgin Danaë was locked in an underground bronze chamber to prevent pregnancy but to no avail. Zeus got to her in the form of a golden beam of light. She begat Perseus, the hero who beheaded Medusa. Thousands of years later, Christian painters depicted Jesus's conception with a beam of heavenly light. Even today, we associate the birth of an idea with an illuminated lightbulb.

Whatever the local details, winter solstice was evidently an occasion for public ceremony at Newgrange, although limited chamber space meant few of the living could witness the solar shaft firsthand. Access was likely restricted to religious adepts. Nowadays the Office of Public Works (OPW) in County Meath conducts an open lottery for the opportunity to observe from inside the burial chamber. In 2007, more than 28,000 applications were received for the hundred available tickets. For the first time, OPW offered a live webcast of the event as well. That's what got me out of bed in the wee small hours.

A trio of commentators, bundled and sniffling in the freezing chill, stood outside the monument with a couple hundred visitors and conducted a thoroughly modern play-by-play. Cameras panned the quartzite face of the mound and the lightening horizon across the misty river. Inside with the lottery winners, other video eyes watched the dark entrance passage. The sun soon peeked above the distant trees. Moments later the promised sunbeams appeared and strengthened impressively along the passage wall and floor.

In my half-awake state, the golden ribbons seemed almost tangible: yellow brick roads linking the heavens with the underworld. Maybe the honored dead or shaman in charge of the solstice ceremony traveled them. Why not? Irishmen have been known to chase leprechaun gold at the end of rainbows. Could the tri-spirals have signified a triple reality consisting of the mundane world and otherworlds above and below inhabited by spirits? Who knows? It was all so long ago.

What Light through Yonder Window?

ANCIENT IRISH FARMERS knew the meaning of solstice sunbeams. Any European Catholic in the Middle Ages could raise her eyes in the cavernous space of a Gothic cathedral and read God's contract in the light streaming through a rose window high above the entrance.

Ours is not always such a time. That's why the Newgrange tri-spirals intrigued me enough to leave a comfortable bed at an unreasonable hour. I wanted to learn which trinity welcomed the sun at the entrance and sanctified its penetration to the rear wall. And I wondered what I'd see in that event, a cleverly showcased natural occurrence, a triumphant re-affirmation of spirits in the land, or what.

I stared into my seventeen inches of liquid crystal display as the grainy yellow beam appeared and inched toward me in the virtual depths of the tomb. To my relief, there was a welcoming magic in it. I felt the others who travel the golden road wherever and whenever it appears. We may disagree about how to explain the experience, but what's constant is the certainty of connection. Dressed in whatever mythic clothes, empathic connection is at the heart of Newgrange.

As to the meaning of the tri-spiral, I drifted back to sleep no wiser after the video feed went dark. In the morning, an answer came. It fits the minimalist facts of modernity and wouldn't have made sense to the ancient divines who carved potent symbols and crouched in the darkness waiting for omens in the year's first light. Perhaps their world was triple, maybe not. But the reality available to the intellectual descendents of Galileo and Dostoevsky most definitely is.

A virtual reality of symbols controlled by implacable algorithms has joined our worlds of nature and subjective awareness. These three realms are as conjoined and interactive as the tri-spirals, if not as well balanced. People live and have lived without the information otherworld but, without it, the planet couldn't support anywhere near the seven billion of us it does. Those numbers may yet prove unsustainable if we don't do a better job of attending to problems in the natural and subjective spheres.

The remedy, as the animists knew, is harmony, balance in how we value and tend the realms of our triple reality, a concept beautifully illustrated in the tri-spiral. The enfeebled state of empathy in the subjective world deserves special attention too. Spiritual connectivity was so important to the builders on the Boyne that they labored for decades to celebrate it in awesome displays of engineering and astronomical prowess. But their skills in discernment are at least as humbling. To this day, who has conceived a more evocative sign of cosmic reassurance than a beam of light?

MICHAEL HOPPING's short fiction and creative nonfiction have appeared in *Spoiled Ink, The Great Smokies Review, fresh,* and the *Mad Hatters' Review Blog.* He is the author of a novel, *Meet Me in Paradise* (WastelandRunes, 2007) and a collection of short stories, *MacTiernan's Bottle* (Pisgah Press, 2011).

MIKE RAMM

Monday Is Garbage Day

If it weren't for garbage, I would never look at stars.
Every Monday morning before dawn,
I carry my two garbage cans down
the dark driveway and set them by the road
in exactly the same spot week after week.
I could take them down Sunday afternoon
when there's plenty of light, but then the dogs
and raccoons will knock over the cans,
scattering coffee filters and disposable diapers.
I could take them down after sunrise,
but by then I'm ready for work and
inevitably I stain my slacks or tie with
mud or mustard or something
smeared on the cans I don't even recognize.
That's why early Monday mornings
I'm hauling garbage under the stars.
I've performed this routine for so many years
I know a little about celestial cycles.
For instance, when I set down the trash
in October, Orion is almost overhead.
To find Betelgeuse and Rigel
all I have to do is look up from the garbage.
But now that Orion has moved on,
the garbage cans point out the Big Dipper.
There's Polaris. There's Mizar—a double star.
And to the east, twenty degrees
above the lids of my monolithic monuments,
there's the comet Hale-Bopp—its trail of debris
streaming a million miles across the heavens.

MIKE RAMM teaches high school English in Foresthill, California.

*View of the Summer House
in the Garden to E. Swedenborg's Residence at Stockholm.*

ANDERS HALLENGREN

E pluribus unum
Mauritian Reflections

Harmony makes a family a paradise; discord makes it a hell.
—EDMOND DE CHAZAL

IN HIS POST-PRIZE INTERVIEWS, a Nobel Laureate of literature in 2008, J.M.G. Le Clézio, arriving in Sweden from his home in Mauritius, expressed his admiration for Swedenborg. The first thing he had done on this visit to Stockholm was to inquire about the house of Emanuel Swedenborg. "You know, the Swedish genius, the scientist, philosopher, and theologian," as he explained to the uninformed journalists. "And," he continued, "then I was shown to the house where Swedenborg used to talk with the angels. How marvelous! That communication with the world of spirits reminded me of another author writing in French, the great Senegalese poet Senghor, who likewise spoke with the spirits, angels, and demons of his African country."

Sometimes the lack of knowledge among us Swedes is embarrassing, but we may perhaps be excused if we did not know that in Le Clézio's island home on Mauritius there had been an active *Société de la Nouvelle Jérusalem* since 1859, an active Swedenborgian movement with many unique facets and unknown literary connections. As background to the laureate's surprising remarks, I have taken down the following notes, which explain his strong esteem for Swedenborg.

Illustration: *Swedenborg's Summer House in His Garden Residence, Stockholm.* Glencarin Museum, Bryn Athyn, Pennsylvania.

IN 1763, an eighteenth-century alchemist, mystic, and Rosicrucian named François de Chazal de la Genesté left France, set out across the Indian Ocean, and settled on the French *Ile de France,* fifteen hundred miles from Africa, later known as *Ile Maurice,* the present-day Mauritius. Before long, he connected with his younger brother

Antoine Régis de Chazal de Chemarel; his brother died in 1772, leaving two sons of tender years, Toussaint and Charles Antoine. Their uncle François, who was known as a philosopher and who had built up a large library on his estate, became their tutor. The books and the tenor of thought both fell to the inheritance of Toussaint, who in turn bequeathed the ever-growing library to his son, the learned Joseph Antoine Edmond de Chazal (1809–1879). Edmond, as we will see later, eventually established the Swedenborg Society mentioned above, became its first chairman, and opened the first Swedenborgian church on Mauritius. This was on his own property, St. Antoine, where he built a "Hall for Worship" *(Salle de Culte)* and preached.

The Roman Catholic Church, to which Edmond belonged, regarded him harshly. We can see this in pamphlets that have come down to us from the latter 1850s in which Edmond states his faith (for example in his public declaration of faith made in *Riviere du Rempart* in 1857). He later explained, "I am an Apostate" *(Je suis Apostat,* 1859), signing himself as "a disciple of the Lord's New Church."[1] The "Lord's New Church" is Swedenborg's term, used in his reports on the world of spirits, meaning a loving community of all humankind.

ON 11 JANUARY 1859, the first Swedenborg Society was founded in the capital city of Port Louis. The gathering was held at the home of the Lesage brothers, Napoléon and James. Also present was Émile Michel, a painter, and in addition, there in the background was Edmond de Chazal with the important and inspiring George Herbert Poole, who had arrived from Adelaide in Australia in 1846 and from the very beginning of his visit had propagated Swedenborg's thought. That is not to say, though, that it was Poole who had brought Swedenborgianism to the island. There are strong indications that the spiritual soil had already been prepared by earlier influences, initially by the import of books by the de Chazal family, and especially by Edmond's father, Toussaint.

At that time, the greater part of Swedenborg's works had been published in French, and even earlier, during Swedenborg's own lifetime, French mysticists, occultists, hypnotists, and Freemasons had been fascinated by the Swedish theosophist (1688–1772). Swedenborgianism's deep roots and wide branches in the de Chazal family are clear from the fact that the name crops up among the most active Swedenborgians in the twentieth century, both in France and on Mauritius. It seems, however, like Lesage, that the artist Émile Michel also had significant contact with France. In fact, Michel began the importing of Swedenborgian literature into Mauritius.[2] To some extent, too, Swedenborgianism on Mauritius can be traced back to the Englishman Charles Augustus Tulk, as profound a thinker as he was controversial, the son of John Augustus Tulk, one of the very first Swedenborgians in the world.[3]

To understand this, we first turn back to the "mystic Australian," Poole. Research in Swedenborgian sources shows that George Herbert Poole was an Englishman, was trained in languages, and had held a teaching post from 1846 to 1849 at the Royal College, a high school on the then-British possession of Mauritius. In England, he had been a close friend of C.A. Tulk; and when Poole returned to Mauritius in 1859, he won many converts to his own faith in Swedenborg's teachings. Among them was Émile Michel, who started a correspondence with Jacques-François-Etienne Le Boys des Guays (1794–1864), known for his many French translations of Swedenborg and for having founded the New Church Society at Saint-Amand-Mont-Rond (the Department of Cher in central France) in November 1837—and also for his correspondence with George Sand and Alexandre Dumas.[4]

Poole took up his teaching profession in Australia from 1850 to 1865, first in Sydney, as reflected in the history of the New Church in New South Wales, an organization that survives at the present day. Poole then fully immigrated to Mauritius in 1865, where we find him on the Rue du Rempart, in a house owned by Edmond de Chazal, who earlier had been, by all testimony, a thorough-going skeptic. It was probably Poole, Lesage, and Michel who finally convinced Edmond, and he became the central figure of the society.[5]

The Echo of the New Jerusalem

After that founding meeting in Port Louis in January 1859, almost a decade after Poole left the island after his earlier visit, Edmond de Chazal donated a piece of land for the proposed society. A year earlier he himself had started corresponding with Le Boys des Guays and the New Church Society in France. In consequence, the little group of friends built *La Société de la Nouvelle Jérusalem* in the capital city of Port Louis. In the fateful year 1861—America's Civil War, the emancipation of the serfs in Russia, the unification of Italy— Edmond de Chazal was not only the leader of the active Swedenborg Society, but also the editor of its monthly journal, *L'Écho de la Nouvelle Jérusalem*, the very first purely religious periodical on Mauritius. Here the liturgy of the New Church was published; here one learned of baptisms and marriages. The journal introduced many contributions from France, including some by the lawyer J.A. Blancheet of Tarbe, who had founded a Swedenborgian society in the Pyrenees. Its columns even took note of General Aleksandr Muraviev's labors for spiritual and humanitarian reform in Russia.

Until his death, Edmond de Chazal was the driving force of Swedenborgianism on the island, a distant outpost two thousand *lieu* from Paris. The results were evident. A year after the purchase of the meeting building bought in 1876 in Port Louse, we find Ordinance No. 4 of 1877, signed by Victoria, Queen of Great Britain and Ireland, Empress of India. This was the official recognition of The New Church and its constitution on Mauritius. A Methodist pastor had joined the New Church. De Chazal had won the hearts of both Protestants and Anglicans, even of Hindus. When his own heart stopped after seventy years, in February 1879, he left behind a love and devotion that are clearly portrayed in his obituary in the periodical, *Le Cernéen*. It is particularly emphasized that even with the Indian hired hands on his sugar plantations, Edmond de Chazal lived in a unique moral and spiritual fellowship.

The people here are extraordinarily helpful. If you ask for directions, they will get in the car with you and direct you to your destination and then accept no money and walk a mile or more back to where you met them. Not once has anyone ever been rude to us. Without exception people have gone out of their way to be helpful. It's hard to believe they are so nice and don't want any money in return. . . . I have never met a more generous people. They are always welcoming. They do not look at North Americans with dollar signs in their eyes.

The people here apparently do not have an identity crisis —they seem to like being Mauritian. They feel unique, are proud of their country in a non-militaristic way, and seem content with their life. They know that they are a third-world country and look at the U.S. and England as rich places but don't seem interested in being like anybody but themselves. Every person I have met has asked me with genuine excitement, "How are you liking Mauritius?" I have traveled in poor countries where people were proud of their country, but I also sensed shame and disappointment, and some bitterness and resentment toward me because I came from a place more economically well off. Here I sense absolutely nothing but self-assured pride and contentment.

ERIC ALLISON from The Manse,
New Jerusalem Church, Remono Street
and Curepipe Road, Mauritius.
Excerpted from
"Mauritius: What is it Like"
New Church Messenger, February 1993.

AFTER EDMOND DE CHAZAL'S DEATH, the Lesage family was dominant in the Societé, and the jurist and political figure Auguste Châteauneuf, a member of the legislative assembly, succeeded him as its leader. On the initiative of the Lesage family, a second church building was erected at Curepipe, where Leona Lesage had donated some land. Since the time of its first pastor, Father Ferkin, Swedenborgian ministers from various parts of the world have from time to time officiated there.[6] One example of the international character of this ministry was Cornelius Bécherel, a member of the island's Indian population, pastor of the church in Curepipe. Like his predecessors, he fastened his hopes on his son and baptized him in the name Espérance. But this Espérance Bécherel, a Frenchman on his mother's side, wound up devoting his life to a quest for earthly treasures in Baie de Tombeau—more precisely, a gold treasure, which, according to a map handed

The island of Mauritius is located off the southeast coast of Africa, east of Madagascar. It is the main island of the Republic of Mauritius, with Port Louis as the capital. Photograph of Mauritius by Shardan, 2008 (Creative Commons Attribution 3.0 Unported).

down from his grandmother, had been hidden by a Dutch sailor in the seventeenth century.

This was the era of pioneers. When the Portuguese had landed in the sixteenth century, the island was unpopulated but rich with exotic animal life. The delicious giant dodo birds (named *Didus ineptus* by Linnaeus) were exterminated by the next colonists, the Dutch, who planted sugarcane, that baneful crop which is associated with slavery in the colonies and with the conditions that accompany it. This is how Africans came to Mauritius. The island had no indigenous population, so in that land a "genuine Mauritian" could have whatever appearance one chose. This was pointed out by one of Cornelius's later successors, Eric Allison, to whom I owe most of my knowledge about this congregation, in a lively, lovely, and memorable report on his pastorate in paradise, where the concept of a "standard of living" lost its American meaning. Eric experienced a sense of fellowship, freedom, and generosity in a multitude of differing people and onlookers, on one place out in the ocean, where people observed each other's holidays and found delight in helping and pleasing others, whoever they might be.[7] (See sidebar on page 78.)

Surrealism and Swedenborgianism

The name of de Chazal has never been forgotten in Mauritius. Nor has it been forgotten outside Mauritius. In 1961, a descendant with the name Maurice de Chazal baptized twenty-one people at the New Church in Paris; he was an officially chosen pastor of the English General Conference of Swedenborgians, who eventually left Paris to continue his work in South Africa. Henry de Geymüller dedicated his noteworthy book, *Swedenborg et les phénomènes psychiques* to the well-known French Swedenborgian, a book also renowned in German translation owing to the acclaimed historian of philosophy, Paul Sakmann.

By no means the least contribution to the international fame of the de Chazal name has been made by the Mauritian surrealist poet and Swedenborgian, Malcolm de Chazal (1902–1981), a descendant of Edmond, a man whom André Breton defended and honored as one of the greatest poets: "nothing so powerful has been heard since Lautréamont." Malcolm de Chazal too sought for wisdom, the infinite, the meaning of birth and death. He experienced revelations, interpreted the Scriptures, albeit in his own surrealistic way; he sought the light of the beginning, had visions of seeing face to face, groped for sensory truth in the supernatural world of nature and in the sensual as the great delight.[8] Malcolm de Chazal and his kindred spirits saw in sensory nature the face of both life and death, the only possibility of freedom.

High above the volcanic island rises a mountain named Le Morne Brabant, wreathed with legends, where year after year escaped slaves hid themselves from their owners and hunters. When slavery was abolished in 1835, English soldiers climbed up to them to bring them the good news. But the slaves, who believed they would be taken prisoner and transported back to the sugarcane fields, threw themselves down from the cliffs in a collective suicide. Similar stories about fugitives recur in our own times: such is the value of freedom.

Malcolm de Chazal was allowed to witness the declaration of independence of the island in the revolutionary year of 1968. Since March 1992, the Mauritius has been a republic with over a million inhabitants who celebrate their independence far beyond any coast or horizon, an island of *tolerance,* according to Pastor Allison, where, in a community of Indians, Africans, Chinese, and Europeans, the motto of the United States once was realized to a greater degree than in America: *e pluribus unum,* a unity out of multitudes.

As the inheritance from father to son in the de Chazal family was of such immense spiritual and historical significance, as we have seen in the case of the first generation on the island, Edmond de Chazal gathered his most important writings under the title, *À Mes Enfants,* "To My Children." As the father of twelve children, however, he included in his spiritual testament all his survivors, his whole succession. The pages are written in the spirit of "holy optimsm";

Swedenborg is present on every page, but the introductory motto was composed by de Chazal himself: "Love one another: the family is the first degree of Christian love, for that is where the first modeling of the angelic heaven happens on earth. Fathers live in their children; children live in the father who loves them. Harmony makes a family a paradise; discord makes it a hell."

Notes

1. *To My Children,* by Joseph Antoine Edmond de Chazal (1809–1879). Translated from the French by Claude Jack Smith, with an introduction by V. F. Taylor. (Place and date of publication missing.) Copy in the archives of the Lord's New Church in Stockholm. See further his pamphlets *Ma défense contre les injustes aggressions dirigées contre ma liberté de conscience par l'église catholique romaine de Maurice.* [Dat.: 1859.;]; *Réponse à … : P. Lebrun, à sa brochure intitulée: Réponse aux deux catéchismes swedenborgiens,* Maurice 1860; and *Réponse de M. Edmond de Chazal et de la Société de la Nouvelle Jérusalem à M. le révérend P. Le Brun,* Maurice, 1861.

2. Karl-Erik Sjödén, *Swedenborg en France* (Stockholm: Almqvist & Wiksell International, 1985), pp. 111, 128, 147f., 198. As late as the 1960s we find New Churchmen in France by the name of Maurice de Chazal and Louis de Chazal, and today there are still families named Chazal, living in different parts of the world, some of them Swedenborgian. The deep philosophical interest of that family is still indicated today by works such as *Les lumières et l'idée de la nature: textes réunis par Gérard Chazal,* Editions universitaires de Dijon, 2011; and as it happens the Nobel Laureate Jean-Marie Gustave Le Clézio coauthored *Les années Cannes : 40 ans de festival* (Renens: 5 Continents, 1987) with the cineast Robert Chazal.

3. *Arcana* (USA), Vol. I, No. 2 (1994), pp. 19ff., 42ff.; Vol. II, No. 4 (1996), pp. 29ff.

4. On this society and the creation of a French manuscript collection (now in the Swedenborg House in London), cf. K.-E. Sjödén, "Ett århundrade av den Nya Kyrkans historia i Frankrike," offprint of *Nya Kyrkans Tidning* No. 3–4, Stockholm 1977. After Le Boys des Guays' death, the collection passed to Edmond Chevrier, author of the valuable *Histoire sommaire de la Nouvelle Église chrétienne* (1879), which has a description of Edmond de Chazal in an informative appendix (pp. 238–243). The Swedenborgian woman author Anna Fredrika Ehrenborg tells the story of the French Swedenborgians in her book of travel, *Tjugufyra Bref från Frankrike, Tyskland och Sweits* (Upsala, 1856).

5. In his introduction to *To My Children,* V. F. Taylor mentions letters and diaries that testify how long and severe was the hesitation before Edmond was finally converted and took part in the founding of the New Church.

6. "The Swedenborgian Church in Mauritius," *The Messenger* (Newton, Massachusetts), February 1993, p. 21.

7. *The Messenger,* February 1993; and February 1994.

8. Malcolm de Chazal was eventually brought to the attention of people in Sweden by the Surrealist Press's *Mannen på Gatan, Surrealism* 1994, with an introduction by Bruno Jacobs and Carl-Michael Edenborg.

ANDERS HALLENGREN is a Swedish author, scholar, and composer, a fellow of The Linnean Society, and president of the Swedenborg Society of London. His most recent book is a collection of poetry published in English and German, illustrated by Paris artist Madlen Herrström, *Pentagrams-Pentagramme* (Éditions Sander, 2012). "E pluribus unum" was translated from the original Swedish by George F. Dole and revised by Anders Hallengren (2011).

THOMAS R. SMITH

The Dragonfly

In the river, we swam up to the floating
emerald, a dragonfly. On its back,
jointed legs in air, its body struggled.
Thinking to rescue, I scooped it up,
conveyed it aloft in one hand, while
paddling with the other. Life appeared
to persist in the green upperparts,
peacock-blue abdomen, deep garnet
of the long, convulsive tail. It was
only when we clambered ashore to set
it on a sun-warmed rock that we noticed
the head was missing. Poor flier! Feet still
twitched for purchase on my wet palm, tail
curled reflexively, and transparent
yellow wings trembled feebly.
I laid it back on the water, then
looked up at the cornflower sky over-
arching the river at the heart of summer,
saw the mercy in your eyes and knew
we love in each other a kindness
that is in us but does not come from us,
the sun we do not see behind the sun.

THOMAS R. SMITH's books of poetry include *Waking Before Dawn* (Red Dragon Press 2007) and *The Foot of the Rainbow* (Red Dragonfly Press 2010). He has just edited *Airmail: The Letters of Robert Bly and Tomas Tranströmer,* to be published by Graywolf Press in 2013. He believes that poetry has room for—and must include—all of life.

Money
on the Table

THIS HILL LOOKS LIKE AN IMPATIENT CHILD, Anna thought each time
she glanced out the window of her room. She remained by the cooking plate, the potato soup simmering, the night falling, slow and hot
on her shoulders. She tried hard not to think of the bills she had to
pay at the end of the week, of the broken chair in the kitchen, and her
old shoes that needed polishing. Her sons, five-year old twins, were
finally fast asleep, and she thought of the fairy tale she'd tell them at
breakfast: on the top of the hill, just over there, a long time ago, the
sun was born. Good fairies and August rains lived in the Sun's palace.
That would be a happy tale.

"No, just now we don't have money for magic swords," she told
her sons when they objected that the Sun was a planet and had no
palace at all. They'd seen that on TV. The Sun had an orbit as far as
they knew; besides, it never rained in August. "No, we don't have
money for toy trucks now. We'll think about it when Daddy comes
back from Madrid. He'll buy you a pedal car for kids . . . Yes, I understand. You are not kids anymore. You've grown up . . . Yes, the car will
have a big battery. One day very soon we'll climb to the top of the
hill."

"And visit the good fairies there?" the twins asked.

"We sure will."

"But the bad witch Yaga can steal the money from our bag! What
about the small laptop you've promised to buy when we get rich,
Mommy O? Don't say we don't have money."

"Wait till Daddy comes back from Madrid."

The boys were arguing heatedly who'd be the first one to drive
the baby car when the front doorbell rang. It sounded for a couple of

83

seconds so powerfully that the two kids rushed to the door, shouting, "Daddy! Daddy's come back!"

It wasn't their father. Old Uncle Vesko stood at the door with a box of chocolates in hand. Uncle Vesso worked in Madrid, too. It was very hot there, they knew, the houses were enormous indeed, and instead of bricks their walls were built of icecream.

"Hi, Vesko," Anna said. "It's good to see you after all this time. Come in quickly and have coffee with us." She fell silent then suddenly added, "Tell me how my Misho is doing."

Vesko didn't answer right away. His eyes took in the faded wallpapers, the torn linoleum on the floor in the corridor, the boys' old shoes arranged neatly by the wall.

"You need to paint all this," he muttered. "Misho's doing fine . . . I can see your sons have torn all their sneakers. Good for them."

Sharon Sprung
Empty Cup.
Oil panel, 42 x 40 in.,
Gallery Henoch,
Greenwich Village.

"Uncle Vesko! Do you know what?" the children prattled on. "Do you know who lives on the top of that hill over there? Yaga the witch! But we can wield big swords! Not little kids' swords, Uncle Vesko. Big ones, you can take our word for it. And they blaze all the time! They flash and glow!"

"Daddy will buy you swords after he comes back from Madrid," Anna cut them short. "You know that."

"Uncle Vesko," the smaller twin, the more cunning one of the two, said. "Tell Daddy to come back home right away. Not tomorrow, Uncle Vesko. Tomorrow will be too late. Let him come today before it gets dark. Tell him to catch the airplane of the good fairies, and land it directly on the balcony of our flat."

"Tell him to buy Mommy a dress: green like the one Danny's Mommy has," said the taller twin who was obviously not as clever as his brother. "We take Mommy to the shop, and she looks at this dress a hundred and million times a day."

"Tell Daddy that Alex and I eat a lot of spinach, and we'll become as strong as him," the cunning twin said. "When we have a lot of money, we eat a lot of icecream, too. But it's not good for our teeth, so we don't eat it often."

"The coffee is ready, Vesko. Please take a seat," Anna said.

Vesko looked around the kitchen: the brown linoleum on the floor, the cupboard on which the twins had drawn Zorro, and a toy truck that cost one million euros. He saw chipped porcelain plates and tea cups with broken handles on the table. There were drawings of the good fairies glued to the door, and a big watercolor picture of a monster who was perhaps the evil witch Yaga.

"Misho has sent you money, Anna," Vesko said. "Buy the boys new shoes and . . . and a big toy truck for each kid."

"You see, Mom!" the cunning twin cried out. "Daddy knows better than you what we need. Don't waste money on sneakers. Buy us swords—big ones that blaze and flash and glow!"

"And you, Annie? How are you?" Vesko asked. "It's not easy with these little kids. But you look great. You do."

He left money on the table, a thin wad of banknotes, and the children were suddenly silent, their eyes big with happiness. Anna counted the money and gasped, unable to believe her eyes.

"Tell Anna to buy a dress; that's what Misho said," Vesko added.

"Oh, did he say so?" Anna breathed.

She imagined she'd bought the green dress from Pretty Women Boutique. A magnificent thing it was. Nonsense! She'd better save the money. She'd prepare sandwiches for the boys and take them to the top of the hill. She'd show them the bend in the road that took the winter away every year and let the spring fly to their windows.

"Your dress was the most beautiful thing at the senior prom," Vesko said. "You looked great in it, honestly."

"All this happened a century ago," Anna said quietly. "You've lost weight, Vesko."

"My truck costs twenty hundred and twenty million euros!" the cunning twin shouted. "Daddy's given us a lot of money. It'll be enough to buy my truck."

"Mommy's dress costs one million hundred euros, and Mommy will be prettier than Danny's mommy."

"Mommy's prettier than Danny's mommy," the cunning twin pointed out. "Why waste money on a silly dress. We'd better buy ice-cream."

"It feels like our prom was yesterday," Vesko said.

It had started raining, and a stranger could not start his car in the street. The engine choked and spluttered in the mist.

"I have to go," Vesko said. "You have to feed your sons." He left his empty cup on the table, the only one with a good handle in the whole set. "We were happy at school. You look great, Annie, really," he cleared his throat and said, "Your husband's doing fine. Don't worry."

He stood up abruptly and started for the door.

"You've got to paint all the walls. . . . Well, don't worry about the walls. Look after the kids well."

The twins were happy as if Vasko had given them a house all built of chocolate and hazelnuts.

In the evening, Anna called her husband up, her face beaming.

"Hi, Misho," she said smiling at the telephone. "How are you, dearest? Thank you! Thank you so much for the money you sent us. I'll buy the children a toy car. I don't know about that dress. They said on the radio the winter would be long and cold."

"What?" Misho shouted from the other end of the world, from the great warm city of Madrid,. "What are you speaking about? I haven't sent you any money. Do you have any idea how one makes money here, in the scorching heat? I'll bring everything you need when I come back home. You have to save up every penny, do you hear me?"

Three months passed, autumn came, the hill became golden, and the bend in the road climbed closer to the sun. The twins went to kindergarten, and Anna went to work. She didn't buy the green dress; she painted the walls of the children's room instead. New and bright, the place looked like a smiling face. Anna didn't buy toy trucks for her sons; she chose a toy car, as small as a matchbox, but its tiny tires screeched dangerously on the linoleum in the kitchen, and its lights blazed, flashed, and glowed!

It was Saturday morning, the wind was strong, it had started snowing when the doorbell rang.

"Uncle Vesko!" the twins shouted at the top of their lungs. "Look at this car! Isn't it gorgeous! Isn't it huge! It roars and it can burst into flames! When did you arrive? Was it very hot in Madrid? How's Daddy doing? Is chocolate in Madrid better than ours?"

"Hi, boys! Annie, you look great," Vesko fell silent. Behind the window, the autumn tried to wrap the street in thick white fog. Disco music boomed from the flat next door. "This door handle is broken," Vesko muttered looking at the thing. "So is the knob. It doesn't matter really. You take good care of the children, Annie." He smiled. "Listen, Annie, Misho has sent you money. Take it."

"Did Daddy say Mommy was to buy us Batman costumes?" the cunning twin asked, staring happily at the small roll of money.

Anna glanced at Vesko. He's lost weight, she thought. The winter would be long and cold, they'd said on the radio. She tried to say something, tried to smile at him, but failed.

"It will be okay," Vesko said.

She didn't meet his eyes and didn't reach out her hand for the money.

ZDRAVKA EVTIMOVA was born in Bulgaria, where she lives and works as a literary translator from English, French, and German. Her short stories have appeared in twenty-one countries. She has translated several short-story collections into English: *Bitter Sky* (SKREV Press, 2003), *Somebody Else* (MAG Press 2005), *Miss Daniella* (SKREV Press, 2007), *Pale and Other Postmodern Bulgarian Stories* (Vox Humana, 2010). Her novel *God of Traitors* was published by Book for a Buck Publishers, 2008.

Sister it Up

What the carpenter will do
to the beams under the porch,
the tired wood, shore it up close and tight
next to new-hewn wood.

What we do for our own sister, broken apart
from her husband, her children, tired
from holding up, diminished with wear.

The body the house. We see hers
large from eating blame, nails
chewed out, yet every eyelash
wet with the dew of the unshed.
Inside, unseen, the heartwood,
which will never rot.

We come close, ear to ear,
hand to hand, reassembling
frame, lintel, crossbeam,
space for new windows,
a hearth not yet lit.

SUE ELLEN KUZMA grew up in upstate New York. She was an opera singer in Europe and the U.S. and directed opera for Young Audiences, Inc., and the Portland Opera in Maine. She teaches singing at her studio in Natick, Massachusetts. Her poetry has appeared in *The Christian Century, Rock & Sling, Blueline, Off the Coast, Avocet, JAMA,* and other publications. In 2002, she won the Diner Competition first prize judged by X.J. Kennedy.

PART III

Stuck in a Pattern

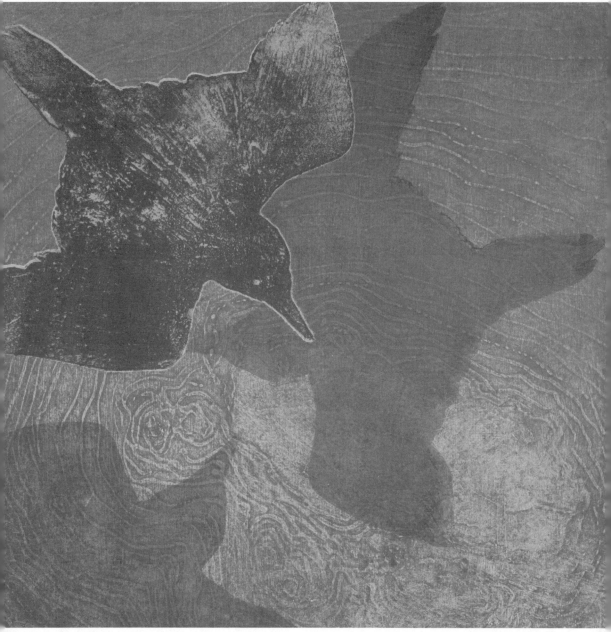

KATE CHAPPELL

RABIUL HASAN

Counting

I envision
you would come
to wake me
any day, any time now.

January gone
and I am counting.

Each leaf:
how it changes color,
how it falls
and how it gathers
on my doorsteps
and on my yard.

I sleep long winters alone
in my house
at the end
of the graveled road.
How long a man can live like this!

December gone
and I am counting.

Published in the U.S., Canada, and Malaysia, RABIUL HASAN's work has appeared in more than forty journals and anthologies, including *Mississippi Writers: Reflections of Childhood and Youth, The Rockford Review, Widener Review, Coe Review, The Macguffin, The Texas Observer, Borderlands, The Black Fly Review, Modern Images, Poet Lore, Permafrost, Aura Literary Arts Review, RiverSedge, Eclipse,* and *Louisiana English Journal.* He is the author of a collection of poems, *Madonna of the Rain* (Rockford Writers' Guild Press, 2008), and a critical book, *Rediscovering Hemingway in Bangladesh and India, 1971–2006* (University Press of America, 2010). Hasan earned a doctorate in English at Texas Tech University and is associate professor of English at Southern University in Baton Rouge.

About June

LET ME TELL YOU ABOUT JUNE. "Eep!" was one of her favorite expressions. She used it for horrific things: rapes, murders, terrorist attacks, or simple everyday occurrences: a caught fingernail, a magazine slipping off a footstool. I called her "The Girl from Eep-anema," although not to her face. June had a very prickly sense of self; a casual remark could easily lead to a *discussion*—really a cunning form of punishment reserved for boyfriends and the cat. The cat didn't mind. It thrived on any attention. Her boyfriends came and went like mayflies. From stories she told, two or three *discussions* seemed to be the limit.

June was an odd, but gifted, cook. She'd throw open her recipe box, banging the lid on the countertop as if to say, "I see you in there! You can't hide from me!" She'd riffle through until she found a recipe that matched her mood. It could be baklava, an *osso bucco* requiring twelve hours in the oven, or peanut butter sandies, which she claimed were an invention of her grandmother's. The necessary ingredients were seldom on the premises, and she never went out for more.

"Eep! I'm out of . . . ," she would say. "Wait, I can substitute . . ."

Canola oil could substitute for butter. Crackers could substitute for bread crumbs. Bread crumbs could substitute for flour. Dried fruit and baking powder, blended together, once stood in for eggs. Another time she put an herb, I forget which, into a batch of chocolate-chip cookies. To my dying day, I will never forget that flavor. Not bad, not good; it was *memorable*.

June had no use for sex and told me as soon as we got to know each other. She wasn't frigid; she was tepid, and stayed that way throughout our relationship. As she told me this detail about herself, I thought it was a point of pride, that she bucked trends so completely that even the most basic human responses were fair game.

June did have the most wonderful sense of humor. She mispronounced words constantly, usually playfully, though sometimes it was hard to tell. Faux was *fox*. Mauve was *moooove*. We lived in a doggy-dog world where you might pick a bouquet of *spit-tunias*. I gently corrected her once—*prostate* for *prostrate*—but all I got was a look of pity.

Her favorite poet was T. S. Eliot. All that early-century anomie, language as flexible as an old shoe and just as tough; she devoured it. June would have made a splendid flapper. Occasionally, she'd wear a cloche hat that made her look adorable. She also was addicted to *People* magazine and would read it on the sly in the library. I still remember her look of delight when I called her a trash hound. Still, twenty minutes later, she began a *discussion*.

June had spinal meningitis as a child; she spent an entire year out of school. The main thing she remembered was the endless time in bed; afternoons were the worst, sun streaming in the window, the sounds of children playing outside. One of the side

George Grantham Bain.
*Vilma Banky in Cloche
Hat,* 1927. Library of
Congress.

effects of her medication, she found out later, was depression.

"Imagine that," she'd say with a quick head shake and a tone caught between irony and despair, "a depressed eight-year-old."

In the beginning, June persisted in seeing only my good points, and even more, in seeing everything I did as good. I should have anticipated what was to come. In the end, I was all bad. Up to that point if I happened to trip over a curb, she would comment on the agility of my recovery. She took my side in any conflict. Once we were given a ticket—I was driving and clearly in the wrong—and she called the police station to argue. That part of her was fierce. I realized her fierceness would come around to me eventually. After all, we were a couple, and couples reveal all in time.

We were both poets; June waited on tables, and I worked in a bookstore. Her restaurant was a fad, in my opinion: raw, vegan, yet the place turned a bank-like profit. We'd eat there from time to time. Wheatgrass shots, "live" nachos, sunburgers, bowls of quinoa or Bhutanese red rice seasoned with coconut-curry or lemon-ginger sauce. It was all wonderfully nutty and healthy in a self-absorbed way that June never acknowledged until she quit in a dispute over a Gratitude Bowl.

Of my job, little good could be said. I told people I was paid ten-fifty an hour to look up books on Amazon. I was often asked to "recommend." After discovering what the customer had been reading, I always suggested Scarlett Thomas—*The End of Mr. Y* or *PopCo*—a wonderful writer; she was my answer to everything. One September I sold forty-three of her novels. That's how I stayed sane.

June's music. Oy! Imagine characters in a seventies sitcom grooving to a network-TV beat. She loved anything with a wah-wah pedal, a cheesy organ. It moved. It had energy. For her, funk never died.

June had a hard-to-define glamour combined with a flair for clothing and a playful, yet attentive, watchfulness. One byproduct of her beauty: upon meeting her, my friends always had to reevaluate me. It was both enjoyable and painful to watch. A flicker, a barely conscious judgment and *voilà*, hearty invitations would flow. She brought out a chthonic yearning in people, as if for childhood, or a lost adolescent love. In the end, her beauty made me sad. I wanted to love what was behind the allure, but there was nothing there to grasp. Whenever I tried, she evanesced, leaving sparkles like a genie in a Disney film. She told me her father had died when she was just a child. I think all of her relationships recreated that loss.

WE MADE PLANS TO DRIVE UP HIGHWAY 1 to a bed and breakfast north of Bodega Bay. We started out early, planning to drive slowly and make lots of stops. We called it the "beach cure." It was a beautiful late-September morning. Fall was in the air, so the warm breeze carried trace odors of moldering leaves along with the tang of the Pacific.

At Olema we pulled into the Vedanta retreat to see the white deer and walk up to the site of their temple, yet unbuilt. We passed ancient buckeye trees, their lower limbs touching the earth before curving back up to the sky. There were still blackberries. We each found and ate a perfect one. It was a specimen day. We were walking hand-in-hand, swinging our arms like a couple in a Viagra ad.

As we came back down, we passed a massive buckeye that had split in two. Both halves of the trunk lay flat on the ground, making a sort of platform or stage. The tree had continued to grow as if nothing much had happened. I said the spot would make a great place to photograph the Dalai Lama for a "Free Tibet" poster—I'd heard he'd visited the retreat in the past. For some reason June became quiet. At the time, there were reports out of Dharamsala that he was suffering from an illness, possibly stomach cancer—I thought that might have been the reason for June's silence.

We returned to the car. She didn't say a word until we'd passed Point Reyes where she replied to one of my sallies with a meaningless sound. I let it go and fell silent. The carefree mood was gone; I feared for the rest of our weekend. June's moods were brutal, but I could see she was making an effort. She searched for music on the radio. She began to chew a piece of gum. She turned and watched the ocean as if it were a movie she might lose herself in. As she struggled, I thought about the Dalai Lama, how he might have approached this change, what the mention of his name had triggered.

We had planned to have lunch at a seafood place called "The Catch." When I mentioned it, she just moved her hand in a wave that said, "Don't bother," "I'm not hungry," "Are you kidding?" and "Just drive."

We got to the bed and breakfast in less than an hour. Conversation had been limited to a few inconsequential remarks. Better than nothing, it gave me hope things might improve. The place consisted of four private cottages, nicely landscaped, each with an ocean view and a petite woodstove of French design: tubular, enameled; I'd seen them before; they gave out tremendous heat. The pictures on the website made the place look like a rustic paradise, and it was. What the pictures didn't show was Highway 1, twenty feet away. June waited until we were inside. I imagine it was because she was always polite in front of strangers.

She sat, slumped in a chair, fiddling with a small silver necklace her grandmother had given her. She asked a simple question, with her voice raised in an incredulous whine, "Why didn't you ask?" I started to explain how great the place looked online but at that moment a truck passed, winding out on the grade. It sounded as if it were coming through the wall. I jumped up to shut the nearest door and glanced in. It was a bathroom, decorated with driftwood and shells. There were sand dunes on wallpaper that looked scrubbable.

"Look! There's a tub with a Jacuzzi," I said brightly. We both hated Jacuzzis.

To no avail. June continued to complain, growing more vehement, making us both miserable. I felt I should say something profound or calming, but I really wanted to strangle her. I suggested lunch at a place a few miles up the road. I lowered my voice; sat behind her; began to rub her shoulders. She allowed this. They felt like wood. I realized we were both conspiring to defeat this other—this thing, which was also her. The rules were she could only offer the tiniest bit of help; anything overt was forbidden. Gradually her shoulders softened. She was wearing a white silk blouse, and through an unbuttoned collar, I could see the top of her bra. Stupidly, I reached down and began to rub her breast. A spark of desire arose. We both felt it. The moment was instantly submerged under a cold wave of anger.

"I want to go home," she said. "Now."

On the drive back I felt I was playing a movie in reverse. The sea and the sky were as beautiful as ever. At one point, I pulled over to walk on a small, stony beach. I was attracted by its isolation and by the fact it was deserted. June stayed in the car. I played for about twenty minutes, getting my feet wet, feeling the weight of her emotions, listening to the ancient, mournful cry of the gulls, at odds with the day, perfect for my mood. I dug out handfuls of wet sand and threw them at the breakers. I stood and let the freezing water run over my ankles. The horizon was a bank of fog standing far out to sea. The timelessness, the incessance—everything seemed like a metaphor for eternity and powerlessness. When I got back to the car, I felt somewhat purified.

There was less traffic going south, so we made good time. There was nothing to say. She was sad now. A tragic sadness. She had been defeated. We had been defeated. It had won.

I knew when June would leave me; I saw it as clearly as a stranger might. We were like a cellphone with its battery winding down: lights failing, desultory beeps. Her moods, always changeable, grew darker. There was nothing I could do. In mammals, females do the choosing. June had made it clear from the beginning all her choices came with a half-life. When the end did come, my main emotion was surprise— not at the break-up, but at the cold-blooded timetable that held sway over her as much me. Somewhere a bell rang and that was it. It was over.

MARK MCKENNA's work has appeared in *The Poetry Warrior* and *Rose & Thorn Journal*. Three of his stories were featured in *Ancient Paths Literary Magazine* (January 2011); one of these stories, "The Aubade," was nominated for a Pushcart Prize. McKenna's novel, *The Word Gang* (Precipitation Press, 2010) describes lives transformed by friendship and good vocabulary.

Orpheus After

I wake before morning.
It's the weighted month of winter
when night falls like a dead tree
and lingers like the loud silence that follows.
Nothing sings tonight.
There are no crickets purring
in the black bones of the oaks. The moon
grins at no one with its perfect yellow teeth.

I remember my heart and make a small noise
turning over. It's too dark to see if I'm lonely.
I think of the whale-mouthed
piano of my childhood, where I played
the simple melodies from Bach's minuets
in the luxury of summer afternoons. Never
using the black keys. Of how the piano sat
for so long after those fresh days,
and the extravagant song held in its wooden lungs
each night in the soundless, empty room. It is the silence
that has followed me most strictly, but from somewhere
behind dawn, I hear faint music again.
It may just be the sun keening
against the dead cold. Or perhaps the sound of the widow
across the hall brushing out her braid.
Or the sad hum of your shadow, which follows me everywhere
but can never be seen.

Or maybe I am only remembering
the way the peaches outside the window sing
in May mornings as they ripen—and oh,
how they sing in their untouched flesh weeks later
as they begin to rot. And to all of this I say,
music nonetheless.

KATHERINE NOBLE is currently studying English literature at the University of Texas in Austin. This poem was nominated for the foundation's Bailey Prize by Professor Kurt Heinzelman, who is the editor-at-large for *Bat City Review*. She received the 2012 Roy Crane Award for Outstanding Creative Achievement in the Literary Arts, University of Texas.

I Am Elizabeth Proctor

UP IN THE BACK, my eye catches a mosquito-sized stage beam illuminating the lightboard for the op, the only light in the house besides the dim aisle markers. As the last words of John/Ben's speech bring me back to Massachusetts, I draw a breath for my next line and immediately begin coughing. The haze in the air outlines the shafts from first and second electrics, creating eerie cones of blue light, but the same chemicals irritate my sinus infection. My diaphragm pushes against the long narrow sash, bound crisscross over my ribs. Finally I've expelled enough mucus to spit out my bitterness against my husband. Phrased in the grammar of seventeenth-century Salem, my accusations of deception have the tang of Scripture, but they tumble out automatically by now, my lips drawing out the w's and bouncing off the b's, my throat cutting off the harsh k's, my tongue snapping every d and t.

Use the sounds. Our director's reminder circles in my brain amid the jumble of other thoughts.

I'm so tired of being sick. Will the antibiotics ever start working?

Stay in the moment. What are you saying?

Crackling. *Someone has chips. Really! Second row? We're live up here, not a movie.*

Put your frustration into your character. What is John/Ben saying? How dare he! Now guilt him. He can't say that to me.

Angered by my husband's stubbornness, I turn out, gazing beyond the fourth wall of my home into the shadows, glimpsing a silhouette by the exit before honing in on an aisle light. Fairly short, one foot on the floor, leaning casually against the wall, shocks of hair forming individual outlines—I guess the silhouette to have been the

MALASPINA UNIVERSITY-COLLEGE THEATRE DEPARTMENT PRESENTS
the CRUCIBLE
BY ARTHUR MILLER
OCTOBER 27th THROUGH TO NOVEMBER 5th
TICKETS AND RESERVATIONS ~ 250.740.6100

show's technical director. He seems magical, really, appearing inexplicably at first one entrance and then another with no time to travel between.

Mary/Lindsay enters, and I shuffle to the cane-backed chair, knocking the hard heel of my shoe against the floor louder than I intended. Her eyes stay down, her hands meet and press together at the waist, the dutiful servant; she looks near tears, and her voice has reached whine-pitch, but I can't tell who is struggling more, Mary or Lindsay. It's been a rough week, she told me offstage, as I guzzled water sympathetically.

OUTSIDE, THE SUN WAS SHINING, a crisp October Wednesday. Inside, heavy scents of wood smoke, honey, and chicken dimmed the restaurant. The four-vegetable entrée came sliding from our teenage waitress to me over the nicks and burns in the wooden table. My gaze shifted back up. Mom's expression was the same as when she used to ask me to wash the dishes or tell me my dog had died. Dad had paused too long, and I already guessed what his flat, matter-of-fact tone was about to tell me.

I found out in a Cracker Barrel on the first day of fall break during my college sophomore year that my father had prostate cancer. We were driving to Kentucky to eat chicken salad with grapes and drink chai in a cabin built a full story off the ground and then to hike between formations of soft red clay and maybe find one of those tiny, stick-out-like-a-sore-thumb Baptist country churches for Sunday. I was the last of the six kids to know.

WHEN I WAS SMALL and could just reach five keys, I thought my dad's ability to reach an octave and one note meant he was basically a concert musician. He was embarrassed when I told my teachers that he was a pianist. He always claimed his kids were smarter than himself, but he helped me with algebra and could tell me how to check my oil from over the phone. His patience both with his kids and his employees always impressed me, the way his voice became so quiet and controlled when he was upset. He made me think through my decisions and answer for myself whether I thought a late movie before 7:30 AM driver's ed would be smart, and he would drive two hours to hear my choir sing two songs in a concert and then give me his honest opinion over coconut lattes afterward. As much as he may like to waive the honor, my dad is one of my heroes.

Illustration:
Crucible Poster
created in Illustrator
and Photoshop from
www.deviantart.com.

THIS SILENCE IS MINE TO BREAK, and I revel in it. My next line will nullify my one chance to discredit my crazed rival, prove I'm less virtuous than I thought, and hopefully, elicit a pitying sigh from the audience. It's a yes-or-no question. Did my husband cheat on me? Or did he not? Only if I corroborate his story that he had an affair will this nightmare trial end. John/Ben's back is to me, his twisted black belt sharply outlined against the leather vest, which I imagine to be from a deer he killed. He stands rigid, and I cannot see his eyes, intensely azure, to know what answer I should give.

An image of John/Ben hanging from a rope, his muddy knee-high boots twitching, suggests itself to my scrambling brain.

What would my three sons do without a father?

What if I say yes? My husband will be charged with adultery. Furthermore, the other actors will have to cover for me, and they'll hate me forever, and I'll get a huge fine.

Better stick to the script.

Wait one more second. Listen. They're not breathing.

My eyebrows, darkened with "charcoal" eyeliner, draw together. The dry stage air combined with my cough is drying out my lips, gluing them together when I try to open my mouth. I touch my tongue to my lips so they will open and take a careful breath. I don't want to inhale anymore chemicals from the haze machine than absolutely necessary.

"No," I whisper. A woman on the floor to my right gasps. She knows before I do that my answer is the wrong one. *[Editor's Note: Elizabeth Proctor doesn't realize that by trying to protect her husband, she actually condemns him to hang and places herself in prison.]*

I swing my elbows and try to keep my non-tread Puritan shoes from slipping off the ramp as Willard/Doug propels me by the shoulders to the dark dungeons of backstage. Babbling phrases not in the script, I beg for a do-over, just one mulligan per show. My voice cuts out in a sob, almost choking me as we pass the orange glow tape that marks the end of our visibility to the audience.

"Are you actually crying?" Willard/Doug sounds impressed. I'd like to tell him yes.

"No," I admit. "I can't."

I HAD QUESTIONS, too, of course, posited as we pulled back onto I-71 and later as we spread chicken salad into flatbreads and rearranged Scrabble tiles, still swarming through my mind as we pushed along overgrown trails and hunted down Daniel Boone's cabin. Most of my questions my parents couldn't answer because they hadn't yet decided on a treatment. Some of my questions I never asked because they seemed premature and pessimistic; they packed themselves into tiny labeled boxes to be stored in a back lobe of my brain, assembling into rationally organized rows. Some nights I lie in bed hunting for the file containing tears—the ones you're supposed to cry when your father has cancer—but I can never find the file.

I like to think that I'm like the Cameron Diaz character in *The Holiday,* and actually cannot cry. Maybe it's a physical disability or I'm shell-shocked or something. But I know that's not true, because I do cry on occasion. Many occasions, actually. I bawled to the point of embarrassment through the "Children of the World" program, with their colorful tribal outfits and traditional choreography. A good love story makes my throat feel all oatmeal-like. And if someone offers an unexpected compliment on an exceptionally rotten day, I have to grind my teeth and tense my neck so I don't lose it in front of them. Biologically, I have to cry to protect my eyes, right? Maybe I use up all my necessary tears on the trivial things, and then my body can't produce for the more momentous occasions. That must be it.

AFTER THREE MONTHS IN A DARK CELL I wince at the bright lights on stage. Danforth/Matthew and Hale/James seat me on the rough wooden bench, and I scoot to the very end, rubbing dried mud off my hands onto my apron, which is already covered in mud and sawdust. Picking at the mud pulls the tiny hairs on the back of my hand. I'll wash after the show, the brown swirls sliding down the drain of a porcelain sink undreamt in 1692, removing any reminder of who I was minutes earlier. For now the dirt under my fingernails suggests misery, and Hale/James's voice cloys on, inspiring real shivers. My husband will die, he tells me, unless I persuade him to confess to something for which he has no guilt.

I'm cold. I'm three months pregnant. Exhausted from sleeping on a wooden board. Nauseous.

Turn a little so the right balcony can see your face.

Try to pay attention to what he's saying. John/Ben will die if you don't.

This place smells sick.

Danforth/Matthew references the rising sun, and I glance up, my body going rigid at the intensifying orange fixture, recognizing an Ellipsoidal and not the actual sun in only part of my mind. The amber is too hopeful. My eyes drop back to the floor, searching the wooden planks of the jail and the first few rows of audience for a focal point, and find a painted knothole in the boards. Tim and his crew have woodgrained the sheets of plywood with lines and swirls in black and shades of brown until I forget that illusion only separates me from the fuchsia-sweatered woman in the front row to my right.

IT'S A FAIRLY NEW PROCEDURE, in the experimental stages, but not, as far as I can tell, dangerous. Side effects should be minimal, none of the incontinence or impotence to be feared of other treatments the doctor suggested. The doctor did not in fact approve hyperthermia, this localized application of heat supposed to render the leeching cancer cells defunct, because the U.S. does not yet allow this procedure. So my parents decided to make a vacation of it and travel to Bad Aibling, a German spa city and health resort where the nurses are only too happy to insert prostate-warming catheters. Even with the airfare, the week-long treatment was a tenth the price of the cheapest options. Their week's absence coincided with their twentieth anniversary, spent in a most romantic location, but celebrated "in ways differently than one would care to," to quote Dad's e-mail. (Though he disliked school in general and English in particular, my father must be at least partly responsible for my impulse to write, judging from his e-mails that even now have me cackling in appreciation.) I roamed the crimson-carpeted hallways of my university and chuckled aloud at his daily reports of missing trains and talking turtles with his "German partner in prostata," a fellow sufferer from a gland heated to fifty-two degree Celsius.

When I told friends that my dad was in Germany for prostate cancer treatment, they adopted an anxious look, eyes wide and eyebrows high, lips slightly open. This expression both gratified and concerned me. Gratified, of course, that my friends cared about me, but troubled that they seemed more worried than I was.

"Is he going to be okay?" they asked. "Are you okay?" My explanation of the process assured them on the first count.

For the second answer, my own mouth would tighten into a smile, squinting my eyes, and after a full breath I could admit, "I'm fine." They think I'm not sure, which is what I want them to think. But really, I was fine. No nightmares. No deep questioning of my faith. No cliché of tears threatening to spill over. Just preoccupation and a few good laughs from Dad's e-mails.

WHEN I WAS SIXTEEN, a girl on my basketball team was killed in a car accident. I cried throughout the whole funeral and still remember a white casket every time I hear the duet her sisters sang. Sometimes I tried to induce tears by imagining my father's funeral—the mahogany casket and sickly-strong stench of funeral lilies, processing with my siblings to the front pews while two hundred people observe our loss in awkward silence. It didn't work. Maybe prostate cancer didn't seem to be life-threatening, or maybe I just didn't love my dad enough.

JOHN/BEN IS RAGING NOW, shouting, weeping, protesting that he will not sign his name to something he did not commit. In the background, my knees weak, my body shakes. Each breath catches, like a child sobbing.

Breathe faster.

This is my fault. He sees himself as a failure, and it's my fault. My lie put him here.

I force the breaths, spasming my diaphragm into near hyperventilation. The amber light has peaked in brilliance and casts the shadow of jail bars onto the wood planks. Sunrise. They will hang him. I lunge forward to touch my husband once more before the marshal drags him to the gibbet, grip his hands and see wetness in his eyes, and feel his warm air on my face but cannot absorb what he says as Willard/Doug shoves between us. I stumble back.

This child will never see his tall, beautiful, tortured father.

Keep your eyes wide. If I stare at the light and don't blink my eyes might water.

They escort him violently from the dingy cell, and I turn outward to the sun/Ellipsoidal, unwilling to watch as they load him into a wagon, to see his empty stare as the twenty-foot panels of darkness open on glaring daylight. But I cannot keep myself from hearing the inexorably pulsing drum, the snare rattling louder and louder, marking time to his death. Behind me, Hale/James has tears in his voice.

If Hale/James and John/Ben can cry, you would think I could muster up a tear.

I am cold. My chin and lips and knees are shaking beyond my control. My teeth clench. My roaring ears beg for quiet. The snare reaches its final crescendo and breaks into silence. John/Ben is dead. My eyes are still dry. Blackout.

KRISTIN TROYER's essay incorporates her acting role as Elizabeth Proctor in Arthur Miller's 1952 play *The Crucible,* an allegory to the McCarthyism of that era. She is finishing her undergraduate studies in theatre and worship, with minors in Bible, church music, and creative writing at Cedarville University in Ohio. Her work has been published in *bio* Stories.

BEN MACNAIR

Blue in Green

It is 3 AM in the morning
in a student house.
Someone is playing an old jazz LP,
but it means nothing to them.
They are just playing it
because they think they have to.
The students are out reading poetry.
They talk about their journey,
and their voice,
and how forty-year-old poetry is really, really, like cool,
but Shakespeare is nothing to them
because they forgot about him when they left school.

Miles played "Blue in Green"
in the 1950s, but it still speaks to me.
More than the students, whose voices are new,
digging away at the same old ground.
For all of their talk of breaking boundaries,
they are getting headaches from banging
their young heads against old walls,
and in a few years, when new students come,
and talk about their journey, and their voice,
Miles will still talk to me
because there is something to be said
for keeping it simple.

BEN MACNAIR resides in the U.K. His poetry has appeared in *Purple Patch, Raw Edge,* and various other small-press publications and websites. His short stories have appeared in *Twisted Tongue* and in Forward Press anthologies. His journalism and reviews have appeared in *Blues in Britain* and *Verbal* magazines, as well as in various local newspapers and *The Independent.* Four of his short plays have been performed in London and America, and another has been adapted into a short film.

Shoe Store

HE WAS A WRITER who liked to walk himself through the past whenever he sat down to work. Even when he went downtown, he tended to see the streets and buildings as if remembering them from long ago rather than as they were. Young women were real enough though. It was due to what they possessed—a vitality powerful enough to dispel his reveries and pull him completely into the present.

In a sandwich shop, on a Monday in August, he found himself entranced by one such woman working the register. She wore skin-tight jeans, a sleeveless shell tighter still, and running shoes with bolts of lightening sewn along the sides. It was this logo that expressed, in an image, how quickly she could obliterate the past. For in her presence, he'd nearly forgotten what he knew so well, that long ago this place had been a shoe store with a machine that x-rayed people's feet. What, he wondered, would she think of that and, even more, of *him*, in this very place, examining a ghastly image of his own boyish toes? He imagined her bringing a hand to her mouth in astonishment.

But now she was everything, and everything was present. He collected himself, put down a five-dollar bill and fished for change. "Two pennies short," he said, wondering if he might filch a couple from the spare change cup.

"That's okay," she told him. "Close enough."

"Thank you," he said, wishing he could stretch time, wishing he never had to turn away. The bag containing his sandwich sat between them on the counter.

"Would you believe me if I told you that this place was once a shoe store with a machine that X-rayed people's feet?" He couldn't help himself. It just came out. "Right over there," he added, pointing to the wall of raw brick directly behind her. She turned and looked, as if his gesture might cause the thing to reappear.

"A what?" she replied. Her stare was acute but filled with interest.

"An X-ray machine," he said, making it sound wondrous.

"You mean hospitals had shoe stores?"

He struggled to parse her conclusion.

"No. I mean it wasn't at all uncommon for shoe stores to have a little X-ray machine, and this place was one that did."

"They x-rayed people's feet?" He couldn't tell whether she was indignant or perplexed.

"Believe it or not they did." She pushed the sandwich in his direction. Her hair swayed like a golden curtain. "I remember it," he went on. "Even tried it once myself." She pulled back and folded her arms. He trembled. She looked at him longer and blinked. He could feel it, could feel her thinking about what he'd ventured to win in their hasty exchange.

"Hm . . ." she said and shook her head. "How long ago was that?"

He looked off, counting back the years. "Nineteen . . . fifty . . . five, I guess. Maybe fifty-six." Her eyes filled with something akin to reverence, as if by some miracle she found herself in the presence of Thomas Edison or one of the Wright Brothers.

"Wow!" she said. "You were alive in nineteen-fifty-five!" His eyes fell to her sneakers and, on them, the bolt that had just slain him where he stood. He smiled, picked up his lunch, went out the door.

Early in the twentieth century commercial uses were found for medical X-ray technology, including machines for measuring a shoe's fit as described in this story. Psychographs, devices for measuring a person's head, were another novelty found in department stores and theater lobbies during the Great Depression. The catch phrase of the phrenological age is still heard today: "You ought to have your head examined!" MuseumofQuackery.com.

After a while, he found an empty bench and sat down. A lanky boy on a skateboard rolled by, rising and settling, as he went, like a human spring. Suddenly the board shot out from under his feet. He stumbled, managed to retrieve it, and rolled on. *Not a bad save,* thought the man who remembered so much as he pulled his sandwich from the bag and took a bite.

He chewed thoughtfully, felt the moment receding behind the glimmer of a little story he might have found. Carefully, he rested the sandwich on his leg and fished for a pen. "Remembering this shoe store . . ." He scribbled the phrase on a corner of the flattened bag and tore it free. He was about to slip it into his pocket when something else came. "A young woman, her beauty makes time stand still." He scratched it out and tried again, "Lightning . . . X-rays. . . ." He saw the bolt on her sneakers, felt again what he had when her glance coursed through him.

He took another bite from his sandwich and sat there. "I am chewing sedulously," he said to himself. Sedulously—it was a word James Joyce had used to describe how a boy chewed chocolate in "An Encounter," one of the stories in *Dubliners.* Our writer longed to use this perfect word himself in the little story he intended to write detailing his own brief encounter. But Joyce owned *sedulously.* It was his and always would be.

He thought a while longer, trying to come up with a title. After a while, he smoothed out the shard of torn paper and, in bold caps, wrote "Shoe Store," then sat back and opened himself to the din of the day.

VINCENT DECAROLIS has set the literary life aside to restore an old house and garage. His aging joints remind him daily that he should get back to writing as soon as possible. His lifelong interests have centered around the works of James Joyce, *Ulysses* in particular, C. G. Jung's various writings (Bollingen editions), and the Greek New Testament. He has taught comparative religion, philosophy, and English courses at the college level and has enjoyed photography for decades. His enduring but lately neglected interest in cosmology has recently been recharged with the announcement of the Higgs boson, a field he hopes to get back to as soon as the house is finished.

DWAYNE THORPE

Rented Space, Second Floor Rear

To discourage theft, my New Orleans friend
going out leaves his radio blaring at night.
Some rely on pit bulls, but he
trusts hip-hop more than bark or bite.

Sometimes I wake, windows still black
with Jerry Vale or Don Cherry in my head.
Then I know my mind isn't mine
but a cheap burglar alarm instead,

which the Landlord, keeping thieves away,
has turned on, leaving me awake,
alert for thoughts up to no good,
to save me from myself until daybreak.

DWAYNE THORPE, one of the student founders of *Tri-Quarterly* at Northwestern University, writes for a variety of journals, most recently *Beloit Poetry Journal, Prairie Schooner, Poem, Chautauqua,* and *Cider Press Review.* His collection of poems is titled *Finding Pigeon Creek* (Monongahela Press).

Bread, Ashtrays, and the Psychic

HEY. HEY! The loaf of bread is calling me. It is lonely.

It is the round, flat loaf of rosemary focaccia on the top shelf of the bakery manned by a bored teenager in a hairnet.

I move another loaf beside it, a cranberry focaccia. The rosemary loaf quiets down, and I am free to leave the store. I feel rain dotting my hair and face and rain jacket, and I wonder how many more voices I will hear today.

THE MAN IS SHORT AND THIN AND HAS KIND BROWN EYES, though my own eyes go immediately to the narrow white scar above his upper lip, from some old surgery. He drops his head and holds out his hand for Hana to sniff, and he smiles at her and doesn't recoil from her eager, wagging tail. He glances at my lovebirds twittering in their cage and clears his throat. "Nice place you got here."

I do not know if he means what he says. People care more about their cars and clothing size than the earth under their feet. Other visitors have complained about the bird smell in the air and the animal hair on the sofa. Hana sits beside my chair, and I pet her. "Thank you."

He clears his throat. "I, uh, brought you a few things."

I point at the table. He checks my face for permission. Good. He is respectful, at least.

He pulls off his army surplus backpack and sets it in his lap. "You need something she made, right? With her hands?"

I nod. My telephone instructions are very clear, and I usually only take clients by referral. A friend sent this man, so he should be all right, but you never know.

"This sounds funny, but she doesn't make a lot. That's what took me so long. She doesn't like to draw. She doesn't even make dinner."

I feel my self, my inner self, curling inward like a cat curving into a ball. This is a bad sign.

"I had to get creative. We went to her mother's house, and I made them take out a box of elementary-school stuff. She made this ash-tray." His scarred mouth jerks up into a smile. "Can you imagine? They'd never let kids make ashtrays now, but back then . . . anyway, I took it."

I look at the flat lump of gray with crude gray and yellow markings. I do not want to touch it, but hiring out my talent represents heating oil and pet food. I take it from his hand and immediately relax.

MOMMY?

I pet the ashtray before the man stares at me, and I realize what I'm doing. "This person is okay. She is very young, but she just wants to please her mother."

He smiles and runs a hand through his brown hair and suddenly, I realize he is not so bad looking, despite his scar and his tendency to talk. "Great. I mean, you might think I'm crazy, but I just want to be sure. You know, once bitten and all that."

I stare at him. Why would he think I would call him crazy? It's what *I* have been called my whole life.

He shifts in his chair. "Never mind. I don't know if we need to bother with the other stuff. She finally made me a Valentine yesterday after I made her one."

This man is paying me a lot. I hold out my hand.

"It's nothing, really. Like I said, she doesn't like to make stuff. She already bought me a card, but I thought it would be fun, and I had the construction paper and scissors out."

He hands me a plain red heart. It is small but neatly cut out. The writing is spiky for a woman's, but written perfectly legibly in black ballpoint pen. "For Rob. Love, Sara."

As soon as the paper brushes my palm, I flinch.

—*nooooooo*—

Oh, no. No, indeed. Not this nice young man who is paying me well. But it is always this way. Even so, I hold my breath and poke the valentine one more time.

NO.

I make a sound at the back of my throat, almost inaudible, but Hana presses against my legs. "She is not the right one for you."

"What is it? What do you see?"

I shake my head. I am no good at counseling. They ask, and I answer, but no more than I can. "She doesn't want you."

"But—" He reaches for the card and knocks the ashtray, catches it before it hits the ground. "You said she was okay!"

I point at the ashtray. "I said she was okay. They are not the same person." I turn away from the pain in his eyes. "Sometimes, people bring me objects made by different people. They try to trick me."

"I didn't. That would be a waste—" He stops, drops in his chair, visibly thinking. "She has a sister, Amy. I suppose their childhood things could have been mixed up."

I nod. "She would be better for you."

"She's fat!" He looks at me, winces. "Sorry. I mean, hell, it would look pretty bad—"

I shrug. My fat shields me from curious eyes and chilblain winters. I am not offended. I am more conflicted by his human pain. This

René Magritte.
La Victoire.
Gouache,
$17^7/10$ x $13^3/4$ in.,
1938 or 1939. Private
collection. ©2012
C. Herscovici, London /
Artists Rights Society
(ARS), New York.
Photograph: Herscovici /
Art Resource, New York.

is why I always guarantee my fee with a credit card. The richest people can be the most slippery.

He runs out of words and stops pacing the room. Fortunately, he is not violent. Hana will bark and growl, but she is very gentle and does not know how to handle angry human beings. The birds are pretty but can do little but chirp, although their flight is something more than we can ever achieve with our own limbs.

He shakes his head again. "This is what I get for chasing after fairy tales." He scoops up the ashtray, hesitates at the valentine, but shoves them both into the backpack. He drops an envelope of money on the table.

"Thank you," I say to the money.

After he slams the door, I lock it and pet Hana until my fingers stop trembling. Then I count the money. It is correct. Next time, I will ask for more. Oil is getting more expensive and every client weighs on my mind and heart and spine.

THE MAN IS BACK. He is older and, if anything, thinner. He still has mouse-brown hair, although it has grown thinner too. I remember the scar. I remember everything. He says, "I'm sorry about how I behaved the last time. Thank you for seeing me again."

I nod.

He seems to be waiting for a response, but then he goes on. "You were right. I married her anyway, but the divorce papers should go through next month. Anyway, we have a son, Jeremy, and—" He stops. "I guess you don't care. Your dog still looks good."

I shake my head. Hana's ashes rest under a maple tree. I point to the golden lab at my feet. "This is Jake."

"I'm sorry. I seem to go about everything all wrong. Anyway, as you know, I'm worried about my business partner. I didn't know if you could work with computer programs, but I printed out the code. I also brought my laptop, and we can run the program if you think you can get anything from it."

It is a strange world we live in, where creation is limited to microchips. Not an improvement. He passes me a folder of white computer paper. I read the strange words and pass my fingers over the raised print. I go through several sheets of paper. The man shifts in his seat. Jake flops over on his side. I do not feel anything. Perhaps this modality is wrong, although I have worked a little with electronic-related objects recently. I open my mouth to apologize, as the man is always doing, and then I get a glimmer:

TAKE

Just a breath, but it is enough. I run my fingers over more lines, and I feel it again.

"He is greedy, whatever that means to you."

He closes his eyes. "Do you always give bad news?"

I do not answer. It is their fault, really. They would not come if they did not have a suspicion. I wait for the money. My fee has doubled since the last time.

"YOU RUINED MY PARENTS' MARRIAGE."

It is not the first time someone has said this, or a variation on it. I have grown even more wary. I employ a sophisticated spam filter so most e-mails go in the trash. I order groceries online and have them leave the bags outside so I don't even talk to the delivery clerk. When I need clients, I meet them at a neutral public place—a library room with a door is good—so they don't see my house or my animals. I take cash only.

This is the first time in a long time someone has rung my doorbell and refused to go away.

"I want to talk to you."

From my webcam, I see it is a boy in that adolescent stage where he seems all legs and spidery fingers and tenor voice.

"I won't hurt you."

Then why are you here? I wonder. I should call the police, but I don't know if they would help me. They might not understand why I have over a dozen love birds, eight cats, and two dogs. They might turn them all over to the humane society. I could not bear that.

"Go away," I say, but I say it softly. From the hallway, I know he won't be able to hear me.

"You did us a favor," he says. "I can talk through the door if you want. I don't care."

I walk up to the door. I hesitate. What if he can see me through the peephole? What if he shoots me through the peephole? I once read that in a book. You never know with people. I stand off to the side, away from the peephole, and I decide to speak. "Talk."

He stops. "Well, okay. I, um . . . you remember my dad?" He says the name. It is the man with the cleft lip scar.

"Yes," I say into the silence.

"He died." His voice breaks.

Even I feel a soft measure of sorrow. My cat, Zulu, stares at me from the bathroom door frame. I wish she would let me pet her, but she stalks over to the litter box instead. My dogs are sleeping in the bedroom.

"He was only fifty-seven. I've been going through his notes, and I found his diary. He talked about you and what you said about my mom. I want to know how you do what you do."

I laugh. It is a silent huff, unaccustomed to use, but a laugh nonetheless.

He continues as if he didn't hear me, and maybe he didn't. "I did a eulogy for my dad, but it sucked. I don't think I ever really knew him. I brought this pen he made for me. He was no good with his hands, but he took a course because he wanted to give me something he made himself. And . . . I brought one of my drawings. It's nothing, but I thought maybe . . . I don't know."

He is crying, the boy outside my doorway. My dog, Sasha, wakes up and begins to bark.

What does this boy want from me? Can he not see that I failed to help his father and everybody else, that even if I tell them the truth, the plain truth, they continue to walk their own crooked ways?

Sasha growls and stalks out of the bedroom. I shush her. She leans against my legs.

The boy raises his voice. "I can pay you. He left us good money after you spotted his rotten business partner, and he made my mom sign a pre-nup, I think because of what you said."

Ah.

Still, I have no answers for this boy. Ahead of him lie heartache and fear and loneliness.

I pet Sasha. She growls one more time. Her ruff smoothes out. She sits up with her ears pricked and wags her tail. Silly dog. I pet her.

"Oh, forget it." He rubs his nose with the back of his hand and starts to turn away. His dull green backpack is the same one his father once wore.

It is foolishness. You can never trust people. They lie, they scream, they die. But perhaps I grow a little weary of my apartment and can risk death, although I will miss my animals. It seems that despite my best barricades, I can never resist the call of a lonely loaf of bread, no matter what shape it takes. Holding onto Sasha's collar, I unlock the door.

MELISSA YUAN-INNES tries to balance emergency medicine practice, writing, a headstrong six-year-old, and a twenty-month-old baby while living in the Canadian wilds outside Montreal. Yuan-Innes was inspired to write this story after a student named Cayleigh said she thinks loaves of bread get lonely in the grocery store.

EARL CAMPBELL

The Hug

I wonder if it's always been like this:
The insistent force with which she
Draws me close, showing me the shape
Of her love by clasping her arms up
Around my neck, standing up
On the tips of her toes to whisper
Into my right ear as I lean to the left:
I wish I could hold your brother like this.
I know what she's saying.
I love you. I need you. Don't go.
It's late November, and the savage wind
Raps against the kitchen windows
Like a late-arriving ghost. I hear
The sign, and I miss him. Turning
From my mother's incessant chatter
And the typical Thanksgiving table clatters,
I catch sight of my old, beige Buick
Parked in the driveway, the crack
In the front windshield running
Diagonally down the driver's side, attesting
To the fact that I tend to
Put off fixing what I'd rather get used to.
She gives me a soft pat on the back as
I carve out a piece of carrot cake, sinking
My fork down through an inch
Of cream cheese frosting, smashing
The rich denseness of sugar,
Cinnamon, carrots, and pecans against
The persistent and present shadow of my

Younger brother, Henry, who
Shot himself in his bedroom closet
When he was twenty-two years old.
Clinging to the side of the refrigerator
In my apartment there's a picture of him
When he was eight. Christmas morning,
Circa 1978, and he'd just opened a
Star Wars Millennium Falcon toy.
His reach around my mother as open and wide
As a clear, blue Colorado sky.
On the couch behind them and holding
A television remote, is our second stepfather,
who my brother and I
Secretly called Karate Chop Joe (because
In order to maintain "order,"
He hugged us into headlocks).
Outside the picture window,
The front yard, across the street, the whole
Wide world for all we knew
At the time—embraced by nothing,
Nothing at all,
But white.

EARL CAMPBELL works at First Merchants Bank in Indiana. He serves on the board of a local theatre group, Carmel Community Players, as the assistant artistic director. He is an award-winning actor and loves riding roller coasters, taking photos, and meditating on the Word of God. Recently, his work was published in *The Polk Street Review.*

STEPHEN GRAF

Building the Perfect Nest

THE PACKAGE CAME IN A PLAIN WHITE PADDED ENVELOPE. His address hand-printed on the front. That surprised Gene. He'd expected it to come in some sort of official package from the government. Then he remembered the government package went to Sarah; as the wife, next of kin. That seemed odd to him. Nobody in the world has closer blood ties to a person than his parents, but once married, the spouse somehow becomes next of kin. He didn't dwell on it. Instead, good retired bookkeeper that he was, he filed it away. After nearly seventy years of compartmentalizing, Gene's mental file system had become quite intricate and labyrinthine.

Sandy Belock-Phippen.
The Empty Nest.
Oil on board,
11 x 14 in., 2009.

The mid-morning sun shone on the package, resting unopened in the center of the breakfast table, exactly where Peggy had left it a half-hour earlier when she carried in the mail. Peggy strolled into the room, and Gene pretended to be immersed in the morning newspaper. Pouring herself a cup of coffee, she sat at the small, circular table and looked at him as she stirred in some milk. Finally, she cleared her throat and asked, "Are you going to open that, Gene?"

Taking a sip of coffee, Gene pretended not to have noticed her. Sometimes he feigned being hard of hearing so that he didn't have to answer questions he didn't like. But Peggy was on to him. After forty-six years of marriage, she knew all the little tricks. "Not opening it isn't going to change anything," she persisted.

He flipped the page of his newspaper as if he still hadn't heard her. "If you're not going to open that package, at least can you prune the apple tree today? It's getting warmer, and if you don't trim those branches back soon it's going to look like the Amazon jungle in the backyard."

Gene glanced up from the paper as if he'd just noticed her. Pushing the glasses back on his nose, he replied, "I can't. A couple of birds are making their nest in it."

"The birds won't mind if you prune the apple tree. And if they do, there are plenty of other trees around for them."

"I don't know," Gene shook his head doubtfully. "They might be rare birds. At least, I can't remember seeing this specific kind of bird around the yard before."

"What kind are they?"

"I'm not sure. I'm going to drive over to the library today to get a book on birds so I can find out."

"Which one?"

"How will I know until I get there?"

"No," she couldn't help chuckling. Nearly seventy years old and still acting like a child when he didn't want to deal with something. "I mean which library?"

"The main one."

"And when do you plan on opening that package?"

Standing up and moving toward the door, he replied, "I don't know. Later."

Gene returned a few hours later with a book, *Birds of the Northeast,* selected because it had the best pictures. Once he started reading, he realized the book he'd chosen was geared toward elementary school children. But while the tone was whimsical, the book did contain detailed photographs that would help him identify the birds in their apple tree.

Passing through the kitchen, he noticed the package had been opened. Standing out starkly in the middle of the otherwise clear table was a rectangular-shaped, brown jeweler's box. Sandwiched between that and the padded envelope were neatly folded sheets of canary yellow and white stationery. He paused to appraise the box and letters for a moment. He knew what they contained, more or less. Recalling that today was April first, he wished they were just an awful April Fool's Day trick. Still, he assured himself as he walked briskly out of the room, he wasn't avoiding them. He just didn't feel like dealing with them at the moment.

At the top of the stairs, he turned into their bedroom. The large picture window adjacent to his side of the bed looked out onto the apple tree. A wooden fence ran behind it, separating their yard from the Kleins'. The apple tree had been there ever since they purchased the house as newlyweds. The tree had survived the bitter cold of more than forty Pittsburgh winters, not to mention several blizzards and the remnants of several tropical storms.

He'd moved a straight-backed wooden chair alongside the window from which he'd been observing the birds for the past couple of days. The pair was out there, singing as they worked. The larger one, a brilliant dark blue with a bright reddish chest, sat on a branch and chirped orders while the smaller one, a drab gray-blue with a duller reddish chest darted around adding bits to the nest. Sitting on the chair, he leafed through pages of the book until he came to illustrations that matched his birds. They were Eastern Bluebirds, *Sialia sialis*. He began to read about them, glancing outside from time to time to monitor their progress.

A little later, Peggy walked in carrying a wicker laundry basket. Setting the basket on the bed, she remarked: "I see you got your book."

"Yep," he nodded, still following the birds.

Walking over to the window, she looked out and said, "They are beautiful. What kind are they?"

"Eastern Bluebirds."

"Bluebirds? I could've told you that without going to the library. They're not that rare; I think you could risk pruning the tree."

"Actually, this book says they were endangered for a time and are just now coming back."

"So we're stuck with them? What're they doing now?"

"Building their nest."

"They're still at that? That's going to be one swanky nest. Anyway, it looks to me like one is doing all the work and the other is just sitting there."

"The book says the female typically does most of the construction while the male oversees and protects her."

Bending over to pick up a pair of Gene's dirty underwear and socks from the floor, Peggy tossed them in the laundry basket and replied, "Typical."

Several days later Gene noticed the eggs. He'd gotten into the habit of checking on the birds when he rose in the morning. This morning the adult bluebirds were away somewhere, but he could make out within the nest tiny bluish-white ovals. Gene waited by the window until the mother reappeared.

RETIREMENT DID NOT SIT WELL WITH GENE. He preferred to stay busy, but there simply was not enough to do around the house. The weather had been unseasonably warm, and he'd just finished trimming the front hedge when he walked up to the bedroom to check on the bluebirds. He could have done it from outside, but he could see directly into the nest from the bedroom. He noticed the jeweler's box and letters had been moved from the kitchen table to the top of his bureau. He still hadn't opened either.

From the picture window, the bluebirds were nowhere to be seen, but it appeared the nest was now finished. Walking over to the bureau, he picked up the box and carried it to the bed. Sitting on the edge of the bed, he placed the box in his lap and snapped the lid open. Inside were two medals pinned on gray felt backing. One he recognized as a Purple Heart. The other was a five-pointed bronze star hanging down from a red ribbon with blue piping down the center. He ran his finger absently around the points of the star. As he did so, he thought: *If only the mill hadn't closed. If he could've just kept his job in the mill.* . . .

It had been nearly twenty years since the Duquesne Mill had closed. A generation. Most people in Pittsburgh didn't remember the mills. They were a distant memory, like something seen in a movie or read about in a book. There was little work in Pittsburgh in the eighties; that was true enough. But why'd he have to go and join the Army? Still, he'd survived nearly seventeen years. He'd made it through the first Gulf War okay, and was nearing the end of his second tour in Iraq during this second damned war. He just had a little over three years to retire; then he said he was going to use the GI Bill to finish college and become a schoolteacher.

The medals began to look like a kaleidoscope. He sniffled, drew his fingers across his eyes and snapped the case shut. He hoped Peggy wouldn't walk in and catch him like this. It was unseemly—effeminate. He placed the medals back on top of the bureau and left the room.

EARLY ON APRIL 15 Gene was awakened by the sound of chirping. Going to the window, he noticed the eggs had hatched. He could make out four tiny, gray heads singing madly for their breakfast. Gene was worried for the young chicks because it had turned cold the previous night and was supposed to get close to freezing again this night.

But his first order of business was dropping off their tax returns. The forms had been completed for more than a month, but when he owed, he always waited until the last minute to mail them. It was little things like doing their taxes, paying bills, and tidying the yard that gave Gene pleasure; he liked the feeling of accomplishment that a task done properly gave him. Upon returning home, he'd grabbed a cup of coffee and immediately made his way up to the bedroom.

Shortly after he'd positioned himself in his normal spot by the window, Peggy entered the room. "You're back? Did you mail the taxes?"

"Mmm-hmm," he nodded, not taking his eyes off of the mother bird feeding her chicks.

"I just talked to Sarah."

"Oh?" he turned to look at her. "How's she doing?"

"About as well as can be hoped. She's a rock, thank God." Peggy crossed the room and stood at the window beside Gene. "They finally hatched?"

"Yep."

"So that's what all the racket was this morning." Noticing something outside, she leaned toward the window for a better look, and then turned to Gene and asked incredulously, "Is that your shoe?" There was a brown leather Oxford, resting on its side at the foot of the apple tree.

"Yes," Gene replied sheepishly.

"Do you mind telling me what it's doing out there?"

"The Kleins' cat was climbing up the tree to get at the nest."

She laughed. "Did you hit him?"

Gene bristled momentarily, still angry at his near miss. "No, but he got the message."

"Say, I thought they were a couple. I only see one."

"I haven't seen the male in a few days."

"Typical male. Got what he wanted and left."

"The book says the male usually stays until the chicks are raised. I think that dirty cat may have gotten him."

"Oh. Well, keep your chin up. You've got plenty more shoes left."

AS GENE STARED OUT THE WINDOW, his mind flashed back thirty years. He could see Stanny, a skinny little ten-year-old. He'd just fallen out of the tree and broken his collarbone. He remembered hearing the boy's cries and running outside to carry him into the house. What struck him at the time was how little he'd wept after those first shocked shouts of pain. He'd been a tough little S.O.B., even then. Not tough like the tough guys in the movies, because he was a gentle boy, but tough on the inside where it counted—like his mother.

Gene got up and walked over to the bureau. Lifting the box with the medals in it, he removed the letters from underneath it. Carrying them over to the bed, he sat down and opened them for the first time. The top one was on stationery from Sarah and simply said:

> _Peggy and Gene:_
> _Stan would want you to have these._
> _Love,_
> _Sarah_

He then opened the other letter on government letterhead. He noticed a couple of blotches on the paper and wondered if they were Sarah's or Peggy's. Underneath the masthead was the heading: _Award of Bronze Star._ Below that, it stated: _The following award is announced posthumously._ He skipped down to the _Reason,_ which read:

> _For heroism in connection with military actions . . . Sergeant First Class Stanley E. Holderlin distinguished himself by valorous actions while serving as element leader on a reconnaissance mission outside the city of Baghdad. While in convoy, the lead vehicle in SFC Holderlin's element was disabled by an improvised explosive device, and his unit simultaneously came under intense small arms fire by a numerically superior rebel force . . . . Upon hearing cries of distress from one of his fallen comrades in the disabled lead vehicle, SFC Holderlin, without regard for personal safety and fully realizing the perils of the situation, dashed across the bullet swept road to pull the injured soldier from the vehicle and carry him to safety. And though grievously wounded, SFC Holderlin continued to direct the defense of his element as well as personally return fire . . . . SFC Holderlin's personal bravery and devotion to duty were in keeping with the highest traditions of military service and reflect great credit upon himself and the United States Army . . . ._

There was more. Gene couldn't read it. For a moment, he was there. He could feel the oppressive heat and the stifling air thick with fear. He could hear the bullets whizzing by and the cries for help from his fallen comrade. He tried to imagine what went through his head as Stanny made that mad dash, bullets skipping past him. But he couldn't follow it through to those last desperate moments. It was more than he could bear. The letter slipped from his hand and floated to the floor.

A LITTLE LATER, Peggy walked into the room. Seeing the letter on the floor and Gene staring listlessly out the window, she sat on the edge of the bed beside him. Placing her hand on his knee, she asked, "Are you okay, Gene?"

Gene started, as if he had only just noticed her. Then he said, "It's supposed to get cold tonight; it may even go below freezing."

"I heard."

"I was thinking maybe I should go out and rent one of those outdoor heaters. You know, the ones they use outside bars and cafes. I thought I might run an extension cord from the kitchen and set one up under the apple tree. The cold's going to be hard on those baby bluebirds."

Peggy smiled and patted his knee. "Those birds are wild, Gene. It's nature. You have to let nature take its course."

"I guess you're right. I just thought . . ." The tears Gene had been carefully filing away since they'd first gotten the news of Stan's death finally began to escape their compartments. "I miss Stanny," he said, no longer trying to hold them back.

Peggy wrapped her arms around him and pulled him toward her. He placed his face on her shoulder and let the emotion finally wash out of him. "I know. I miss Stanny, too." Peggy stroked his thinning hair. After a few moments, she added, "You know, maybe an outdoor heater isn't such a bad idea after all."

LATER THAT AFTERNOON, Gene stood in a back aisle of Gary Hardware surveying outdoor heaters. A tall, thin teenager wearing an apron approached him: "Can I help you, sir?"

For a moment, Gene was taken aback by the boy's similarity to Stan at that age. But upon closer scrutiny—the acne scars, the curly brown hair—Gene realized the lad looked very little like Stan. Clearing his throat, Gene replied, "Yes, I'd like to rent an outdoor heater. A tall one."

STEPHEN GRAF served as a captain in the U.S. Army Reserves and currently teaches English literature at Robert Morris University in Pittsburgh. He has been published in *Cicada, AIM Magazine, The Southern Review, Mobius, Fiction, SNReview,* the *Willow Review, The Wisconsin Review,* as well as *The Black Mountain Review* (in Ireland), among others. His short story "Hadamard's Billiards" won the editor's choice award in the Spring 2010 issue of *The Minnetonka Review* and was awarded an honorable mention for the 2012 Pushcart Prize.

DEBORAH H. DOOLITTLE

Indian Summer

A sunny and cloudless morning
of autumn. The students clutch
pencils, press thick lead in wobbly
curls upon yellow paper.

In the classroom, a row of
CCCCC slants across the chalk
board, the entire alphabet
waltzes above it on the wall.

Mrs. Gordon paces the floor,
peers over the bent heads through
thick eyeglasses that drop the length
of their chain upon her breast.

Even the open windows lean
in the same direction. While outside,
the tall grass wavers, a few orange
leaves drift to the ground.

A sunny and cloudless morning
of autumn. Who's to say that girl
wasn't me, watching the slow progress
a caterpillar makes across the glass.

DEBORAH H. DOOLITTLE holds master's degrees in women's studies and creative writing. She teaches at Coastal Carolina Community College in North Carolina. Her chapbooks, *No Crazy Notions* (Birch Brook Press 2001) and *That Echo* (Longleaf Press 2003) won the Mary Belle Campbell and Longleaf Press Awards, respectively. Recent work has been published in *Atlantic Pacific Review, Backstreet, The New Renaissance, Poets' Espresso, Potomac Review, Pinyon,* and *Smartish Pace.*

Home
and Away

I'VE ALWAYS LOVED THE IDEA OF TRAVELING. As a kid I'd stand close
to the road so that I could smell the Greyhound fumes when a bus
swept through our small Illinois farming town during the Second
World War. The reek and fumes of gasoline evoked visions of exotic
places, promised adventure, and escape.

It wasn't that I didn't love my family and our little clapboard
house perched on a bank high above the Kankakee River, but I knew
there were more exciting places than the fields and farmland about
us, the town with its movie theater, hardware store, and elegantly
dressed mannequins in the window of the Begay Shop—and I wanted to see them.

Before Illinois, we'd lived in England, a tiny Michigan town, and
a suburb outside Cincinnati. Perhaps it was the exposure to new
places that made me long for a change of landscape. But there's a severe downside that comes with this longing for adventure—an embarrassing tendency to be horribly, gut-wrenchingly homesick.

I've done a good deal of traveling in the years since I wistfully
watched the Greyhound bus roar across the railroad tracks and out
of that small town, and although I no longer get high on bus fumes,
the sight of a jet's con trail against an October sky still sets me dreaming. . . . despite my homesickness when I travel.

This pattern expressed itself at an early age. In 1940, when my
parents packed up their five children and as many possessions as
could be easily transported, I knew little of the war then beginning
in Europe except for air-raid drills that were made exciting by the
piece of candy we each were given if we were well behaved while in
the shelter. I had no idea of Hitler's expected invasion of England

Horace de Callias.
*Young woman looking at
herself in a mirror while
standing in front of a
window.* Miniature oil
painting on ivory panel.
5³/10 x 4¹/2 in., ca. 1909.
Louvre Museum, Paris.
Photograph: ©RMN-
Grand Palais /
Art Resource, New York.

or that as Americans and all other aliens in the area, we had seventy-two hours to leave the ancient military town of Colchester, a city near the coast where for twelve years my father had ministered to his small congregation. I only knew life had changed, and it was a lot more interesting.

In London, while my father scrambled to arrange passage to the U.S., he and mother spoke with muted eagerness of going home. Home? Home was our house on Lexden Road fronted by a low brick walled enclosure where we collected conkas, as we called the glossy brown horse chestnuts that littered the grassy circle beneath a great horse chestnut tree.

The ensuing bustle was marvelously entertaining, but by the time we were on a train bound for Ireland, where we would board our American ship, my excitement dwindled. When my father got off the train to see if he could find food for us, I felt an anxious twinge watching mother look for him out the smoky window. As the engine chuffed and snorted and the train began to move, I was suddenly terrified that it—and we—would to go hurtling through the night without him. At the last minute my father clambered aboard (minus any food). Mixed with tremendous relief, I felt an awful, hurting pang in the pit of my stomach. It wasn't hunger. I wanted to be back in my bed, I wanted the family, all seven of us, safely back in the house on Lexden Road. It was my first encounter with homesickness.

EVEN TODAY MY HOMESICKNESS CAN BE TRIGGERED by something as prosaic as jet lag. After arriving in northern Scotland recently, I was unable to sleep. I drew back the curtains to look out at the harbor below. As I gazed at the black, glistening waters of the Loch, at the shadowed fishing boats lit by tall sodium lights, a bleak desolation swept me. The scene was beautiful and exotic. But I didn't want exotic. I wanted familiar—the soft glow of our neighbors' house lights in our Chicago suburb, the comforting curve of the street as it circled the grass at the end of our cul-de-sac. I wanted home.

The next morning came with its crisp sunshine. My homesickness doesn't last long when I'm well breakfasted and driving through Scottish Highlands where mirror-still lochs reflect heather-clad mountain peaks. Yet . . .

A few days later, I looked out the kitchen window of a fifteenth-century stone cottage at four plump, speckled pheasants pecking at the greenery of the enclosed garden. As my gaze traveled to sheep dotting the steep, grassy hills above, I decided the sleepless first night had been a minor glitch; my homesick demons were well and truly gone.

But like me, they were only vacationing. During that week, my husband decided to help our host, Alstair, mark sheep while I, accompanied by Ben, the farm's Labrador retriever, walked the dirt road up to the ridge that ran along the Pentland hills behind the farm. When Ben and I reached the crest, I stood in the bright, chill sunlight and gazed at yet another line of blue-purple hills in the distance. Then I turned back to see the tiny figures of my husband and Alstair as they guided sheep from cram-packed pens and marked them with splashes of bright blue paint. I told myself how lucky I was to be able to savor such a scene, but what edged out of that appreciation was a sense of isolation that escalated to a fierce longing for home.

As I stroked Ben's black head, I told him what an astonishingly silly woman his companion was, a disgrace to all the brave people who left this wild land for the wilder shores of a new, untamed country. It was only after we trekked down the dirt track through the gorse back to our snug stone cottage and I started preparing stew for dinner that my homesickness subsided.

On another trip my husband and I traveled to Colchester and found the house on Lexden Road our family had left so precipitously so many years before. We parked our rented car beside the low-walled brick enclosure where chestnut trees still stood and conkas still littered the grassy oval. Half relieved when no one answered my timid tap on the rose-hung front door, I showed my husband to the narrow lane alongside the house that led to a field overlooking the countryside. Finding that field after some thirty years seemed miraculous. I'd fully expected a view of new roads and newer houses, but there it was, just as I remembered, the field where I'd played with my brother and sisters. Interestingly, I felt only a smidgen of nostalgia. This wasn't home. Home was now half a world away in a Midwestern suburb.

The hunger for home can be brought on by an unexpected sight or smell. It attacks lightning fast and often leaves as abruptly. On occasion, however, it can linger. One time on Italy's Amalfi coast, what started as a prickling of apprehension deepened to a somber, almost sinister sensation that stayed with me for days. The memory disturbs me even now, though I'm not sure what actually happened on that hillside above an impossibly blue Mediterranean.

We didn't need the privacy of the lemon trees that grew beside the porch of our tiny cottage, for it was late October, and except for the caretaker and his family who lived by the iron gates at the top (and spoke not a word of English), the cottages sprinkled down the steep hill were deserted. It was a night or so after our arrival that I woke out of a sound sleep to a conversation. The words, though I couldn't quite make them out, were most certainly English, and the accent sounded American. Steps echoed on the steep, flagstone path. Late arriving renters? I checked the alarm clock. Two AM.

The footsteps receded. And then returned.

"Claire!" a man called plaintively. There was silence. The call came again, sharp, anxious. "Claire!"

I reached for my sleeping husband. Before I succeeded in rousing him there was another call and then a reply in low, authoritative Italian.

"Claire!" came a last desperate call before stillness fell like a curtain mid-act. My husband opened the door and peered into the velvety blackness, but there were no more calls for Claire, no more footsteps. Nothing but silence. We went back to bed and before dawn I slept. There were no new renters. For days I thought of Claire. Had they found her? Did she want to be found? All I wanted was to flee that beautiful hillside and the memory of those eerie calls, to be transported back to my own familiar territory, to my Midwestern space.

During another trip, we lived on a vineyard between Florence and Siena and explored the hill towns of Tuscany. We learned to appreciate Chianti *classico* and Italian football (soccer). Homesickness didn't intrude when we sat in the stands among screaming, madly partisan fans and painlessly expanded our limited Italian vocabulary. (How is it one is able to understand profanity in a language one does not know?) We didn't need the policemen sporting Uzis as they strolled the stands to tell us Italian fans take their sport seriously.

It wasn't only at soccer games that I found an antidote for homesickness. When interacting with people, you don't have time to long for home.

I'll always remember a conversation with an elderly gentleman on a sheep farm in the English midlands where we were staying in his remodeled granary. When I mentioned that I had to cut short our chat to put a joint in the oven, Mr. Havard said, "Cooking a joint, are you? Good on you!" Then he eyed me hopefully and added, "Is it lamb then?"

I nodded, feeling inordinately proud that not only had I remembered to call the roast a 'joint', but that it was indeed lamb.

"Good on you!" he said again. "And will you be having mint with it?"

"Of course," I said.

"Good on you!" he said a third time. "And you made the mint sauce yourself?"

"Now you're reaching," I said.

Mr. Havard laughed—and I did too.

I've been astonished how easy it is to communicate with people in other countries despite a lack of fluency in their language. My halting French has met with an amazingly gracious reception. You don't have to be a language expert to learn to say "good morning" or "thank you" in your host country's language. The Japanese don't mind if your pronunciation isn't correct when you say, *"Ohayou gozaimus,"* and any Greek will respond with smiles to *"Efkharisto."* It is these tiny connections, these smiles that make me want to pack my suitcase and venture into the unknown once again.

No matter what stratagems I've devised to circumvent it, however, there are still times when homesickness obtrudes. Like the clear, unseasonably warm Austrian afternoon in Innsbruck, when I found myself surrounded by passing shoppers cheerily discussing who knew what with their companions. I suddenly felt that pang of aloneness that presages homesickness. I didn't want to be on that busy street among those cheery shoppers: I yearned to be on my way to our house where I could put my parcels on the kitchen table and think about cooking supper. The ache was partially assuaged when I returned to the refuge of our hotel where we'd spent the past few days. There on the bedside table was the novel I'd left half finished, and by the time I'd hung my coat in the closet and had taken a clean shirt from a drawer filled with my neatly folded clothes, I felt better. It wasn't home, but, for the time being, it was good enough.

As I've become older, moments seldom escalate to the gut-wrenching homesickness experienced in times past. Yet on the flight home, I'll find myself gripping the airline seat arms in a ridiculously irrational effort to make the plane fly faster. And on returning home, a neighbor's "Good to see you back" can sound like the Hallelujah Chorus, and the simple act of driving to the store for milk and corn flakes makes me dizzy with happiness.

Given a few months, however, and the familiar pattern resurfaces. Homesickness seems a small price to pay for the opportunity to explore worlds outside my own. As St. Augustine said, "The world's a book and those who don't travel read only one page."

I've come to accept that I'll always have moments of melancholy when I travel. And I've come to appreciate the upside—that wonderful feeling when I return to the very ordinary part of the Midwest I call home.

One night not long ago I got up about three in the morning and looked out at the rain-swept street. Although I shivered against the cool, damp air, a startling spike of joy swept me. What was the difference between the night I looked out at the dark waters of that Scottish lock and this moment gazing at a sodden, gleaming street?

I was home.

It was a while before I turned away and went back to bed. The next morning I sat at the table a bit longer than usual, just to sip an extra cup of coffee, to admire the green holly bushes that spiked the blue sky and marked the perimeter of our backyard—to revel in being home.

NAOMI GLADISH SMITH's essays have appeared in various publications. She has read several on National Public Radio's WBEZ. Her short story, "Lamartine's Wife" will be featured in an upcoming issue of *Soundings Review*. She has written three novels, *The Arrivals* (2004), *The Wanderers* (2007), and *The Searchers* (2011). Her latest novel about the afterlife is a finalist in USA Best Books 2011, Visionary Fiction.

RONALD F. SMITS

On My Brother's Bicycle

Handed down to me,
I converted my brother's bicycle
into a chrome-and-yellow masterpiece,
perfect for an odyssey,
a forty-mile trip
from Bayonne to New Brunswick.

At fourteen, an artist, a mechanic, a hero,
I got what I wanted—
brand new chrome fenders and handlebars.

I flew over the Bayonne Bridge,
floated over Staten Island
with the ham sandwich
my parents packed—
pickles, fruit, cookies, cake.

But on US 1, I succumbed to the heat,
angry honking from drivers—
no respect for a hero.
Constant horns, curses, skidding
forced me to walk my iron horse.

My brother's bike, a burden,
I became a burden to myself.
Frustrated and frightened,
I stopped at corner stores to prolong
the agony—
wanted them to worry.

One store owner threatened
to call the police—
I was a runaway.
My odyssey took too long.
Everyone was worried,
my mother, frantic.
I took the whole day
to reach New Brunswick.

There, my brother waited with his family,
a chemistry major at Rutgers,
where years later, I would follow
to major in English.
Not hailed a hero by family—
an early lesson in irony.

The late RONALD R. SMITS was emeritus professor of English at Indiana University in Pennsylvania. His poems have appeared in many anthologies and journals including *College English,* the *Journal of the American Medical Association, North American Review, Poet Lore, Poetry East, River Styx, The South Carolina Review, The Southern Review, Tar River Poetry,* and *The Texas Observer. Push,* his book of poems, is published by the University of Scranton Press (2009).

PART IV
Patterns in Process

KATE CHAPPELL

Natural Order

If you're paying attention, you may notice the way all things
move around you, but there are no guarantees.

You can't remember childhood—so you stand in another's
    memory, silent movie
turning back on itself. You begin learning a language that's always
    lived in you.

Then a teenager, and everything is wrong—endings of your life
all too common. Will you ever ask the right questions?

You leave home—parents anxious and aware. And it's boy
meets girl—all moves forward without ever moving a frame.

You get married.
You fall in love.

You bring a child into a world you think you understand,
but you're always wrong about certainty.

Then the night comes when you walk into and away
from yourself at the same time:

Holding that familiar hand—children gone the way you went away—
you look up: that helm turning all these years behind a shroud.

One light you do not remember being there, pulsing little pearl.
You're slow enough to wonder what you might have missed.

And you ask it to fall, so you can wish this life to live again all over.

DAVE HARRITY is the author of a forthcoming book on devotional meditations and writing exercises, *Making Manifest: On Faith, Writing, and
the Kingdom At-hand.* The founder of Antler—a teaching and resource platform devoted to instructing people in religious communities how to use creative writing as a devotional practice for spiritual formation—Harrity trav-
els throughout the U.S. conducting workshops on the intersection of faith
and imagination.

Baghdad Blues

IT WAS HARDLY A HOMECOMING: no hoopla, no key to the city, no sharp affinity for those things left behind; only the fat drops of rain splattering the tarmac, splashes of memory popping up here and there, bubbles in a well. I walked carefully off the plane, my right hand gripping the wet rail, the empty left sleeve of my uniform flapping in the April breeze.

Then my wife's arm was around my neck, her other arm cradling our ten-week-old son. Her lips were warm, softer than I remembered, like velvet against my ear. "Welcome home, Joe," she whispered. I moved back just enough to focus: wet, tangled hair curling around her pale face like dark ivy, emerald eyes rich with curious light, one brow always endearingly higher than the other. Gina was half Italian, half Irish—often a volatile mix.

She held up the baby for me. He gurgled along with the chorus of rain, lips moving in amoeba fashion, gazing up at me skeptically. Struggling with a half-smile, I pressed a forefinger on his belly.

"Hi there, Chad," I said.

He shifted his blue eyes back to his mother for verification. Apparently, I passed, for the lips formed into a tentative smile.

"He's got your eyes," she said. She toyed with a dark tuft of newly-hatched hair at the back of his head. "And my hair." She smiled with that shyness that, in the beginning, had rocked me like a truck.

I was silent all the way home. Gina chattered on about the baby, new friends. I heard little. She asked when I'd be going to Walter Reed to be fitted for a prosthesis. Coldly, I told her I didn't know, didn't even know if I wanted one. After a moment, she wondered aloud if they could give me an attitude adjustment at the same time. Turning into the driveway of our small house, she suggested a welcome home party. Discussion on this point was brevity itself. "No," I said. She said fine but told me not to expect her attendance at my pity party. And so it went.

Later, I peeked in on Chad, awake in his crib. But I wasn't seeing my son; I was mesmerized by the gray shadows within his eyes, swirling like smoke rising from ruins into the sky. Baghdad blue. I was still there, a prisoner of the images that haunted me.

For weeks, I showed little interest in my wife or son. I assumed a civil manner, a pretense which Gina, unsuccessfully, tried to penetrate. Despite her occasional outbursts, she never gave up reaching out to me, but I didn't respond. I paced around the house for no reason and drank too much. I visited old friends leading normal lives, which only made me feel worse.

There were cold sweats at night from Technicolor nightmares: rocket-propelled grenades exploding, house-to-house firefights, the surreal carnage of a suicide attack, the charred corpses of children, the slow-motion horror of the land mine that took away our Humvee, my left arm, and my best friend, Tim. And the guilt: shooting two suspects in the back as they fled, how troubled I was by how good it had felt; a bullet of mine ricocheting off a wall and just missing a small boy, his mother wailing and pointing at me.

Like unwanted companions, depression and anxiety followed me. I was edgy in traffic, anxious in crowds, uncomfortable around strangers.

Still Gina tried. One morning, she pointed out the kitchen window. "Oh Joe, look! Calvin's back." Calvin was a cardinal who had seemingly adopted us. Gina had come up with the name. I looked out and, sure enough, there he was: impossibly red against a lingering smudge of snow, twittering and showing off his wings. Gina looked up at me hopefully—maybe Calvin could set off a spark. He didn't.

Later, I said, "Maybe I should go see a shrink."

She was rocking the baby on the bed and never looked up. I was becoming an outsider.

"Save your money, Joe, and go talk to Tony."

So I did. Tony had become a surrogate father of sorts after my parents were killed in a car accident seven years ago. Tony's Pizzeria had been an institution in our town for as long as I could remember. I got there at four when things would be slow. The place hadn't changed: cozy booths dressed in red-checked tablecloths, drip-candles in Chianti bottles, and, of course, Buddy, Tony's old basset hound, who patrolled the perimeter.

Tony spotted me right away as I came in, greeting me with his customary Italian schmooze-fest: arms open, head cocked in happy surprise. "Joe, where you been?" Tony looked a bit older, a bit grayer, but the brown eyes were as lively as ever. After a long look, his smile collapsed; his hug was tighter, lasted longer. Over a beer, I spilled everything. He was a good listener.

"Joe, listen to your old Tony now. I was in Korea, as you know, and I see many things. Bad things. Horrible things. A friend of mine died in my arms, Joe. Some of the closest friends you ever make are during wartime. Your Tony knows this. Your friend Tim will never be gone, Joe. That's because you got him locked up nice and safe right here." Tony thumped his chest. "Be thankful you had the chance to have such a friend—many people never do. My closest friend in the world was your father. He always lives right here." He thumped his chest again. "In fact, your old Tony wouldn't be surprised if he walked through that door right now."

He lowered his voice. "Forget the bad things, Joe. It was war. I do some things I'm not proud of either. It's time for the living now, Joe. I know you're afraid. You don't want to lose anyone else you love, but none of us know how long we have someone for. All we can do is love them while they're here. You get that new arm, and you hold your Gina that much closer, no?" He gave me a conspiratorial wink. "You think about all this now, Joe, while your Tony gets you a nice pepperoni pizza."

Tony left for the kitchen. Buddy placed his front paws on my knee, cocked his head, and whimpered softly. Just as animals could sense earthquakes in advance, was it possible that Buddy had become alert to some seismic shift taking place within me?

Tony brought the pizza. My first bite of crust sounded like the crunch of boots over rubble and, suddenly, I pushed the pizza away and buried my face in my arm. The tears came fast and furious. Tony came by and placed a hand briefly on one of my shaking shoulders. "That's it, Joe," he said. "You have a good cry now." A member of a combat stress-control team had once told me to expect such a breakdown but that it would come unexpectedly.

Afterward, I sat back up. Tony came back and sat down. "Everyone hungry now?" Buddy barked in the affirmative. The three of us ate every crumb.

Tony patted his stomach. "How about a little song now, huh?"

I smiled. "Why not," I said, and Tony got up and slid in beside me. He placed an arm around my shoulder, and we launched into our little song and dance act we'd do sometimes. Heads together, we sang:

Bill Ward.
Soldier at Rest
Clay sculpture, 13 in. high, 2011.

When the moon hits your eye
Like a big pizza pie
That's amore!

Buddy bayed along as best he could. For the middle section, we held up our invisible little bells between thumb and forefinger. "Ting-aling-a-ling, ting-aling-a-ling, ting-aling-a-ling."

I got up. It was finally time to go home. I hugged Tony one more time and scratched Buddy behind the ears.

"You no be a stranger now, huh?" Tony asked. I nodded.

Outside, it was raining again, but this time I knew it wouldn't last forever. Sometimes we are fortunate enough to experience moments of absolute purity, so singular that they are rarely forgotten. One of those moments was in the making, filling quickly with redemption, reconciliation, and surrender.

Driving back, I spotted an old woman selling flowers at a roadside stand. She wore a big, floppy red hat that flapped in the wind; it reminded me oddly of Calvin. I got out, dancing my way toward her around the puddles. In the rising orchestration of wind and water, I felt something else emerge, something I hadn't felt in a long time— joy. I told the woman that I liked her hat,and then bought flowers for Gina, white roses.

MICHAEL BARBER retired from the publishing industry after a heart transplant in 2006 and now lives on a lake where he sails his boat. When the wind isn't blowing, he writes short stories. Michael graduated from the University of Connecticut with a bachelor's degree in English. His stories have appeared in *The Berkshire Review, Storyteller, NEWN, Midnight Times, Nuvein,* and *Ascent Aspirations,* among other publications.

ADEN ROSS

First Eclipse

The fall I learned to bicycle, my father
whistled me awake, hoisted me piggyback,
promised all in one night moon and earth
passed every phase, shadow game spirals.
Cricket rattles snaked the moonlight; darkness
edged the yard, us. I gulped for his hand.

Caught years ago in gears, fingers missing, his hand
taught me bicycles, balanced like an egg. My father
had scorched with drought, cricket clouds—a darkness
rising like dust from the plains to settle back
on his green winter wheat. When tornado spirals
licked his farms, he plowed new patterns into earth

and planted each seed in season. Now the earth's
shadow smeared the moon's face, like a hand,
with dried blood dust. A hummy spiral
I squirmed in his loose, hooped arms while my father
squatted—afraid to trot barefoot back
to the farmhouse, webbed in crickets and rosy darkness,

or sidle the windmill's ghostly stilts. That darkness
crossed Iphigenia when her father, needing earth's
fair winds, turned his silent shadow and his back
on her. She burned through ancient hands,
bonds strong as membrane. Born breech, her father's
scream with her pyre's smoke spiraled

the rising breeze. My bicycle wheels spiraled
every smoky dusk that fall to darkness.
The chain caught my dress: grounded. Father
unwound the gears, wobbled me upright, wiped the earth
from my face, taught me to let go his hands.
That first eclipse, as he promised, changed back

to moonlight, but the farm would not spring back
to shape. Roads, children, years spiraled
from that yard, like sunlight charred my hands
blacker each appointed, passing darkness—
but none so blank as the spring the newly-turned earth,
whistling with furrow crickets, fell away from my father.

Through time, moons spiral, never circle back.
Each darkness glints differently; like the earth's
shadow, we drop through our father's hands.

ADEN ROSS recently retired as a university professor of English and the humanities and now writes full time. Her poems have appeared in numerous journals including *The New York Quarterly, The Atlanta Review,* and *The California Quarterly.* Twenty-five of her plays have been produced nationwide, and *Dreamkeepers,* the Utah Centennial opera for which she wrote the libretto, was nominated for a Pulitzer Prize. She has just completed her first novel. Aden Ross writes, "I wanted to write a poem about my father, which quickly circled outward to other fathers and very different treatments daughters had received in their hands. A subject of such archetypal recurrence really demanded a 'circular' structure: a triolet felt too trivial, and a villanelle too short. So I ended up with the most difficult form of all, the sestina. It is a thirty-nine line poem comprised of six six-line stanzas and a three-line envoy. The end words of each line must occur in a predetermined but different sequence in each stanza, and all six end-words must occur in a specific order in the last three lines."

Coffee

I SCREAMED WHEN I CAUGHT MY REFLECTION in the elevator mirror. Strings of hair had escaped my perfect bun and now clung to my shiny face like freshly chewed gum to the underside of a cafeteria table. The brown stain on the front of my designer blazer had soaked through to my blouse, which had come untucked from my skirt. I limped closer to the mirror, the broken heel of my pump dragging across the floor. Just thirty minutes ago I was a smartly dressed advertising executive, and now I looked like a deranged nutcase. Feeling defeated, I slumped against the wall and watched the numbers light up, lifting me closer to the sixty-second floor.

It had all begun when I reached for the carafe in the office kitchen. Before I could pour myself a cup, Ryan, my coworker, pegged me with a foam football.

"I don't want to play," I complained, holding up my hands to protect my face. "Plus, I don't have time. The meeting starts in forty-five minutes, and I want to arrive early to prepare."

Ryan wasn't listening. The ball smacked my forehead. I lunged at him and seized the football. When I had him cornered, I pulled back my arm in preparation of an epic launch and released. The ball spun toward Ryan's face, but he ducked. The football smashed into the coffee machine, which tipped onto its side with a hideous crack. Steaming coffee gushed from the full carafe and splashed onto the floor. I hastily picked up the carafe and shook it. Empty.

"Look at that mess," muttered Ryan. "It's going to take us forever to clean up."

"Us?" I shouted. "I don't have time, and now I don't have any coffee." Fuming, I glanced at my watch. To arrive at my meeting early, I would have to leave pronto. I stormed out of the room, stuffed my presentation materials into my briefcase, grabbed my purse, and headed out of the office.

I rushed to the sidewalk edge and flung my arm out to hail a cab. Just as one screeched to a halt in front of me, I spotted the sign across the street. Starbucks. Surely, I could spare a few minutes to quickly grab a cup of coffee. I backed away from the cab, smiling at the angry driver who flipped me off. I dashed across the street as soon as I saw a break in the stream of traffic. Unfortunately, I misjudged my timing. Halfway across, I froze as a fleet of yellow taxis sped straight toward me. The cabs swerved and screeched to a stop. Amidst blaring horns and nasty cuss words, I crept across the street.

I entered Starbucks to see a long line snaking through the store. Sulking my way to the back of the line, an idea struck me. I slyly rubbed my ear against my shoulder and felt my earring slip from its hole.

"Oops! I seem to have lost my earring," I said to no one in particular. I dropped to the floor, pretending to search for it. On my hands and knees with my purse and briefcase dragging along beside me, I slowly crawled to the front of the line. When the customer in front walked away, I popped up. "I found it," I announced. I turned to the cashier. "Mocha Frappuchino, double-shot, please."

"Excuse me," said an angry voice in my ear.

I fumbled with my purse, trying to pay before anyone realized what was going on.

"Excuse me, but you just cut to the front of the line."

I pivoted and met the ugly scowl of a large woman. I flashed her my best 'I'm-a-really-friendly-person' smile and held up my earring. "I dropped my earring. You must not have seen me because I was on the floor looking for it."

The woman's expression didn't change. "We've been waiting all morning for our coffee, and you've got to wait, too."

My brain was too fried from lack of sleep to continue the lie, so I opted for a less glamorous approach. Begging. "Please, I'm in such a hurry, and I have a terribly important meeting this morning that could change the course of my career!" I took a deep breath. "Plus, my auntie is in the hospital, dying," I added for good measure.

"Get in the back of the line!" demanded the woman.

"If you'll just let me pay, I'll be out of your way in two seconds." I frantically pulled out a wad of bills, which fluttered to the floor.

"Ma'am, you're going to have to wait in line like the rest of the customers," said the cashier.

Embarrassed, I picked up my money and snuck out of the store.

In the fresh air, I regained my sense of purpose. I had an important meeting to get to! I quickly forgot about my coffee and hailed a cab. Once settled in the backseat, I perked up at the opportunity to review my presentation notes. But by the time I flipped to page two, my eyelids were drooping. I shook my head and glanced through the windshield. Traffic was at a dead stop. I had only twenty minutes before the start of the meeting, and we were still ten blocks away. Slightly alarmed, I reached for my purse, and then I saw it. Another Starbucks! It was so close I could almost smell the coffee grounds.

"Sir, would you mind pulling over for a few seconds while I run in to grab a cup of coffee?" I asked in my sweetest voice.

"Pull over? It's Fifth Avenue in Manhattan, honey."

I stared longingly through the glass door at the empty cashier counter and made a snap decision. I threw some money into the driver's lap, grabbed my purse and leapt out of the cab.

A couple of minutes later I swept my steaming Grande Mocha Double-Shot Frappuccino off the counter. I had coffee! After a brief

143

Coffee

Ruth Bernard. *Time Disintegrating, Hollywood, California.* Gelatin silver print, 11^{13}/16 x 10^5/8 in., 1942. Princeton University Art Museum. Bequest of Ruth Bernhard. ©Trustees of Princeton University. Photograph: Princeton University Art Museum / Art Resource, New York.

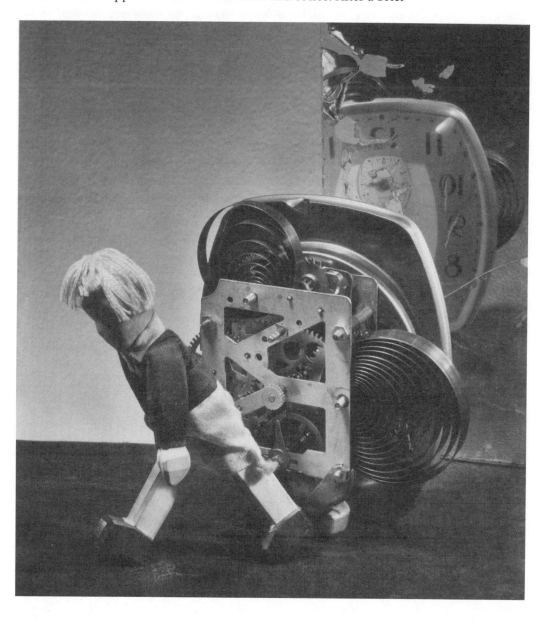

celebratory fist-pump I headed back outside. Standing in the morning sunlight, I felt revitalized. I wouldn't arrive early as planned, but so what? As long as I arrived on time, everything would be fine. Plus, I would be totally focused after drinking this glorious cup of rejuvenation now warming my palm. Finally at ease, I slowed down to take a sip and enjoy the moment.

Just as my lips touched the rim of the cup, a kid on his skateboard hit me square in the side. My purse went flying, and I tumbled to the sidewalk. Miraculously, my coffee cup remained firmly in my grasp, but its contents had splashed down the front of my blazer.

"Sorry," said the skateboard kid before taking off.

Near tears, I peeled myself off the ground. I was checking my belongings for damage when I realized I didn't have my briefcase—the one that held my notes to the most important presentation in my career. I frantically looked around, as if the sidewalk would suddenly spit out my briefcase. No luck. I was about to run into Starbucks to see if I'd left it on the counter, but the vision appeared in my mind like a flash of lightning in a dark sky. I had left it in the cab. I stared hopelessly at the fleet of stagnant, honking yellow cabs in front of me.

As I sulked on the crowded sidewalk, I had a thought. I lost my notes, but I had most of it memorized anyway. My watch told me I had ten minutes. I could still make it. I started to run.

Soon, the tall building came into view and, clutching my purse, I sprinted the rest of the way. My hair jostled out of place and my skirt suit twisted in odd ways, but I didn't care. After weaving in and out of pedestrians, I hopped up the steps that led to the entrance, not daring to glance at my watch. I leapt to the last step, and there was a loud crack. I stumbled sideways. I paused briefly, afraid a broken ankle might slow me down a bit. But it was only my heel, dangling from my shoe by a thread. Without a second thought, I quickly hobbled through the revolving doors.

Ignoring strange stares, I lunged into an empty elevator and the doors slid shut.

Then I glanced in the mirror and screamed.

After the initial shock of my appearance, I forced myself to examine the damage. I pulled my hair down, fluffed it up a bit, wiped the smeared makeup from under my eyes and straightened my clothes as best I could. I held my purse in front of my stained blazer and stood on my tiptoes to create the illusion I still had a heel. The elevator dinged. I turned, took a deep breath, and stepped into the fancy lobby.

I swiftly passed the receptionist and popped my head in the conference room, hoping to enter undetected. But the room grew quiet, and all heads turned in my direction. Across the room, my boss's jaw dropped in silent shock.

"There she is," announced Mr. Brock, the president of Sudz and our most important client, who stood at the head of the table.

I did a little wave, scanning the room for an empty seat where I could collect myself.

"Why don't you join me up here," said Mr. Brock, waving me over.

Hugging my purse, I made my way to the front.

"We were just discussing the campaign," he explained. "We are most anxious to hear the tagline you've created."

I smiled tentatively, carefully avoiding the dagger-like gaze of my boss.

"Well? What is it?" he prodded.

Stalling for time, I looked around and caught my reflection in the window. Despite my attempt to repair my appearance, I still looked like I had been spun through a muddy dryer. How could any of these men take my proposal seriously? The tagline I had been so proud of seemed to vanish in a swirl of the morning's horrible events—the foam football, the waterfall of spilled coffee, the yellow cab near-death experience, the "lost earring," and the skateboard collision.

When had the most important morning of my career turned into an uncontrollable circus?

And then it hit me.

I dropped my purse, revealing my stained and wrinkled clothes to a burst of gasps and stifled laughs. My boss turned ghostly white. "Sudz," I said, smiling confidently. "Because stains happen."

Silence.

And then laughter—cacophonous, breathtaking, tear-producing laughter.

Mr. Brock clapped a hand on my shoulder, wiping tears from the corners of his eyes. "It's refreshing to see someone so dedicated to her work. We would be happy to have you on the team to head our new ad campaign."

I stared at him, stunned but thrilled.

After introducing me to the group, Mr. Brock motioned to a small table in the back of the room. "Would you like a cup of coffee?"

SOPHIE SHULMAN has always been an avid reader with a vivid imagination. During her senior year at University of California, Davis, she began writing short stories. She is a freelance writer and working on her first novel.

Special

After publishing his Special Theory of Relativity,
Einstein continued working as a patent officer for several years,
     & if I'd been working next to him
I probably would've asked questions about time all the time,
     & Einstein would've responded:
     Greenhause: Leave me alone already!,
though in German it would've been: *Greenhause: Lass mich*
                                                  in Ruhe!,

& maybe after work, we would've shared our short walks home,
     & at some point
he'd have to turn right & I'd have to turn left,
& I'd say something like: *Alright, Albert. Guess I'll see you*
                                                  tomorrow,
     & he'd reply: *Ya, Johann,*
or he'd nod his head & look slightly annoyed,

& I'd wish I could invent my own Special Theory of Relativity
     or any kind of special theory,
& maybe sometimes I'd turn back towards Albert
& ask him if he thought any of this mattered,
& he'd turn toward me again & say: *Greenhause: Lass mich*
                                                  in Ruhe!

& the years would pass by, & one day I'd arrive to work,
     & instead of seeing Einstein,
there'd be a new employee where he used to be,
     & he'd have no special theories,
& he wouldn't know how to play the violin
nor how to answer my questions about theoretical physics.

146

He'd just sit there & either approve or not approve patents,
    & the two of us would share our short walks home,
& at some point he'd have to turn left & I'd have to turn right,
& I'd say something like: *Alright, Jörg. Guess I'll see you*
                                          tomorrow,
    & he'd reply: *Guess so, Greenhause,*
& I'd wonder why neither of us had any special theories
                                    of anything,
    but when I'd get home & see my wife & kids,
I'd remember theories aren't the only things that are special

Twice-nominated for the Pushcart Prize, JONATHAN GREENHAUSE was a runner-up in the 2012 *Georgetown Review* Prize and a semifinalist for the 2011 Paumanok Poetry Award. He's the author of a chapbook, *Sebastian's Relativity* (Anobium Books 2011), and his poems have recently appeared or are forthcoming in *10x3 plus, Acumen* (U.K.), *The Believer, The Bitter Oleander, JAAM* (N.Z.), *The James Dickey Review, Nimrod, Other Poetry* (U.K.), and other publications. He works as a Spanish interpreter.

New Wine/ New Wine Skins

Pattern and Growth in Spirituality*

IN 1962, the Benedictine monastic community at Weston Priory in Vermont was not quite ten years old. In its founding years, Abbot Leo Rudloff had laid out the pattern of spirituality for forming the community. He put it succinctly: follow the Rule of St. Benedict as closely as possible and be open to the Holy Spirit. The Rule was a pattern of life and spirituality drawn up in the sixth century for monastic communities, i.e., families of Christian men dedicated communally and wholeheartedly to the search for God in the spirit of the Gospels and following the way of Jesus of Nazareth.

This pattern, traced out by Benedict in seventy-three brief chapters, detailed the daily life for Weston Priory: times and forms of communal and private prayer, the fraternal relationships of the brothers, the balance and kinds of work, the process of decision-making, the sharing of meals and care for the sick, the young, and the elderly, the reception of guests, the concern for nature and neighbors. Even the spirit of enthusiasm and joy of sharing burdens found their place in this extraordinary blueprint for community life.

*The subtitle of this essay is adapted from *Pattern and Growth in Personality* by Gordon Allport, professor of psychology in the Department of Social Relations at Harvard University and past president of the American Psychological Association. His works were a major influence on the School of Psychology at Ottawa University.

Abbot Leo emphasized that a unique characteristic of Benedict's Rule is discretion. The pattern was not rigid. The pattern was not the last word. There were invitational openings for adaptation to place and time—opportunities for change and growth. But the emphasis in the foundational years at Weston Priory was adhesion to the Pattern.

In 1962, after five years of training and living with the Benedictine community in Weston, my life felt secure. Following the pattern for monastic life and spirituality found in the Rule of Benedict and so convincingly taught by Abbot Leo enabled my solemn commitment with final vows of obedience, stability, and common life *(Conversatio morum)* with the priory community.

Other applicants to the community were numerous and young, usually college dropouts. There was such a continuous coming and going that brothers joked that the front entrance to the Priory was a revolving door! Evidently, we needed clearer criteria for community entrants. Recent studies in psychology were addressing this question, and it was suggested that insights from the study of psychology could benefit the Weston Community. In light of this suggestion, Abbot Leo agreed to send me off for a few years of study in psychology. The community, however, had recently reduced its farm operations and was economically barely surviving and without the means for such a major undertaking.

Some of us began to search for a solution. We visited William Bier, S.J., at Fordham University where he pioneered in psychological research for religious vocations. He confessed that studies at Fordham in this field were still largely theoretical and recommended the School of Psychology at Ottawa University in Canada as being more practical and suited to our situation.

We had friendly relations with faculty at Ottawa University because of my seminary studies there in the 1940s. At that time, I became acquainted with Raymond Shevenel, O.M.I., director of the School of Psychology. When we approached him in 1962, he welcomed our community interest in vocational studies and offered me free tuition to enter studies there. My earlier seminary experience also provided a solution to the cost of housing. A seminary classmate, Tom O'Rourke, was pastor of the parish in Ottawa East. He offered room and board in exchange for weekend ministry in the parish.

This venture, from 1962 to 1964, proved to be a departure from the monastic pattern of life—simple and enclosed, rustic and somewhat secure—that had engaged me at Weston Priory.

The household of the rectory included the pastor, his retired predecessor, Monsignor O'Neil, myself, and another Benedictine from St. Peter's Abbey in Saskatchewan. Three capable women did the cooking, secretarial work, and household chores. The choir director and organist, who were struggling with the first liturgical changes emerging from Vatican Council II, were frequent visitors. The spirit of the place was congenial and efficient.

On Saturday afternoons and evenings, I offered the ministry of sacramental forgiveness in the church confessional. On Sundays, I celebrated Eucharist, preached at several masses, and taught Gregorian chant to the congregation before the High Mass. (Congregational singing of Gregorian chant was considered a bit avant garde by liturgists during that early period of Vatican Council II.) During the rest of the week, I was free to attend classes and to study in the comfortable room assigned to me.

An early problem was transportation to the university, which was downtown and a few miles from the rectory. I purchased a second-hand bicycle that served well until the Ottawa snows and slush took

over the roadways. A few good textbooks suffered significant water damage as I slipped and spilled on the messy pavement.

Thanksgiving holiday at Weston offered a more viable solution to the transportation problem. Naturally, I did not bicycle back to Weston in December, but the bus trip by way of Montreal seemed interminable. When Jean and Chuck Savage, young owners of the Colonial House Motel in Weston, learned of my bicycle plight, they generously offered a car they no longer needed. Though not in perfect shape, it served the purpose and was a great improvement over the bicycle. At the same time it provided occasion for my first encounter with the Canadian Mounted Police.

Back in Ottawa, I drove blissfully and leisurely along the Rideau Canal to attend class. In the rearview mirror, I noticed a police car tailing me. After a short distance its lights started flashing. I pulled over. A Mountie confronted me at the window. When he spotted my Roman collar and clerical garb he looked a bit embarrassed and asked to see my license. As he returned it, I asked why he had stopped me, since obviously I was not speeding. His reply made sense. "Excuse me, Father, but that license plate number 'B-25' does look a little suspicious." We parted with friendly understanding.

Classes and lectures at the university were fascinating and mind expanding. Alongside several notable Canadian scholars, the professors, with names such as Ramounas, Sidlaskas, Verblosky, and Wyspianski, represented psychological scholarship from Estonia, Latvia, and other countries behind the Iron Curtain. Ottawa University had offered refuge and recognition to extraordinary thinkers fleeing repression and seeking creative social and religious freedom and advancement. Courses in methodology, developmental psychology, diagnostics and mental testing, personality, pathology, and even dreadful statistics opened students to new perspectives on human life and the world.

Besides the class work, there were experiences of monitored interviews and testing procedures. Even more significantly, students were encouraged to organize small discussion groups to share insights and pursue questions raised in class. I joined a diverse and stimulating group that met weekly at the home of Truda and Imrich Rosenberg, refugees from Poland under Nazi domination. A Jewish rabbi, an Irish-Canadian school superintendent, a young gay Episcopalian, and I rounded out the circle. We became good friends and challenging dialog partners. Differing viewpoints became en-riching insights rather than threatening competitors for truth.

I still have my old letter back to the community at Weston that captures the sense of adventure of my Ottawa assignment. It says in part:

Nov. 25, 1962

Dear Brethren,

> *Greetings from the Ottawa expedition!*
> *. . . There was considerable excitement in the church . . . when a couple of little anarchists set fire to one of the confessionals. Father O'Rourke had to form a bucket brigade with the house-keepers to put it out. Fortunately they were able to extinguish it before it spread any further.*
> *We have been doing some IQ testing in the school lately, which may be somehow related . . . to improving our admission process at the Priory. My last assignment was at a Protestant school out in the countryside. The teachers pick out special sub-jects for us—they seem to be little characters that might be caus-ing the teachers to have psychological problems.*
> *The principal was dragging a ten-year-old along the corridor by the arm, trying to convince him that he had not done anything wrong and that she wasn't going to punish him. Finally she was*

able to shove him through the door of the examining room where
I was anxiously waiting, and she introduced us with the words,
"This man is going to ask you some questions."

I don't know which of us was more frightened! (By the way,
the principal's name was Mrs. Stickler. . . . Anyway, Clayton
and I finally got adjusted to one another—maybe because
of a common feeling toward Mrs. S . . .)

As we were about to start the test, Clayton started to rub his
hands together in great glee. "Ya know," he confided, "I just love to
get into trouble. It's just so much fun to get into real mischief!
I got a big pocketful of balloons, and I've been busting 'em all over
the place. Maybe I otta start busting 'em in here, eh?" Well this is
the signal for me to get out a package of Lifesavers—these, I have
found, are the most powerful psychological tool that has been
discovered since the law of specific energies. It was just a matter
of getting over each little crisis with poor Clayton.

By the end of our testing session, we were good pals—and I
was just about out of Lifesavers. His teachers figure that he will be
twenty years old by the time he reaches the eighth grade—
if nothing happens to hinder his present rate of progress!

I'm looking forward to seeing you all soon. The time is short
before the holidays—just a few exams and a lot of Lifesavers. The
weather is fine, and so far the B-25 behaves like a contented cow—
I just hope that it won't swallow any of its loose hardware. We
have very little snow, and the weather is quite mild. I'm still able
to ride the bike a couple of times a week and let the B-52 rest on
the landing strip for the harder days.

Hoping you are all fine and happy. Please pray for me.

Fraternally in Our Lord,
Fr. John

New horizons of learning and friendly relationships with persons
of differing religious, ethnic, and social backgrounds strengthened
my monastic identity that had begun with the pattern of the Rule and
monastic tradition. Weekly letters to and from the brothers at Weston
with joyful holiday visits to the Priory helped to integrate this adventure beyond the set pattern of the Rule into a constructive part of our
life and growth as a Benedictine community. The mutual love,
interest, and concern of the brothers made it possible for us to go beyond fears of difference and to become a more inclusive, open, and
creative community.

In the tough economic years of the 1930s, my mother had made
simple clothing for all five of her children. She laid a pattern out on
the material, followed the outline and fashioned well-fitting shirts,

skirts, and trousers. Patterns were productive and constructive. They were also eventually outgrown. Patterns needed adjustment. New styles were created going beyond limits of old patterns.

In a similar way, our monastery was outgrowing its original outfit of rules. We needed to adjust and adapt the pattern. The experience of sending a brother into an unexplored field at that point of community fragility was an act of trust. A sense of humor and openness to other perspectives, experiences, and understandings made it possible to go beyond the fear of what is different—the fear of change.

The Ottawa experience began with a question before the young community at Weston Priory, "What to do about the revolving door at the entrance to the monastery—candidates coming and going in great numbers?" The two years of studies in psychology provided no easy answers, although creation of a program of psychological tests and screening did emerge from the studies to help in the discernment process. The experience also opened the door to new and crucial questions: how to value the spiritual pattern of the Rule and at the same time be open to change and the challenges of a changing time, how to embrace new opportunities to grow, not only numerically, but in the quality and meaning of the monastic way of life?

Fifty years later, the words of Gordon Allport continue to shed light on the connection between pattern and growth:

> Both humor and religion shed new light on life's troubles
> by taking them out of the routine frame. To view our problems
> humorously is to see them as of little consequence; to view
> them religiously is to see them in a serious scheme of changed
> meaning. In either case a new perspective results.
> (*Pattern and Growth in Personality,* Holt, Reinhart, Winston,
> New York, cfr Chapter 12, *The Mature Personality,* p. 301.)

BROTHER JOHN HAMMOND is a Benedictine monk in Weston Priory in Vermont. He served as prior of the Weston Community from 1964 to 1998. He completed studies in philosophy, theology, and psychology at St. Paul University Seminary and Ottawa University. He is the author of the book *A Benedictine Legacy of Peace: The Life of Abbot Leo A. Rudloff* (Weston Priory 2005). The pen-and-ink illustrations (2012) were created by Mike Taylor, a cartoonist, songwriter, and haiku poet living in San Francisco.

JOAN KRESICH

Sand Painting

In the white tent where a Tibetan monk
is making a sand painting, his face
absent expression, I am not reminded
of impermanence. I'm enthralled
with the tool he's using. It's a tool
just for making sand paintings.

A small metal cone imprinted
with swirling designs holds the sand,
and when he rubs serrations on the cone
with a stick, the sand drops its trail.
The rubbing sound is the sort children
love to make on table edges, on boulders.

The tool has permanence. It looks like
it might be hundreds of years old.
It was carefully wrought
by human hands, wrapped in cloth
and carried across the big ocean.
It must have a beautiful case.

It doesn't seem odd to use a tool
with permanence to teach impermanence.
We've always made tools, and they outlive us.
Once our son found an arrowhead
in the mountains, and the museum
said it was four thousand years old.

As I leave the tent I want to touch the cone,
to lift it and feel the serrations. It's true,
all the people in the tent are destined to die
and the tent will crumble to dust, but I want
to see if I can make the sand draw
a perfect blossom-red swirl.

JOAN KRESICH has been a general and special-education teacher for thirty-
five years. As a poet, she attempts to pare the words down to the moment
they heat up, a sort of alchemy of language. Joan is currently working to
bring restorative justice to her communities in Livingston, Montana, and
Berkeley, California; in one place listening to the cries of wild geese overhead, and in the other, to the intriguing mix of dialects and languages heard
on urban streets.

BERNIE SIEGEL

The Power
of Words

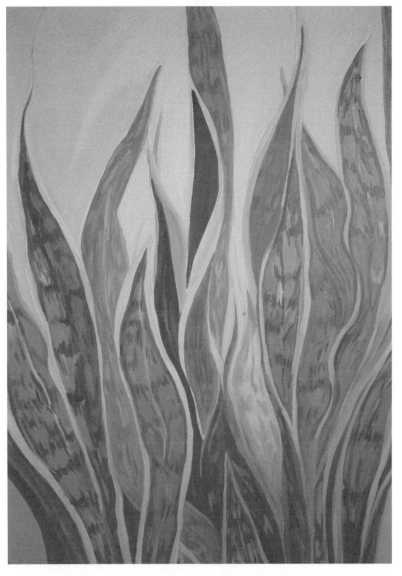

MOST DOCTORS ARE NOT TRAINED to communicate and understand the power of their words as they relate to a patient's ability and desire to survive. Doctors are not the only authority figures who impact patients' lives and their abilities to survive the diagnosis of a disease.

Shelia Geoffrion.
Mother in Law Tongue.
Oil on canvas, 2006.

157

Parents, teachers, and clergy also have the ability to change lives with their words. It can be hypnotic for a child or patient to hear an authority figure's words. As I am fond of saying, *"wordswordswords"* can become *"swordswordswords."* Doctors have the ability either to cure with or kill with words or swords.

Up to the age of six, a child's brain wave pattern is similar to that of a hypnotized individual. To quote a woman I know, whose mother gave her only failure messages and dressed her in dark colors and who as an adult has more trouble with her mother's words than she does with cancer: "My mother's words were eating away at me and maybe gave me cancer." We know from recent studies that loneliness affects the genes which control the immune system. So it is incumbent upon doctors to ask the right questions and know what patients have experienced and are experiencing in their lives.

I recently received two e-mails related specifically to physicians' words. One was from a woman who had a recurrence of her cancer and had decided to not undergo chemotherapy again. Her doctor told her, "Then you might as well go home and commit suicide." The other e-mail came from a woman who asked her doctor if they could become a team. He told her no, that he was the doctor and in charge of her care. She packed her belongings, walked out of the hospital, and has found a caring oncologist with whom to work. She is a survivor and not a submissive sufferer or, from the doctor's perspective, a so-called "good patient."

Doctors need to listen to their patients' words and treat their experiences. Helen Keller stated it very well: "Deafness is darker by far than blindness." Doctors also need to understand that patients do not live a disease—they live an experience. Doctors need to ask how patients would describe their experience and then treat them accordingly. The words patients use, such as "draining," "failure," "denial," "pressure," "gift," and "wake-up call" are always about what is happening in their lives. Doctors can help patients to heal their lives and thus improve the chances of curing their disorders.

I did a great deal of children's surgery earlier in my career. When I meet many of these children today, as young adults, I am amazed at their vivid memories. It is obvious how important this event was to them by the details they recall. I learned how powerful my words were when I began to notice children falling asleep as we wheeled them into the operating room. One boy turned onto his stomach and fell asleep as we entered the O.R. I turned him over on the operating table, and he said, "What are you doing? . . . You told me I would go to sleep in the operating room, and I sleep on my stomach." I replied, "I need to operate on your stomach to get to your appendix." So we reached a compromise.

I would rub an alcohol sponge on a child's arm and say it would numb his or her skin. A third of the children would not feel the needle and ask why other doctors didn't do that. I called it deceiving people into health. Give someone who has faith in you a placebo and call it a hair-growing pill, anti-nausea pill, or whatever, and you will be amazed at how many respond to your therapy.

Dr. Milton Erickson, from his childhood experience with polio and hearing his doctor's dire predictions to his mother that he wouldn't see the sunrise, knew how important words were. His childhood anger led him to defy the doctor's predictions. As a psychiatrist and hypnotherapist, he knew how to talk to patients to achieve the best outcome. One of many books about his work is entitled *My Voice Will Go with You.* And our voices do. At the conclusion of an operation, while patients were still under anesthesia, a time when they still hear their surgeon's words, I would say, "You will awaken comfortable, thirsty, and hungry." I did that until I noticed many of my patients were gaining weight, and then I added these words, "but you won't finish everything on your plate."

Erickson would write in a patient's chart and then excuse himself and leave the room. Of course, he expected the patient would get up and go look at what he had written, so he would write, "Doing well."

Give your family mottos to live by, such as "Do what makes you happy," so they pay attention to their feelings and keep an open mind about the future. Don't be afraid to remind your doctor that his or her words have the ability to hurt, but also, more importantly, to heal.

DR. SIEGEL, who prefers to be called Bernie, attended Colgate University and Cornell University Medical College. His surgical training took place at Yale New Haven Hospital, West Haven Veterans Hospital, and the Children's Hospital of Pittsburg. In 1978, Bernie began talking about patient empowerment and the choice to live fully and die in peace. As a physician who has cared for and counseled innumerable people threatened by life-threatening illness, Bernie embraces a philosophy of living and dying at the forefront of medical ethics and spiritual issues. He retired from practice as an assistant clinical professor of surgery at Yale and from general and pediatric surgery in 1989 to speak to patients and their caregivers. He continues to assist in the practice and field of healing and personal struggle.

RICHARD N. BENTLEY

Snowstorm in Eden

The first whisper of snow
At the gates, every creature
Wants out. Shuddering. Murmuring.
Snow falls on the Garden's clipped hedges,
Topiary shrubs, and the dwarf peach trees
Nailed to their trellises.
Martyred lovers, the blizzard is coming on.
You see it descending, circling,
Here within the lush garden
Of childhood.
High winds, whiteout, squall.
That tree is already rising,
Raging like music.
The Opera of the Angels is finished.
The applause is fading.

RICHARD N. BENTLEY's fiction, poetry, and memoirs have been published in over two hundred publications on three continents. He served on the board of the Modern Poetry Association (now called the Poetry Foundation) and was prizewinner in the International Fiction Awards sponsored by the *Paris Review* and the Paris Writers' Workshop. He has written two books: *Post-Freudian Dreaming* (Amherst Writers & Artists Press 2002) and *A General Theory of Desire* (Patchwork Farms Press 2007). Bentley's latest book, which includes graphic poetry, is *All Rise*. It will be out in early 2013.

CHARLENE WAKEFIELD

Mouth

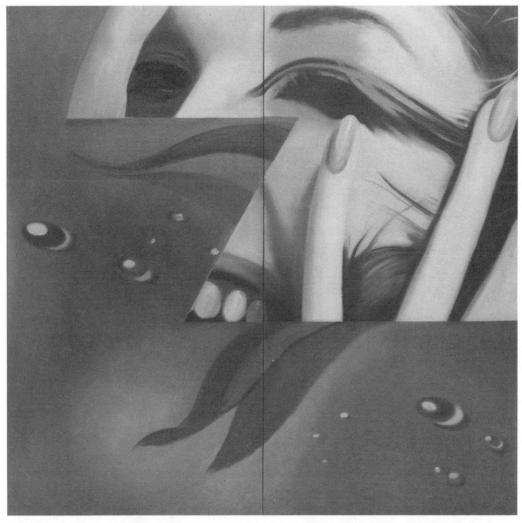

WE'RE LULLED BY THE PATTERNS OF OUR LIVES—it's easy to know what's coming next and to deal with only the details instead of the entire picture. We know what time we're getting up in the morning, what we're going to have for breakfast, where we're going to go, and who we're going to see. We even anticipate the changes to usual patterns—vacations, sleeping in, attending events, adjustments to the seasons, or unexpected weather. Despite our adjustments to differing details, all things considered, we know pretty much what to anticipate.

Then suddenly something comes along and breaks a comfortable pattern so badly that we're shaken out of our easy acceptance of the flow of things—we're blasted into having to actually accept that there's more to what's going on than our daily routines, be they hectic or benign, be they emotional or practical.

You can think that you're an aware person—someone who notices your surroundings and puts them in a special brain space so that they become more and more familiar with each visit. This awareness is especially true about your own body—the parts of yourself that you visit continually and, therefore, know so well. What's the expression—"like the back of your own hand"? You say you could recognize your own hand anywhere, anytime. Likewise your knees, perhaps, or the unique shape of your chin, or tilt of your cheekbones.

I COULD HAVE TOLD YOU ANY OF THOSE THINGS ABOUT MYSELF, but who would even think to consider the familiarity you have with the inside of your own mouth? It's something that's just there, comfortable but out of sight, familiar but out of mind; that is, until its applecart is somehow upset.

The applecart of my own mouth was upset when a trailer truck struck the car I was driving, and both sides of my jaw were broken. That wasn't when the comfortable relationship I'd had with the inside of my mouth became apparent—that happened six weeks later when the clamps, wires, and elastics holding it stationary came off, and I tried for the first time since the initial fractures to chew food.

To my horror, it wasn't the same old mouth that I'd had my whole life, the mouth that was so much a part of me. The change was beyond my imagination, beyond any comprehension. For the first time ever, I was aware of the inside of my mouth. It was full of teeth bumping into each other in odd configurations, a tongue that was too short, cheeks that bulged inward. It was jammed with stuff that didn't fit right.

My lips didn't close well around its new shape. I had to keep reminding myself to shut my mouth, but it was so crowded in there, it was hard to do. My teeth seemed to take up so much space! They didn't fit together right anymore, and the ridges were bumping into each other. When I attempted to talk, chew, or swallow, it felt like a mouthful of marbles.

The crude meshing of the uppers and lowers prevented my front teeth to meet for biting things: anything from fingernails to pizza. When I tried to bite off a length of thread after sewing on a button— oh no!—now I need scissors. To bite off a forkful of pasta, now I needed to do it with the pressure of my tongue against the top teeth, the bottom teeth being unable to close the gap. No more apples, no more

corn on the cob, no more sandwiches, no more brownies. Not that I
wanted the sandwiches or brownies anyway. Even when I was able to
get them inside my mouth using creative maneuvers, I found that the
misaligned teeth just got all gummed up. Bready products seemed to
pack into the gaps where the teeth no longer met precisely, creating
an unappetizing muck inside that unfamiliar mouth space that I now
seemed to be stuck with.

It was probably no different than a prosthetic hand or an artifi-
cial hip only right there inside my own head, about as close to where
I reside in this body as it could get.

The dentist said he couldn't do anything until my whole mouth
had finished its own attempt at adjusting to the new conditions,
which would be a few months. He didn't want to change the shape of
my teeth only to have my jaw creep toward its new configuration and
have them quit fitting all over again. I was stuck with this stranger's
mouth for a while.

I'm getting familiar with it now, but it isn't a familiarity that I
cherish. I'd rather be back in the comfort of unaware acceptance I'd
had for all the years I'd lived with it—the years when I'd missed my
opportunity to appreciate what I had, while I busily noted the earrings of the cashier at the grocery store, the placement of new fash-
ions in a store window, the patterns on the water as a breeze passed,
or the crooked smile on a stranger's face.

CHARLENE WAKEFIELD is a writer and visual artist. She is president of Write
Action, a group that promotes, fosters, and encourages writing. Her work
has appeared in *The Best of Write Action, The Cracker Barrel, Winter* (a publication of Write Action short stories) and in The *Commons,* a weekly reader. Her artwork, a piece created from broken dishes, appeared on the 2002
cover of the Chrysalis Reader, titled *Chances Are . . . : Providence? Serendipity?
or Fate?*

ERROL MILLER

Summer Left Last Night

Summer left last night.
In the early morning mist
of the dawn we stood together
in the new-found coolness
of an early winter.

In silent
splendor we discovered
the quiet solitude of the wind,
the rain, the stillness.

And we were
thrilled by the change
and knowing also that we
had lived and loved into
a brand-new season.

ERROL MILLER's recent work has been included in *Southern Humanities Review, Aura, Borderlands, Arkansas Review, Harpur Palate, Skidrow Penthouse, Kestrel, Big Muddy, Chattahoochee Review, Louisiana Review, Portland Review, Cairn, Riversedge,* and *Birmingham Arts Journal.* Three larger collections of Miller's poetry have been published as *Downward Glide,* (1998), *Forever Beyond Us* (1997), and *Magnolia Hall* (2000). A featured artist in the 2000 *Poet's Market,* he has been nominated for several Pushcart Prizes.

From a Different World

ALONG THE RIVER ROAD, LONG AGO, outside the village of Oak Hollow, North Carolina, small whirlwinds stirred the dry, red dirt. They were caused by a ripple and then a tear in the membrane separating this universe from a parallel one in which time had three dimensions, matter had properties unknown here, and the creatures on at least one world experienced birth, death, and life in ways unimaginable to humans.

The chances of such an event happening were infinitesimally small, yet on that midmorning, it happened. And by further chance, little Guntrel, while playing with some other Shingaru children, fell through the momentary rip.

Suddenly finding himself in linear rather than multidimensional time, he sat dazed, facing the Catawba River, feeling grass tickling his bottom. *What happened?* he wondered in Shingaru. He was missing some of his senses—or rather some of his senses had nothing to do here. He tried altering his shape, but nothing happened. Linear time passed by relentlessly.

He pulled himself upright and walked forward, right into the Catawba. Unable to alter the change in temperature or the water's force, he turned and walked back out of the river, confused by the absence of the parts of his mind that should connect to his environment. And the death feeling was missing, as was the birth feeling. There was, instead, another feeling he would only later learn to name.

Back on the road, he chose a direction, and after a while, he ran across his first human.

SHE SEEMED A SENTIENT BEING trapped in linear time just as he was. She had, to Guntrel, a very odd shape, but because he was used to altering his own shape, this didn't alarm him. His shape, however, did alarm the woman. When he approached her, she fainted. He sank to the ground next to her to observe and contemplate. It was not possible to alter shapes, he surmised, as there were only three spatial dimensions. He could not speak the human language, but he retained the ability to communicate thoughts without words. His "conversation" with the woman, when she awoke, amounted to this:

"What are you?" she cried.

"I'm a sentient being like yourself, but I've lost many of my senses and don't know how to describe my present circumstance."

"Where are you from?"

"As far as I know, I'm from right here. But 'here' suddenly changed."

"What do you mean? When did it change?"

"Ah! I notice you have an expression for this entrapment. 'When' it changed was just back there in this linear time, which seems to have no speed, strength, or direction that I can touch." ("Touch" might translate more closely to "manipulate.")

"What is your name?" the woman asked, beginning to realize she was not dreaming.

"Guntrel," he said. "I'm a child," he added tentatively.

"You don't look like a child," she said. "You look old, and you don't look human."

"Human? You mean to name your species of sentient beings?"

"Well, yes."

Guntrel thought for a moment. No, he decided, he was not human. This woman not only looked odd, but had a completely different experience of sentience from his own. She did not, for example, seem to miss her other senses, if she'd ever had them.

"No," he said to her telepathically. "I'm not a human. I'm a Shingaru."

The woman said it aloud. "Shingaru?"

"That's right," he sent her. He opened up his mind to her, and she understood what a nice being he was, even if not human, and finally she relaxed.

"I'm Beatrice. I'm taking you home to meet my husband," she said.

Walking down the River Road toward her farm, he sent to her, "I notice we have to move our bodies through these, what, three dimensions of space in addition to this single dimension of time?" It seemed not to register on her, though.

After a little while, she said "You say you're not from around here?"

"Here?"

"Catawba County."

"No," he sent. "I'm pretty sure I'm not from around here."

IT WAS NOT SO EASY TO COMMUNICATE with Beatrice's husband. Unlike his wife, Carlos had a maze of thoughts to negotiate before he was able to receive any new information. He was in the barn pitching hay to the cows when Beatrice arrived with Guntrel, and the first thing he did was hurry across the loft and grab his rifle. But soon he settled down and understood the situation.

At noon, Beatrice called her three children in from the garden for dinner. Guntrel didn't understand this ritual, so he stood in the corner and observed. The three children, Hector, Clyde, and Jewel, possessed minds different from their parents'.

"Because they're children," Beatrice told him, having heard his thought.

"But I'm a child, too," Guntrel communicated to the whole family. The children laughed, their mirth almost filling the void in Guntrel currently occupied by this other, rather unpleasant feeling, where the birth and death feelings belonged.

"No, you're very old!" little Jewel insisted.

"Jewel, be quiet," her mother told her.

After dinner, Guntrel played with Clyde and Jewel. (Hector was older and had to work all day with his father.) Guntrel taught the little ones a Shingaru game, but Jewel said it was silly and no fun.

"She's right, Guntrel," Clyde said. "It's not a good game. Let me show you our baby turkeys. They're fun to watch."

Guntrel struggled to understand. He learned much, but he was uneasy about the passage and irretrievability of one-dimensional time.

GUNTREL MOVED ON FROM THE FARM. The unpleasant feeling, which Beatrice had suggested was a feeling of loss and being lost, slowly merged with the linear time annoyance. He found he could ignore it better if he kept busy acquiring knowledge.

Decades went by. He'd learned that the humans gave birth to "new" people. It took Guntrel a long time to grasp that individual humans ceased to exist after a period of time, and that others came into existence from not having existed previously. It was so counterintuitive that he finally just had to accept it, as it was evidently true.

Beatrice and her family had long since grown old and died. Guntrel, however, was finding that he did not age the way humans did. By the year 2000, Guntrel had a deep understanding of the properties of this universe. He had accepted that his knowledge was just covering up his lostness. Even so, he always felt like a fish out of water here, to use a human expression he liked. So, he sought out the humans who were reputed to know the most about existence, and he talked with as many of these as possible—philosophers, theologians, artists, and—very helpful, he found—the scientists. He learned of one scientist named Stephen Hawking, whom he conversed with at length.

Stephen was amazed that Guntrel was even in this universe. Though he wasn't sure, he did speculate about a rip in one of the membranes separating multiple universes. (He was correct, of course.) At any rate, given the extremely low chances of such a rip happening again, they agreed that Guntrel was simply never going to get back to his universe. Meanwhile, Stephen pumped Guntrel for information but supplied little in return. Guntrel moved on.

Finding a secluded spot high in the Rocky Mountains of Colorado, Guntrel sat down on a rock. His lostness, he realized, had turned to despair.

GUNTREL SURVIVED IN THE ROCKIES for a few years, licking his wounds. Then he traveled to Los Angeles and found a psychiatrist, Dr. Bernard Procise, to help him.

Dr. Procise, duly astonished at Guntrel's ability to communicate ideas without words, began firing questions, sometimes in words and sometimes through telepathy, often giggling with excitement. Guntrel gave him a while to get over it, and then kindly sent the message, "Look, Doctor, I'm here to get help, not to amuse and amaze you, all right?"

"Of course," Dr. Procise responded, sobering quickly. "Why don't we begin. Would you like to lie down on the couch?"

Once Guntrel began telling his story, Dr. Procise found himself torn between beliefs based on his training and experience (e.g., when someone says he came from another universe a hundred and fifty years ago, you suspect he is delusional), versus what his eyes, ears, and his very consciousness were telling him.

"And this lengthy experience of life in this universe," Dr. Procise said, "how does it make you feel?"

"It does very little to alleviate my despair," Guntrel replied.

Sometimes Guntrel would try to express a feeling but get frustrated because humans had no context for understanding it. After all, these were Shingaru feelings, not human ones. Although he visited Dr. Procise twice a week for three years and four months, ultimately he found no help.

DR. PROCISE'S OFFICE was located in a cluster of offices and clinics near a large hospital complex. When Guntrel was in the neighborhood waiting for his appointment, he sometimes went to the hospital and roamed around the hallways, taking the elevator to every floor that wasn't off limits. Even after he had quit Dr. Procise, he went back to the hospital to revisit floors he'd found interesting. One was the neonatal unit, where he saw rows of new humans wrapped snugly in blankets and stored in open plastic boxes behind a window through which family members could adore them.

Standing at the viewing window, Guntrel studied the babies. By now, of course, he knew that they would learn things from scratch more or less, as they had just entered the universe from somewhere that many people tried to explain as "heaven," or "nowhere," a place to which they would finally return. These explanations always became unclear when Guntrel pressed for details, and there were about as many versions of it as there were humans telling it.

A man came in and stood next to Guntrel. He was smiling broadly, looking at one particular baby.

"Boy or girl?" Guntrel asked in English.

"Boy," said the man. "Right there, see?"

"Very handsome," Guntrel said. He was familiar with most human rituals by now.

"Yours?" the man asked politely.

"None of them," Guntrel sent him. The man noticed the mental communication and looked at Guntrel with mild surprise.

"Wow," he said. "Are you an alien?"

"Definitely," Guntrel said aloud, and then elaborated mentally for the man.

"Amazing."

The man returned to admiring his new son. Guntrel (mentally) asked the man if he minded being mind-read, and the man had no problem with it. Guntrel "heard" the man's pride, his ebullience about the possible future his son might experience (always this future and past!) and some passing concern about his wife, who lay in a room nearby recovering from the birth.

"Where I come from," Guntrel thought to the man, "there's no such thing as this kind of birth, and there is no counterpart, death. We come into being and go out of being, but because of the various dimensions in which we exist, we experience birth and death as a sort of blanket experience shared by all, all the time."

The man looked at him and said, "That's about the most confusing thing I've ever heard. How could you remain an individual?"

"The individuality of the Shingaru is preserved through other dimensions that are completely unknown here." Guntrel registered the man's lack of comprehension. "It's impossible to explain it," he said, feeling that familiar sense of loss. Directing his gaze at the man's baby boy, he smiled and said, "Goochy goochy goo."

GUNTREL HAD LIVED OVER A CENTURY AND A HALF in this universe, had accumulated knowledge in almost every field of learning, yet he looked about the same as he had when he fell through the membrane. He detected some signs of aging, but he was "growing old" at a much slower rate than the humans. For a long time now, he'd been wondering what he should do with his life, and why. He had no answers.

One day he decided to revisit the River Road where he had landed in this alien universe. He took his time (he happened to be located in Seattle when he got this idea) and did some sightseeing along the way, but finally found the place in Catawba County, North Carolina, on the bank of the Catawba River, where he and some unimpressive dust devils had quietly materialized.

The place looked entirely different. Instead of the quiet dirt road, a paved four-lane, set much farther back from the river, carried a nasty rush of cars and trucks. Oak Hollow had spread outskirts to the river and beyond. The Catawba itself looked murkier, polluted. Still, he easily located the very spot where he'd arrived. It was all weedy, with trash in the undergrowth.

He picked up a paper cup, a straw sticking through the lid, and looked around for a place to dispose of it, but found none. He looked at the cup closely, and pondered how it fit into this universe. He smiled as it occurred to him to question how it would fit into his long lost universe. It hinted at the human word *now*. Like the piece of trash, Guntrel mused, *now* had scant relevance in this universe, though the humans were always using it. *Now* simply meant the general area along the linear time line that was nearby, either in what was called the future or the past. But while *now* certainly would be a good word in his universe, almost a synonym for the Shingaru word *renitke, now* itself did not exist here—it was the same as the humans' strange concept *nowhere.*

Just by virtue of being here, I'm essentially the same as the humans, he thought, dropping the cup back into the weeds. *Though I look different, have some different abilities and lack some of their qualities, those things don't really matter. Like the humans, I arrived here from what is, for all practical purposes, nowhere. And although it is taking me longer, I will finally return to nowhere—but really nowhere.*

And that inescapable fact, Guntrel knew, was the origin of the first feeling he had acquired right here in this spot along the River Road, that quality he had long since learned to identify as alone.

JERRY STUBBLEFIELD received a bachelor's of fine arts degree in playwriting from the University of Texas. His plays have been produced in New York City and elsewhere. Jerry has published short fiction and nonfiction, and a novel, *Homunculus* (Black Heron Press, 2009). He has conducted workshops at public schools, for The Writers Workshop, and the International Thespian Society Annual Festivals and has lectured at various colleges. He taught creative writing at The Asheville School, and has mentored writing students at the University of North Carolina–Asheville and The Boston Latin Academy. The pen-and-ink illustrations (2012) were created by Mike Taylor, a cartoonist, songwriter, and haiku poet living in San Francisco.

SALLY CLARK

Neighborhood Dogs

I remember when the house was full
of braces and acne and turn down the stereo!
and get off the phone! and not pizza, again;

in those days, our neighborhood was
punctuated with barking dogs who'd wake us
with their yowls and howls,

who'd yip at the moon and growl at
feet in the street in the middle of the night,
running wild with the darkness;

how we labored for our rest in those
restless years when the wind banged the gate,
coming and going at all hours of

the breeze-less night and the moon
spotlighted snaking adolescent shadows
behind the trees

and now the neighborhood dogs are quiet,
having grown mellow with the years,
waddling to investigate the mailman,

sleeping soundly through the night and hardly
sniffing the squirrels that scuttle beneath their noses,
no alarms to raise and shake the air.

SALLY CLARK's poetry has been published in *Relief, Weavings,* in three years' issues of the *Texas Poetry Calendar,* and numerous other magazines, gift books, and anthologies. Before she started writing poetry, she and her husband owned a restaurant in Fredericksburg, Texas, where both of their teenage children worked with them, like it or not. A memory of those exhausting years served as inspiration for this poem.

Alpha Test

PAUL REDFORD had wanted to visit a desert ever since seeing the movie *Lawrence of Arabia*. So he was glad to finally be in one, even though the part of the Mojave he was traveling through was splattered with small vegetation that gave it the equivalent of a five o'clock shadow.

Redford had rented a car in Las Vegas and was on his way to a meeting at New Charon Research Corp. Their public relations director, Anna Flores, had called him the prior afternoon at his office in New Jersey and offered him $500 an hour, plus expenses, to drop everything and fly to Nevada.

A Google search of "New Charon Research" produced nothing he didn't already know: the company was seeking to extend the human lifespan through physics; it had a twenty-mile-long particle accelerator, the Moorlock Disperser-Compressor, buried under the Mojave; and it was owned by Toby Moorlock, a multi-billionaire global telecommunications mogul who was notorious for his cutthroat business practices and anachronistic espousal of social Darwinism.

It took Redford two hours of driving on secondary roads to reach the New Charon campus, which consisted of a high chain-link fence enclosing a vast expanse of desert and two structures—a small booth at the entrance gate and a large building a mile away. The guard at the gate told him to make a U-turn and park in the small visitors' lot where Ms. Flores would pick him up.

Ten minutes later a tan, expedition-type Range Rover with Anna Flores at the wheel drove into the lot and pulled alongside his rental.

"Hi Doctor Redford. I'm Anna," she said with a sunny smile. "May I call you Paul?"

"Sure. I'm happy to meet you Anna."

Still single at thirty-eight, Redford processed that she was pretty, about his age, and wasn't wearing a ring on her left hand. The combination of the vehicle and her outfit—a khaki blouse and slacks—made it look as if she were on safari. Redford felt overdressed in his black suit, white shirt, and dark tie.

As soon as he climbed into the Rover, she handed him a non-disclosure agreement and waited until he read and signed it before driving away.

While she drove, she explained that her boss, New Charon's president, Bob King, told her to find an expert on religion who wasn't a fanatical nut job. Redford was a practicing psychologist with a doctorate in theology whose specialty was religion-related mental illness. Flores chose him on the basis of his performance in a televised criminal trial at which he had testified as an expert for the defense. Privately she was glad he looked as distinguished in person as he had on television.

"Bob wants an expert on religion who can be objective about it. I hope that's you."

"Let me put it this way. I'm continually testing and wrestling with my own beliefs to the point that I feel as much of an affinity to atheists as to true believers. But I don't like the smug, aggressive version of either. There's way too much that's profoundly mysterious in the universe to allow for complacency about the existence and nature of God."

"Good. That's about where I am. Now we have only ten minutes, so I'm going to talk fast and keep it simple. Physicists have long known that the particles that make up the reflected light and sound waves that enable us to see and hear and the electrical waves emitted by the synapses in our brains all drift off into space. All this information from the past was thought to remain in the universe but was considered to be too distant for retrieval. New Charon scientists have discovered that when these particles, consisting of electrons and protons, leave earth's gravitational field, they merge and morph into a stream of what they call 'Stark-Neutrino Hybrid particles'. The stream combines with other similar streams to form a river of chronological data, which, instead of heading off into the outer reaches of the universe, circles round the earth. We call this river the "Reel" because we think of it as a three-dimensional movie film that is continuously playing our past."

"Can you retrieve data from it?"

"Better than that. Our scientific team under Harold Stark has developed a process of particle modification that enables us to insert humans, "quantum-nauts" or "Q-nauts" we call them, into the Reel and bring them back by converting them from electrons and protons to Stark-Neutrinos and then back again. And we're able to locate specific dates on the Reel through a technique that's analogous to carbon dating."

"Time travel!"

"No, we aren't visiting the past, only a record of it. So if we disrupt things nothing is affected in our time."

"But I thought you're looking for ways to expand life expectancy."

She flashed a proud little smile. "We hope to soon have the capability to go into the Reel and bring a person back after his or her death at whatever age he or she specified in advance. 'Return to Life' or 'RTL' is our tentative name for the service, which will be affordable only by the very wealthy."

"But what you bring back won't be real, it'll only be a simulacrum."

"Call it what you like. The important thing is it'll be identical to the original in all respects, including its memories."

Redford doubted this was possible but knew he had to suspend his skepticism if he wanted to earn a fee. "Well I can understand why you hired me. Offering a secular way to achieve what is arguably a kind of eternal life could have a disruptive effect on organized religion. It might trigger a turf war."

"And we'll need your help in managing that."

"I'll do my best, but it's a can of worms. Populist politicians may also be a problem, considering RTL will benefit only the wealthy upper class."

She smiled. "Oh but that's not the case! Toby will also be using it pro bono to retrieve eminent individuals whose return would benefit all of humankind. It's what I like most about RTL."

"That could help or hurt a lot, depending on whom he chooses," Redford said grimly as he recalled reports of Moorlock subsidizing a flattering biography of Joseph Stalin and praising Hitler's charisma.

She pulled into a parking space in front of a low, windowless building with four enormous dish antennas on its roof.

"This is headquarters. It's built on the same theory as the desert Indian pit houses—ten percent above ground, ninety percent below. Both our business offices and the operations center for the accelerator are here."

THE MEETING TOOK PLACE in a beige, windowless room containing a circular conference table. Dazzling Navajo rugs were spread around the floor, and ornately framed photos of Toby Moorlock hung on three walls like Byzantine icons. Redford thought votary candles would not be out of place. On the fourth wall there was a large, flat-screen monitor wirelessly connected to a player on the table.

Bob King, New Charon's president, greeted Redford and introduced him to Asher Barr, general counsel; Harold Stark, head of research; and Jack Bold, the owner of Bold Security, an outside contractor. All were in their late forties or early fifties, impeccably groomed, and dressed in business casual attire—long-sleeved, collared shirts and creased trousers—with the addition of a white lab coat in Stark's case.

King, who was in high spirits, asked Bold to bring Flores, Barr and Redford up to speed on an unexpected development. Bold rose and walked to the wall-mounted monitor.

"The Q-naut I assigned to Alpha Test 5 is Dave Santini, a thirty-year-old ex-Navy Seal. Up till now the Alphas have been quick in-and-out affairs. But this time the Q-naut was to travel around and find a specific individual, engage him in conversation, and return alone by activating a new Max-2 launcher-converter. It was a test of the Max-2 and a dry run for the Beta Test during which the Q-naut will find a deceased individual, probably Mr. Moorlock's mother, and bring her back. Alpha 5 would have been a piece of cake but for the point of entry, which, I understand, was selected as a kind of lark by Mr. Moorlock."

Bold used a remote to start the disc player. A steel booth with a glass front appeared on the monitor. It contained two barely discernable human figures who appeared to be caught in a blizzard. The picture cleared, and the men came into sharp focus. Both were lean, bearded, and dressed in long-sleeved Arab-style tunics. One stood slightly stooped as though he were injured. The other had the remnant of a monk's bag slunk over his shoulder looking as if it had been blown apart by something it contained. The booth opened, and the man with the bag remnant stepped out and spoke: "I'm sorry everyone, but I just couldn't let them crucify him."

Barr gasped, "Jesus Christ."

"Exactly," King said, and everyone laughed, except Redford and Flores.

"Of course, that will be the last time we send one of Bold Security's muscle heads on a mission," Stark said.

Bold turned red. "You don't know what you're talking about. Santini has a 130 IQ, and it took him only three months to learn Aramaic from Iraqi goat herders. Problem is that his specialty in the Seals was hostage rescue, and in the heat of the moment, he reverted to it."

"Where is the Passenger now?" Flores asked Bold.

"He's resting in the infirmary. We treated him for head and back wounds and dehydration, and he's fine. He's remarkably composed and talks a lot with Santini, the only one here who speaks Aramaic.

But we don't know what he's saying because Santini is being extremely protective and not very forthcoming. He'll only say that the Passenger has lots of questions."

"He's bonded with him. It was a mistake to assign a Christian to this mission," Stark said angrily.

Bold howled with delight, apologized for the outburst, and announced, slowly and softly, that Santini was a Jew.

"Let's get back to business," King said. "Toby is due here in three hours, so we don't have much time to put together an action plan. The situation in a nutshell is that Santini's impulsiveness has turned an alpha test into a successful beta. So we are now able to announce the RTL capability in the context of a spectacular extraction. I also see an opportunity for Toby to build a profit center around the Passenger, who is about to become the world's number-one celebrity. I'm thinking of books, speaking engagements, inspirational CDs and DVDs,

Jesus Ascending into Heaven, detail. Wallpaper. www.free jesuschristwallpapers.com.

product endorsements. Asher, I want you to draft an employment contract as soon as we finish here."

"Sure. In English and Aramaic. Santini can help."

"Santini only speaks Aramaic," Bold said. "The guys he learned it from couldn't read or write."

"Find someone who can," King said. "Maybe Dr. Redford can help." He turned to Flores. "I want a plan for operationalizing all of this on my desk within the hour."

"Right," she said. "I expect Toby will want to introduce the Passenger to the world on television. They would each make a statement and then answer questions from a panel of prominent journalists, academicians, and religious leaders."

She paused to allow King to comment and then continued.

"I assume Toby would report the successful beta test, describe the technology, and announce RTL. I'm open to ideas on what the Passenger, who will be speaking through an interpreter, might want to say. I suppose he would refer to his biblical message, the main points of which were . . ."

"Get ready for the Kingdom of God," Barr offered jovially.

Redford was happy for the opportunity to contribute. "There are also his ethical teachings and his characterization of God as a loving father, which was new and not part of the Jewish tradition or, as far as I know, of any other religious tradition."

"A tsunami kills 200,000 Indonesians. I call that extremely tough love," Stark said.

"Read the Book of Job," Redford snapped, wishing he could have thought of something better.

King shook his head. "No, all that's old news. Everyone has heard it already. He needs a new message. Something meaningful and exciting to people today. Toby will want to draft it himself."

"The Passenger's wardrobe will require some thought," Flores said.

Barr chuckled. "Yeah, the tunic and beard make him look like a terrorist."

King thought about it. "Maybe something a New Age shaman would wear, or the Maharishi yogi. Or even a business suit. Anna, have the art department do sketches of him in different kinds of outfits for Toby to consider."

Redford was amazed by their obliviousness to the wonder and the mind-boggling potential of the situation.

"With all due respect, I think you're overlooking a couple of things," he said, determined for Flores's sake not to sound like a fanatical nut job.

Everyone turned to him.

"You're assuming he'll do what you tell him and, even more important, you seem to be forgetting that he, or the original version of him, is sacred to over two billion Christians worldwide."

King stared at him blankly. "Your point?"

"That you're about to walk into a minefield. If the public believes the Passenger is what you say he is and you disrespect him, there will be riots. There will also be riots if they consider him a fraud or, even worse, the Antichrist. He probably won't match their preconceptions of him and his second coming."

"We could apologize for perceived disrespect," Flores said gravely, "but it would be a disaster if the public thinks the Passenger is a fraud. It would ruin the market for RTL."

"That's right," Barr said, "and the Christian churches might lobby for a law prohibiting RTL as a form of human cloning."

King was unfazed. "I'm sure our fellow Christians will prove to be more adaptable than you think. The Tibetan Buddhists have no problem with having the Dalai Lama, a laid-back, regular guy, as a kind of demigod."

Redford figured King did not like being contradicted, and he proceeded gingerly. "You're right about the Tibetans, sir. That's part of their ancient tradition and is supported by their religious leaders. But my best guess is that the Christian clergy will be skeptical and maybe even worried about the Passenger's identity, and that the Vatican will convene an investigatory proceeding like the ones they use to vet potential saints. It could go on for years."

Stark was still bristling from the Book of Job retort and wanted another round. "It takes them so long because they need to find miracles they can attribute to the candidate. But our man can perform them at will, isn't that so, Doctor Redford?"

"I'm not convinced you really have him, or all of him, in the infirmary. As I understand it, the Passenger is comprised of a pattern of particles that you have converted from a different pattern of different kinds of particles. There must be some possibility of error, of things falling between the cracks."

"The algorithms give us back our Q-nauts exactly as they were before, and the same is true of the Passenger," Stark insisted.

"Suppose the Passenger represents a genetic mutation, an anomaly with particles that differ from the norm in some way. Say an evolutionary process that God, or a blind primal force if you prefer, set in motion produced a human with special psychic or intellectual capabilities that connect him in a unique way to the Deity or the cosmos. Can you be sure your algorithms would be up to handling that?"

"No, I can't, because your supposition is too vague, besides being reminiscent of the Nestorian heresy and, therefore, outside the pale of Christian orthodoxy. Let's suppose, on the other hand, that he was, in fact, processed correctly and completely. Is it your position that he would he be able to perform miracles?

"Well, the most significant ones—the post-crucifixion appearances—can't be replicated because he was rescued."

"Suppose he gives a speech, and some screwball takes him out with an assault rifle. Would that be good enough?" Barr asked with a grin.

Stark chuckled. "And what about walking on water?"

Flores, who knew Redford was dodging the issue for her sake, came to his rescue. "It doesn't matter. New Testament-type miracles won't be enough to impress a public that's been jaded by movie special effects, high-tech stage magicians, and faith-healing televangelists. Let's move on. We're wasting time."

Stark removed a vibrating smartphone from his pocket, read a text message, and left.

"I don't mean to pile on, Bob," Barr said "but since we are looking at risk factors, I need to point out that the Passenger is an undocumented Palestinian alien, and we are right this minute violating immigration law by harboring him."

"Don't quit on me, people," King pleaded. "Profit motive aside, don't you think we have an obligation to introduce this fascinating man to the world?"

"Shouldn't we let him decide that?" Redford asked.

Barr agreed. "If we hold him against his will, he can sue us for damages in civil court on grounds of what's called 'false imprisonment'. You know how litigious Jews are. He could recover millions, and it would be no consolation to Toby if he gave it all to the poor."

"Wouldn't it make sense to help him stay out of the limelight until he's been taught English and modern history and gradually exposed to our society?" Flores asked

"He could stay with me," Redford said eagerly. "That would protect you from immigration law problems."

Flores saw that King was floundering and threw him a life preserver. "But this is really Toby's call."

"Right," he said, "and I need a PowerPoint presentation that tees up the pros and cons of going public and that outlines a public relations and marketing plan in case Toby chooses that option. You have an hour. Asher and Dr. Redford will help."

Stark returned.

"Problem's solved," he said to King with mock cheerfulness. "He's gone."

"What?"

"He's broken up and presumably drifted back to the Reel."

"How could this happen?"

"Remember, Santini was converted from electrons and protons to Stark-Neutrinos and then back again. The Passenger was a one-way conversion that, for some reason, hasn't held."

"Damn, this is terrible. Toby will be furious."

"May I speak with Santini?" Redford asked Bold, who nodded his consent.

"Me too," Flores said, and the three of them left the room.

"How much of a setback is this?" King asked.

"I don't know. It may have happened because he was going to die soon after we extracted him. Or maybe we reached back too far on the Reel. Our next probe should be into a much more recent date, say one in the 1950s. The Stark-Neutrinos may be more susceptible to permanent conversion. And we should pick a passenger with at least twenty years of life left on the Reel. But you're right about Toby. Someone's head will have to roll, and we have to make sure it's not one of ours. First thing when you talk to him say Bold screwed up by supplying a mentally unbalanced Q-naut. I'll beat the same drum when he gets here."

"Good, I'll call him now. You get ready to convince him you have a good handle on what went wrong and can fix it. It'll help if you focus his attention on the details of the next mission, which has to include an extraction."

"Yeah, but I don't want it to be Toby's mother until we're sure we've got it right."

"How about Elvis?" Barr asked.

BILL FINNEGAN has written one novel, *Saving Frank Casey* (Barn Swallow Press 2009) and nine science fiction and fantasy stories that have appeared in small magazines and literary journals in the U.S. and Australia, including *Barbaric Yawp, Studio—A Journal of Christians Writing, First Class, Cover of Darkness, The Nocturnal Lyric, The Ultimate Writer, Tough Lit*, and *Adventures for the Average Woman*. In the course of his legal career, he served as staff counsel for major corporations, such as American Broadcasting Companies, ITT World Communications, and AT&T. He also served as a pro bono attorney at Legal Services of New Jersey and was awarded an Equal Justice Medal for his work with the needy.

JAY GRISWOLD

The Piano

The piano sits in the center of space
Like a black square on an empty canvas
Hanging on a museum wall. Outside,
Snow is swirling against windowpanes,
Slowly erasing the Hudson River.

A bored schoolboy is seated at the piano,
Absently tapping a single note.
Is it C major, the note from which
All of his compositions ultimately begin?
He gazes out of the window.

He would like to paint the river, and the snow.
He would like to paint the yellow glow
Given off by the lights of the train station
Downhill from the house, their solitary warmth
In the gathering dark.

He taps his monotonous note again,
And thinks of ice floes out on the river.
He doesn't know what his art is yet.
The note continues to grow in the darkness.
It grows until it fills the house.

JAY GRISWOLD holds a master's degree in creative writing from Colorado State University. His published books are *Meditations for the Year of the Horse* (Leaping Mountain Press, 1987) and *The Landscape of Exile* (West End Press, 1993).

PART V

Making New Patterns

KATE CHAPPELL

RODGER MARTIN

Rohrschach Alumnus

Intermission
of the school play
and the lead

has gone AWOL,
left on stage a drawing
of the audience.

Principals search bathrooms,
the halls. I ask to check
my old locker,

gray, empty except—
behind a flap of metal
stand kitchen utensils.

I pull a steel serving spoon,
return to the office
where they examine the drawing.

"Do you see?" they ask. "Do you see?
See the children sitting?"

"No," I said.
"I see their empty chairs."

RODGER MARTIN has been published in literary journals throughout the U.S. and China. His most recent poetry collection is *The Battlefield Guide* (Hobblebush, 2010). He has received an Appalachia poetry award, a New Hampshire State Council on the Arts Fiction fellowship, and fellowships from The National Endowment for the Humanities. Recently, his poetry appeared in *Imago Dei: The Best of Sixty Years of Christianity and Literature*. Rodger serves as an editor in The Granite State Poetry Series.

The Road to Livingstonia

THE DAY, LIKE MOST DAYS IN AFRICA, had not gone as planned. We had taken a long time to say our tearful goodbyes to Tukombo Village. We basked in the afterglow of being welcomed by so many strong, friendly people and of leading successful writing workshops with four hundred teenage girls. Lunch of chambo fish and chicken at the Sunbird Hotel in Mzuzu took longer than expected, and then Sylvia discovered the gas can under the seat was leaking—leading to an unplanned stop across from the sprawling Mzuzu market.

Our driver, Maurice, pulled over and, out of nowhere, two men appeared—one with a proper gas can lid to replace the soggy plastic bag that a gas station attendant had wrapped around the can's opening. The other had a crowbar to open the tiny trunk of our van, where he placed the can. When the fumes had lessened and we were once again on our way, we were behind schedule. We had planned to be nestled into our accommodations before sunset. It was estimated that it would take us, at most, three hours to reach Livingstonia, and it was now 2 PM. We all agreed it was best to get there before dark, so we plunged ahead on the slick highway leading out of Mzuzu.

But the left turn we took was much bumpier than any we had found on this trip. It wasn't until the next day that we learned that rather than the "popular" route with its twenty hairpin turns, we had turned onto a narrow, winding, rutted trail that also served as a dry creek bed. The stares should have been a clue. Every person we passed looked after us with more than the usual long glances. Janet and I waved and wondered about the jaw-dropping stares.

"Maybe there aren't a lot of visitors up this way?" she said.

"That must be it," I said.

Eric Schambion.
*Rough Ride to
Livingstonia, Malawi.*
Photograph, 2007.

Of course, we later learned there were almost *no* visitors up this way because it was not a real road.

The staring villagers waved and then the children ran after our van, waving both arms and smiling as if they had never known hardship. They yelled "Coaster! Coaster!" and chased after us until they disappeared in the great billows of red clay dust that had followed our vehicle everywhere. Elizabeth, a local woman who never ceased to astound me with her knowledge of all things Malawian, told us that children call vans like ours "coasters" and that most children had never seen a motor vehicle, since there was no proper roadway up here.

We kept waving back, with me in the window seat, my right ear and cheek plastered with that swirling dust, and Janet sitting next to me, trying to play a round of Scrabble on her iPad. All around us was the constant chatter to which we had grown accustomed on a long journey with a group of women writers.

"This scenery is amazing, every part of Malawi is so different," said Sonya, who traveled from the U.S. to Malawi frequently to visit her son who was a doctor in Malawi.

"They call it 'God's country' up here," Elizabeth said, and I thought it interesting how Americans reserve that same designation for the more scenic and isolated parts of our own country. "You'll see when we get to the top."

"Do you think they'll have Wi-Fi in Livingstonia? I need to write home," said Sylvia, as she adjusted the volume on her iPod.

"My guidebook said it's a university town, so there should be a cyber cafe," I said.

Most of what we were to learn on the journey came, not from guidebooks, but from actually being there together. It was on that coaster that we learned about a recent death in Rachel's world; learned about Jody's big decision; and, as we bumped our way along, learned things about my marriage and divorce that I hadn't told anyone. It was on that coaster that nine women melted into a family.

We bounced along, with Maurice at the wheel, plumes of red dust billowing behind us for one, then two, then three hours. Every so often, we passed a cluster of huts and a small, splintering-plywood store that called itself a "Shopping Centre," with some goats and a few wind-blown cows, so we knew we were not all alone. As the sun began to sink over the towering Livingstone Mountains, which we were just beginning to climb, we saw residents of the villages walking in from the fields with hoes and scythes swinging from their arms, their clothes swathed in that swirling red soil that made farming so good and staying clean impossible. With the oncoming darkness, some members of our group grew quieter and quieter until they were silent—shutting down with fear of the unknown and with the frustration that nothing is easy in Africa.

The winding creek bed went on and on, growing narrower, until we were one, then two hours late, and still chugging ahead in the shiny white van that was now red-brown. The stunning, rugged mountains ahead and behind and all around us were dotted with orderly specks of green that became coffee and banana plantations and maize fields as we drew close and passed. To our sides, everywhere on that drive, were tall shrubs with red, purple, and yellow flowers that I called wildflowers and some others called weeds. The plants thumped the sides of the van and reached long tendrils through our open windows, leaving giant green ants, small red beetles, and fuzzy honeybees on our seats. When Elizabeth suggested we close the windows so that poisonous snakes didn't also fling in with the heavy branches, everyone briskly shut their windows. My window stayed closed until the van, with its ten humans and heaps of dust, felt stifling.

The sky began to turn a deep orange and purple, and the sun disappeared below the tall mountain to our west. Silence enveloped the van, replacing laughter with the return of fear. I watched the wildflowers slide past along with deep crevasses in our route that could easily gobble up a tire and topple us over the steep cliffs we skirted if Maurice wasn't watching. But I knew that he was. The quiet man who spoke only Chichewa and wore T-shirts with English sayings like "Smart Girls Rule," had earned my respect. He was one of the best drivers I had known.

By the time darkness fell in earnest, the quiet and fear in the van were palpable. Someone wondered aloud if we were just driving in circles. I learned later that I was the only woman in the van who wasn't afraid. Too many childhood adventures with my family in Nova Scotia and in the deserts of the American Southwest, in which my dad calmly drove down unmarked trails or dry canyon creek beds, had prepared me well for this journey. To the women in the van, I pointed out the nearly full moon and the brilliant upside-down constellations and the fireflies that were rising from the jungle floor, their flashes of hope against the black velvet sky. This all drew some interest, for a while.

"Wow, look at that sky," I said. "I bet you can see a million stars tonight."

"Lovely, but I wish we could see some real streetlights out there, somewhere," Sylvia said.

"But look at the mountains. It reminds me of California," I said.

"This does not look like anyplace I've ever seen in California," said Diane, who lived in the Bay Area. But then Maurice stopped. The van just stopped, and when I leaned over Janet to look out the windshield, I could see the reason—there was one enormous crater half as big as our van and other slightly smaller holes, right in our path. We could not go around this time, and we couldn't go through. There wasn't even room to turn around to back up on this path that Janet kept likening to a hiking trail.

We all got out and listened to the sounds of the African night competing with the sounds of insect repellant being sprayed on bare arms and legs. To our right, we could hear croaking sounds that felt both reassuring and warning; I was pretty certain those were the calls of crocodiles. Soon enough I learned this was true.

"What do you think is going to happen?" Diane said, with tears in her wavering voice. "Is there any chance we'll get there tonight? I'm not comfortable sleeping in the van."

"I'd rather stop here and sleep in the van than keep going in the dark," Jody said. "We could end up driving all night and then slip off a cliff. Who would ever know?"

"Right—probably no one would even know to look for us for days and then they wouldn't know exactly where we were," Rachel said, and we all shivered.

I did not have any answers. While I had been enjoying the adventure, I, too, wished we were tucked in for the night with electric lights, our familiar belongings strewn around us, and a meal of squishy nsima and greens.

Then, out of the darkness, they appeared: teenagers, women, preschoolers. We were all alone in the world, and then they were suddenly there, just like the guys who helped solve our leaky-gas-can emergency. They were there, though it was past normal lights-out and we could see no signs of a village.

Without a word, each teenager, woman, and child began picking up stones that recent rains had left in the washout. The boys lifted stones as heavy as me, while a three-year-old girl searched until she found a perfect round rock, the size of a chicken egg. They filled the holes with these stones and then dragged boards from somewhere and laid them across while we awkwardly tried to help them help us. And, although it was two more hours before we reached electricity and beds, the power of the human spirit took the stage with the songs of crocodiles playing in the background.

KARI KYNARD-RIDGE is a journalist, editor, photographer and fiction writer. She has been published in literary journals, metropolitan newspapers, national magazines and websites. She leads Amherst Writers and Artists-based writing workshops. "The Road to Livingstonia" is a chapter in her book about her experiences in Malawi, volunteering with the nonprofit VoiceFlame, which helps African women to create writing workshops in their villages and towns. She will never forget the moonlit drive to Livingstonia when the crocodiles sang sweet lullabies, and they learned about the a mysterious power of a village.

DEBORAH MURPHY

Detour

After driving for hours
we cross the line,
pass through places
we've never been:
Portland, Westbrook,
Ogunquit, Lisbon Falls.
We flip a coin, choose an exit
abandon the dull rush of I-95.
At the end of the ramp
we pause, weigh our options.
You shrug your shoulders;
either way is foreign territory.

But I tell you, no, I have a feeling.
Turn east, toward the ocean.
In my mind I imagine the perfect spot—
a village green lined
with park benches, sheltered
by large oaks, elms, maples.
There'll be a general store—
Del's or Smith's—on the left,
with a jumble of homemade breads,
jams, pies, soda, penny candy, fishing rods,
bait, soap, nails, rakes, linens, corn flakes.
And an all-night diner must be on the right—
probably meatloaf or fried steak
on the blue plate tomorrow.

And somewhere close
a long dirt road will wind its way
up a steep hill to a wide white farmhouse
that sits on a bluff overlooking the sea
and Ruby, Empress of The Wildflower Inn,
will throw open the heavy oak door,
welcome us in.

DEBORAH MURPHY's poetry has appeared in *Connecticut River Review,*
Concrete Wolf, Smoky Quartz Quarterly, Soundings East, and *Flash!point.*
Holding a bachelor's degree from the University of Pennsylvania and a master's degree from Tufts University, she works as a freelance writer and as a
writing instructor.

KAREN CORINNE HERCEG

Knitting in Transit

Albert Anker.
Little Girls Knitting.
Oil on canvas,
24²/5 x 27 in., 1892.
Museum Oskar Reinhart
am Stadtgarten,
Winterthur, Switzerland.
Photograph, bpk, Berlin /
Museum Oskar Reinhart
am Stadtgarten,
Winterthur, Switzerland /
Braun / Art Resource,
New York.

TETHERED BY LARGE RUBBER WHEELS and the tenuous attention of a union driver, our commuter bus pulled out of the park-and-ride lot with relative promptness each morning at the unholy hour of 5:30 AM. Each morning we acknowledged sleepy gazes and each evening equally dazed states of exhaustion. Deep in my heart I was certain we were not born for this. Otherwise, I would feel joy. Joy was a two-hour commute because there were no accidents or weather delays. I had been keeping this routine for twenty years, advancing toward the glory of my middle years.

Miriam stood out from the crowd immediately. She was a new commuter with a smile for everyone before the sun had the decency to rise. Nothing else distinguished her: straight, brown hair in a clip, pale skin, fine but plain features and drab, inexpensive business attire. She carried a lunch tote and folding umbrella. Her vibrant morning greeting to the bus driver shocked him into a semiconscious state.

One morning Miriam found an empty seat next to mine. She introduced herself explaining she was a "city transplant" like most of us. Although we'd grown up in the boroughs, most of us had become financially disenfranchised from living there with any quality of life. We were priced out of our homes by the nouveau riche, Ivy executives from the right clubs, and foreign nationals who seemed to own more and more of a Manhattan I was convinced the Indians did well to have sold off. So we had migrated to upstate New York. The Hudson Valley was scenic and rural compared to the concrete blocks of Brooklyn and Queens. But there were no comparable jobs.

It was a conundrum of distance for quality either way you sliced the suburban pie. Miriam hadn't been worn down enough by the long hours and potholes, which accounted for her enthusiastic demeanor.

Reluctantly, I responded.

"I'm Janine," I said, "welcome to the Netherworld."

"Here we go again!" she said, settling into her seat.

"Indeed," I replied, leaning back and closing my eyes. She didn't take the hint.

"Well, the time change will be helpful," she said cheerfully.

The clocks would spring ahead on Saturday, garnering more daylight during our morning commute.

As Miriam beamed at me, I noticed her clear and compelling blue eyes.

"It beats tomb-like darkness," I replied.

"Well," she said pensively, "everything is relative. Imagine people in Scandinavia. In winter there are only a few hours of daylight."

"And they have the highest suicide rate and have probably cornered the market on alcohol consumption," I responded.

Miriam laughed.

"That might be true. I guess we are luckier."

She simply had not endured enough hardship to appreciate that if anything was relative it was luck. She reached into her bag and pulled out a small skein of knitting and began manipulating two long needles through a small square of periwinkle colored patch.

Once in the city Miriam wished me a wonderful day and disappeared into the massive crowds pushing toward the streets.

On Monday morning our group clustered in the park-and-ride lot once more discussing a late-season snowfall for our anticipated evening commute. That meant traffic delays and arriving home even later than usual.

"This winter just won't quit," someone remarked, and we all agreed.

A small, brown car pulled into one of the remaining spots. Miriam stepped out, gathered her things and put a key in the driver's side door. Most of us hit the automatic lock button on our key chains. This often caused a synchronized cacophony sounding like small dogs barking.

Miriam smiled and, glancing back at her car, sighed, "Well, it's an old model but very faithful. And I don't have to worry about anyone stealing it!"

We all smiled politely. Someone noted the bus was unusually tardy. Our regular driver was likely out, and substitutes were typically bad news.

"Well," someone piped up, "be prepared for a long haul tonight."

"That's why it's good to bring knitting or a book." Miriam said as if it were the first time anyone might have thought of this idea.

Later that afternoon I glanced out the office window. A light snow began drifting and growing heavier within minutes until a steady, white brew began sweeping, by enveloping the streets and pedestrians below. I noticed a familiar tightening sensation in my stomach and began planning an escape before the five o'clock hordes emerged and descended the subway.

I left around 4:45 and navigated slushy streets down into the musty smelling platform where a train was pulling in. The crowd surged, propelling me as the doors opened.

We unloaded at Port Authority, making our way through turnstiles and ramps. I joined the end of a very long line hoping I would make it onto the 5:20 bus.

"Oh, you had the same idea," a familiar voice said behind me.

I turned to face Miriam, whose smile was barely diminished from a full day and a rush to the Port.

"Yes," I responded sarcastically, "you, me, and several thousand others."

A garbled voice began announcing unexpected delays due to bad weather. I marveled at how it was always "unexpected" when I expected it daily. Fortunately, the 5:20 bus pulled in by 5:30. Miriam and I got the last two seats in the back amidst grumblings and complaints of those who would have to await the next bus.

"That was lucky," she said, patting my arm.

"Absolutely," I sneered, "I think I'd better buy a lottery ticket as soon as possible."

She laughed as the driver gave a honk and maneuvered his way toward the Lincoln Tunnel.

Once on the highway it was obvious the trip was going to be long. Various vehicles crawled along slippery roads as heavy snow fell. I noticed Miriam was not doing her knitting but was staring through the streaked window. Her reflection was pensive amidst the cascading precipitation. Her eyes had a faraway look. She turned to me.

"What do you do?" she asked politely.

I hesitated.

She clarified. "I mean what kind of work do you do?"

"Oh," I replied, "I'm an office manager for an investment firm on 50th Street near Third Avenue."

"You have to get across town then," she replied.

The Port was west on Eighth Avenue near Times Square.

"Yes," I answered morosely, "adding another hour onto this trip."

Miriam nodded sympathetically.

"And you?" I asked.

She paused letting out a breath of air, looking straight ahead when answering.

"I'm doing something temporarily also on the east side," she said.

"I did temp work in my teens. You'd be surprised how often that leads to permanent offers," I responded.

She smiled but became quiet and took out her knitting.

I leaned back as the snow turned to a pounding hail.

Despite a grueling ride home Monday, we awoke Tuesday to sunshine and warmer temperatures which miraculously melted whatever snow remained. Warmer air mixed with aromas of new foliage producing a fragrant atmosphere. It was the first sign of spring and a morale booster as we boarded the bus only two minutes behind schedule.

Miriam was missing that morning. It occurred to me that I felt an absence of hope. How ridiculous, I thought. I leaned back dozing and found myself thinking of my childhood and memories from years ago. I woke with a start when we pulled into the Port.

"I've never seen you out like that before," said Jim, smiling as he walked past me. Jim was a long-haul commuter like me.

I rubbed my eyes, remembering not to smudge my makeup, and, gathering my things, I pushed toward the escalator and marched to the turnstile only to realize my metro card had expired. I waited in line five minutes to reinstate it.

When I arrived at my desk, I was still the first one in the office. I wondered why I was so upset to have "wasted" five minutes.

All of that week Miriam was not on the bus. Her absence left a subtle void.

One day at lunchtime I took a walk and spotted a shop with knitting and needlepoint. On impulse I stopped.

"May I help you?" asked a salesperson.

"I'm not sure," I replied. "I have no experience with this stuff."

This seemed to delight the woman, an older lady in her late sixties, who advised I was about to enter a world of calm and meditation. I laughed.

"No, really," she smiled, "it's always good to open up to something new. We have classes here, too."

It seemed I could fit in classes on my lunch hour a couple of days each week. Inexplicably, I signed up.

That night at the Port I looked for Miriam. I felt compelled to tell her about the class. I had a momentary vision of both of us flipping needles around on the bus while passing the commuting time. But she was nowhere to be seen.

I began my classes the following week. At first I felt as if I had two left hands. Gradually a rhythm came in the thrust of needles and spinning of the colorful yarns and a satisfaction in its practicality. It gave me a focus during the ride.

One evening, two weeks later, I boarded the bus and, once seated, saw Miriam hurriedly enter the aisle. She saw a seat next to me and sat down with a large sigh.

"I thought you were on vacation," I said.

She caught her breath and turned to me smiling faintly.

"I wish," she said, "no, just some things to take care of."

I reached into my bag for the knitting I was working on as the bus backed up. Miriam turned to me and caught her breath slightly.

"How wonderful," she said, "you've taken up knitting."

I explained my chance lunch-time walk and the class I was taking.

"I can show you some pointers, if you don't mind," she said.

"Sure," I responded, "after all you're the expert."

She showed me some movements with the needles and different stitches. It seemed to lift her spirits, which were less than exuberant when she boarded the bus.

On Monday I looked for Miriam to arrive. She had given me excellent advice on my knitting, and it was coming along much better. In class I had been complimented on how quickly I'd progressed. I was making a sweater for myself and was proud of making something by hand on my own.

That evening on the bus I fussed at the seat next to mine, realizing I was trying to hold it for Miriam. I glanced out the window and saw her approaching just before the bus was leaving. I motioned to her as she boarded.

"Oh, wonderful," she said, looking at my progress in knitting.

"Do you think so?" I asked.

"I can't believe how good it is for such a novice," she said then looked at me and smiled.

"I'm so sorry," she said, "that must seem terribly condescending. We never know our talents until we explore them. There are many stories of students excelling their teachers. I'm jealous!"

We both laughed.

"You're just being kind," I replied.

"We don't have to be kind," Miriam said, "we are kind."

I felt my eyes well up, as if she'd touched on my forgotten humanity diminished by divorce, supporting children, growing older, and taking care of mundane things that had a way of taking precedence in our lives.

"Don't be so hard on yourself," Miriam said. "we're all hard on ourselves, especially women."

I don't know where it came from, but I replied, "We forget ourselves, living for others and obligations."

"Obligations," she stated flatly. "We all have them. Nothing wrong with them, except when they make us forget everything else."

"Everything else?" I asked.

"Like our daily lists of what needs to be done," she said, "instead of getting on with what is practical but remembering our connections to one another and to life itself."

"I'm sorry," she said, adding, "it's unfair to be so judgmental. We should never judge, but we do need boundaries. It took a long time to realize the difference."

"Boundaries?" I asked.

"We give so much to others," she said, "spouses, children, parents, and friends."

"Is that wrong?" I asked.

"No," she said, "but if we don't consider ourselves part of the circle of life, what right do we have to worry about others?"

I thought about this. I'd raised three sons after my divorce and tried making amends in many ways for perceived deficits.

"We can't compensate for all the losses in the world," she continued, "each life makes its own way and its own difference."

I took a deep breath. She touched my arm in a comforting gesture.

Miriam's words reverberated in my mind the entire weekend. There was a wistfulness about her, something transitory that disturbed yet comforted me. After all, everything is very fleeting. I recalled the words of my mother when I was in my early twenties saying I would blink and be older, and it all would seem like a dream.

Along the Irish coast, Aran Island fisherman wore sweaters knit by their families with specific patterns. This custom helped to identify the men if they drowned and were washed ashore.

That reminder jolted me back to the moment. When my youngest returned home that evening, I hugged him hard. I felt time pass as I held him and then released him from my grasp. He would start college that fall, the last to leave home. I would have to redefine the meaning of home.

I settled myself into the seat on the bus the next morning and anticipated Miriam's arrival. She wasn't on the bus that morning or the rest of that week. I thought it odd since she had been out the week before.

I continued my knitting and was pleased with it. I found those lunch hours in class truly enjoyable. I wanted to share this with Miriam. There was no way to be in touch with her other than the bus, so I waited. She showed up the following morning. She looked pale, but gave everyone her cheerful morning greeting. I assumed she had been ill with some bug that was going around. We weren't able to sit next to one another, but she was one row opposite me and gave me a thumbs up on my knitting as I held it up.

"Keep up the good work," she said encouragingly, adding, "and you'll be just fine."

I thought that an odd comment and meant to ask her about it.

When we arrived at the terminal, Miriam got off the bus before I did. I lost her in the shuffle but then caught sight of her as she stepped onto the escalator. I noticed she had a small overnight bag and guessed she must be visiting someone. Then I saw her getting into a cab. I rushed over and stuck my head in the window.

"Since we both go to the east side," I said, "do you want to split the cab with me?"

Miriam hesitated. After an awkward moment she said, "Sure," and shifted over in the seat.

During the ride, we commented on the great spring weather and talked about our knitting projects. As we approached Third Avenue, I asked where she needed to stop.

"Oh, you first," she said, "I need to go a little further today."

"Okay, thanks," I said handing her some bills. She stuffed them back into my hand.

"No," I protested, but she cut me off.

"It's fine," she replied, "you can get the next one."

"Okay," I said reluctantly, "but that's a promise."

I closed the door and watched the taxi pull away. She gave me a slight wave.

I didn't see Miriam for the rest of the week. By Sunday evening I had completed my sweater. On Monday our usual group waited for the bus, but Miriam wasn't there. Just as we boarded Jim came dashing onboard. He put his briefcase down and reached inside taking out a small brown bag. He spotted me and made his way down the aisle.

"Hi, Jim," I said.

He held out the bag.

"What's this?" I asked curiously.

"It's from Miriam," he said slowly.

I looked perplexed.

"Janine," he began, then faltered, "Miriam passed away this weekend."

I stared at him as if he'd just announced something utterly preposterous.

"She belonged to my church," he continued. "She gave this to me and said I should give it to you after . . ." He stopped.

"What happened?" I asked incredulously.

"After she moved here and joined the church we found her name on the prayer list. She had cancer and was going to the city for treatments. She didn't want anyone to know."

I felt as if I was about to be sick.

"No," I said helplessly, not making any sense.

"I'm sorry," Jim said and returned to his seat.

I sat holding the bag, my hands trembling. We were on the highway before I opened it. I pulled out a pair of knitted mittens and a scarf that matched the sweater I had made. I stared at my lap. Involuntarily, tears welled up. Then I saw white paper sticking out of a mitten. It was a note from Miriam: "There are no goodbyes, only bridges to the future. You are gifted. Be joyous every day."

I stared out the window. I knew I did not feel joyous, but I felt an obligation to feel joy.

We arrived in the city and I decided to walk amid the bright spring morning of the bustling streets. I stuffed the note and gifts into my knitting bag and looked up to see patches of angel-blue sky peek between the buildings. I clutched the bag against me and made my way through the crowds. I thought how warm I would be in my sweater, scarf, and mittens when the skies grew dark and cold and I waited for the bus next winter.

KAREN CORINNE HERCEG graduated from Columbia University. Her poetry has appeared in *Inkwell* (Manhattanville College, 2012), *From a Window: Harmony* (Eber & Wein Publishing, 2011), among others. Herceg published a poetry volume, *Inner Sanctions* (First East Coast Theatre, 1979) and recently completed her first novel, *Diva!* Currently she is collaborating with famed Palm Beach psychic and spiritualist Barbara Norcross on her extraordinary life as the first book in a biographical series Beneath the Psychic Veil.

Southern California

Hot spring rain,
wet asphalt, damp exhaust, and—
strawberry blossoms.

The snails have overtaken
the young garden.

Slowly, slowly,
they eat away the labor
of hours.

Swiping plastic cards,
and bagging plastic merchandise.

The grocers
smile—
and check their watches.

Two hours now
until it's over.

Far from home,
the young man watches a bus window
while rain falls.

Where he came from, sprouts
are just beginning to appear.

NATHANIEL HUNT is a freelance writer and editor. His poems have been featured in *Iconoclast, The Houston Literary Review, Poetry Quarterly,* and *Pennsylvania Literary Journal.* He is the cofounder and coeditor of a literary journal *Cartographer.* Nathaniel Hunt writes: "Renku is a linked verse form in which each stanza forms overlapping poems with the preceding and following stanzas. Renku are usually collaborative; this one is not, nor is it as formal as traditional renku."

TIM CHAMPLIN

All the Difference

JOHN MCKINNEY DOWNSHIFTED his old 1999 Dodge pickup and leaned forward in a vain attempt to see the road through the misty fog blanketing the top of the mountain.

"Need fog lights," he muttered.

He'd seen no cars in at least a half hour. "Anybody with good sense is in bed." He sighed. "Wish I were." But home was still a hundred miles away with midnight approaching.

He should pass somewhere in the vicinity of St. Teresa of Avila, a boarding school where his wife, Susan, and her sister went to high school in the sixties. It was now a home for the elderly, still staffed by the same order of nuns who'd since done away with wearing traditional habits. *Nothing,* he reflected, *stays the same for long.*

Then, fifty miles into his trip, he was forced to stop and change a slow-leaking rear tire; a brass screw had punctured it. But the spare was low, too. *How stupid,* he thought, *but who regularly checks the air in a spare tire?* The old saying came to him that it wasn't the physical effort of scaling a mountain that would defeat a climber but, rather, the rock in his shoe. It was the small things—little daily habits—that formed the pattern of an individual's life. What if he awoke one

Edward Hopper. *Gas.* Oil on canvas, 26¼ x 40¼ in., 1940. The Museum of Modern Art, New York, Mrs. Simon Guggenheim Fund. Digital Image ©The Museum of Modern Art / Licensed by SCALA / Art Resource, New York.

morning, recognized all his bad habits, and somehow had the will to break every one of them? *Reform.* Did that word mean to make better or just to change? It could be either.

He shook his head and banished these ruminations. Slowing to thirty-five miles per hour to ease pressure on his low tire, he dimmed the headlights to help see under the fog.

Never mind breaking bad habits. At age seventy-two he was probably too old to do much changing. At this point, he'd be satisfied just to escape the financial situation now pushing him to the brink of bankruptcy. It wasn't his fault; the deep recession had hurt him. But falling into the clutches of the usurious credit-card companies with their 30 percent interest *had* been his fault. Charging things he wanted or needed, he slid down the slippery slope, selling his soul to the cloven-footed financial demon. Now was the day of reckoning. In fact, he and Susan, his wife of forty-four years, were scheduled to meet a lawyer Monday to talk about bankruptcy.

He shifted his focus back to driving. There should be a sign pointing toward the interstate pretty soon. This state highway was unfamiliar. If he'd ever been this way before, he didn't recall it.

Bridge repairs had forced a detour—a detour that offered two choices, either of which should eventually lead back to the interstate. At random, he'd chosen State Route 16, but there were no more signposts. Confused by the tendrils of vapor swirling past his headlights, he was afraid he'd mistaken an unmarked fork for Route 16.

He wished he could drive on and on and never reach home—drive right off into eternity and leave his troubles behind. What awaited him and his ailing wife was humiliating: they'd lose the house they couldn't sell and couldn't pay for, uninsured medical bills, unexpected repair bills. It went on and on—a depressing list. A life of work and trouble shouldn't wind up like this. Well, thank God for his health, if nothing else. *Discipline*—he had to banish these depressing thoughts.

Two more miles of blacktop unwound beneath his wheels. The steady, low rumble of the truck exhaust, the late hour and his solitude lulled him into drowsiness. *This won't do. I have to stay awake.*

He switched on the radio. Static. He twisted the knob. The mountains, the fog, and distance from towns limited his selection. Anything to keep him awake.

Suddenly, a station came in clearly.

"And now," the announcer was saying, "a live concert from Cobo Hall in downtown Detroit, brought to you by Marlboro cigarettes. It's *The Beatles!*"

McKinney smiled. They were replaying some of the old radio shows. The wildly popular British group that had defined an entire generation burst into one of its original songs, *A Hard Day's Night.* Marlboros? Wasn't it against the law to advertise cigarettes on the air?

The music took him back to the sixties. His sense of isolation on the foggy mountain, combined with the old radio show, made him feel disconnected from the present.

The program ended, followed by Dinah Shore's singing commercial, *See the USA in your Chevrolet!*

The fog thinned and turned into a fine mist. The road dipped and wound downhill through a dense forest. He saw a light ahead. As he drew closer, he identified a blue-and-white circular neon sign advertising PURE OIL. He turned into the service station and switched off the ignition.

A lean man in overalls and a John Deere cap appeared. "I was fixin' to close up," he said, looking at McKinney. Then his eyes lit on the truck. "Say, now, is this one of them custom jobs?"

McKinney climbed out. "Naw. Just a twelve year-old Dodge with 200,000 miles on it."

"Slick," the man commented, pursing his lips. "Can't say as I've ever seen one like it. Fill 'er up with Ethyl?"

"Regular. And put some air in that right rear tire."

"Sure thing."

These country folk were certainly accommodating. He never got this kind of service at home.

"Can you tell me if this road connects with the interstate up ahead?"

"Interstate?" The attendant shook his head. "Dunno that place. Grab yourself one o' them maps off the rack inside."

"Can I use your phone to call my wife?"

"Pay phone's out of order." A bell dinged as the man cranked a handle on the side of the pump to turn the gauge back to zero.

"You got a cell phone I could borrow? I'll pay you for it."

The man paused with the nozzle in his hand. "What's a sell phone?"

McKinney went inside and selected a red state map. Champlin Oil Company was printed on it. When was the last time he'd seen a free map put out by an oil company? These were once a common promotion. He unfolded and spread it on the counter. No interstates marked. No wonder these maps were free—they were outdated. He pulled off his bifocals and used them to magnify the tiny red lines. He'd locate the state highway he was on and go from there.

The attendant came inside, wiping his hands on a rag. "I put 32 pounds of air in that tire. Your oil's okay. Cleaned the windshield."

This was a real, old-time service station. "How much do I owe you?"

"That'll be $4.18 on the gas."

"What? Didn't you fill 'er up?"

"Sure did. Took a tad over ten gallons."

McKinney's mind whirled. But he said nothing as he pulled out his billfold and counted out five ones. "Keep the change." McKinney noted he had $75 left, which would have to hold him until his pension check came in later that week.

"Thanks." The attendant went behind the counter and rang open the cash register.

Numbly, McKinney walked outside and climbed into his truck. His mind was foggy as the night air. He had the oddest feeling he was watching a rerun of *The Twilight Zone.* Maybe he'd had a slight stroke. Strokes were painless and, at his age, anything was possible. Surely, there was no way he could have actually traveled back in time to the early 1960s. Maybe this service station attendant was playing some kind of practical joke. But why? If so, he'd short-changed himself on the gas: the gauge showed the tank was full.

He pulled back onto the highway. If he stayed on this road, it would take him home, even though he guessed the route was at least thirty miles longer than the interstate he couldn't find.

He had briefly forced money worries from his thoughts, but now the chronic stress of impending ruin returned and pressed on his sternum with the weight of an anvil.

If he could diagram his life on a chart, what kind of pattern would it make? Zigzag lines, false starts, blind alleys, swirls and humps, reverses, ups and downs. Wrong choices must have outnumbered right, or he wouldn't find himself in a financial tangle without an exit. As much as he wished it, there were no do-overs, as in some game where he could make up the rules. Free will or determinism? Certainly he had free choices, but who could see the overall pattern his life would take? Philosophers had been pondering this question for centuries. He didn't believe in happenstance. On the contrary, he attributed dozens of incidents in his life to the guidance of divine providence— to a caring God who worked beyond his sight and understanding. But the benefits of providence couldn't be ordered up like a pizza.

Distracted by his thoughts, he automatically guided his truck into a sharp curve. Two dark figures leapt past the front of his hood. He slammed the brake pedal. Tires squalled, wheels locked, and the truck slid sideways. The white face of a girl flashed in the headlights— then disappeared.

Shaken, he stomped the parking brake and got out.

"Sue!" a girl cried. She flung herself at the figure on the ground.

"Oh, my God!" he breathed. He knelt beside her.

"You almost hit my sister!" the girl said, cradling the figure that was swathed in a cape.

"I . . . I'm, okay, Donna," the girl on the ground said, blinking in the headlights.

"Thank God you're all right." Donna helped her sister to her feet and retrieved a backpack with a broken strap.

"Do I need to take you to the hospital?" McKinney asked.

"No, really, mister. I've taken harder falls in field hockey." She brushed the brown hair out of her eyes and smiled weakly.

McKinney sighed with relief, his knees feeling shaky. "Where you girls going? Can I give you a lift? I won't hurt you. I promise." He hoped he appeared more grandfatherly than predatory.

"We'll just be on our way," the taller, blond Donna said, taking her sister by the arm.

"Wait." McKinney was curious. "It's after midnight. You live close by here?" As the shock wore off, he noticed both teens wore knee-length capes with attached hoods, and green plaid skirts and saddle shoes. School uniforms of some kind.

"No. We'll just be going."

"Where?"

"To visit our aunt. She's expecting us."

Donna was doing the talking for both.

McKinney hadn't lived more than seventy years to be taken in by such a story.

"What're you running from?"

"Nothing. We're not running." She pulled Sue as they edged away. "Like I said . . ."

"I heard what you said. You're not going to visit any aunt. Why don't you tell me what you're really up to? I won't stop you."

McKinney thought Sue was blinking away tears. But a mist was beginning to fall again, so he couldn't be sure.

"Come on, Sue, let's go."

"Wait," McKinney said. "What's the problem? Can I help?"

"We don't have a problem. We gotta go." Donna started away.

"If we tell you, will you go on and leave us alone?" Sue asked.

"Sure."

"You won't report us?"

"Of course not. As far as I'm concerned, you're free to do whatever."

The girls looked at each other.

"All right," Sue said, wiping the moisture from her face with the sleeve of her blouse. "We're running away from boarding school. We hate it. We're going to walk to the next town and catch a bus somewhere."

"How long you been walking?"

"I don't know. Two hours, maybe. Since right after curfew and bed check."

McKinney nodded, recalling his own rebellious youth.

"What are your plans?" he asked.

"To get away where we can't be found."

"No idea where you'll go?"

"We'll decide later. Maybe St. Louis."

"A long ways."

"That's the whole idea," Donna said.

"You have enough money to live on?"

"We'll get jobs."

He could imagine what was in store for two young girls in some big city. He'd seen runaways before.

"Let me move my truck over on the shoulder in case another car comes around this curve," McKinney said.

"Okay, we told you our story. Now we're leaving," Donna said.

"Hold on just a minute, and then you can go," McKinney said, jumping into the truck, cranking it up and pulling over to the side. He left the motor running.

The girls stood together, watching him.

He got out and came into the light beam. "What's so terrible about school?"

"The nuns are too strict."

"Some are mean," Sue added. "Can't talk at meals. We're only allowed to go into town once a week on the bus to a movie. No boys. No dances . . ."

"No life," Donna summed up.

"What kind of music do you like?"

"Besides the Beatles?"

"Yeah."

"Oh, lots of others—Peter, Paul and Mary; The Kingston Trio; The Brothers Four," Donna said.

"I really like Glenn Yarbrough," Sue said. "What a voice!"

"Pretty nasty night out here," McKinney remarked, wiping a sleeve across his face and looking through the mist into the dark beyond the headlights. "Cold."

He moved to open the truck door, then hesitated.

Sue was shivering—either from the cold or nerves—or both.

"I have a granddaughter about your age," he said. He had to try again. He'd never forgive himself if he just left them standing on this wet mountain road at midnight.

He pulled out his billfold and extracted all his remaining money—what he'd saved as a retainer fee for his bankruptcy attorney. "Here." He handed the bills to Sue.

"We can't take your money, mister," Donna said.

"You'll need a little cash for bus tickets, motel rooms, meals—whatever," he said, ignoring her statement. "When you get settled and have a place to play them, you could buy a few CDs . . . uh, I mean . . . records of your favorite music." He shrugged. "Of course, by then you'll be working and making your own money." He moved out of the headlights and reached for the driver's-side door handle. "I wish you all the best. May none of your bosses in the future be tougher than those nuns."

The girls didn't move.

McKinney watched them and pretended to fumble with his key ring before opening the door.

Sue whispered something to her older sister, and the pair had a quick, urgent exchange McKinney couldn't hear.

"Be glad to drop you off somewhere," McKinney offered.

"I think . . . maybe I'll go back to school for now," Sue said.

The older girl glared at McKinney but finally sighed with resignation. "I'll have to go with her."

"It's late," McKinney said. "I'll give you a ride. I'm guessing you came from St. Teresa's. Right?"

"Yeah," Sue said. "Here's your money back." She held out the crumpled bills.

"It's yours to spend on anything you want." He opened the door. "Jump in. I'm getting wet."

"Okay, but we're riding in the back," Donna said.

McKinney wondered if the girls knew that St. Teresa of Avila had run away from home as a child when she and her brother were determined to become martyrs among the Moors. They'd been caught and brought home by an uncle. He decided not to bring up the story.

They climbed into the bed of the truck and sat down.

"You can run away tomorrow," he said, "or as soon as I drive away from the school. But I think you made the right choice—$75 and a warm bed in a dorm room sure beats hiking in the dark and cold, miles from anywhere."

TWENTY MINUTES LATER and with the help from Sue, who gave directions from the back, they arrived at the school. McKinney watched through a rain-streaked windshield as the girls slipped through a hole in the fence and fled silently, capes flying, to the end of a large building where a security light was burning. They either had a key, or a co-conspirator was watching for them. They disappeared inside.

McKinney shifted into low gear and pulled away from the darkened campus.

He wondered what would happen to these sisters, now that he'd interrupted their plan. He didn't even know their last names. But no matter. Maybe there was a reason providence—his only explanation for this time-travel experience—had allowed him to return to 1964.

Was he an old man then, or was he an old man now? Circumstances had to be just right or he wouldn't have met these girls on their journey of escape. And yet . . . somehow they looked very familiar to him——especially Sue, the younger brunette. She was probably about sixteen. The short, brown hair that framed her face, her general appearance, her voice—who did she remind him of?

Like a physical blow, the realization struck him. The girl, Sue, was a dead ringer for his wife, Susan, as she looked when he'd first met her some forty-five years ago. And her older sister Jean, wasn't her full name Donna Jean?

The winding road descended from the foothills and leveled out. He saw a red, white, and blue sign that announced the interstate ahead. Still stunned by the realization he'd just met his wife in 1964, he glanced into his rear-view mirrors at the fog bank he was leaving behind on the mountain. "Well, whatever I just passed through, it's gone now," he said, aloud, turning on his blinker as he approached the on-ramp.

He'd broken the pattern of Susan's life when she was a high schooler, and now he would break the pattern of both their lives. "I discovered tonight things don't always have to be a certain way," he said aloud. *The course of future events can be altered, and I can change them for the better,* he thought. *Tomorrow I'll call the bankruptcy attorney and cancel that appointment.* Immediately, he felt better. No patterns were inevitable. He'd take charge of his own future or die trying. *There're things I can sell to raise some cash—my coin collection, my antique typewriters, Grandpa's Colt revolver that's worth at least $8,000.* He smiled with a confident resolve. An image leapt to mind of the little dark-haired teenager from long ago. They'd been through a lot together, and they weren't done yet. Tomorrow, if she agreed, they'd order the realtor to reduce the price of their house.

> *"I shall be telling this with a sigh*
> *Somewhere ages and ages hence:*
> *Two roads diverged in a wood, and I—*
> *I took the one less traveled by,*
> *And that has made all the difference."*
> —ROBERT FROST, FROM "THE ROAD NOT TAKEN"

TIM CHAMPLIN received a master's degree in English from Peabody College, Nashville. He is the author of thirty-one historical novels, twenty short stories, and twenty nonfiction articles. He retired after thirty years with the U.S. Civil Service and now enjoys sailing, tennis, and shooting.

MAUREEN BUCHANAN JONES

Beans Like Peace

This is one of those weeks
when a bowlful of beans
looks like salvation.
The speckles on the lima beans
keep company
with the eyes on the black peas.
I have been hurried and rushed
small bits of me escaping—
my gloves, the lid for the sauce pot,
my hairbrush.
I show up for an appointment.
I am told it is the wrong day.
I am not wrong.
The beans sift into one another,
make soft music as they jostle
into better friendships.
The navy beans and pinto beans
curve like smiles,
their skins not too tough for softening.
I am on the expressway.
A knobbed, metal sphere drops
from a truck three lanes away.
It bounces; it rolls.
I have no options.
A jolt. A bang.
It flies off to the left.

I wait for the calamity.
The rain comes down hard.
I slow, inch right.
The wheels stay on.
I remember the bird I almost hit,
swooping in too-early spring madness,
diving under my bumper.
I don't know.
I know the beans look like peace.
Great Northerns smooth and luminous
next to the hazy green of whole peas.
Everywhere an extra dot,
a funny little line,
a tiny jot of color.
The rain slaps,
and I remember this same day,
a different day,
my lifetime ago.
I drove into the sun
late in the afternoon
and knew he was gone.
I knew all the diving birds,
the lost pieces,
the random, flung obstacles,
the botched appointments
add up to nothing. His death
means I pay attention
to exactly how a yellow pea
splits.

MAUREEN BUCHANAN JONES is executive director of Amherst Writers &
Artists and leads creative writing workshops. Her poetry has appeared in
*Woman in Natural Resources, 13th Moon, Peregrine, North Dakota Quarterly,
Letters from Daughters to Fathers, WriterAdvice, Equinox,* and *Calyx.* Her
book of poems, *blessed are the menial chores,* was recently published (AWA
Press, 2012). She holds a doctorate in English literature.

Quantum Entanglement and the Individual

AS I PREPARE TO MEET WITH A CLIENT, I let my intuition select symbols from my altar, and I place them in our meeting area. The client's response to their presence often takes a direction I could not have anticipated. It is as if my inner (and unconscious) connection with my client knows in advance what will be needed.

Interconnectedness

THIS BOND WITH OTHERS occurs at a deep, unconscious human level, through a psychological field, analogous to a magnetic field, which spreads out beyond us wherever we go. Whether this field is open and inclusive or closed and aversive, it is always there. This idea parallels the statement that pioneering psychologist C.G. Jung carved into the door lintel to his house: *vocatus atque non vocatus deus aderit,* that is, "Invoked or not, God will be present." That deep psychological field is who we truly are in our own depths.

The inspiration for this essay comes from the fact that this interpersonal bond that lies deep within us has now acquired powerful scientific support. There is a remarkable quote from *Scientific American:*

In the quantum effect called entanglement, two electrons establish a kind of telepathic link that transcends space and time.

And not just electrons: you, too, retain a quantum bond with your loved ones that endures no matter how far apart you may be.[1]

Who would ever have thought that a statement on the quantum bond *between persons* would appear in a scientific venue?

Quantum entanglement is one of the central principles of quantum physics. It states that multiple particles are connected in such a way that the measurement of one particle's quantum state determines the possible quantum states of the other particles.

In psychotherapy, as in the quantum physics of the entanglement of electrons, the wholeness remains when the two persons (particles) separate. Einstein called this "quantum weirdness," but it has been experimentally verified on the microphysical level, not just existentially on the interpersonal level, as has long been the case. At this level of contact, it is possible to assert that *every person with whom you have ever interacted is still with you, still a part of you.* Quantum entanglement can explain what can happen when persons meet. They are no longer separate persons but a unity, a wholeness that has the potential to heal spiritually, mentally, or physically.

In a more recent *Scientific American,* it says that quantum entanglement *may be the primary physical principle of the entire cosmos,* more fundamental even than space and time.

> If anything, the general belief is that if a deeper theory ever supercedes quantum physics, it will show the world to be even more counterintuitive than anything we have seen so far.
>
> Thus, the fact that quantum mechanics applies on all scales forces us to confront the theory's deepest mysteries. We cannot simply write them off as mere details that matter only on the very smallest scales. For instance, space and time are two of the most fundamental classical concepts, but according to quantum mechanics they are secondary. The entanglements are primary. They interconnect quantum systems *without reference to space and time* . . . We must explain space and time as somehow emerging from fundamentally spaceless and timeless physics. [my emphasis added in italics].[2]

Illustration:
Lise Aubry.
Dancing Blossoms.
Acrylic on paper,
2003.

By implication, the primacy of the entanglements has to go all the way back to the Big Bang. Since everything came from that origin, *all things* are thus interconnected.

Individuality

MARY GERGEN (my emphasis added in italics) describes the individual as "*defined* as the intersection of multiple matrices of relations."[3] This situation is easily mapped onto the meaning of quantum entanglement as given in the quotes from *Scientific American.* That intersection is always with us whether or not we are conscious of it and live accordingly. Mostly, it must be assumed, we do not live it consciously.

That complex intersection is certainly unique to each of us and thus contributes to the definition of our individuality, but it is our *social* uniqueness that is thus framed. It is the "nurture" component of our nature/nurture wholeness. There are two other components, at least. One is our *genetic* uniqueness, our DNA. From that perspective we are initially a mix of mother and father, but they each were derived from their parents, and so on all the way back to the origin of life. The genetic structure evolving at each turning point of life somehow records the sum of the effects of quantum entanglement in our progenitors, and so also represents that entanglement in very concrete form. We thus have that uniqueness from conception, and that is the "nature" component of our individuality. It is certainly different from the temporal intersections that pervade our lives, even as prenatal beings and which accumulate more and more from birth onward through the years.

Another symbol of individuality comes through the phenomena of *synchronicity,* the symbolic resonance, or *congruence of meaning,* of outer and inner events. The inner component is the experience of meaning itself, when an outer event connects deeply with one's inner situation. Many people find such connections in consulting *The I Ching* or a tarot card spread.

For me, the symbolic system that connects most clearly with the local cosmos is astrology, where I find many inexplicable resonances in the horoscopes of my clients. I have practiced in the field of psychology for over thirty years and find the astrological symbols in each chart highly individual. Astrology is a symbolic system relating the configuration of the solar system (the relationships of the positions of the planets to each other as seen from the Earth) to the life of a person born at a specific time and place. It functions by means of synchronicity, as defined above. The configuration of the solar system at the moment of birth is the outer event, and the inner event with the same meaning lies in the psyche of the newborn person. Each of us is a unique component of the solar system.

Is there an even more expansive level of individuality? As we have known ever since Einstein's relativity became standard physics, the cosmos is fundamentally spaceless and timeless. Thus, the connections may be with any place and time. Perhaps our dreams come from clear across the universe. This, too, may be understood as attributable to quantum entanglement, since the whole emerged from a single point in the Big Bang. Thus, each level from which our individuality emerges may be the product of the fundamental entanglement or interconnectedness of everything in the cosmos.

Ongoing Entanglement and Individuality

FOR MANY YEARS I have reread Paul Tillich's sermons, especially those in *The Shaking of the Foundations* (1948). I credit one chapter in this book, "You are Accepted," with saving my own psychological and spiritual life. The title of another chapter, "Nature Mourns for a Lost Good," comes from Schelling, who says, "A veil of sadness is spread over all nature, a deep unappeasable melancholy over all life." Tillich also quotes him as saying, "The darkest and deepest ground in human nature is *longing*." While I agree that longing is indeed very deep in the core of human being, I disagree that it is a longing for something *lost* that needs to be *redeemed*. I believe, instead, that we long for something that is present but not yet found, that pulls us toward our own sense of fulfillment (a somewhat different term from redemption). Although we have intimations of it and sometimes actually touch it, it is bound to remain permanently elusive because our lives are finite, and what we long for is the infinite that we sense as the ground of all that is. Tillich reports being with a great biologist in the presence of a tree:

> Suddenly he exclaimed, "I would like to know something about this tree!" He, of course, knew everything that science had to say about it. I asked him what he meant. "I want to know what the life of this tree is for itself. I want to understand the life of this tree. It is so strange, so unapproachable. He longed for a sympathetic understanding of the *life* of nature.[4]

That same longing can also be applied to a need for an unmediated experience and understanding of how cells, neurons, hormones, neurotransmitters work. Our consciousness is only the endpoint built on these miraculous entities, only the visible surface of a vast and ultimately intangible realm. It is becoming clear intellectually that quantum physics has much to do with the life of the cosmos, but it still does not give us the direct experience of what that is. We intuit that something miraculous is there, and at times it seems almost within our grasp.

Whether or not we have physical children, we live in the world and by that very fact we contribute to the ongoing evolution of the whole toward consciousness. In one sense it means that we have no choice not to belong. If we commit suicide, that act is also recorded and is a part of the whole. Tillich quoted a theologian in his sermon: "Corporeal being is the end of the ways of God." Of course, "end" has two possible meanings; it can mean the destruction or demise of something, or it can mean the *goal* of something, the *telos*, or culmination, as in our word "teleology." The latter meaning could be the interpretation of God wanting to become human or the ongoing evolution of species into new species. A suicide would then be a mani-festation of God's desire *not* to become human. In any case, life-forms are all part of a universal incarnation. As the poet Kenneth Patchen put it:

OTHEEYESOFGODWATCHOUTOFEACHONEOFUS[5]

I believe that this is our own ultimate longing.

Quantum entanglement shows us the interconnectedness of all things. It also appears that quantum entanglement is the origin of in-dividuality on all levels, genetic, social, and cosmic, which is appropri-ate for the most profound principle of physical reality. We *are* involved whether or not we are open to it or defend against it, and if the latter, we diminish our own being, as well as our ability to be present to the world in which we reside and to its own ground, nature. So the task is continually to check ourselves for our defenses with respect to the darker aspects of life and to open ourselves to the tragedies around us that do indeed wound and sadden us. In that case, paradoxically, those wounds can become *gifts* to us, as harsh as that may sound.

What we need in order to be ourselves fully in our own individ-uality is dependent on what Jung's colleague, Erich Neumann, in *The Place of Creation* called "personal evocation," which is "dependent by its very nature on fateful encounters in the form of relationships which are, as it were, prepared for [us] with other individuals who are fulfilling and suffering their own destiny."[6] It is then our task to see each relationship as potentially one of these "fateful encounters" for the other as well as for ourselves. This will surely be the case if we are indeed fulfilling and suffering our own destiny.

Notes

1. Musser, George. "How Noise Can Help Quantum Entanglement." *Scientific American* Nov. 2009, p. 25.
2. Vedral, Vlatko. "Living in a Quantum World." *Scientific American,* June 2011, p. 43.
3. Gergen, Mary. "Finished at 40: Women's Development within the Patriarchy." *Psychology of Women Quarterly,* 1990, 14, pp. 471–493 (quote on p. 486).
4. Tillich, Paul. "Nature Mourns for a Lost Good." In *The Shaking of the Foundations,* New York: Charles Scribner's Sons, 1948, p. 79.
5. Patchen, Kenneth. *Sleepers Awake.* New York: New Directions, 1946, p. 362.
6. Neumann, Erich. *The Place of Creation.* Princeton University Press, 1989, pp. 358–359.

JOHN L. HITCHCOCK holds graduate degrees in clinical mental health coun-seling, phenomenology of science and religion (doctorate with Jung, Kierkegaard, and Niels Bohr as major dissertation figures), and astronomy. He has taught mythology and astronomy at San Francisco State University and physics at the University of Wisconsin at La Crosse. Since 1968 he has led seminars with the Guild for Psychological Studies of San Francisco, spe-cializing in mythology and in science as a source of numinous symbols for personal growth and daily living.

DAVID LAWRENCE

A Just Meal

If I settle for your coming and going,
Would you find a nest in my wings?

Could we share branches,
Twine love,
Turn the sharing of worms into a just meal?

Would we plant the tree we land on
In another spot?

Would our kisses be deciduous and lovely?

DAVID LAWRENCE earned a doctorate in literature from The City University of New York Graduate Center. He was the CEO of Allied (Insurance) Programs and a professional boxer. He starred in the movie *Boxer Rebellion*, which played at the Sundance Film Festival, and currently teaches boxing at Gleason's Gym in Brooklyn. He has published over six hundred poems in magazines such as *Poet Lore*, *Green Hills Literary Lantern*, *Nimrod*, *North American Review*, *Shidrow Penthouse*, and *The SouthCarolina Review*. His last poetry book was *Lane Changes* (Four Way Books, 2007). His memoir, *The King of White Collar Boxing*, was published by Rain Mountain Press (2012).

Two New-Church Patterns

Hindmarsh versus Clowes

Robert Hindmarsh\
(1759–1835).
Portrait painted
by Joseph Allen.
Engraved by Samuel
William Reynolds
and Samuel Cousins.
Published by Agnew
and Zanetti, Manchester.
Mezzotint,
20 x 12½ in., 1824.
©National Portrait
Gallery, London.

IN HIS LAST PUBLISHED WORK *True Christian Religion* (*True Christianity* in the New Century Edition) Emanuel Swedenborg wrote of a "New Church" that was to be "the crown of churches." In the supplement to that book he wrote: "It has pleased the Lord to show himself to me, and to send me to teach the doctrines of His new church, which is meant by the New Jerusalem in Revelation" [paragraph no. 851].

Explaining why he had consistently written "new church" with a lowercase "n" and a lowercase "c," John Chadwick, the most recent English translator of *True Christian Religion*, wrote that it was important to grasp that:

The new church which the Lord established after the Last Judgment [which Swedenborg claimed to have witnessed in 1757] was not intended to be a separate body of people with new doctrines, but rather a transformation of the existing Christian churches from within, leading to the acceptance of a common set of doctrines derived from the Word, in many ways a restoration of the unity of the Apostolic church.

Swedenborg, the son of a Lutheran clergyman who became a bishop, never sought ordination himself. He did not attempt to gather followers or to form a religious sect. Yet fifteen years after his death (in 1772) there was organized in London a distinct denomination separate from the Church of England and the dissenting churches called the "New Jerusalem Church" or simply the "New Church." While the establishment of this new denomination was the work of a number of men and women, it was above all one man, Robert Hindmarsh, who was the driving force behind the founding of the New Church in Great Britain "in a distinct form for public worship." The church that Hindmarsh was instrumental in founding, the General Conference of the New Church, is still in existence today, although the total of its congregations in Great Britain numbers well under one thousand people. But such was the historic influence of this church and its control of the dissemination of Swedenborg's writings through the Swedenborg Society (founded in 1810 but never a part of the Conference) that scholars usually think of "Swedenborgianism" as Swedenborg's religious teachings are often called, as synonymous with the organized New Church, despite the fact that Swedenborg's influence has been most widespread in literature.

As important as Hindmarsh was in the early dissemination of Swedenborg's works in England so too was the Anglican clergyman John Clowes, rector of St John's Church, Deansgate, in the northern English city of Manchester. Born in Manchester in 1743 and educated at Cambridge University, Clowes first read *True Christian Religion* in the Latin original in 1773. He became a strong advocate of Swedenborg's teachings and at the same time formed an ardent desire to translate Swedenborg into English. But he was a man for whom the New Church was not "a mere visible building of wood and stone, nor yet any mere visible forms and ceremonies of worship" (from a letter to the separatist minister Reverend Joseph Proud quoted in *The Life and Correspondence of the Reverend John Clowes, M.A.*, by Theodore Compton, 1898). Clowes was the foremost early translator into English of Swedenborg's religious works. His first translation was *True Christian Religion*, published in 1781. The following year he formed the Society of Gentlemen in Manchester for the translating, printing, and publishing of Swedenborg's works. Clowes translated *Arcana Coelestia (Secrets of Heaven)*, the first volume of which was published in 1783 and the last (volume 12) in 1806. He did the first English translation of *Conjugial Love*, which was published by Hindmarsh in 1794. After the establishment of the London Printing Society in 1810 (later renamed the Swedenborg Society), Clowes translated *Heaven and Hell* and other works for the Society.

Robert Hindmarsh was born in Alnwick, Northumberland, in 1759. His father, James Hindmarsh, was a Methodist preacher, and Robert was educated at the Methodist academy, Kingswood School near Bristol, where his father had previously been a writing master. Here Robert gained proficiency in Latin and Greek. At the age of fourteen he left school and was apprenticed to a printer in London. While still a young man, he established his own printing business, and in 1787 he was appointed "Printer Extraordinary to the Prince of Wales" (the future Prince Regent and later King George IV). Hindmarsh first came across Swedenborg's name in 1778 when he was an apprentice to Josiah Collier, a Quaker. A fellow Quaker who was also a printer and a friend of Collier was at that time printing the translation of *Heaven and Hell* done by the Rev. Thomas Hartley and William Cookworthy. It was through this connection that Hindmarsh first came to hear about Swedenborg, but it was not until 1782 that he procured copies of translations of *Heaven and Hell* and *Intercourse of the Soul and the Body.* Reading both books avidly, he became convinced of the truths contained within them, in particular the unity of God manifested to humankind as the Lord Jesus Christ.

Within a year Hindmarsh had formed a small Swedenborg reading group, meeting first at his house in Clerkenwell (not far from where Swedenborg had died), then at the London Coffee House on Ludgate Hill (near St. Paul's Cathedral), and finally in the Inner Temple just off Fleet Street. In January 1784 this group was formally constituted as "The Theosophical Society, instituted for the purpose of promoting the Heavenly Doctrines of the New Jerusalem, by translating, printing and publishing the Theological Writings of the Honourable Emanuel Swedenborg," Hindmarsh becoming its secretary. Its members were laymen, not clergymen, although some London Anglican clergymen, notably the Rev. Jacob Duché, chaplain of the London Asylum for Female Orphans, and the Rev. A.S. Matthew of St. Martin in the Fields, were sympathetic to Swedenborg's religious teachings. The Theosophical Society was a reading group and publishing house and no attempt initially was made to form a religious sect or denomination. The membership reflected the cosmopolitan nature of London society which was evident in the eighteenth century as it is today. There were the Swedes Carl Bernard Wadström and Augustus Nordenskjöld, both famous later as antislavery campaigners; the Frenchmen Bénédict Chastanier and François Hippolyte Barthélemon (the former a surgeon and the latter a musician and composer); John Flaxman, a young artist and sculptor who had not yet found fame; and Lieutenant-General Rainsford, who was later the Governor of Gibraltar.

Thus far the London society ran in parallel with the Manchester society led by Clowes, but by early 1787 Hindmarsh began to agitate for the formation of a separate religious denomination in which the

Lord Jesus Christ in His Divine Human could be openly worshipped. Clowes, on the other hand, felt that to separate at this stage from what many adherents of the new doctrines called the "Old Church" was both hasty and premature. He himself had been summoned by his bishop, Beilby Porteous, Bishop of Chester, to answer charges of heresy, that he denied the Trinity and the Atonement. After a full and frank discussion of doctrine, the bishop concluded that Clowes's views had been misunderstood. What was at issue was the interpretation of these two doctrines, not their denial. Contrary to the views of some commentators, Swedenborg never denied the doctrine of the Trinity. In fact, he explains that doctrine at length in *True Christian Religion.* Swedenborg's explanation of the Atonement as an act of supreme love by God, a giving of himself as it were, and not a "vicarious" or "penal" atonement by which an "angry" Father sent his Son to suffer for humankind's sins, is widely (if not universally) accepted among Christians today, albeit without recognition of Swedenborg's contribution to the development of the modern doctrine.

Fortified by the support of his bishop, Clowes had the confidence to remain a clergyman of the Church of England and to argue the case for non-separation against Hindmarsh and his supporters. He traveled to London and did his best to dissuade Hindmarsh and his friends from taking a step he considered would retard rather than advance the New Church. Clowes emphasized the importance of charity over creeds and forms of religious worship. After the last meeting Clowes attended at the Temple, one of those present remarked that Clowes was like a cuckoo. He could only repeat the single refrain of charity. Clowes believed that the New Church, represented by the Holy City the New Jerusalem in the book of Revelation, was God's tabernacle with humankind, and that God's true church is not limited by outward forms of worship. The one kind of separation which Clowes recommended was "a separation from all evil and false principles of heart and life." He believed that the liturgy of the Church of England was taken principally from Holy Scripture and that the differences of doctrine were formal and verbal rather than real or essential. The apparent tri-theism in the creeds and in some prayers stemmed from an erroneous

John Clowes, 1743–1831. Portrait (detail) painted by Joseph Allen. Engraved by Edward Scriven. Line and stipple engraving, 18½ x 13⅜ in., 1820. Given by Thomas Agnew, 1932. ©National Portrait Gallery, London.

understanding of the term"'person" (the Latin word *persona* means a "mask"), as though the three persons of the Trinity were separate beings.

Clowes's arguments did not persuade Hindmarsh and his friends, and they went ahead to form (on 7 May 1787) the Society for Promoting the Heavenly Doctrine of the New Jerusalem Church. This society celebrated the sacraments of baptism and the Holy Supper for the first time on 31 July that year. Hindmarsh later drafted a liturgy for this new church, and they moved into a chapel in Great East-Cheap in the City of London where public worship was first performed in January 1788. The next step taken was the ordination of ministers. All the members of the Great East-Cheap congregation were laypeople, but two of them, James Hindmarsh (Robert's father) and Samuel Smith, were Methodist preachers who had been "commissioned" by John Wesley, and they were considered by the other members to be well qualified and called by the Lord for this task. It was agreed unanimously at a meeting held on Sunday, 1 June 1788, that these two should be ordained as ministers of the New Church. It was further agreed that they should be ordained by the laying on of hands by twelve male members of the church chosen by lot from among sixteen members. One of those chosen was Robert Hindmarsh. The other eleven agreed that Hindmarsh should read the service. Unknown to his colleagues, Hindmarsh wrote upon one of the tickets to be drawn by lot the word 'Ordain'. It was Robert Hindmarsh himself who drew this ticket, and this satisfied him that he had been chosen by the Lord to perform the ordaining ceremony. He considered that thereafter he was not only the principal ordainer, but that he was also an ordained minister of the New Church, although he did not use the title "Reverend" and did not claim recognition from his colleagues until the Conference of 1818 by unanimous resolution placed his name at the head of the church's ordained ministers.

The New Church thus established felt the need to set out their reasons for separating from the Church of England, and, in a document dated 7 December 1788 and printed by Robert Hindmarsh, those reasons were stated and signed by seventy-seven members of the Great East-Cheap congregation. The document purported to be an answer to a letter from "certain persons in Manchester" (clearly Clowes and his supporters) dated 14 November 1787. It is couched for the most part in a spirit of charity toward those brethren who had not separated from the "old church," but it is insistent on the need to make a fresh start, just as the primitive Christian church separated from the Jewish religion and the Reformed and Protestant churches established in the sixteenth century separated from the Roman Catholic Church. It declares that the faith of the old church is diametrically opposed to that of the New Church so that those receiving the new teachings cannot "remain together in the same house, much less in the same mind, without the most dangerous consequences to man's spiritual life." The central point of the argument in the letter seems to be that the old church worshipped a "trinity of Gods," and that this gave rise to the "pernicious doctrine of justification by Faith alone." To the letter were appended numerous passages from Swedenborg's religious writings which, in the opinion of the writers of the letter, demonstrated the necessity of a complete separation from the old church. The document is a defensive and forensic one, giving reasons which appeared to justify the conduct of Hindmarsh and his friends in establishing an entirely new organization.

In April 1789 the New Church held its first Conference at Great East-Cheap. It is most famous for the fact that the poet and artist William Blake and his wife Catherine were present. If they could ever be said to have been members of the New Church, they left very soon afterwards. The Conference ended with the unanimous passing of thirty-two resolutions signed by fourteen members (Hindmarsh was not one of them) and all appeared to be sweetness and light. But within a few months the majority of the Great East-Cheap society had excluded Hindmarsh from membership, together with Wadström and Nordenskjöld, and also John Augustus Tulk, Henry Servanté and Bénédict Chastanier, the five last-named gentlemen being signatories of the thirty-two unanimous resolutions.

The cause of the dispute was apparently the interpretation of certain passages in Swedenborg's book *Conjugial Love* which seemed to sanction the taking of mistresses in certain circumstances. Those excluded were among the most intelligent and the best-read of the members of the society. *Conjugial Love* had not yet been translated into English, and the presentation of Swedenborg's teaching on irregular sexual conduct came as a great shock to the more conservative members of the Great East-Cheap chapel. The translation of this work into English became a matter of urgency, and Tulk, Servanté, Chastanier, Nordenskjöld, and Wadström set up in August 1789 a new group called the Universal Society for the Promotion of the New Jerusalem Church. The first and only fruit of this new society was a remarkable publication called the *New Jerusalem* magazine, which appeared in 1790. The "crown" of this new magazine was to be the publication in monthly parts of an English translation of that invaluable work, the *Treatise on Conjugal Love*. In the event only three sections of the translation were published, and the magazine itself ceased publication that year. It was superseded the following year by the *New Magazine of Knowledge*, published by the more businesslike Hindmarsh. But the demise of the *New Jerusalem* magazine led to a remarkable collaboration between separatists and non-separatists resulting in the publication by Hindmarsh in 1794 of the first full English translation by John Clowes of Swedenborg's book on marriage and the relations of the sexes, now entitled *Conjugial Love,* from Swedenborg's use of the rare Latin form *conjugialis* instead of the more usual *conjugalis.*

It appears that Hindmarsh may have enlisted the help of the Anglican parson (a supporter of the government of William Pitt the Younger) against the radical Swedenborgians like Wadström and Nordenskjöld who wanted to give Swedenborg's views on "concubinage" a distinctly liberal interpretation, although Hindmarsh had been one of those excluded from membership of the Great East-Cheap chapel. There is an interesting footnote in the translator's preface to the 1794 edition of *Conjugial Love* in which Swedenborg's teachings are distanced from the mischievous reasoning of the author of the *Rights of Women* [sic] that "the female sex are equally qualified with the male for every intellectual attainment." This was a reference to Mary Wollstonecraft's *A Vindication of the Rights of Woman,* which had been published in 1792. The footnote may have been the work of Hindmarsh rather than of Clowes. Feelings ran high in the New Church at that time on the concubinage issue. One of William Blake's biographers records that he had proposed to his wife that he should add a concubine to their household and that this had caused Mrs. Blake to cry. Interestingly, this biographer adds a reference to the passion that Mary Wollstonecraft had for Blake's fellow artist Henry Fuseli. Clowes, gentle Anglican cleric, although a bachelor, was no misogynist and had no special regard for celibacy. He was later to write a treatise on marriage, *The Golden Wedding Ring,* published in 1814.

One of the most remarkable achievements of Clowes and the non-separatist Swedenborgians was the establishment in 1806 of the annual Hawkstone Meetings. These were held each July at an inn on the edge of the beautiful Hawkstone Park in Shropshire for the study of the religious writings of Swedenborg. At the first meeting the Declaration of the Manchester Printing Society (Clowes's Society of Gentlemen) was adopted:

> That all ought to be regarded as members of the Lord's New
> Church who believe in the sole Divinity of Jesus Christ, and in
> the internal spiritual sense of his Holy Word, as revealed to his
> servant E. Swedenborg, and who live a life according to the
> Decalogue, by shunning Evils as Sins against that great and
> Holy God; and that everyone ought to be left at perfect liberty
> to use his own external forms of Worship, whether in the
> Establishment [the Church of England] or out of it, and thus

be judged from his life and conversation, rather than ceremonious Observances.

The non-separatists were later joined at Hawkstone by separatists, particularly after the founding in 1810 of the London Printing Society, in which both separatists and non-separatists participated. In 1814 the chair at Hawkstone was taken for the first time by Charles Augustus Tulk (1786–1849), the son of John Augustus Tulk, both of them being founders of the London Printing Society. The younger Tulk is a very important (if sometimes misunderstood) figure in early English Swedenborgianism. Although his father was an early separatist, Charles was sent to Westminster School and then to Trinity College, Cambridge (Clowes's old college), at both of which conformity to the doctrines of the Church of England would have been required. At Westminster he was an abbey chorister and became captain of the school. In adult life Tulk worshipped neither in the Church of England nor in the New Church, but preferred private family worship which he led himself, including the administration of the sacrament of Holy Communion. Tulk became a close friend and confidant of Clowes. In later years they had sharp theological differences when Tulk began to develop an idealist interpretation of Swedenborg, influenced probably by his close friendship with the poet, critic, and philosopher Samuel Taylor Coleridge and their common reading of Berkeley, Kant, and later German idealists. But these differences did not destroy their friendship. Clowes, on the other hand, although he never left the Church of England, held theological views which were much closer to those of the separatists in the New Church.

The Hawkstone Meeting continued until 1865, long after Clowes's death in 1831, and the tradition of non-separatist Swedenborgianism was maintained into the later nineteenth century by two important figures in the Swedenborg Society, the Rev. Augustus Clissold (1797–1882), another Anglican clergyman, and James John Garth Wilkinson (1812–1899), a homeopathic physician and prolific writer who declined to join the New Church and remained a member of the Church of England. Because of his translations of Swedenborg, his own books, and his wide circle of friends in the intellectual and literary world, Wilkinson was perhaps the most influential Swedenborgian in Victorian London. The General Conference of the New Church continued to thrive throughout the nineteenth century and reached its highest membership (a little under seven thousand) just before the First World War. One of its most distinguished members, Edward Broadfield (1831–1913), chairman of the Conference Council for over thirty years, was, like Clowes, a distinguished citizen of Manchester. An important figure in the political, educational, and cultural life of the city, he was ecumenical in his religious views, being a close friend of the Anglican James Fraser, Bishop of Manchester from 1870 to 1885 and known as the "bishop of all denominations."

Broadfield was the president of an International Swedenborg Congress held in London in 1910 to celebrate the centenary of the Swedenborg Society. In his summing-up at the conclusion of the congress he spoke to his audience of changed attitudes to Swedenborg that had occurred in his lifetime. He mentioned a conversation he had had recently with a very distinguished Anglican clergyman who had asked him for a brief summary of Swedenborg's teachings. After listening to Broadfield's account, the cleric had said, "Those views might be preached in any pulpit of the Established Church." Broadfield went on to mention how the old doctrine of the vicarious atonement had been replaced by a Swedenborgian view of the incarnation and atonement as works of love. Referring to Tennyson's great poem "In Memoriam" as "rich in New Church teaching," he also pointed to the direct influence that Swedenborg's writings had had on the poetry of Robert Browning and of Elizabeth Barrett Browning. One hundred years on, it would be difficult to find Anglican clergymen like John Clowes who are devoted readers and students of Swedenborg. Even the poetry of Tennyson and the Brownings is not as widely known and read as it once was. But, as I have written elsewhere, "as the incoming tide creeps up the estuaries and the rivers, teachings that were outlandish and unacceptable to eighteenth-century Christians have, as Kathleen Raine put it, 'permeated the spiritual sensibility of the English nation.'"

At the same time, the denomination based on Swedenborg's teachings that was founded by Robert Hindmarsh still survives in Great Britain and in countries of the Commonwealth and outside the Commonwealth. The Swedenborg Society (like its counterpart Swedenborg Foundation in the U.S.) continues to publish new translations of Swedenborg's religious writings, both for New Church adherents and for readers of English throughout the world.

RICHARD LINES was educated at Oxford University and was called to the Bar by Gray's Inn. He worked as a lawyer in the Civil Service until his retirement in 2002, whereupon he became secretary of the Swedenborg Society, having previously served on its governing council for nearly eighteen years. He was president of the society from 1991 to 1994. He has published numerous articles on Swedenborg, his influence on nineteenth-century literature, and on early Swedenborgians, including biographical essays about Charles Augustus Tulk and James John Garth Wilkinson. He has contributed to the *Journal of the Swedenborg Society* and has given papers at academic conferences at the universities of Oxford and York, University College London, and the Royal Swedish Academy of Sciences in Stockholm. He is active in the Blake and George MacDonald Societies.

FRANK DE CANIO

Madrigals

I worship at the Juilliard.
For there my music god resides
amidst allegro and retard,
Fidelio and Bartered Brides,
in a community of saints.
I visit there to warm my heart
and not to cleanse my soul of taints
which lore says devil's trills impart.
Therein the maestro's acolytes
can play along as he says Mass,
while music-loving anchorites
submit to blessing from the brass.
And better than to be absolved
of sin, is dissonance resolved.

FRANK DE CANIO loves music from Bach to Dory Previn, Amy Beach to Amy Winehouse, world music, Latin, and opera. Shakespeare is his consolation, writing his hobby. He enjoys the poetry of Dylan Thomas, Keats, Wallace Stevens, Frost, Ginsburg, and Sylvia Plath. Frank De Canio writes, "Since I've always admired the musician as the highest exemplar of art, I gain some satisfaction from creating music out of words and metrics. Furthermore, the Shakespearean sonnet form almost mirrors the classical sonata form. You have your first and second 'subjects' in the first two quatrains, and the development in the third quatrain—which constitutes traditionally the 'turn' of the argument."

Lost

Checking Out

"PLEASE HELP ME!" she sobbed to the policeman. "I got lost. They left without me!"

She tried explaining her terror calmly, but her words stampeded. Why was he staring? Couldn't he understand she was an Englishwoman lost in a maze of shops? That she had a plane to catch and couldn't find her way to the rendezvous point? That she could not speak more than two words in Mandarin? That in her fear of being left behind, she had run in stocking feet after the heel of her shoe broke off? Run until she thought her heart would burst. And worst of all, what would Rollo think as he ended his meeting with a smart snap of his briefcase and returned to the hotel to check out? What would he think when he stood in the lobby with the other directors, and the wives told him she had not shown up at the agreed-upon hour?

"*Papers.*"

She choked back a sob. "Yes, of course," she managed, rummaging through her large bag. She had bought it expressly for the company trip to Shanghai to carry all the essentials. Now its depths yielded up only nonessentials: hairbrush, crumpled tissues, lipstick, museum brochures no longer needed, half a Hershey bar—and her shoes, one with a broken heel.

"*Papers.*"

She was on her knees now, emptying the bag's contents, her hands skittering about. *We've missed our flight! Rollo will be furious with me. Oh, God! They've stolen my passport—and my wallet!*

Her hands rummaged again through the trash of her few possessions. Even the little notebook with the scribbled name and address of the hotel was gone. "Stolen, all stolen!" she gasped.

Illustration:
Shelia Geoffrion.
View of Shanghai.
Conte on rag paper,
2003.

229

"People like you not allowed here."

"What? Oh!" Her hands shot up to her wild hair. She staggered to her feet. "I must look a mess!" She flushed with embarrassment at her tea-stained blouse and slacks, unaware of the black mascara now streaking her wet cheekbones. She remembered being jostled somewhere in the labyrinth of stores, and that the tea had burned as it spilled from the Styrofoam cup. "But . . . I assure you I'm not like those homeless people out there!" Reaching for her enormous bag, she laughed self-consciously. "I'm no bag lady."

"Move! No can stay here!" The official poked her with his billy club.

"No! I have to wait here for my husband!" She slumped to the floor. Another thought prodded her more fiercely than the man's club: *What if Rollo doesn't come looking for me? What if he leaves me here?*

Lady Baglady

Two other uniformed men arrived. One of them smiled as he offered his hand to help her rise.

"Come with us. We'll help you." She was comforted by his command of English and his smile.

"Oh, thank you! Thank you! I must get to the airport!"

Moments later they were back in the hot, humid street.

"At what time is your flight, Madame?" The official opened a car door for her.

"Actually, I rather suspect I've missed it. But if you would be so kind as to get me there, I'm certain my husband has booked us on another flight by now."

The backseat was comfortable, although an enormous gash ran across the entire backrest. They drove at a fast clip. *But why aren't they using the highway instead of backstreets?* As if reading her mind, the official tapped his stick to the brim of his cap.

"Shortcut."

They traveled deeper into China's largest city, leaving behind the high-rise skyline. The streets narrowed and twisted. The car stopped abruptly. And there in front of an abandoned building, somewhere on the outskirts of a dismal slum, the two men finished the job others had started—robbing her of her rings, earrings, and pendant. When she resisted, they beat her mercilessly. By the time the rain found her curled up in a ditch, she could only mutter through swollen lips, "Lady. Not bag lady!"

Over the next few days, whenever people passed by her, eyes hard with indifference to her blood-stained blouse and slacks, she would

mutter her mantra. *Lady. Not bag lady.* She might have stayed in the
ditch until starvation desiccated her cheeks; she would have stayed
there through the sweltering heat and sulfur-tinged nights, mutter-
ing her mantra, chasing language and memory away from horror,
withdrawing ever deeper into the safety of childhood. But she could
not ignore the blast of thunder that suddenly forced her swollen eyelids open.

A rush of recognition lit her from within. For all her many fears,
she had never been afraid of thunder or lightning. On the contrary.
She had loved them intensely since those early days, the fragrant,
sweet days when her grandmother taught her to sit by a window and
revel in the spectacle of sound and light. She sat up. Pressing her back
to a crumbling wall, she let the wind caress her swollen face and rus-
tle through her hair. The sky smiled with a second and third bolt of
lightning. Sitting on the cracked sidewalk of a forgotten street, she
felt her spirit rush out to meet old friends. People scurried indoors.
Doors slammed shut, and all the while Lady Baglady, as the locals
would come to call her, threw open her arms to the rain.

She remained a child, a harmless oddity whose bright smile and
pale blue eyes had the effect of inspiring some of the women to feed
her table scraps. When it was noted that she had no fear of the many
thunderstorms that struck that season, the rumor spread that the
crazy foreign woman who only spoke three words was a talisman for
good luck. Women who hoped to get pregnant had only to look into
the pale eyes of Lady Baglady when a storm threatened, and they
would conceive that very night. If they wanted a boy child, they had
to brave one or two thunderbolts under the open sky, gazing into
those steady eyes. Because the neighborhood bore more boys than
girl babies for the next few years, Lady Baglady was fed. The empty
building where she curled up at night had no door or windows, but
local women gave her a mat, old clothes, and quilts to shield her when
Siberian winds prowled winter streets. One spring night when Lady
Baglady was smiling at the thunder with outstretched arms, a small
child ran up to her. In seconds, the little girl had climbed her like an
apple tree, clinging tightly to her neck as the child shrieked her terror.

Lady Baglady carried her into her shelter. Wrapping herself and
the child in the same blankets, she had the little girl sit her on her lap
by the open doorway to watch the sky. The child nestled, pressing her
face to the large, friendly breasts. By morning they were still huddled
together. By the end of the month Lalu was clapping and laughing
with the thunder. By winter three more children were huddling under Lady's blankets, homeless boys of uncertain origin. The two older ones spoke Wu; Lalu and the third boy, Mandarin. None spoke

English, but then neither did the Englishwoman. If she still retained any words in her native tongue, she no longer seemed interested in using them. Lady Baglady learned both Mandarin and Wu. In time she became almost as fluent as the children who shared her shelter.

Seasons came and went. The children grew streetwise and learned how to beg for food and later how to earn it. When the government opened a school nearby, A Fa, Chen, and Lalu began to attend classes, while A Cai, the eldest boy, swept the floor of a small restaurant and disposed of its garbage. Lady Baglady followed A Cai to work and was eventually employed to dice onions and other vegetables when she demonstrated her dexterity with knife and chopping board. She was never paid, but she smiled happily at the table scraps she was allowed to take back to her shelter. At night she and the children would sit on their mats, sharing food and stories. Sometimes she surprised them with stories they had never heard, Perrault or Brothers Grimm fairytales she told in Mandarin or Wu. And if it happened to thunder, little Lalu knew to bring their tea to the doorway, where they would gather under the quilts to applaud the sky's performance.

Rollo

He almost escaped a return to China. He had informed the head office that health issues would prevent him from attending the meetings in Shanghai. Since he was scheduled to retire by the end of the month, no one seemed upset. Then Sibyl derailed his escape plan by personally phoning the office to say that she had rescheduled his doctor's appointments for *after* the business trip.

"But I don't want to go to China!" he protested that night. "Why did you have to meddle?"

"Far from it, darling. I simply thought you should retire with a blaze of glory. With the company paying your expenses one last time, this is the perfect opportunity for you and Godfrey to travel together."

"What's Godfrey got to do with it?"

"It's a chance for the two of you to bond and for Godfrey to practice his Mandarin."

Bond? That was something best left to adhesives or cement, not to his stepson.

"Godfrey can practice his Mandarin without me. Mandarin. Of all the useless . . ."

"Sino politics is hardly useless! Godfrey needs this trip. He's got to find a focus for his thesis. Please be a dear. Let him go with you. You've been there before, so you can show him the ropes. And as he's been studying intensive Mandarin at university, he'll be a wonderful traveling companion! Don't look at me that way, Rollo."

Shanghai! He had carefully avoided it for years. What was it now? Twenty-two . . . no, twenty-three years since Daphne had disappeared.

He had stayed behind to search for her. A full nine days. The company had been supportive, deeply pained for him, then pained by him. When sympathy waned and he sensed the silent ultimatum—come home or look for employment elsewhere—what choice had he? As the years passed and his occasional queries at the British embassy turned up nothing, he decided that she had to be dead, needed to be dead, so he could get on with his life. Discarding Daphne's photos, he had her legally declared dead and set off to enjoy a new freedom.

He had not intended to marry Sibyl. When she bullied her husband to sue for divorce and retain custody of the boy, she became just as insistent on marriage. Her voice sometimes grated on his nerves, but she was not all bad. Encumbrances and all, she was levelheaded, and she had an income that would allow for a comfortable retirement. Despite his total devotion to the company, he had never made it past assistant vice president, a title shared by a dozen. He had no intention of living the rest of his life in mediocrity.

At the Shanghai airport, after separating from Godfrey to go to the men's room, he got lost. Every turn in the airport, every gate and luggage carousel looked identical to all the others. He was haunted by the image of someone making off with his bag. He began to sweat and to breathe heavily, going up and down escalators and long corridors that never went where he needed to be. Panting and mopping his face, he finally heard a familiar voice.

"Where the deuce have you been, Rollo?" a young man laughed.

"Looking for my damn bag! What kind of an airport is this? These people have no logic! None!"

"Really?"

It seemed to Rollo that his stepson, who used to fear him, now found him vastly amusing. When had the change started? When had he morphed from feared tyrant to miserable buffoon?

"Don't worry. We'll find your bag." And, of course, they did. Godfrey—like Sibyl—was capable and unfazed by most things.

Rollo sat back in the passenger seat, content to let the younger man drive to the hotel. He stared furtively out the window, staring into the dark as if to catch the hint of a ghost.

When the company meetings were finally over, Godfrey announced a schedule change.

"Peking can wait. It's just another city. If you want to see the real China . . ."

"I don't."

In the manner in which he crossed his arms and smiled, Rollo was sure Godfrey was laughing at him silently. "Correction, since I want to photograph the real China, I'm heading out to some fishing villages off the beaten track. I've booked us at a small inn."

It was stay alone in Shanghai or tag along. Rollo accepted the long bumpy drive to nowhere.

When they spotted the village, Godfrey pulled over and practically leaped out of the car.

"My God! It's like a print from the Ming Dynasty!" the young man gasped.

Godfrey was drinking it in: the steep mountains, the small bridge that didn't just span a narrow river, but connected two buildings to each other; the fishermen who stood in the stern of gondolas, poling their way through the narrow channels; the willows that dipped gracefully into the water.

For the next few days Rollo hardly saw Godfrey. Then one afternoon the young man plopped down next to him on the narrow sofa in their sitting room. "Rollo, you've got to see this!" He flicked through his digital camera. "Here!"

"What about it?"

"Look at her face."

"What about it?"

"Get your glasses on."

Rollo dug them out of his pocket and glanced at the picture, quickly, more annoyed than interested. The woman was thin and gray haired. No one he knew. Yet something about her . . . His heartbeat accelerated.

"We're in a fishing village where time has stood still for several hundred years," his stepson continued. "Few if any foreigners come this far. Yet this woman who looks like any of our old marms in England serves me Chinese tea in a teahouse just up the road. I shot the image just as she was putting the tray down in front of me. She was all smiles until I spoke to her in English. Then she hurried off."

A fugitive . . . Rollo wanted to smirk, but his throat constricted. Jumping up, he thrust the camera aside and hurried down the stairs to the narrow streets below, walking fast without destination. And then, because he feared getting lost in the twisting alleys, and because too many eyes were touching him, he turned back to the inn.

"Which teahouse?" he asked Godfrey the next day.

"Which teahouse what?"

"Where did you find your strange woman?"

"Lady Baglady? That's what they call her around here. Only I don't think they have the faintest idea what it means. She seems to be highly respected. It's over there. The house with the green balcony. Do you want to go in?"

"No."

The next day, alone, Rollo walked back and forth along the canal that fronted the teahouse, back and forth: if it's her, what then? Take her home and be charged with bigamy? *She made me think she was dead. What then?*

He hurried back to the inn and up the rickety stairs. *We're leaving tomorrow. So that's the end of it!*

And that would have been the end of it, except for Godfrey.

"You know that Lady Baglady I told you about? I talked with her daughter."

"She has a daughter?"

"The owner of the teahouse. Lalu and her husband own it; the old lady helps out."

"How old is the daughter?"

"How should I know?"

"Would you say she's younger or older than twenty-three or twenty-four?"

"I didn't ask. But she did introduce me to her oldest brother, a fisherman named A Kai. They mentioned that he had just celebrated his thirtieth birthday."

"Thirtieth!" Rollo broke into one of his rare smiles.

"Is that so wonderful an age?"

An hour or so before they were to leave, Rollo agreed to have tea with Godfrey at Lalu's teahouse. A pretty young woman greeted them at the door and seated them on the balcony that overlooked the river. Godfrey immediately engaged her in conversation. Being able to hold his own in Mandarin, he grew expansive. The young woman, for her part, laughed and chatted readily enough. When she turned to other guests, Godfrey turned to his stepfather with a glow of satisfaction, "I asked her to tell me her mother's story. It's quite extraordinary."

"Why can't these people make proper tea? It's bath water!"

"We're the ones who insist on using old tea!" the young man laughed. "But anyway, it turns out that Lalu was adopted by Lady Baglady. They all were, all four siblings. But here's the extraordinary part. You know how Lalu met Lady? On a stormy night in a Shanghai slum. There was Lady with her arms spread out to the rain with great thunderclaps sounding all around her as if . . ."

Rollo sputtered as he swallowed the hot tea. He went into a paroxysm of coughing. Lalu and a young servant hurried to him. Rollo waved them away. Moments later when Godfrey left to pay the bill, Rollo remained on the balcony, struggling to regain his composure. A slender woman with silver hair and a lovely face stepped onto the balcony and took the seat opposite him.

"Daphne?" he gasped. She studied his face closely. "Don't you know me?" he asked.

Her pond-calm eyes rested on his face. Then there was the unmistakable flicker of recognition. He braced for the cry of joy, her leap from the table to embrace him, to smother him with gratitude. He would be forced to plead with her not to return with him to disrupt his life. But just as quickly as her eyes flared with recognition, she doused the flame. Still sitting opposite him, she gazed at him with a placid smile. Then she rose, bowed, and walked away.

He left hurriedly, almost knocking his chair over. "Let's go!" he gasped to Godfrey as he got into the car. "Drive! Drive!"

He was aware of a moral failing of epic proportions.

THE SILVER-HAIRED WOMAN returned to the empty balcony. She sat very still, listening to the river, to the fishermen as they glided past her, their faces well known to her, their greetings clear and friendly. A little girl ran to her with outstretched arms.

"Grandma!" the child nestled into her, enjoying the fragrance of the gardenia she wore in her hair. After a moment, the child leaned back and asked in Mandarin,

"Who was the man who ran out of here? He almost knocked me down the stairs!"

"Rollo."

"Who's Rollo?"

Brushing her lips against the child's hair, Daphne smiled. "No one important."

SYLVIA MONTGOMERY SHAW has numerous short stories in print. Winner of the Rupert Hughes Award in fiction, her first novel, *Paradise Misplaced,* was published this year. This story, "Lost," was inspired by A.S. Byatt's brilliantly horrific story, "Baglady," and by a passage from Swedenborg's *Divine Providence:* "The Lord's divine providence works things out so that what is both evil and false promotes balance, evaluation, and purification, which means that it promotes the union of what is good and true in others" (paragraph no. 2:9).

JOHN GREY

Climbing the Mountain above the House

How high I climb
and still feel no wind . . .
My jacket wraps around me
in anticipation,
in wasted effort.

When I think of all
the chilly breezes blowing
in the house below,
this feels like rescue,
like an easier road to travel
than going from
one room to another.

And those are faces at the window,
wondering will he do it this time,
or die of exposure,
or lose his footing and fall.
Those faces are like cliffs
that have never been climbed
and they wonder about these elevations,

where everything is calm,
where the higher I scramble,
the easier the ascent becomes.

Yes I'm a little tired,
a little out of breath.
But that just leaves
a lot of everything else I am.

JOHN GREY works as a financial systems analyst. His work has been published in numerous magazines, including *Weird Tales, Christian Science Monitor, Agni, Poet Lore,* and *Journal of the American Medical Association,* as well as in *What Fears Become: An Anthology from The Horror Zine* (Imajin Books 2011). Other poetry is upcoming in *Poem, Prism International,* and *Potomac Review.* His has plays have been produced in Los Angeles and off-off Broadway in New York. He won the Rhysling Award for short genre poetry.

EPILOGUE

KATE CHAPPELL

CHRYSALIS

JOURNAL OF THE SWEDENBORG FOUNDATION

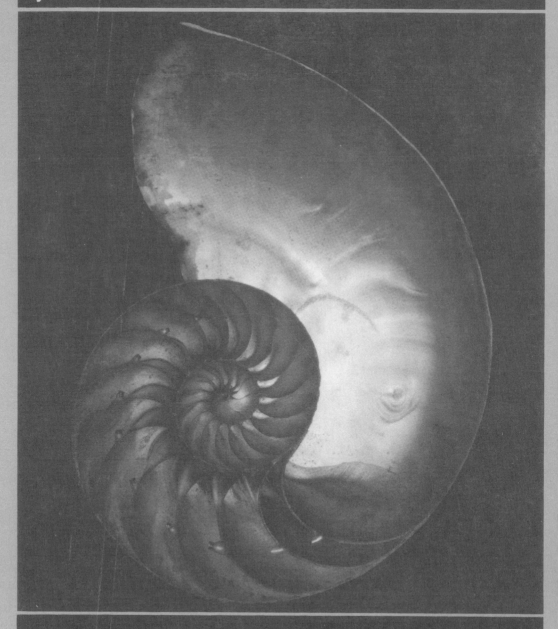

Introductory Issue · In Search of the Soul

WINTER 1985

ROBIN LARSEN

My Grandmother's Magic Ducks

In the rush and chatter of the waterfall,
do I hear the secretive quacking
of our grandmother's magic ducks?
They're recalling in chorus those old tales we've lost.

Do I hear the secretive quacking
of something wild out beyond the young moon's edge?
They're recalling in chorus those old tales we've lost.
Leaves crackle beneath our feet; we hold hands, listening.

There's something wild out beyond the young moon's edge—
I might have missed its song, but you whispered, "Wait—"
Leaves crackle beneath our feet; we hold hands, listening.
At last my heart's ears open to the unbidden message.

I might have missed its song (but you whispered, "Wait—")
in the rush and chatter of the waterfall.
At last my heart's ears open to the unbidden message
of our grandmother's magic ducks.

Illustration:
The introductory issue of the *Chrysalis Journal* was published by the Swedenborg Foundation in 1985. Its theme was "In Search of the Soul." With its continuous geometric spiral curves and perfect ratios between each of the chambers, the nautilus shell symbolizes life's unfolding mysteries. The cover illustration was a photograph by Edward Weston, titled *Shell* from The Art Institute of Chicago.

ROBIN LARSEN is an exhibiting artist and art historian, former faculty at the State University of New York (SUNY) New Paltz, SUNY Dutchess and Marist College. Dr. Larsen began the Image Archive at the Swedenborg Foundation and was editor-in-chief of *Emanuel Swedenborg: A Continuing Vision*

(1988), a volume celebrating the tricentennial of Swedenborg's birth in 1688. Dr. Larsen coauthored with her husband, Stephen, *A Fire in the Mind: The Life of Joseph Campbell* (1991). Founding director of the Center for Symbolic Studies, Larsen is also co-author of *The Fashioning of Angels: Partnership as Spiritual Practice.* "The pantoun," Larsen explains, "achieves its timeless dignity by the repetition of simple lines, using a specific sequence, through four stanzas, each a quatrain. You may use alliteration, rhymes, assonances, woven within this structure, which will make it stronger, more memorable. You may also echo images, statements, questions among the lines. Composed in a garden house nearby rushing water in New Hampshire, 'My Grandmother's Magic Ducks' was my first pantoun, written at a solstice dream-sharing event."

CAROL S. LAWSON

Taking Flight

WITH THE SUPPORT of the Swedenborg Foundation board of directors, executive director and staff, the *Chrysalis Journal* editors embarked on a new venture, as expressed in the publisher's statement:

> Welcome to the pages of *Chrysalis*, a journal of ideas for readers interested in Swedenborgian perspectives on basic questions of our times. These pages are addressed to those who are looking for creative approaches to the spiritual dimensions of life as well as to those who want to know more about Emanuel Swedenborg's contributions, *Chrysalis* will draw upon the reflections of writers and artists of many faiths and on the treasure-trove of Swedenborgian archives and contemporary resources. . . . May *Chrysalis* enable you to continue on your own journey with wings of new insight and a rejuvenated spirit.

Ten years later, in 1995, the journal morphed into an annual book series, as we continued to develop themes for each issue that inspired prose, poetry, and illustrations bridging Swedenborg's world of spirit into contemporary experiences and insights. Now, after nearly thirty years, we trust that we have fulfilled, at least in part, our mission to capture and illuminate the presence of the spiritual world—through the words and deeds of so many individuals committed to the literary arts and to Swedenborgian thought.

"Swedenborgian thought" is sharper and better communicated today because, more than a quarter-century ago, the foundation envisioned Swedenborg's theology in contemporary terms. We made a series of films and initiated a scholarly translation of Swedenborg's work—the New Century Edition, now in production.

A small part of that exciting visionary period was the foundation's publication of *Chrysalis*—a journal for the database of some 30,000 respondents to our films. Five editorial departments were formed and directed to gather articles for each issue from New-Church (Swedenborgian) authors addressing non-Swedenborgian readers. The *Chrysalis* departments were Image and Vision, Things Heard and Seen, Patterns, Vital Issues, and Fringe Benefits. The editors soon discovered, however, that the envisioned supply of New-Church authors who could write for the general public did not exist: the editors had to write the articles themselves! The indefatigable Don Rose (department editor of Things Heard and Seen) suggested that we advertise for writers in *Writers' Market,* which we did. The foundation, thus, encountered new authors who wrote fiction, non-fiction, and poetry based on *Chrysalis* themes related to Swedenborgian concepts about spirit. The authors did not, of course, use our traditional New-Church terminology.

Today, marvelously, there are many New-Church and non-New-Church writers describing Swedenborgian ideas in everyday language. This turnaround is fully evident in recent *Chrysalis* issues.

WITH DEEP APPRECIATION I will always remember Alice Skinner for her vision to set *Chrysalis* in motion and for her thoughtful choices of many of our illustrations. I feel profound gratitude for our first editors (George Dole, Robert and Marian Kirven, Steve and Robin Larsen, and Donald Rose); my son Rob Lawson, who became my co-editor and poetry editor; managing editor and designer Susanna Buschmann; fiction editors Robert Tucker and John Welliver; art editor Shelia Geoffrion; editorial associate Constance Eldridge; editorial assistants Jane Kennedy and Richard Butterworth; cover designer Karen Connor; contributing editors Morgan Beard, Patte LeVan, Perry Martin, Dirk Spruyt; and marketing associate Carol Urbanc.

These many years of publishing *Chrysalis* would not have been possible without the generous support of the board of directors and its staff, a gift from Esther Blackwood Freeman (Mrs. Forster Freeman Jr.), the literary and artistic contributions of many writers and artists, and our devoted readers. As we take flight, we trust that we have left a timeless literary treasure for many generations.

STEPHEN LARSEN

Vale
for Chrysalis

THE YEAR 1984 SEEMED A TIME of great creative and intellectual renaissance at the Swedenborg Foundation. My father, the Rev. Harold B. Larsen, whose "place" I took on the board of directors, had always cherished the vision of a far greater outreach for the Swedenborg Foundation's activities than merely keeping Swedenborg's books in print. The Writings, he thought, contained universal human truths that could inspire and transform the world! But the McLuhan revolution was in full force, and literacy seemed on the decline, while films and television captured mass audiences.

An unprecedented film program began, first with Elda Hartley of Hartley Films, a company with a dedication to films about thoughtful topics, and then with her successor, Harvey Bellin, who had a particular fascination with Swedenborg's influence. First was *The Man Who Had to Know,* on Swedenborg's life and transformation from scientist to spiritual visionary and writer. Then, in succession, films about Swedenborg's influence on literature, the arts, and culture encompassing William Blake, Johnny Appleseed, and two beautiful shorter films with scripts by George Dole: *Images of Knowing,* on correspondences between the material and the spiritual, and *The Other Side of Life,* on Swedenborg's central reassurance that what we call death is simply a transition to a deeper, spiritual existence that has always been there.

In a coincidence that now seems just a little spooky to us, the eminent mythologist Joseph Campbell was our guest at the annual meeting of the Swedenborg Foundation, the year that the latter film was first screened (1987). He would pass away five months later. Campbell said what he liked best about the Swedenborg Foundation's films was that they introduced a spiritual perspective without prose-lytizing for a particular organization. He was truly moved by what he saw as our effort to deepen the spiritual perspective, without hype or salesmanship.

I believe this service or "use" to the spiritual side of humanity, without coercion, is the core of what my father envisioned. If the ideas Swedenborg apprehended in his visionary activities and docu-mented in his writing are practical, useful, and durable, they will in-fluence the world, and ultimately empower the regeneration of hu-manity.

This was, then, also the core impulse in 1984 that moved Alice Skinner (vice president), Darrell Ruhl (executive director), George Dole, Robin (my wife), me, and Carol Lawson, as we sat in that little restaurant across 23rd Street from the Foundation offices in New York City. How could we capitalize on the considerable foment we had occasioned in the larger culture around Swedenborg and his in-fluence? A publication such as *Parabola,* which reaches hundreds of thousands of people all over the world, with deep subjects, but with-out proselytizing, offered a model (*Parabola,* by the way, is still in print). But we needed a name. Robin and I were not long back from a transpersonal psychology conference in Europe, where we had met Elizabeth Kübler-Ross. The great thanatologist told us a moving sto-ry: When, as a seventeen-year-old, just after the fall of the Third Reich, she had bicycled across the border from neutral Switzerland into Germany and had actually visited the concentration camps, she saw one symbol repeated over and over—and particularly in the aw-ful dorms where children prepared for realities that even adults could not imagine: It was the butterfly breaking free from the chrysalis. There it was, undeniably over and over (Robin and I confirmed this, a few years later, looking at children's diaries from the Terezin death camp in Czechoslovakia). Without theology, or philosophy, the chil-dren seemed to find a core symbol affirming the immortality of the soul.

As we told the story at the table there was a pregnant silence. I can't remember if it was Carol, or Darrell, or all of us together that said, "That's the name: Chrysalis!"

It is sad, as Carol notes, that the mailing list of thirty thousand reached and inspired by the films, somehow was lost. But the early editions of *Chrysalis* did indeed reach thousands. The journal, dedi-cated to the regenerative potential of humanity, touched lives both inside and outside the bourne of the New Church; further it empha-sized that, as Swedenborg himself said, the new spirituality awaiting us transcends institutional boundaries and exists in every human heart. I still have those beautiful early editions on my bookshelves (along with years of *Parabola* magazine) and they have been perennially available for perusal in my counseling center waiting room at the Center for Symbolic Studies. *Chrysalis* has offered spiritual wisdom, consolation, and creative inspiration to many writers, and, as George Dole says, "helped to break us out of a traditional insularity" and widen the conversation about what it means to be a spiritually attuned human being.

My only regret is that I did not write more for *Chrysalis,* beyond those early years (other projects supervened, including two biographies: *Emanuel Swedenborg: A Continuing Vision* and *A Fire in the Mind: The Life of Joseph Campbell.*) But I greatly applaud Carol's vision and perseverance in seeing it through all of these years since its birth and transformation into an annual book series in 1995. I have read many inspiring and thoughtful pieces in its pages, and I believe it has in many ways furthered the outreach and the literary stature of the Foundation, which, after all, is a publishing house. In more than one case, writers who appeared first on the pages of *Chrysalis* became published in the Foundation's "corollary publications" (by writers other than Swedenborg himself). Since this is consistent with a new direction the Foundation has taken, I heartily endorse any effort to see *Chrysalis* digitized and available to future generations in that form. In this way, the love and wisdom is perpetuated and made (usefully) available.

STEPHEN LARSEN is a SUNY psychology professor emeritus, a licensed mental health counselor in New York, board certified in neurofeedback, and the author or editor of some ten books in print, including *A Fire in the Mind: The Life of Joseph Campbell.* His wife, Robin, was the editor-in-chief of *Emanuel Swedenborg: A Continuing Vision,* to which he was also a contributor. The Larsens also co-authored *The Fashioning of Angels: Partnership as Spiritual Practice,* published by the Swedenborg Foundation. He is also a past and current member of the board of directors of the Swedenborg Foundation.

GEORGE F. DOLE

Epilogue from
a Translator

WHEN IT WAS FIRST PROPOSED more than a quarter of a century ago
that the Swedenborg Foundation should publish a journal, part of my
own dream was that it would help us break out of our insularity by
including translations of some of the excellent work being done in
Sweden and Germany. This proved impracticable, but the fundamental philosophy remained intact. *Chrysalis* has broken out of a traditional insularity, and it has done so by a consistent effort to find
"Swedenborgian" principles translated into "non-Swedenborgian"
language. As the late board member Bill Woofenden was fond of saying, "Any fool can quote Swedenborg. Show me you understand it by
putting it in your own words."

There are countless thoughtful conversations going on all around
us, conversations to which we believe we have a great deal to contribute. They may be in unfamiliar "languages," so it behooves us to
follow the Golden Rule by listening and learning before we butt in.
May this legacy of *Chrysalis* be recognized, and may it be wisely in-
vested in new creative efforts toward a world that is very much in
process, a world that is becoming.

GEORGE F. DOLE was professor of Bible, languages, and theology at the
Swedenborg School of Religion until his retirement in 1999. His recent pub-
lications include *Freedom from Evil: A Pilgrim's Guide to Hell; A Book about
Us: The Bible and Stages of Our Lives;* and translations from the Latin of
Swedenborg's works: *Heaven and Hell, Divine Love and Wisdom,* and *Divine
Providence.*

ROBERT BLY

It Takes
a Long Time

Let the insects go on shouting their hallelujahs;
Let the crickets go on hiding their parents;
Let the goats complain they can't find Jerusalem.

Eternity waits for the moose to start moving.
The mouse keeps circling around for its own tail.
Finally it just curls up and goes to sleep.

We know how long it takes to make a waterfall,
How many years the oak tree waits in the orchard,
How long the caterpillar takes to wash his feet.

The sitarist's head bends over the skinny sitar.
Notes come in from a hundred Indian villages.
The long notes sweeten the sea bottom.

It will be years before the great dragon returns.
Meanwhile, our grandmother has a lot to do,
And the tired birds keep flying over the ocean.

It will be years before the busy sea calms down,
And the wind stops blowing ships landward,
And the goats give up looking for Jerusalem.

ROBERT BLY's new book of poems, *Talking into the Ear of a Donkey* (W. W. Norton), includes many poems written in his American adaptation of the Mideastern ghazal form. In 2013 Graywolf Press will be publishing *Airmail*, his correspondence with the Swedish poet Tomas Tranströmer. In its classic form, each stanza of a ghazal stands alone—has its own landscape, so to speak—and the theme of the poem is never stated. Thus, connections between stanzas are purely associative.

Swan Song

Patterns: Make 'Em and Break 'Em is the twenty-eighth and last edition of CHRYSALIS, which includes its nine years as a triannual journal and nineteen years as an annual book series. To the writers, artists, and editors involved with the creation and publication of CHRYSALIS: *we give our sincere thanks.*

As a thank-you to our readers for their abiding support, we are extending a special offer:

> Receive any back issue
> of the Chrysalis Reader
> for **50%** off the retail price.
> Enter code **"CHRYSALIS"**
> at checkout.

Order online: www.swedenborg.com

800.621.2736

773.702.7000 (U.S. & Canada)

773.702.7000 (outside U.S. & Canada)

"'The veil between worlds is thinner at some places and at certain times' according to ancient Irish Celts (p. 68). This Chrysalis presents a veil so thin as to permit encounter with the eternal patterns of our being and knowing."

—*Arlene Laskey, artist, retired arts educator,*
freelance arts columnist and sometime poet

"For this valedictory Chrysalis, patterns are broken, perpetuated, endured, made new—all on vivid display, as we watch Woodstock take its organic shape; explore the triple world of Irish myth; witness an Iraq War veteran's homecoming. We are reminded in poem after essay after story that 'no pattern is inevitable.' As Chrysalis takes flight, the closing lines from Errol Miller's 'Summer Left Last Night' (p. 164) seem especially fitting: 'we were / thrilled by the change / and knowing also that we / had lived and loved into / a brand-new season.'"

—*Craig Challender, professor of English, Longwood*
University; director, Longwood Authors Series

"Like birds, Laurence Holden's poem (p. xvi) 'Thistle and Seed' ends, 'seeds take flight, loft // into the emptied sky / like birds / going home.' The poems and art in *Patterns* carry just this way. The music in *Patterns* moves quietly, like the relief of the bird in the woodcuts that serve to tie the sections together, repeating and varying the theme, rara avis—a rich and wonderful gathering."

—*Steve Lautermilch, poet and photographer*

"A wise man said, 'Change is the only constant in life.' Gautama the Buddha went one step further: 'The life of an individual lasts but for the period of one thought; after that a new being is said to exist.' The patterns of our lives often change. The reasons are many, as this issue of Chrysalis so apply illustrates."

—*David D. Jones, fiction and nonfiction writer*

"In this final Chrysalis, poets, essayists, and storytellers exquisitely weave new meaning from the seeming randomness of life. Through elegant verse and evocative prose, they aspire to heal the broken places, beckon the hidden pieces, and resurrect trapped potential from obsolete forms."

—*Jonathan Odell, novelist and author*